# All Along the River: A Novel

M. E. Braddon

# ALL·ALONG·THE·RIVER

M. E. Braddon

ALL ALONG THE RIVER

A Novel

BY THE AUTHOR OF

"ISHMAEL," "VIXEN," "LADY AUDLEY'S SECRET,"
"THE VENETIANS," Etc.

Stereotyped Edition

LONDON
SIMPKIN, MARSHALL, HAMILTON, KENT & CO. LIMITED
STATIONERS' HALL COURT

LONDON:

PRINTED BY WILLIAM CLOWES AND SONS, LIMITED,
STAMFORD STREET AND CHARING CROSS.

CONTENTS.

CHAPTER

I. "The Rain set early in To-night"

II. "But the Days drop One by One"

III. "Oh Moment One and Infinite!"

IV. "Dreaming, she knew it was a Dream"

V. "And the Child-cheek blushing Scarlet for the very Shame of Bliss"

VI. "A Love still burning upward"

VII. "Look through mine Eyes with thine, True Wife"

VIII. My Frolic Falcon, with Bright Eyes

IX. "Lies Nothing buried long ago?"

X. "Of the Weak my Heart is Weakest"

XI. "Where the Cold Sea raves"

XII. "Far, too far off for Thought or any Prayer"

XIII. "Under the Pine-wood, Blind with Boughs"

XIV. "Say the False Charge was True"

XV. "My Life continues yours, and your Life mine"

XVI. "Sorrow that's Deeper than we dream, perchance"

XVII. "The Year of the Rose is Brief"

XVIII. "No Sudden Fancy of an Ardent Boy"

XIX. "I have you still, the Sun comes out again"

XX. "Thou Paradise of Exiles, Italy"

XXI. "The Woods are round us, Heaped and Dim"

XXII. Ecco Roma

XXIII. "Seek Shelter in the Shadow of the Tomb"

XXIV. "Oh, Old Thoughts they cling, they cling!"

XXV. "We'll bind you Fast in Silken Cords"

XXVI. "So, Full Content shall henceforth be my Lot"

XXVII. "Gone Deeper than all Plummets sound"

XXVIII. "Though Love and Life and Death should come and go"

XXIX. "I, you, and God can comprehend each other"

# CHAPTER I.

## "THE RAIN SET EARLY IN TO-NIGHT."

It had been raining all the morning, and it was raining still, in that feeble and desultory manner which presages a change of some kind, when the postman came with the long-expected Indian letter.

He was later than usual. It was nearly two o'clock, and Isola had been watching for him since one, watching with an unread book in her lap, listening for the click of the gate. She had been sitting by the open window, looking out at the wet landscape, the glistening hedgerow and dull grey river, with the great, green hill beyond, a steep slope of meadow land, dotted with red cattle, and so divided by hedgerows, as to look like a Titanic chessboard.

At last she heard the familiar tread of the postman's heavy boots, and saw his shining oilskin hat moving above the edge of the hollies, and heard the click of the iron latch as he came into the little garden.

She called to him from the window, and he came tramping across the sodden grass and put three letters into her outstretched hand.

One from her married sister in Hans Place. That would keep. One from an old schoolfellow. That would keep. And one—the long-looked-for Indian letter, which she tore open eagerly, and read hurriedly, devouring the close lines, in the neat, black penmanship, with its decided up and down strokes, and legible characters, so firm, so strong, so straightforward, like the nature of the man who wrote the letter.

The tears sprang to her eyes as she came to the end, and her hands crushed the thin paper in a paroxysm of vexation or despair.

"Six months—perhaps a year, before he can come back, and I am to go on living here—alone, unless I like to send for a girl whose face I hardly know, to keep me company, and cheer me with her good spirits. I want no strange girls. I want no one's good spirits. I hate people with good spirits. I want him, and nobody but him! It is hard that we should be parted like this. I ought to have gone with him, in spite of all the doctors in Christendom."

1

She relented towards the letter which her feverish hand had used so badly. She smoothed out the flimsy paper carefully with that pretty little hand, and then she re-read the husband's letter, so full of grave tenderness and fond, consoling words.

He was with his regiment in Burmah, and the present aspect of things gave him no hope of being able to return to England for the next half-year, and there was no certainty that the half-year might not be stretched into a whole year. The separation could not be more irksome to his dearest Isola than it was to him, her husband of little more than a year: but not for worlds would he have exposed her to the risks of that climate. He took comfort in thinking of her in the snug little Cornish nest, with his good Tabitha.

Isola kissed the letter before she put it in her pocket, and then she looked round the room rather dolefully, as if the Cornish nest were not altogether paradise. And yet it was a pretty little room enough, half dining-room, half study, with handsomely bound books on carved oak shelves, and photographs and bright draperies, and cosily cushioned bamboo chairs, and a bird-cage, and a Persian cat. Nor was the garden outside flowerless, even on the threshold of winter. The purple blossoms of the veronica were untouched by frost; there were pale tea roses gleaming yonder against the dark gloss of holly and laurel. There were single dahlias of vividest red, like flaming stars; and close under the open window, last splendour of departed summer, the waxen chalice of a golden lily trembled on its tall stem, and filled the room with perfume.

The rain was over—the monotonous drip, drip, which had irritated Isola's nerves all that morning, had ceased at last. She left the modest little lunch untouched upon the table, and went out into the hall, where her hat and jacket hung handy for any impromptu ramble. No need to look at one's self in the glass before going out of doors, at twenty years of age, and in such a place as Trelasco. Isola took her stick from the stand, a green orange stick, bought in the sunny South, on her way to Venice with her husband last year—a leisurely trip, which had been to them as a second honeymoon after a few happy months of wedlock. Then had come the sadness of parting, and a swift and lonely journey for the young wife—a lonely return to the Angler's Nest, Trelasco, that cosy cottage between Lostwithiel and Fowey, which Major Disney had bought and furnished before his marriage. He was a son of the soil, and he had chosen to pitch his tent in that remote spot for the sake of old associations, and from a fixed belief that there was no locality of equal merit for health, beauty, and all other virtues which a man should seek in his home.

Isola rarely touched that stick without remembering the day it was bought—a rainy day in Milan—just such a day as this, a low, grey sky, and an oppressive mildness of atmosphere. She remembered, with the sick pain that goes with long partings, how she and her husband had dawdled away an afternoon in the Victor Emmanuel Gallery, buying handkerchiefs and neckties, a book or two, a collection of photographs, and finally the orange stick.

She went out to walk down her depression before teatime, if possible. She went along a narrow path by the river, then turned into a road that skirted those green pastures which rose sheer till the ragged edge of the topmost boundary seemed to touch the dim, grey sky. She passed the village inn, deadly quiet at this season and at this hour. She passed the half-dozen decent cottages, and the three or four genteeler houses, each in its neatly kept garden, and she walked with quick, light step along the wet road, her useful tailor-gown well clear of the mud, her stick striking the hedgerow now and then, as she swung it to and fro in dreamy thought.

A long, lonely winter to look forward to—a winter like the last— with her books and drawing-board, and her cottage piano, and the cat and the fox-terrier, and Tabitha for her daily companions. There were a few neighbours within a radius of half a dozen miles, who had been very civil to her; who called upon her, say once in six weeks; who sometimes invited her to a stately dinner-party, and sometimes at a suspiciously short notice, which made her feel she was wanted to fill a gap; who made her free of their tennis lawns; and who talked to her on Sundays after church, and were always very particular in inquiring for news from India. There was not one among them for whom she cared; not one to whom she would have liked to pour out her thoughts about Keats or Shelley, or to whom she would have confided her opinion of Byron. She was more interested in Bulwer's "Audley Egerton" than in any of those flesh and blood neighbours. She was happier sitting by her chimney corner with a novel than in the best society available within a drive of Trelasco.

She struck off the high road into a lane, a lane that led to the base of a wilder hill than that where the red cattle were grazing. The crest of the hill was common land, and dark fir-trees made a ragged line against the autumn sky, and the view from the summit was wide and varied, with a glimpse of the great brown cliffs and the dark, grey sea far off to the west, to that dim distance where the Dodman shut off the watery way to the new world. On the landward slope of that wild-looking ridge was the Mount, Lord Lostwithiel's place, uninhabited for the greater part of the year except by servants, his lordship being the very last kind of man to bury himself alive in a remote Cornish fastness, a long day's journey from the London theatres, and the R.Y.S. Clubhouse at Cowes.

Who was Lord Lostwithiel? Well, in the estimation of Trelasco he was the only nobleman in England, or say that he was to all other peers as the sun to the planets. He belonged to Trelasco by reason of his large landed estate and the accident of his birth, which had taken place at the Mount; and, although his character and way of life were not altogether satisfactory to the village mind, Trelasco made the best of him.

Isola Disney climbed the hill, an easy matter to light-footed twenty. She stood amidst the tall fir columns, and looked down at the November landscape, very distinctly defined in the soft, grey atmosphere. She could see the plough moving slowly across the red earth in the fields below, the clumsy farm horses, white against the deep, rich red. She could see the winding river, bluish grey, between its willowy banks, and far off beyond Fowey there rose the wooded hills, where the foliage showed orange and tawny and russet between the blue-grey water and the pale grey sky.

She loved this lonely hill, and felt her spirits rise in this lighter atmosphere as she stood resting against the scaly trunk of a Scotch fir, with the wind blowing her hair. It was a relief to escape from the silence of those empty rooms, where she had only the sleepy Persian or the hyper-intelligent fox-terrier for company. There was a longer and more picturesque way home than that by which she had come. She could descend the other side of the hill, skirt the gardens of the

Mount, by a path that led through the Park to a lodge gate on the Fowey road. It was one of her favourite walks, and she was so accustomed to seeing the shutters closed at the great house that she never expected to meet any one more alarming than a farm-servant or a cottager's child.

There was a thick chestnut copse upon one side, and the wide expanse of undulating turf, with an occasional clump of choice timber, upon the other. The house stood on higher ground than the park, but was hemmed in and hidden by shrubberies that had overgrown the intention of the landscape gardener who planned them. Only the old grey-stone gables, with their heavy slabs of slate, and the tall, clustered chimneys, showed above the copper beeches, and deodaras, the laurels, and junipers, and Irish yews, and the shining masses of arbutus with crimson berries gleaming amongst the green. Isola had never seen that old Manor House nearer than she saw it to-day, from the path, which was a public right of way through the park. She knew that the greater part of the building dated from the reign of Charles the Second, but that there were older bits; and that about the whole, and about those ancient rooms and passages most especially, there were legends and traditions and historical associations, not without the suspicion of ghosts. The Mount was not a show place, like the home of the Treffrys at Fowey, and of late years it had been very seldom inhabited, except by certain human fossils who had served the house of Hulbert for two generations. She had often looked longingly at those quaint old gables, those clustered stone chimneys, likening the house amidst its overgrown shrubberies to the Palace of the Sleeping Beauty, and had wished that she were on friendly terms with one of those drowsy old retainers.

"I dare say if I were daring enough to open one of the doors and go in I should find them all asleep," she thought, "and I might roam all over the house without awakening anybody." She was too depressed to-day to give more than a careless, unseeing glance at those many gables as she walked along the muddy path beside the dripping copse. The chestnut boughs were nearly bare, but here and there clusters of bright yellow leaves were still hanging, shining like pale gold in the last watery gleams of the sun; and though the leaves were lying sodden and brown among the rank, wet grass, there were emerald mosses and cool, green ferns, and red and orange fungi to give colour to the foreground, and to the little vistas that opened here and there amidst the underwood.

Those final yellow gleams were fading low down in the western sky as Isola turned her face towards the river and the Angler's Nest, and just above that pale radiance there stretched a dense black cloud, like a monstrous iron bar, which she felt must mean mischief. She looked at that black line apprehensively. She was three miles from home, without cloak or umbrella, and with no available shelter within three-quarters of a mile.

She quickened her pace, watching the fading light and lowering cloud, expecting thunder, lightning, hail, she knew not what. A sudden deluge settled the question. Torrential rain! That was the meaning of the inky bar above the setting sun. She looked round her helplessly. Should she dart into the copse, and try to shelter herself amidst those leafless twigs, those slender withies and saplings? Better to face the storm and plod valiantly on. Her neat little cloth gown would not be much the worse for a ducking; her neat little feet were accustomed to rapid walking. Should she run? No; useless when there were three miles to be got over. A brisk, steady tramp would be better. But, brave as she was, that fierce rain was far from pleasant. It cut into her eyes and blinded her. She had to grope her way along the path with her stick.

"Pray let me take you to the house," said a voice close beside her, a man's voice—low and deep, and with the accents of refinement.

Could one of Lord Lostwithiel's fossilized servants talk like that? Impossible. She looked up, as well as she could, under that blinding downpour, and saw a tall man standing beside the pathway with his back to the copse. He was over six feet two and of slim, active figure. He was pale, and wore a short, dark beard, and the eyes which looked at Isola out of the pale, thin face were very dark. That was about as much as she could see of the stranger in the November dusk.

"Pray let me persuade you to come to the house," he said urgently. "You are being drenched. It is absolutely dreadful to see anybody out in such rain—and there is no other shelter within reach. Let me take you there. My housekeeper will dry your hat and jacket for you. I ought to introduce myself, perhaps. I am Lord Lostwithiel."

She had guessed as much. Who else would speak with authority in that place? She dimly recalled a photograph, pale and faded, of a tall man in a yeomanry uniform, seen in somebody's album; and the face of the photograph had been the same elongated oval face—with long thin nose, and dark eyes a shade too near together—which was looking down at her now.

She felt it would be churlish to refuse shelter so earnestly offered.

"You are very kind," she faltered. "I am sorry to be so troublesome. I ought not to have come so far in such doubtful weather."

She went with him meekly, walking her fastest under the pelting rain, which was at her back now as they made for the house.

"Have you really come far?" he asked.

"From Trelasco. I live at the Angler's Nest, a cottage by the river. You know it, perhaps?"

"Yes. I know every house at Trelasco. Then you are staying with Mrs. Disney, I presume?"

"I am Mrs. Disney."

"You?"—with intense surprise. "I beg your pardon. You are so young. I imagined Mrs. Disney an older person."

He glanced at the girlish figure, the pale delicate face, and told himself that his new acquaintance could scarcely be more than nineteen or twenty. He had met Major Disney, a man who looked about forty—a lucky fellow to have caught such a pretty bird as this.

They had reached the shrubbery by this time, and were hurrying along a winding walk where the rain reached them with less violence. The narrow walk brought them on to a broad terrace in front of the house. Lostwithiel opened a half-glass door, and led Mrs. Disney into the library, a long, low room, full of curious nooks and corners, formed by two massive chimney-pieces, and by the projecting wings of the heavy oak bookcases. Isola had never seen any room so filled with books, nor had she ever seen a room with two such chimney-pieces, of statuary marble, yellowed with age, elaborately carved with cherubic heads, and Cupids, and torches and festal wreaths, bows and arrows, lyres and urns.

A wood fire was burning upon one hearth, and it was hither Lostwithiel brought his guest, wheeling a large armchair in front of the blaze.

"If you will take off your hat and jacket, and sit down there, I'll get my housekeeper to attend to you," he said, with his hand upon the bell.

"You are more than kind. I must hurry home directly the rain abates a little. I have a careful old servant who is sure to be anxious about me," said Isola, devouring the room with her eyes, wanting to take in every detail of this enchanted castle.

She might never enter it again, perhaps. Lord Lostwithiel was so seldom there. His absenteeism was the lament of the neighbourhood. The things he ought to have done and did not do would have filled a book. He had been wild in his youth. He had once owned a theatre. He had done, or was supposed to have done, things which were spoken of with bated breath; but of late years he had developed new ambitions, and had done with theatrical speculations. He had become literary, scientific, political. He was one of the lights of the intellectual world, or of that small section of the intellectual world which is affiliated to the smart world. He knew all the clever people in London, and a good many of the intellectualities of Paris, Berlin, and Vienna. He had never married; but it was supposed that he would eventually marry, before he was forty, for instance, and that he would make a great match. He was not rich, but he was Lord Lostwithiel. He was by no means handsome, but he was said to be one of the most fascinating men in London.

Isola pulled off her jacket slowly, looking about her all the time; and Lostwithiel forbore from offering her any assistance, lest he should intensify her evident shyness.

A man in plain clothes, who looked more like a valet than a butler, answered the bell.

"Send Mrs. Mayne, and bring tea," ordered his lordship.

What a slender, girlish form it was which the removal of the tweed jacket revealed! The slim waist and somewhat narrow shoulders betokened a delicacy of constitution. The throat was beautiful, milk white, the throat of Diana, and the head, now the hat was off, would also have done for Diana; a small classic head, with soft, brown hair drawn smoothly away from the low, white brow and rolled into a knot at the back. The features were as delicate as the complexion, in which there was no brilliancy of colouring, only a paleness as of ivory. The eyes were dark grey, with long, brown lashes, and their present expression was between anxiety and wondering interest. Lostwithiel was not such a coxcomb as to appropriate that look of interest. He saw that it was his house and not himself which inspired the feeling.

"You like old houses, I can see, Mrs. Disney," he said, smiling at her.

"Intensely. They are histories in brick and stone, are they not? I dare say there are stories about this room."

"Innumerable stories. I should have to ransack the Record Office for some of them, and to draw upon a very bad memory to a perilous extent for others."

"Is it haunted?"

"I am not one of those privileged persons who see ghosts; neither seventh son of a seventh son, nor of the mediumistic temperament; but I have heard of an apparition pervading the house on occasions, and being seen in this room, which once formed part of a certain small monastery, put down by Henry VIII., and recorded in the Black Book. As one of the oldest rooms it is naturally uncanny; but as I have never suffered any inconvenience in that line, I make it my den."

"It is the most picturesque room I ever saw. And what a multitude of books!" exclaimed Isola.

"Yes; I have a good many books. I am always buying; but I find I never have exactly the book I want. And as I have no librarian I am too apt to forget the books I have. If I could afford to spend more of my life at the Mount, I would engage some learned gentleman, whose life had been a failure, to take care of my books. Are you Cornish, like your husband, Mrs. Disney?"

"No. I was born at Dinan."

"What! in that mediæval Breton city? You are not French, though, I think?"

"My mother and father were both English, but my sister and I were born and brought up in Brittany."

Lostwithiel questioned no further. He had a shrewd idea that when English people live for a good many years in a Breton town they have reasons of their own, generally financial, for their choice of a settlement. He was a man who could not have spent six months of his life away from London or Paris.

The housekeeper made her appearance and offered her services. She wrung the rain out of Isola's cloth skirt, and wiped the muddy hem. She took charge of the jacket and hat, and at Lostwithiel's suggestion she remained to pour out the tea. She was a dignified person, in a black silk gown and a lace cap, and she treated her master as if he had been a demi-god. Isola could not be afraid of taking tea in this matronly presence, yet she kept looking nervously towards the window in front of her, where the rain beat with undiminished force, and where the night was closing in.

"I see you are anxious to be on your way home, Mrs. Disney," said Lostwithiel, who had nothing to do but watch her face, such an expressive face at all times, so picturesquely beautiful when touched by the flickering light of the wood fire. "If you were to wait for fine weather you might be here all night, and your good people at home would be frantic. I'll order a carriage, and you can be at home in three-quarters of an hour."

"Oh no, Lord Lostwithiel, I couldn't give you so much trouble. If your housekeeper will be so kind as to lend me a cloak and umbrella, I can get home very well. And I had better start at once."

"In the rain, alone, and in the darkness? It will be dark before you are home, in any case. No, Mrs. Disney, if I were to permit such a thing I should expect Major Disney to call me out directly he came home. He is in India, I think?"

10

"He is with his regiment in Burmah."

"Do you expect him home soon?"

"Not very soon; not for six months, or perhaps longer. It was that which made me walk so far."

Lostwithiel looked puzzled.

"I mean that I was so disappointed by his letter—a letter I received to-day—that I went out for a long ramble to walk down my bad spirits, and hardly knew how far I was going. It has made me inflict trouble on you, and Mrs.——"

"Mayne. Both Mrs. Mayne and I are delighted to be of use to you. Order the station brougham, Dalton, immediately," to the man who answered his bell. "The carriage can hardly be ready in less than twenty minutes, so pray try to do justice to Mrs. Mayne's tea."

"It is delicious tea," said Isola, enjoying the fire-glow, and the dancing lights upon the richly bound books in all their varieties of colouring, from black and crimson and orange-tawny to vellum diapered with gold.

She was evidently relieved in her mind by the knowledge that she was to be driven home presently.

"If you are really interested in this old house you must come some sunny morning and let Mrs. Mayne show you over it," said Lostwithiel, establishing himself with his cup and saucer upon the other side of the hearth. "She knows all the old stories, and she has a better memory than I."

"I should like so much to do so next summer, when my husband can come with me."

"I'm afraid Major Disney won't care much about the old place. He is a native of these parts, and must have been here often in my father's time. I shall hope to receive you both, if I am here next October for the shooting—but there is no need to postpone your inspection of the house to the remote future. Come on the first fine morning that you have nothing better to do. Mrs. Mayne is always at home; and I am almost always out of doors in the morning. You can have the house to yourselves, and talk about ghosts to your hearts' content."

"Oh, my lord, I hope I know better than to say anything disrespectful of the house," protested Mrs. Mayne.

"My dear Mayne, a family ghost is as respectable an institution as a family tree."

Isola murmured some vague acknowledgment of his civility. She was far too shy to have any idea of taking advantage of his offer. To re-enter that house alone of her own accord would be impossible. By-and-by, with her husband at her side, she would be bold enough to do anything, to accept any hospitality that Lostwithiel might be moved to offer. He would invite Martin, perhaps, for the shooting, or to a luncheon, or a dinner. She wondered vaguely if she would ever possess a gown good enough to wear at a dinner-party in such a house.

After this there came a brief silence. Mrs. Mayne stood straight and prim behind the tea-table. Nothing would have induced her to sit in his lordship's presence, albeit she had dandled him in her arms when there was much less of him than of the cambric and fine flannel which composed his raiment, and albeit his easy familiarity might have invited some forgetfulness of class distinctions. Mrs. Mayne fully understood that she was wanted there to set the stranger at her ease, and she performed her mission; but even her presence could not lessen Isola's shyness. She felt like a bird caught in a net, or fluttering in the grasp of some strong but kindly hand. She sat listening for carriage wheels, and only hearing the dull thumping of her own scared heart.

And yet he was so kind, and yet he so fully realized her idea of high-bred gentleness, that she need hardly have been so troubled by the situation. She stole a glance at him as he stood by the chimney-piece, in a thoughtful attitude, looking down at the burning logs on the massive old andirons. The firelight shining on a face above it will often give a sinister look to the openest countenance; and to-night Lostwithiel's long, narrow face, dark, deep-set eyes, and pointed beard had some touch of the diabolical in that red and uncertain glow; an effect that was but instantaneous, for as the light changed the look passed, and she saw him as he really was, with his pale and somewhat sunken cheeks, and eyes darkly grave, of exceeding gentleness.

12

"Have you lived long at the Angler's Nest, Mrs. Disney?" he asked.

"Nearly a year and a half; ever since my marriage, with just one interval on the Continent before Martin went to India."

"Then I need not ask if you are heartily sick of the place?"

"Indeed, I should not be tired of the cottage or the neighbourhood if my husband were at home. I am only tired of solitude. He wants me to send for his sister—a girl who has not long left school—to keep me company; but I detest school-girls, and I would much rather be alone than put up with a silly companion."

"You are wise beyond your years, Mrs. Disney. Avoid the sister, by all means. She would bore you to death—a scampering, exuberant girl, who would develop hysteria after one month of Cornish dulness. Besides, I am sure you have resources of your own, and that you would rather endure solitude than uncongenial company."

Isola sighed, and shook her head rather dolefully, tracing the pattern of the Persian rug with the point of her stick.

"I am very fond of books, and of music," she said; "but one gets tired of being alone after a time. It seems such ages since Martin and I said good-bye in Venice. I was dreadfully unhappy at first. I stand almost alone in the world, when I am parted from him."

"Your father and mother are dead?" in gentlest inquiry.

"Oh no; they are not dead; they are at Dinan," she said, almost as if it were the same thing.

"And that is very far from Trelasco."

"They never leave Dinan. The kind of life suits them. Mamma knits; papa has his club and his English newspapers. People enjoy the English papers so much more when they live abroad than when they are at home. Mamma is a very bad sailor. It would be a risk for her to cross. If my sister or I were dangerously ill, mamma would come. But it would be at the hazard of her life. Papa has often told me so."

"And your father, is he a bad sailor?"

"He is rather worse than mamma."

"Then I conclude you were married at Dinan?"

"Oh yes; I never left Brittany until my wedding-day."

"What a pretty idea! It is as if Major Disney had found a new kind of wild flower in some cranny of the old grey wall that guards the town."

"You know Dinan?"

"There are very few places within easy reach of a yachtsman that I don't know. I have anchored in almost every bay between Cherbourg and Brest, and have rambled inland whenever there was anything worth seeing within a day's journey from the coast. Yes, I know Dinan well. Strange to think that I may have passed you in the street there. Do you sketch, by the way?"

"A little."

"Ah, then, perhaps you are one of the young ladies I have seen sitting at street corners, or under archways, doing fearful and wonderful things with a box of moist colours and a drawing-board."

"The young ladies who sit about the streets are tourists," said Isola, with a look of disgust.

"I understand. The resident ladies would no more do such things than they would sit upon the pavement and make pictures of salmon or men-of-war in coloured chalks, like our Metropolitan artists."

"I think I hear a carriage," said Isola, putting down her cup and saucer, and looking at her jacket, which Mrs. Mayne was holding before the fire.

"Yes, that is the carriage," answered Lostwithiel, opening the glass door. "What a night! The rain is just as bad as it was when I brought you indoors."

"If you will accept the use of a shawl, ma'am, it would be safer than putting on this damp jacket."

"Yes, Mayne, get your shawl. Mrs. Disney will wear it, I know."

The housekeeper bustled out, and Lostwithiel and his guest were alone, looking at each other somewhat helplessly, as they stood far apart, she in the glow of the hearth, he in the darkness near the door, and feeling that every available subject of conversation had been exhausted. Their embarrassment was increased when Dalton and a footman came in with two great lamps and flooded the room with light.

"I hardly know how to thank you for having taken so much trouble about me," Isola faltered presently, under that necessity to say something which is one of the marks of shyness.

"There has been no trouble. I only hope I got you out of that pelting rain in time to save you from any evil consequences. Strange that our acquaintance should begin in such an accidental manner. I shall be glad to know more of Major Disney when he comes home, and in the meantime I hope I shall have the pleasure of meeting you sometimes. No doubt you know everybody in the neighbourhood, so we can hardly help running against each other somewhere."

Isola smiled faintly, thinking that the chances of any such meeting were of the slightest; but she did not gainsay him. He wanted to say something courteous no doubt, and had gone into no nice question of probabilities before he spoke. She had heard him described by a good many people, who had hinted darkly at his shortcomings, but had all agreed as to his politeness and persuasive powers.

"A man who would talk over Satan himself," said the village lawyer.

Mrs. Mayne reappeared with a comfortable Scotch plaid, which she wrapped carefully about Mrs. Disney, in a pleasant, motherly fashion. The rain had all been shaken off the little felt hat, which had no feathers or frippery to spoil. People who live in the west of England make their account with wet weather.

Lord Lostwithiel handed his guest into the carriage, and stood bareheaded in the rain to wish her good-bye before he shut the door.

"I shall be very anxious to know that you have escaped cold," he said, at the last moment. "I hope you won't think me a nuisance if I call to-morrow to inquire."

He shut the door quickly, and the brougham drove off before she could answer. She was alone in the darkness in the snug, warm little carriage. There was a clock ticking beside her, a sound that startled her in the stillness. There was a basket hanging in front of her, and an odour of cigars and Russia leather. There was a black bear rug, lined with white fleeciness, which almost filled the carriage. She had never sat in such a carriage. How different from the mouldy old brougham in which she occasionally went to dinner-parties—a capacious vehicle with a bow window, like a seaside parlour!

She leant back in a corner of the little carriage, wrapped in the soft, warm rug, wondering at her strange adventure. She had penetrated that mysterious house on Black-fir Hill, and she had made the acquaintance of Lord Lostwithiel. How much she would have to tell Martin in her next letter! She wrote to him every week—a long, loving letter, closely written on thin paper, pouring out all her fancies and feelings to the husband she loved with all her heart.

She sighed as her thoughts recurred to the letter received to-day. Six months, or perhaps even a year, before he was to come back to her! Yet the letter had not been without hopefulness. He had the prospect of getting his next step before that year was over, and then his coming home would be a final return. He would be able to retire, and he would buy some land—a hundred acres or so—and breed horses—one of his youthful dreams—and do a little building, perhaps, to enlarge and beautify the Angler's Nest, and his Isola should have a pair of ponies and a good saddle-horse. He looked forward to a life of unalloyed happiness.

## CHAPTER II.

### "BUT THE DAYS DROP ONE BY ONE."

Next morning was fine, a morning so bright and balmy that the month might have been mistaken for September. Isola ran down to the garden in her neat little morning frock and linen collar, and ran about among the shrubs and autumn flowers in a much gayer mood than that of yesterday. She loved her garden—small and modest as it was in comparison with the grounds and gardens of her county neighbours—and on a morning like this it was rapture to her to run from flower to flower, and from shrub to shrub, with her great garden scissors in her hand, and her garden basket hanging over her arm, clipping a withered leaf or a fading flower every here and there, or plucking up those little groundsel plants which seem the perpetual expression of the earth's fertility.

Alas! those pale tea-roses, those sulphur and flame-coloured dahlias, meant the last crumbs of summer's plenteous feast. Soon winter and barrenness would spread over the poor little garden; but even in the chill dark heart of mid-winter those graceful conifers and shining laurels, the vermilion on the holly bushes, the crimson of the hawthorn berries would give beauty to the scene; and then would come the return of Persephone with her hands full of gold, the abundant gold of crocus and daffodil, jonquil and pale primrose, the rain of yellow blossoms which heralds the spring.

Half a year did not seem such an appalling interval—nay, even the thought of a year of waiting did not scare her so much this morning in the sunlight and fresh clear air as yesterday in the grey dim rain. What an improvement Martin would find in the garden, should he return before the end of the summer! How tall those Irish yews had grown by the gate yonder, a pair of dark green obelisks keeping stately guard over the modest wooden gate; and the escalonia hedge that screened the kitchen garden was two feet higher since the spring! How the juniper at the corner of the grass plot had shot up and thickened! Arbutus, laurel, ribes, everything had been growing as shrubs only grow in the south and south-west of England. What a darling garden it was, and how full of pleasure her life would be by-

and-by, when Martin was able to settle down and buy land, and give her a little herd of Jersey cows! She had always envied the farmers' wives in that fertile valley of the Rance, where her childhood had been passed. And how delightful to have her own cows and her own farmyard, and a pony-carriage to drive up and down the hilly Cornish lanes and into the narrow little street of Fowey, and to ride her own horse by her husband's side for long exploring rambles among those wild hills towards Mevagissey!

She had only to wait patiently for a year or less, and that bright life might be hers. She had no frivolous vanities, no craving for dissipations and fine clothes, no fatal thirst for "smartness." Her ideas were essentially modest. She had never envied her sister, who had married a rich stockbroker, and whose brand new red-brick house in Hans Place towered above surrounding Chelsea as much as her diamonds eclipsed the jewels of other middle-class matrons at the festal gatherings of South Kensington and Bayswater. Gwendolen had married for wealth. Isola had married for love. She had given her girlish affection to a man who was nearly thirty years her senior, her heart going out to him almost at the beginning of their acquaintance, first because he was a soldier, and in her mind a hero, and secondly because he was kinder to her than anybody else had ever been.

He was her first admirer. That delicate loveliness, as of some woodland flower, which distinguished Isola from the herd of women, had been still in embryo when Major Disney spent a summer holiday between Dinard and Dinan. She had scarcely ranked as a pretty girl two years ago. The slight figure was denounced as scraggy; the pale face was voted sickly; and the delicate features were spoken of as insignificant. Gwendolen's big fair face, with its healthy roses and lilies, her bright hair, and well-developed figure, had completely overshadowed the younger sister. Martin Disney was the first man upon whom Isola's low-toned beauty had any power. He was drawn to her from the very beginning. She listened so prettily, with such a bewitching modesty and almost tremulous pleasure, when he talked to her, as they sat side by side on the club ground at Dinard, watching Gwendolen playing tennis, superb in striped flannel of delicate pink and cream

18

colour. He could hardly believe that those two were sisters. Isola was so slim and fragile, of such an ethereal prettiness, owing so little to colouring, and nothing to redundancy of form.

He was told that Miss Manwaring was engaged to one of the richest men in London. That, of course, was a gossip's fable, but it was an established fact that Mr. Hazelrigg had made his fortune in South American railways, water-works, and other public improvements, and could afford to make a liberal settlement.

He showed no indisposition to be generous to his handsome sweetheart. He settled seven hundred a year upon her, and told her that she could spend as much of that income as she liked upon toilet and pocket-money, and that he would invest her surplus advantageously for her.

The two sisters were married on the same day to husbands who were their seniors by more than twenty years in one instance, by thirty years in the other. Daniel Hazelrigg had passed his jubilee birthday when he led Miss Manwaring to the altar; but he was a fine-looking man, straight and tall, like his bride, with a ruddy complexion and iron-grey moustache, and an air and bearing that savoured rather of the mess-room than the city. He had been on the Stock Exchange ever since he came of age; but he had made it the study of his life not to look city or to talk city. Nothing could tempt him to expatiate upon the money market outside his office. He would talk sport, travel, politics—even literature, of which he knew very little—but not stocks and shares, Nicaraguas, or Reading and Philadelphias, Mexican Street Railways, or Patagonian Building Society.

Isola read her sister's glowing descriptions of dinners and routs, gowns by Worth or Cresser, suppers for two hundred people at a guinea a head, from Gunter, waggon-loads of cut roses from Cheshunt or Cheam, and felt no thrill of longing, no pang of envy. Life in the Angler's Nest might be dull; but it was only dull because Martin was away. She would have felt more solitary in Hans Place, had she accepted Gwendolen's invitation to spend her Christmas there, than she would feel in the cottage by the river, even with no better company than Tabitha, Shah, and Tim. She was essentially shy and retiring. Her girlhood had been spent in a very narrow world, among people whom she seemed to have known all her life; for while Gwendolen, who was six years older, and had been "out" for four years before she married, joined in all the little gaieties of the place, and was always making new acquaintance, Isola, who was not "out," spent her days for the most part in a half-neglected garden on the slope of the hill that looks across the Rance towards the unseen sea. The view from that garden was one of the finest in Western France; and it was Isola's delight to sit in a little berceau at the end of a terrace walk, with her books and work-basket and drawing-board, all through the long tranquil summer day, in a silence broken by the sound of wheels and horses' feet on the viaduct and bridge two or three hundred feet below, or by the muffled music of the organ in the convent chapel.

---

Tim, the fox-terrier, and Shah, the Persian cat, were both on the lawn with their mistress this morning. They were not friendly towards each other, but preserved an armed neutrality. Tim chased every stray strange cat with a fury that threatened annihilation; and he always looked as if he would like to give chase to Shah, when that dignified piece of fluff moved slowly across the lawn before him with uplifted tail that seemed to wave defiance; but he knew that any attack upon that valued personage would entail punishment and disgrace. Isola loved both these animals—the cat a wedding-present from an old Breton lady in Dinan, the terrier her husband's parting legacy. "Take care of Tim," he had said, the day they parted on board the steamer at Venice.

The dog loved his mistress vehemently and obtrusively, leaping into her lap at the slightest sign of indulgence in her eye. The cat suffered himself to be adored, receiving all attentions with a sleepy complacency.

It was only half-past eight, and the world was looking its freshest. There was an opening in the shrubbery that let in a view of the river, and just in front of this opening there was a rustic bench on which Major Disney liked to smoke his after-breakfast pipe or after-dinner cigar. The garden contained very little over two acres, but it was an old garden, and there were some fine old trees, which must have shaded hoops and powder, and pig-tails and knee-breeches. Major

Disney had done a great deal in the way of planting wherever there was room for improvement, and he had secured to himself an elderly gardener of exceptional industry, who worked in the garden as if he loved it. Tabitha, again, was one of those wonderful women who know all about everything except books; and she, too, loved the garden, and helped at weeding and watering, in seasons of pressure. Thus it had come to pass that these two acres of velvet lawn and flower-bed, shrubbery, and trim, old-fashioned garden had acquired a reputation in Trelasco, and people frequently complimented Mrs. Disney about her garden.

She was proud of their praises, remembering the straggling rose-bushes and lavender, and unkempt flower-beds, and overgrown cabbages, and loose shingly paths in that old garden at Dinan, which she had loved despite its neglected condition. Her house at Trelasco was just as superior to the house at Dinan, as garden was to garden. She often thought of her old home, the shabby square house, with walls and shutters of dazzling white, shining brown floors, and worn-out furniture of the Empire period, furniture which had been shabby and out of repair when Colonel Manwaring took the house furnished, intending to spend a month or two in retirement at Dinan with his wife and her firstborn, a chubby little girl of five. They had lost a promising boy of a year old, and the colonel, having no reason for living anywhere in particular, and very little to live upon, thought that residence in a foreign country would improve his wife's health and spirits. He had been told that Dinan was picturesque and cheap: and he had put himself and his family on board the *St. Malo* steamer and had gone out like an emigrant to push his fortunes in a strange land. He had even an idea that he might get "something to do" in Dinan—a secretaryship of a club, an agency, or managerial post of some kind, never having cultivated the art of self-examination so far as to discover that he must have proved utterly incapable, had any such occasion presented itself.

The occasion never did present itself. The one English club existent at Dinan in those days was amply provided with the secretarial element. There was nothing in Dinan for an Englishman to manage; no English agency required. Colonel Manwaring settled down into a kind of somnolent submission to obscure fortunes. He liked the old town, and he liked the climate. He liked the cooking, and he liked being out of the way of all the people he knew, and whose vicinity would have obliged him to live up to a certain conventional level. He liked to get his English newspapers upon French soil, and it irked him not that they were thirty-six hours old. He liked to bask in the sunshine on the terrace above the Rance, or in the open places of the town. He liked talking of the possibilities of an impending war, in very dubious French, with the French officers, whose acquaintance he made at club or café. He had sold his commission and sunk the proceeds of the sale upon an annuity. He had a little income of his own, and his wife had a little money from a maiden aunt, and these resources just enabled him to live with a certain unpretending comfort. He had a good Breton cook, and an old Scotch valet and butler, who would have gone through fire and water for his master. Mrs. Manwaring was a thoroughly negative character, placid as summer seas, sympathetic and helpless. She let Macgregor and Antoinette manage the house for her, do all the catering, pay all the bills, and work the whole machinery of her domestic life. She rejoiced in having a good-tempered husband and obedient daughters. She had no boys to put her in a fever of anxiety lest they should be making surreptitious ascents in balloons or staking their little all upon Zero at the "Etablissement" at Dinard. In summer she sat all day in one particular south window, knitting stockings for the colonel and reading the English papers. In winter she occupied herself in the same manner by the chimney corner. She devoted one day in the week to writing long letters to distant relatives. Once a day, weather permitting, she took a gentle constitutional walk upon the terrace above the Rance, with one of her daughters. Needless to say that in this life of harmless apathy she had grown very stout, and that she had forgotten almost every accomplishment of her girlhood.

From the placid monotony of life in Brittany to the placid monotony of life in Cornwall, was not a startling transition; yet when she married Martin Disney, and bade her commonplace father and her apathetic mother good-bye, Isola felt as if she had escaped from stagnation into a fresh and vigorous atmosphere. Disney's character made all the difference. He was every inch a soldier, a keen politician, a man who had seen many countries and read many books, clear-brained, strong-willed, energetic, self-reliant. She felt what it was to belong to somebody who was capable of taking care of her. She trusted him implicitly; and she loved him with as deep a love as a girl of nineteen is capable of feeling for any lover. It may be that the capacity for deep feeling is but half developed at that age, and in that one fact may be found the key to many domestic mysteries; mysteries of unions which begin in the gladness and warmth of responsive affection, and which, a few years later, pass into a frozen region of indifference or are wrecked on sunken rocks of guilty passion. Certain it was that Isola Manwaring gave her hand to this grave, middle-aged soldier, in all the innocence of a first love; and the love with which he rewarded her confidence, the earnest watchful love of a man of mature years, was enough for her happiness. That honeymoon time, that summer of installation in the Cornish cottage, and then the leisurely journey to Venice in the waning brilliance of a southern October, seemed like one long happy dream, as she looked back upon it now, after a year of solitude.

The doctor had decided that, in the delicate health in which she found herself at the end of that summer, it would be dangerous for her to accompany her husband to India, more especially as a campaign in Burmah meant roughing it, and she would in all probability have been separated from him in the East; so they bade each other a sad good-bye at Venice, and Isola travelled quickly homeward, all possible comfort having been secured for her on the way, by her husband's forethought. It had been a long, sad, sleepy journey, through a rain-blurred landscape, and she was glad when the evening of the fourth day brought her to the snug little dining-room in the Angler's Nest, where Tabitha was waiting for her with a cheerful fire and the amber-shaded reading lamp, and the most delightful little composite meal of chicken and tongue, and tart, and cream, and tea. It was pleasant to be among familiar things, after that long journey in stuffy ladies' carriages, with elderly invalids, whose chief talk was of their ailments. Pleasant to see the Shah's solemn sea-green eyes staring at her, and to have to repulse the demonstrative attentions of Tim, who leapt upon her lap and licked her face vehemently every time he caught her off her guard.

She was ill and broken down after her journey, and that sad parting, and she hid her tears upon Tabitha's comfortable arm.

23

"It will be at least a year before he comes back," she sobbed. "How can I live without him all that dreary time?"

Tabitha thought it was very hard upon the girl-wife, but affected to make light of it. "Lor, bless you, ma'am," she said, "a year looks a long time, but it isn't much when you come to grapple with it. There'll be such a lot for you to do. There'll be the garden. We ought to make ever so many improvements next spring and summer, against the master comes home. And there's your piano. You want to improve yourself—I've heard you say so—and you can get up all sorts of new tunes, and won't the major be pleased with you; and then—there'll be something else to occupy your mind before next summer comes."

That "something else" which was to have filled Isola's empty life with a new interest, ended in disappointment. She was very ill at the beginning of the new year, and Tabitha nursed her with motherly tenderness long after the doctor and the professional nurse had renounced their care of her. She regained strength very slowly after that serious illness, and it was only in June that she was able to take the lonely rambles she loved, or row in her little boat upon the river.

Tabitha was a servant in a thousand, faithful and devoted, clever, active, and industrious. She had been maid to Martin Disney's mother for nearly fifteen years, had nursed her mistress through a long and weary illness, and had closed her eyes in death. Martin parted with that faithful servant with reluctance after the breaking up of his mother's household, and he told her if he should marry and have a house of his own—a very remote contingency—she must be his housekeeper. Love and marriage came upon him before the end of the year, as a delightful surprise. He bought the Angler's Nest, and he engaged Tabitha for the rest of her life, at wages which, beginning at a liberal figure, were to rise a pound every Christmas.

"As if I cared about wages, Mr. Martin," exclaimed Tabitha. "I'd just as soon come to you for nothing. I've got more clothes than will last my time, I'll be bound. You'd only have to find me in shoe-leather."

She had never got out of the way of calling her master by the name by which she had first known him, when his father and elder brother were both at home, in the old family house at Fowey. In all moments of forgetfulness he was still "Mr. Martin."

---

And now, in this bright November morning, Tabitha came out to say that breakfast was waiting for her young mistress, and mistress and maid went in together to the cosy dining-room, where the small round table near the window was arranged as only Tabitha could arrange a table—with autumn flowers, and spotless damask, and a new-laid egg, and a dish of honey, and some dainty little rolls of Tabitha's own making, nestling in a napkin, a breakfast for a Princess in a fairy tale.

There was only one other servant in the little household—a bouncing, rosy-cheeked Cornish girl, who was very industrious under Tabitha's eye, and very idle when she was out of that faithful housekeeper's ken. Tabitha cooked and took care of everything, and for the most part waited upon her mistress in this time of widowhood, although Susan was supposed to be parlour-maid.

Tabitha poured out the tea, and buttered a roll, while Isola leant back in the bamboo chair and played with the Shah.

"I never knew him do such a thing before," said Tabitha, in continuation of a theme which had been fully discussed last night.

"Oh, it was very kind and polite; but it was not such a tremendous thing, after all," answered Isola, still occupied with the Persian. "He could hardly stand by and see one drowned. You have no idea what the rain was like."

"But to send you home in his own carriage."

"There was nothing else for him to do—except send me home in the gardener's cart. He could not have turned out a dog in such weather."

"It's a thing that never happened before, and it just shows what a respect he must have for the Disneys. You don't know how stand-offish he is with all the people about here—how he keeps himself to himself. Not a bit like his father and mother. They used to entertain all the neighbourhood, and they went everywhere, as affable as you like. He has taken care to show people that he doesn't want their company. They say he has led a very queer kind of life at home and abroad; never settling down anywhere, here to-day and gone to-morrow; roving about with his yacht. I don't believe any good ever comes of a young gentleman like that having a yacht. It would be ever so much better for him to live at the Mount and keep a pack of harriers."

"Why should a yacht be bad?" asked Isola, lazily beginning her breakfast, Tabitha standing by the table all the time, ready for conversation.

"Oh, I don't know. It gives a young man too much liberty," answered Tabitha, shaking her head with a meaning air, as if with a knowledge of dark things in connection with yachts. "He can keep just what company he likes on board—gentlemen or ladies. He can gamble—or drink—as much as he likes. There's nobody to check him. Sundays and weekdays, night and day, are all alike to him."

"Lord Lostwithiel is not particularly young," said Isola, musingly, not paying much attention to this homily on yachts. "He must be thirty, I think."

"Thirty-two last birthday. He ought to marry and settle down. They say he's very clever, and that he's bound to make a figure in politics some of these odd days."

Isola looked at the clock on the chimney-piece—a gilt horse-shoe with onyx nails; one of her wedding presents. It was early yet—only half-past nine. Lord Lostwithiel had talked about calling to inquire after her health. She felt overpowered with shyness at the thought of seeing him again, alone—with no stately Mrs. Mayne to take the edge off a *tête-à-tête*. Anything to escape such an ordeal! There was her boat—that boat of which she was perfect mistress, and in which she went for long, dawdling expeditions towards Fowey or Lostwithiel with only Tim for her companion—Tim, who was the best of company, in almost perpetual circulation between stem and stern, balancing himself in perilous places every now and then, to bark furiously at imaginary foes in slowly passing fishermen's boats.

"Have you any fancy about lunch, ma'am?" asked Tabitha, lingering with feather-brush in hand over a side-table, on which work-basket, books, writing-case, and flower-vases were arranged with tasteful neatness by those skilful hands.

"No, you dear old Tabbie; you know that anything will do for me. Bread and jam, if you like, and some of your clotted cream. Won't it be nice when we have our very own dairy, and our very own cows, who will know us and be fond of us, like Tim and the Shah?"

She put on her hat and jacket, and went out into the garden again, singing "La Lettre de Perichole" as she went. It was a capital idea to take refuge in her boat. If his lordship should call—which was doubtful—since he might be one of that numerous race of people whose days are made up of unfulfilled intentions and promises never realized—if he should call, she would be far away when he came. He would make his inquiry, leave his card, which would look nice in the old Indian bowl on the hall-table. Such cards have a power of flotation unknown to other pasteboard; they are always at the top.

Isola went to the little boat-house on the edge of the lawn, Tim following her. She pushed the light skiff down the slope into the water, and in a few minutes more her sculls were in the rowlocks and she was moving slowly up the river, between autumnal woods, in a silence broken only by the dip of the sculls and the little rippling sound as the water dropped away from them. A good deal of her life was spent like this, moving slowly up the river through that deep silence of the woodland shores. The river was as beautiful as the Dart almost, but lonelier and more silent. It was Martin Disney's river—the river whose ripples had soothed his mother's dying ears—the last of all earthly sounds that had been heard in the stillness of the death-chamber.

In that tranquil atmosphere Isola used to dream of her absent husband and of that mystical world of the East which seemed made up of dreams—the world of Brahma and Buddha, of jewel-bedecked Rajahs and Palace-tombs—world of beauty and of terror; of tropical forests, tigers, orchids, serpents, elephants, Thugs.

She dreamt her dream of that strange world in fear and trembling, conjuring up scenes of horror—tiger hunts; snakes hidden in the corner of a tent; battle; fever; fire; mutiny. Her morbid imagination pictured all possible and impossible danger for the man she loved. And then she thought of his home-coming—for good, for good—for all the span of their joint lives; and she longed for that return with the sickness of hope deferred.

She would go back to the Angler's Nest sometimes after one of these dreamy days upon the river, and would pace about the house or the garden, planning things for her husband's return, as if he were due next day. She would wheel his own particular chair to the drawing-room fireplace, and look at it, and arrange the fall of the curtains before the old-fashioned bow-window, and change the position of the lamp, and alter the books on the shelves, and do this and that with an eye to effect, anxious to discover how the room might be made prettiest, cosiest, most lovable and home-like—for him, for him, for him!

And now she had to resign herself to a year's delay, perhaps. Yes, he had said it might be a year. All that bright picture of union and content, which had seemed so vivid and so near, had now grown dim and pale. It had melted into a shadowy distance. To a girl who has but just passed her twentieth birthday a year of waiting and delay seems an eternity.

"I won't think of him," she said to herself, plunging her sculls fiercely into the rippling water. The tide was running down, and it was strong enough to have carried her little boat out to sea like an autumn leaf swept along the current. "I must try to lull my mind to sleep, as if I were an enchanted Princess, and so bridge over twelve slow months of loneliness. I won't think of you, Martin, my good, brave, truest of the true! I'll occupy my poor, foolish little mind. I'll write a novel, perhaps, like old Miss Carver at Dinan. Anything in the world—just to keep my thoughts from always brooding on one subject."

She rowed on steadily, hugging the shore under the wooded hillside, where the rich autumn colouring and the clear, cool lights were so full of beauty—a beauty which she could feel, with a vague, dim sense which just touched the realm of poetry. Perhaps she felt the same sense of loss which Keats or Alfred de Musset would have felt in the stillness of such a scene—the want of something to people the wood and the river—some race of beings loftier than fishermen and peasants; some of those mystic forms which the poet sees amidst the shadows of old woods or in the creeks and sheltered inlets of a secluded river.

She thought, with a half-smile, of yesterday's adventure. What importance that foolish Tabitha gave to so simple an incident; the merest commonplace courtesy, necessitated by circumstances; and only because the person who had been commonly courteous was Richard Hulbert, thirteenth Baron Lostwithiel. Thirteenth Baron! There lay the distinction. These Cornish folks worshipped antique lineage. Tabitha would have thought very little of a mushroom peer's civility, although he had sent her mistress home in a chariot and four. She was no worshipper of wealth, and she turned up her blunt old nose at Mr. Crowther, of Glenaveril—the great new red-brick mansion which had sprung up like a fungus amidst the woods only yesterday—because he had made his money in trade, albeit his trade had been upon a large scale, and altogether genteel and worthy to be esteemed—a great cloth factory at Stroud, which was said to have clad half the army at one period of modern history.

Poor, foolish Tabitha! What would she have thought of the tea-drinking in that lovely old room, mysteriously beautiful in the light of a wood fire—the playful, uncertain light which glorifies everything? What would she have thought of those walls of books— richly bound books, books in sombre brown, big books and little books, from floor to ceiling? A room which made those poor little oak bookcases in the cottage parlour something to blush for. What would Tabitha have thought of his deferential kindness—that tone of deepest consideration with which such men treat all women, even the old and uncomely? She could hardly have helped admiring his good manners, whatever dark things she might have been told about his earlier years.

Why should he not have a yacht? It seemed the fittest life for a man without home ties; a man still young, and with no need to labour at a profession. What better life could there be than that free wandering from port to port over a romantic sea?—and to Isola all seas were alike mysterious and romantic.

She dawdled away the morning; she sculled against the stream for nearly three hours, and then let her boat drift down the river to the garden above the towpath. It was long past her usual time for luncheon when she moored her boat to the little wooden steps, leaving it for Thomas, the gardener, to pull up into the boat-house. She had made up her mind that if Lostwithiel troubled himself to make any inquiry about her health he would call in the morning.

She had guessed rightly. Tabitha was full of his visit, and his wondrous condescension. He had called at eleven o'clock, on his way to the railway station at Fowey. He called in the most perfect of T carts, with a pair of bright bays. Tabitha had opened the door to him. He had asked quite anxiously about Mrs. Disney's health. He had walked round the garden with Tabitha and admired everything, and had told her that Major Disney had a better gardener than any he had at the Mount, after which he had left her charmed by his amiability. And so this little episode in Isola's life came to a pleasant end, leaving no record but his lordship's card, lying like a jewel on the top of less distinguished names in the old Indian bowl.

## CHAPTER III.

### "OH MOMENT ONE AND INFINITE!"

Isola fancied that her adventure was all over and done with after that ceremonious call of inquiry; but in so narrow a world as that of Trelasco it was scarcely possible to have seen the last of a man who lived within three miles; and she and Lord Lostwithiel met now and then in the course of her solitary rambles. The walk into Fowey, following the old disused railway, was almost her favourite, and one which she had occasion to take oftener than any other, since Tabitha was a stay-at-home person, and expected her young mistress to do all the marketing, so that Isola had usually some errand to take her into the narrow street on the hillside above the sea. It was at Fowey that she oftenest met Lostwithiel. His yacht, the *Vendetta*, was in the harbour under repairs, and he went down to look at the work daily, and often dawdled upon the deck till dusk, watching the carpenters, or talking to his captain. They had been half over the world together, master and man, and were almost as familiar as brothers. The crew were half English and half foreign; and it was a curious mixture of languages in which Lostwithiel talked to them. They were most of them old hands on board the *Vendetta*, and would have stood by the owner of the craft if he had wanted to sail her up the Phlegethon.

She was a schooner of two hundred and fifty tons, built for speed, and with a rakish rig. She had cost, with her fittings, her extra silk sails for racing, more money than Lostwithiel cared to remember; but he loved her as a man loves his mistress, and if she were costly and exacting, she was no worse than other mistresses, and she was true as steel, which they are not always; and so he felt that he had money's worth in her. He showed her to Isola one evening from the promontory above the harbour, where she met him in the autumn sundown. Her work at the butcher's and the grocer's being done, she had gone up to that airy height by Point Neptune to refresh herself with a long look seaward before she went back to her home in the valley. Lostwithiel took her away from the Point, and made her look down into the harbour.

"Isn't she a beauty?" he asked, pointing below.

Her inexperienced eyes roamed about among the boats, colliers, fishing-boats, half a dozen yachts of different tonnage.

"Which is yours?" she asked.

"Which? Why, there is only one decent boat in the harbour. The schooner."

She saw which boat he meant by the direction in which he flourished his walking-stick, but was not learned in distinctions of rig. The *Vendetta*, being under repair, did not seem to her especially lovely.

"Have you pretty cabins?" she asked childishly.

"Oh yes, they're pretty enough; but that's not the question. Look at her lines. She skims over the water like a gull. Ladies seem to think only what a boat looks like inside. I believe my boat is rather exceptional, from a lady's point of view. Will you come on board and have a look at her?"

"Thanks, no; I couldn't possibly. It will be dark before I get home as it is."

"But it wouldn't take you a quarter of an hour, and we could row you up the river in no time—ever so much faster than you could walk."

Isola looked frightened at the very idea.

"Not for the world!" she said. "Tabitha would think I had gone mad. She would begin to fancy that I could never go out without over-staying the daylight, and troubling you to send me home."

"Ah, but it is so long since you were last belated," he said, in his low caressing voice, with a tone that was new to her and different from all other voices; "ages and ages ago—half a lifetime. There could be no harm in being just a little late this mild evening, and I would row you home—myself, under the new moon. Look at her swinging up in the grey blue there above Polruan. She looks like a fairy boat, anchored in the sky by that star hanging a fathom below her keel. I look at her, and wish—wish—wish!"

He looked up, pale in the twilight, with dark deep-set eyes, of which it was never easy to read the expression. Perhaps that inscrutable look made those sunken and by no means brilliant eyes more interesting than some much handsomer eyes—interesting with the deep interest that belongs to the unknowable.

"Good night," said Isola. "I'm afraid that I shall be very late."

"Good night. You would be earlier if you would trust to the boat."

He held out his hand, and she gave him hers, hesitatingly for the first time in their acquaintance. It was after this parting in the wintry sundown that she first began to look troubled at meeting him.

The troubled feeling grew upon her somehow. In a life so lonely and uneventful trifles assume undue importance. She tried to avoid him, and on her journeys to Fowey she finished her business in the village street and turned homewards without having climbed the promontory by that rugged walk she loved so well. It needed some self-denial to forego that keen pleasure of standing on the windy height and gazing across the western sea towards Ushant and her native province; but she knew that Lord Lostwithiel spent a good deal of his time lounging on the heights above the harbour, and she did not want to meet him again.

Although she lived her quiet life in the shortening days for nearly a month without meeting him, she was not allowed to forget his existence. Wherever she went people talked about him and speculated about him. Every detail of his existence made matter for discussion; his yacht, his political opinions, his talents, his income, his matrimonial prospects, the likelihood or unlikelihood of his settling down permanently at the Mount, and taking the hounds, which were probably to be without a master within a measurable distance of time. There was so little to talk about in Trelasco and those scattered hamlets between Fowey and Lostwithiel.

Isola found herself joining in the talk at afternoon tea-parties, those casual droppings in of charitable ladies who had been their rounds among the cottagers and came back to the atmosphere of gentility worn out by long stories of woes and ailments, sore legs and rheumatic joints, and were very glad to discuss a local nobleman over a cup of delicately flavoured Indian tea in the glow of a flower-scented drawing-room.

Among other houses Mrs. Disney visited Glenaveril, Mr. Crowther's great red-brick mansion, with its pepper-box turrets, and Jacobean windows, after the manner of Burleigh House by Stamford town.

Here lived in wealth and state quite the most important family within a mile of Trelasco, the Vansittart Crowthers, erst of Pilbury Mills, near Stroud, now as much county as a family can make itself after its head has passed his fortieth birthday. Nobody quite knew how Mr. Crowther had come to be a Vansittart—unless by the easy process of baptism and the complaisance of an aristocratic sponsor; but the Crowthers had been known in Stroud for nearly two hundred years, and had kept their sacks upright, as Mr. Crowther called it, all that time.

Fortune had favoured this last of the Crowthers, and, at forty years of age, he had found himself rich enough to dispose of his business to two younger brothers and a brother-in-law, and to convert himself into a landed proprietor. He bought up all the land that was to be had about Trelasco. Cornish people cling to their land like limpets to a rock; and it was not easy to acquire the ownership of the soil. In the prosperous past, when land was paying nearly four per cent. in other parts of England, Cornishmen were content to hold estates that yielded only two per cent.; but the days of decay had come when Mr. Crowther entered the market, and he was able to buy out more than one gentleman of ancient lineage.

When he had secured his land, he sent to Plymouth for an architect, and he so harried that architect and so tampered with his drawings that the result of much labour and outlay was that monstrosity in red brick with stone dressings, known in the neighbourhood as Glenaveril. Mr. Crowther's elder daughter was deep in Lord Lytton's newly published poem when the house was being finished, and had imposed that euphonious name upon her father. Glenaveril. The house really was in a glen, or at least in a wooded valley, and Glenaveril seemed to suit it to perfection; and so the romantic name of a romantic poem was cut in massive Gothic letters on the granite pillars of Vansittart Crowther's gate, beneath a shield which exhibited the coat of arms made and provided by the Herald's College.

Mrs. Vansittart Crowther was at home on Thursday afternoons, when the choicest Indian tea and the thickest cream, coffee as in Paris, and the daintiest cakes and muffins which a professed cook could provide, furnished the zest to conversation; for it could scarcely be said that the conversation gave a zest to those creature comforts. It would be perhaps nearer the mark to say that Mrs. Crowther was supposed to sit in the drawing-room on these occasions while the two Miss Crowthers were at home. The mistress of Glenaveril was not an aspiring woman; and in her heart of hearts she preferred Gloucestershire to Cornwall, and the stuccoed villa on the Cheltenham road, with its acre and a half of tennis-lawn and flower-beds, open to the blazing sun, and powdered with the summer dust, to Glenaveril, with its solemn belt of woodlands, and its too spacious grandeur. She was not vulgar or illiterate. She never misplaced an aspirate. She had learnt to play the piano and to talk French at the politest of young ladies' schools at Cheltenham. She never dressed outrageously, or behaved rudely. She had neither red hands nor splay feet. She was in all things blameless; and yet Belinda and Alicia, her daughters, were ashamed of her, and did their utmost to keep her, and her tastes, and her opinions in the background. She had no style. She was not "smart." She seemed incapable of grasping the ideas, or understanding the ways of smart people; or at least her daughters thought so.

"Your mother is one of the best women I know," said the curate to Alicia, being on the most confidential terms with both sisters, "and yet you and Miss Crowther are always trying to edit her."

"Father wants a great deal more editing than mother," said Belinda, "but there's no use in talking to him. He is encased in the armour of self-esteem. It made my blood run cold to see him taking Lord Lostwithiel over the grounds and stables the other day—praising everything, and pointing out this and that,—and even saying how much things had cost!"

"I dare say it was vulgar," agreed the curate, "but it's human nature. I've seen a duke behave in pretty much the same way. Children are always proud of their new toys, and men are but children of a larger growth, don't you know. You'll find there's a family resemblance in humanity, and that nature is stronger than training."

"Lord Lostwithiel would never behave in that kind of way—boring people about his stables."

"Lord Lostwithiel doesn't care about stables—he would bore you about his yacht, I dare say."

"No, he never talks of himself or his own affairs. That is just the charm of his manner. He makes us all believe that he is thinking about us; and yet I dare say he forgets us directly he is outside the gate."

"I'm sure he does," replied Mr. Colfox, the curate. "There isn't a more selfish man living than Lostwithiel."

The fair Belinda looked at him angrily. There are assertions which young ladies make on purpose to have them controverted.

Mrs. Disney hated the great red-brick porch, with its vaulted roof and monstrous iron lantern, and the bell which made such a clamour, as if it meant fire, or at least dinner, when she touched the hanging brass handle. She hated to find herself face to face with a tall footman, who hardly condescended to say whether his mistress were at home or not, but just preceded her languidly along the broad corridor, where the carpet was so thick that it felt like turf, and flung open the drawing-room door with an air, and pronounced her name into empty space, so remote were the half-dozen ladies at the other end of the room, clustered round Belinda's tea-table, and fed with cake by Alicia, while Mrs. Crowther sat in the window a little way off, with her basket of woolwork at her side, and her fat somnolent pug lying at her feet. To Isola it was an ordeal to have to walk the length of the drawing-room, navigating her course amidst an archipelago of expensive things—Florentine tables, portfolios of engravings, Louis Seize Jardinières, easels supporting the last expensive etching from Goupil's—to the window where Mrs. Crowther waited to receive her, rising with her lap full of wools, to shake hands with simple friendliness and without a vestige of style. Belinda shook hands on a level with the tip of her sharp *retroussé* nose, and twirled the silken train of her tea-gown with the serpentine grace of Sarah Bernhardt. She prided herself on those serpentine movements and languid graces which belong to the Græco-Belgravian period; while Alicia held herself like a ramrod, and took her stand upon being nothing if not sporting. Her olive-cloth gown and starched collar, her neat double-soled boots and cloth gaiters, were a standing reproach to Belinda's silken slovenliness and embroidered slippers, always dropping off her restless feet, and being chased surreptitiously among her lace and pongee frillings. Poor Mrs. Crowther disliked the Guard's collar, which she felt was writing premature wrinkles upon her younger girl's throat, but she positively loathed the loose elegance of the Indian silk tea-gown, with its wide Oriental sleeves, exhibiting naked arms to the broad daylight. That sloppy raiment made a discord in the subdued harmony of the visitors' tailor-made gowns—well worn some of them—brown, and grey, and indigo, and russet; and Mrs. Crowther was tortured by the conviction that her elder daughter looked disreputable. This honest matron was fond of Isola Disney. In her own simple phraseology, she had "taken to her;" and pressed the girl-wife to come every Thursday afternoon.

"It must be so lonely for you," she said gently, "with your husband so far away, and you such a child, too. I wonder your mamma doesn't come and stay with you for a bit. You must always come on our Thursdays. Now mind you do, my dear."

"I don't think our Thursdays are remarkably enlivening, mother," said Alicia, objecting to the faintest suggestion of fussiness, the crying sin of both her parents. And then she turned to Isola, and measured her from head to foot. "It's rather a pity you don't hunt," she said. "We had a splendid morning with the hounds."

"Perhaps I may get a little hunting by-and-by, when my husband comes home."

"Ah, but one can't begin all at once; and this is a difficult country; breakneck hills, and nasty banks. Have you hunted much?"

"Hardly at all. I was out in a boar-hunt once, near Angers, but only as a looker-on. It was a grand sight. The Duke of Beaufort came over to Brittany on purpose to join in it."

"How glorious a boar-hunt must be! I must get my father to take me to Angers next year. Do you know a great many people there?"

"No, only two or three professors at the college, and the Marquis de Querangal, the gentleman who has the boar-hounds. His daughter used to visit at Dinan, and she and I were great friends."

"Lord Lostwithiel talked about boar-hunting the other night," said Alicia. "It must be capital fun." His name recurred in this way, whatever the conversation might be, with more certainty than Zero on the wheel at roulette.

He had been there in the evening, Isola thought. There had been a dinner-party, perhaps, at which he had been present. She had not long to wonder. The name once pronounced, the stream of talk flowed on. Yes, there had been a dinner, and Lord Lostwithiel had been delightful; so brilliant in conversation as compared with everybody else; so witty, so cynical, so *fin de siècle*.

"I didn't hear him say anything very much out of the common," said Mrs. Crowther, in her matter-of-fact way.

She liked having a nobleman or any other local magnate at her table; but she had too much common sense to be hypnotized by his magnificence, and made to taste milk and water as Maronean wine.

"Do you know Lord Lostwithiel?" Belinda asked languidly, as Isola sipped her tea, sitting shyly in the broad glare of a colossal fireplace. "Oh yes, by-the-by, you met him here the week before last."

Mrs. Disney blushed to the roots of those soft tendril-like curls which clustered about her forehead; but she said never a word. She had no occasion to tell them the history of that meeting in the rain, or of those many subsequent meetings which had drifted her into almost the familiarity of an old friendship. They might take credit to themselves for having made her acquainted with their star if they liked. She had seen plenty of smart people at Dinan in those sunny summer months when visitors came from Dinard to look at the old quiet inland city. Lostwithiel's rank had no disturbing influence upon her mind. It was himself—something in his look and in his voice, in the mere touch of his hand—an indescribable something which of late had moved her in his presence, and made her faintly tremulous at the sound of his name.

He was announced while they were talking of him, and he seemed surprised to come suddenly upon that slim unobtrusive figure almost hidden by Belinda's flowing garment and fuller form. Belinda was decidedly handsome—handsomer than an heiress need be; but she was also just a shade larger than an heiress need be at three and twenty. She was a Rubens' beauty, expansive, florid, and fair, with reddish auburn hair piled on the top of her head. Sitting between this massive beauty and the still more massive chimney-piece, Mrs. Disney was completely hidden from the new arrival.

He discovered her suddenly while he was shaking hands with Belinda, and his quick glance of pleased surprise did not escape that young lady's steely blue eyes. Not a look or a breath ever does escape observation in a village drawing-room. Even the intellectual people, the people who devour all Mudie's most solid books—travels, memoirs, metaphysics, agnostic novels—even these are as keenly interested in their neighbours' thoughts and feelings as the unlettered rustic in the village street.

Lostwithiel took the proffered cup of tea, and planted himself near Mrs. Disney, with his back against the marble caryatid which bore up one-half of the chimney-piece. Alicia began to talk to him about his yacht. How were the repairs going on? and so on, and so on, delighted to air her technical knowledge. He answered her somewhat languidly, as if the *Vendetta* were not first in his thoughts at this particular moment.

"What about this ball?" he asked presently. "You are all going to be there, of course?"

"Do you mean the hunt ball at Lostwithiel?"

"Of course! What other ball could I mean? It is the great festivity of these parts. The one tremendous event of the winter season. It was a grand idea of you new people to revive the old festivity, which had become a tradition. I wore my first dress coat at the Lostwithiel Hunt Ball nearly twenty years ago. I think it was there I first fell in love, with a young lady in pink tulle, who was miserable because she had been mistaken enough to wear pink at a hunt ball. I condoled with her, assured her that in my eyes she was lovely, although her gown clashed—that was her word, I remember—with the pink coats. My coat was not pink, and I believe she favoured me a little on that account. She gave me a good many waltzes in the course of the evening, and I can answer for her never wearing that pink frock again, for I trampled it to shreds. There were traces of her to be found all over the rooms, as if I had been Greenacre and she my victim's body."

"It will be rather a humdrum ball, I'm afraid," said Belinda. "All the best people seem to be away."

"Never mind that if the worst people can dance. I am on the committee, so I will answer for the supper and the champagne. You like a dry brand, of course, Miss Crowther?"

"I never touch wine of any kind."

"No; then my chief virtue will be thrown away upon you. Are all young ladies blue-ribbonites nowadays, I wonder? Mrs. Disney, pray tell me you are interested in the champagne question."

"I am not going to the ball."

"Not going! Oh, but it is a duty which you owe to the county! Do you think because you are an alien and a foreigner you can flout our local gaieties—fleer at our solemnities? No, it is incumbent upon you to give us your support."

"Yes, my dear, you must go to the ball," put in Mrs. Crowther, in her motherly tone. "You are much too young and pretty to stay at home, like Cinderella, while we are all enjoying ourselves. Of course you must go. Mr. Crowther has put down his name for five and twenty tickets, and I'm sure there'll be one to spare for you, although we shall have a large house-party."

"Indeed, you are too kind, but I couldn't think——" faltered Isola, with a distressed look.

She knew that Lostwithiel was watching her from his vantage ground ever so far above her head. A man of six feet two has considerable advantages at a billiard-table, and in a quiet flirtation carried on in public.

"If it is a chaperon you are thinking about, I'll take care of you," urged good Mrs. Crowther.

"No, it isn't on that account. Mrs. Baynham offered to take me in her party. But I really would much rather not be there. It would seem horrid to me to be dancing in a great, dazzling room, among happy people, while Martin is in Burmah, perhaps in peril of his life on that very night. One can never tell. I often shudder at the thought of what may be happening to him while I am sitting quietly by the fire. And what should I feel at a ball?"

"I should hardly have expected you to have such romantic notions about Major Disney," said Belinda, coolly, "considering the difference in your ages."

"Do you suppose I care the less for him because he is twenty years older than I am?"

"Twenty! Is it really as much as that?" ejaculated Mrs. Crowther, unaffectedly shocked.

"He is just as dear to me," pursued Isola, warmly. "I look up to him, and love him with all my heart. There never was a better, truer man. From the time I began to read history I always admired great soldiers. I don't mean to say that Martin is a hero—only I know he is a thorough soldier—and he seemed to realize all my childish dreams."

She had spoken impetuously, fancying that there was some slight towards her absent husband in Miss Crowther's speech. Her flash of anger made a break in the conversation, and nothing more was said about her going or not going to the Hunt Ball. They talked of that entertainment in the abstract—discussed the floor—the lighting—the band—and the great people who might be induced to appear, if the proper pressure were put upon them.

"There is plenty of time," said Lostwithiel, "between now and the twenty-second of December—nearly three weeks. Time for you and your sister to get new frocks from London or Paris, Miss Crowther. You mean having new frocks, I suppose?"

"One generally does have a new frock for a dance," replied Belinda, "though the fashions this winter are so completely odious that I would much rather appear in a gown of my great-grandmother's."

Lostwithiel smiled his slow secret smile high up in the fainter firelight. He was reflecting upon his notion of Miss Crowther's great-grandmother, in linsey-wolsey, with a lavender print apron, a costume that would be hardly impressive at a Hunt Ball. He did not give the young lady credit for a great-grandmother from the Society point of view. There was the mother yonder—inoffensive respectability—the grandmother would be humbler—and the great-grandmother he imagined at the wash-tub, or cooking the noontide meal for an artisan husband. He had never yet realized the idea of numerous generations of middle-class life upon the same plane, the same dead level of prosperous commerce.

Isola rose to take leave, after having let her tea get cold, and dropped half her cake on the Persian rug. She felt shyer in that house than in any other. She had a feeling that there she was weighed in the balance and found wanting; that unfriendly eyes were scrutinizing her gloves and hat, and appraising her features and complexion. She felt herself insignificant, colourless, insipid beside that brilliant Miss Crowther, with her vivid beauty, and her self-assured airs and graces.

Tabitha urged her to be of good heart when she hinted at these feelings.

"Why, Lord have mercy upon us, ma'am, however grand they may all look, it's nothing but wool—only wool; and I heard there used to be a good deal of devil's dust mixed with it, after this Mr. Crowther came into the business."

The dusk was thickening as she went along the short avenue which led to the gates. Mr. Crowther, having built his house in a wood, had been able to cut himself out a carriage drive, which gave him an avenue of more than two centuries' growth, and thus imparted an air of spurious antiquity to his demesne. He felt, as he looked at the massive boles of those old Spanish chestnuts, as if he had belonged to the soil since the Commonwealth.

Even the lodge was an important building, Tudor on one side, and monastic on the other; with that agreeable hodge-podge of styles which the modern architect loveth. It was a better house than the curate lived in, as he often told Miss Crowther.

Isola quickened her pace outside that solemn gateway, and seemed to breathe more freely. She hurried even faster at the sound of a footstep behind her, though there was no need for nervous apprehensions at that early hour in the November evening on the high road between Fowey and Trelasco. Did she know that firm, quick footfall; or was it an instinctive avoidance of an unknown danger which made her hurry on till her heart began to beat stormily, and her breath came in short gasps?

"My dear Mrs. Disney, do you usually walk as if for a wager?" asked a voice behind her. "I can generally get over the ground pretty fast, but it was as much as I could do to overtake you without running."

He was not breathless, however. His tones were firm and tranquil. It was she who could scarcely speak.

"I'm afraid I am very late," she answered nervously.

"For what? For afternoon tea by your own fireside? Have you anybody waiting for you at the Angler's Nest, that you should be in such a hurry to get home?"

"No, there is no one waiting, except Tabitha. I expect no one."

"Then why walk yourself into a fever?"

"Tabitha gets fidgety if I am out after dusk."

"Then let Tabitha fidget! It will be good for her liver. Those adipose people require small worries to keep them in health. You mustn't over-pace yourself to oblige Tabitha."

She had slackened her steps, and he was walking by her side, looking down at her from that superb altitude which gave him an unfair advantage. How could she, upon her lower level, escape those searching glances?

She knew that her way home was his way home, so far as the bend of the road which led away from the river; and to avoid him for the intervening distance would have been difficult. She must submit to his company on the road, or make a greater effort than it was in her nature to make.

"You mean to go to this ball, don't you?" he asked earnestly.

"I think not."

"Oh, but pray do! Why should you shut yourself from all the pleasures of this world, and live like a nun, always? You might surely make just one exception for such a grand event as the Hunt Ball. You have no idea how much we all think of it hereabouts. Remember, it will be the first public dance we have had at Lostwithiel for ever so many years. You will see family diamonds enough to make you fancy you are at St. James's. Do you think Major Disney would dislike your having just one evening's dissipation?"

"Oh no, he would not mind! He is only too kind and indulgent. He would have liked me to spend the winter with my sister in Hans Place, where there would have been gaieties of all kinds; but I don't want to go into society while Martin is away. It would not make me happy."

"But if it made some one else happy—if it made other people happy to see you there?"

"Oh, but it would not matter to anybody! I am a stranger in the land. People are only kind to me for my husband's sake."

"Your modesty becomes you as the dew becomes a rose. I won't gainsay you—only be sure you will be missed if you don't go to the ball. And if you do go—well, it will be an opportunity of making nice friends. It will be your *début* in county society."

"Without my husband? Please don't say any more about it, Lord Lostwithiel. I had much rather stay at home."

He changed the conversation instantly, asking her what she thought of Glenaveril.

"I think the situation most lovely."

"Yes, there we are all agreed. Mr. Crowther had the good taste to find a charming site, and the bad taste to erect an architectural monstrosity, a chimera in red brick. There was a grange once in the heart of that wood, and the Crowthers have the advantage of acorns and chestnuts that sowed themselves while the sleepy old monks were telling their beads. How do you like Miss Crowther?"

"I hardly know her well enough to like or dislike her. She is very handsome."

"So was Rubens' wife, Helena Forman; but what would one do in a world peopled with Helena Formans? There are galleries in Antwerp which no man should enter without smoke-coloured spectacles, if he would avoid being blinded by a blaze of red-haired beauty. I am told that the Miss Crowthers will have, at least, a million of money between them in days to come, and that they are destined to make great matches. Perhaps we shall see some of their *soupirants* at the ball. Since the decay of the landed interest, the *chasse aux dots* has become fiercer than of old."

This seemed to come strangely from him who had already been talked of as a possible candidate for one of the Miss Crowthers. It would be such a particularly suitable match, Mrs. Baynham, the doctor's wife, had told Isola. What could his lordship look for beyond a fine fortune and a handsome wife?

"They would make such a splendid pair," said Mrs. Baynham, talking of them as if they were carriage-horses.

Mrs. Disney and her companion crossed a narrow meadow, from the high road to the river-path which was the nearest way to the Angler's Nest. The river went rippling by under the gathering grey of the November evening. On their right hand there was the gloom of dark woods: and from the meadow on their left rose a thick white mist, like a sea that threatened to swallow them up in its phantasmal tide. The sound of distant oars, dipping with rhythmical measure, was the only sound except their own voices.

Did that three-quarters of a mile seem longer or shorter than usual? Isola hardly knew; but when she saw the lights shining in Tabitha's kitchen, and the fire-glow in the drawing-room, she was glad with the gladness of one who escapes from some fancied danger of ghosts or goblins.

Lostwithiel detained her at the gate.

"Good night," he said; "good night. You will change your mind, won't you, Mrs. Disney? It is not in one so gentle as you to be inflexible about such a trifle. Say that you will honour our ball."

She drew herself up a little, as if in protest against his pertinacity.

"I really cannot understand why you should care whether I go or stay away," she said coldly.

"Oh, but I do care! It is childish, perhaps, on my part, but I do care; I care tremendously; more than I have cared about anything for a long time. It is so small a thing on your part—it means so much for me! Say you will be there."

"Is that you, ma'am?" asked Tabitha's pleasant voice, while Tabitha's substantial soles made themselves audible upon the gravel path. "I was beginning to get fidgety about you."

"Good night," said Isola, shortly, as she passed through the gate.

It shut with a sharp little click of the latch, and she vanished among the laurels and arbutus. He heard her voice and Tabitha's as they walked towards the house in friendly conversation, mistress and maid.

There was a great over-blown Dijon rose nodding its heavy head over the fence. Roses linger so late in that soft western air. Lostwithiel plucked the flower, and pulled off its petals one by one as he walked towards the village street.

"Will she go—will she stay—go—stay—go—stay?" he muttered, as the petals fluttered to the ground.

"Go! Yes, of course she will go," he said to himself as the last leaf fell. "Does it need ghost from the grave or rose from the garden to tell me that?"

## CHAPTER IV.

### "DREAMING, SHE KNEW IT WAS A DREAM."

Isola and Lostwithiel met a good many times after that walk through the autumn mists. She tried her utmost to avoid him. She went for fewer walks than of old; nay, she chiefly confined her perambulations to those domestic errands which Tabitha imposed upon her, and such afternoon visits as she felt it incumbent upon her to pay, in strict return for visits paid to her. Major Disney had begged her to be exact in such small ceremonies, and to keep upon the best possible terms with his friends. "I love every soul in the place, for old sake's sake," he told her; and for old sake's sake Isola had to cultivate the people her husband had known all his life.

She tried to avoid Lostwithiel, but Fate was against her, and they met. He was unvaryingly courteous. He said no word which could offend the most sensitive of women. Prudery itself could have had no ground for alarm. He did not again allude to the ball, or his wishes upon that point. He talked of those common topics of interest to which every day and every season give rise, even in a Cornish village; and yet in this common talk acquaintance ripened until it became friendship unawares. And then—as all sense of shyness and reserve upon Isola's part gave way to a vague, reposeful feeling, like drifting down a sunlit river, with never a breath of chilling wind—they began to exchange confidences about their past lives. Unawares Martin Disney's wife found herself entering into the minutest details about the people she had met on that level road of a monotonous girlhood by which she had come to be what she was. Unawares she betrayed all her feelings and opinions, her likes and dislikes, and even the little weaknesses and eccentricities of her parents—her sister—her wealthy brother-in-law. Never before had she found so good a listener. Her husband had been all affectionate interest in the things that concerned her; yet she had often discovered that his mind was wandering in the midst of some girlish reminiscence; and he had a tiresome trick of forgetting all those particulars about her friends which would have enabled him to distinguish the personages of a story. He had to be told everything afresh at each recurrence of those names that were so familiar to her. Nor had he Lostwithiel's keen sense of humour, and quick perception of the ridiculous side of life, whereby many a small social sketch fell flat.

The glimpses she caught of her new friend's past existence enthralled her. It was to see new vistas opening into unknown worlds; the world of university life; the world of society, English and continental, with all its varieties of jargon; the world of politics, and literature, and art. It charmed him to see her interest in all those unknown things and people.

"You would very soon be tired of it, and would come back to Trelasco—like the hare to her form—or like me," he said, smiling at her ardent look. "Believe me, it is all dust and ashes. My happiest hours have been on board a yacht, with only half a dozen good books, and ten or a dozen ignoramuses in blue serge for my companions."

---

She was to go to the Hunt Ball after all; not because he wished it, but because other people had taken her affairs in hand, and decided that she should go. Dr. and Mrs. Baynham had decided for her. Mrs. Vansittart Crowther had decided for her, and had sent her a ticket with her love by that very footman whose appearance when he opened the door always crushed her, and who had given her a frightful shock when she danced into the kitchen to speak to Tabitha, and found him meekly sitting on a Windsor chair, with his knees drawn up nearly to his chin. Lastly, Tabitha had decided; and Tabitha's opinion went for more than that of anybody else.

"You want a little bit of change and gaiety," said the faithful stewardess. "You have been looking pale and worried ever since you had that bad news from Broomer," this was Tabitha's nearest approach to Burmah, "and you'll be all the better for an evening's pleasure. It isn't as if you had to buy a dress, or even a pair of gloves. You've only worn your wedding-dress at three parties since you came home from your honeymoon, and it's as fresh as if you'd been married yesterday. You've got everything, and everything of the best. Why shouldn't you go?"

Isola could advance no reason, except her vague fear that her husband might not approve of her appearing at a public ball without him; but at this objection honest Tabitha snapped her fingers.

"I'll answer for Mr. Martin," she said. "He'll be pleased for you to enjoy yourself. 'Don't let her mope while I'm away, Tabby,' he said to me the day before he started for foreign parts. He'd like you to be at the ball. You'll have Mrs. Baynham to take care of you, and what can you want more than that, I should like to know?"

Mrs. Baynham, the portly doctor's wife, was, in Tabitha's mind, the representative of all the respectabilities. How could a girl just out of her teens—a girl who loved dancing, and had been told she danced exquisitely—turn a deaf ear to such arguments, put forward by the person to whose care her husband had in some wise confided her. If Tabitha approved, Isola thought she could not do wrong in yielding; so the simply-fashioned white satin gown—made in Paris, and with all Parisian *chic*—was taken out of the pot-pourri perfumed drawer. Gloves and fan, and little white slippers were passed in review. There was nothing wanted. The carefullest housewife need not have hesitated on the score of economy.

So the question was finally settled—she was to go to the Hunt Ball. A fly was engaged for her especial service, so that she might not crowd Mrs. Baynham, who was to take two fresh, fat-cheeked nieces, who looked as if they had been fed from infancy upwards upon apple pasties and clotted cream. She was to drive to Lostwithiel in the fly from the Maypole Inn, and she was to join Mrs. Baynham in the cloak-room, and make her entrance under that lady's wing.

This final decision was arrived at about ten days before the event, and for nine of those intervening days Isola's life went by as if she were always sitting in that imaginary boat drifting down a sunlit river; but on the day of the dance, after just half an hour's quiet walk with Lostwithiel on the towpath, she went back to the cottage pale as ashes; and sat down at her little davenport in the drawing-room, trembling, breathless, and on the verge of hysteria.

She opened the drawers of the davenport one after another, looking for something—helplessly, confusedly, as one whose brain is half distraught. It was ten minutes before she found what she wanted — a sheaf of telegram forms.

"To Major Disney, Cornwall Fusiliers, Rangoon. — Let me go to you at once. I am miserable. My heart will break if you leave me here."

This was the gist of a message which she wrote half a dozen times, in different words, upon half a dozen forms. Then she tore up all but the last, threw that into a drawer, and began to pace the room feverishly, with her hands clasped before her face.

What fever-fraught vision was it that those hands tried to shut out from her burning eyes? So little had happened — so little — only half an hour's quiet walk along the towpath, where the leafless willows had a grim, uncanny look, like those trees whose old grey branches seemed the arms of the Erlking's daughters, beckoning the child as he nestled in his father's arms, riding through the night. So little — so little — and yet it meant the lifting of a veil — the passage from happy innocence to the full consciousness of an unholy love. It meant what one kiss on trembling lips meant for Paolo and Francesca. It meant the plunge into a gulf of dark despair — unless she had strength to draw back, seeing the abyss at her feet, warned of her danger.

What had he said? Only a few agitated words — only a revelation. He loved her, loved her with all the passion of his passionate soul; loved her as he had never loved before. They all tell the same story, these destroyers of innocence; and, for that one burning moment, they all mean what they say. Every seducer has his hour of sublime truthfulness; of generous feeling; of ardent heroic aspirations; the hour in which he would perish for the woman he loves; cut off his right hand; burn out his eyes; leap off a monument; do anything except surrender her, except forego his privilege to destroy her.

It was not too late. The warning had come in time — just in time to save her. She knew now to what ocean that drifting boat was carrying her — through the sunny atmosphere, between the flowery shores of dreamland. It was taking her to the arctic ocean of shame and ruin — the great sea strewn with the corpses of women who had sinned, and suffered, and repented, and died — unforgiven of mankind — to wait the tribunal of God.

"Oh, lor!" cried Tabitha, bursting into the room. "I thought you were never coming home. You ought to go and lay down for two or three hours after your tea, or we shall have you fainting away before the night's over. You've not been eating enough for a healthy canary bird for the last week."

"I'm not very well, Tabbie. I don't think I'll go to the ball."

"Not go! and when the fly's ordered—and will have to be paid for whether or no; for Masters told me he could have let it twelve deep. Not go! and disappoint Mrs. Baynham, who has set her heart on taking you; and Mrs. Crowther, who gave you the ticket! Why, it would never do! You'll feel well enough when you're there. You won't know whether you're standing on your head or your heels. It's past five o'clock, and your tea has been ready in the study since a quarter to."

"How do you send telegrams to India, Tabitha?"

"Lor, ma'am, how should I know? From the post-office, I suppose, pretty much like other telegrams. But they cost no end of money, I'll be bound. You're not wanting to send a telegram to the major, are you, ma'am, to ask his leave about the ball?"

"No; I was only wondering," Isola answered feebly.

She shut and locked the davenport, leaving her message in the drawer. She meant to send it—if not to-day, to-morrow; if not before the ball, after the ball. She felt that her only hope of peace and safety and a clear conscience was at her husband's side. She must go out to him yonder in the unknown land. She must get to him somehow, with or without his leave—with or without his help. She would brave anything, hazard anything to be with that faithful friend and defender—her first love—her brave, self-denying, God-fearing lover. She felt as if there were no other safety or shelter for her in all the world.

"God will not help me unless I help myself," she muttered distractedly, as she sat in her low chair by the fire, with her head flung back upon the cushions and the untouched meal at her side. Tabitha had left off providing dinner for her, at her particular request. She had neither heart to sit down alone to a formal dinner nor appetite to eat it; so Tabitha had exercised all her skill as a cook, which was great, in preparing a dainty little supper at nine o'clock; and it had irked her that her mistress did such scant justice to the tempting meal.

Isola fell asleep by the fire, comforted by the warmth, worn out by nights that had been made sleepless by vague agitation—by the living over again of accidental meetings, and friendly conversations—not by fear or remorse—for it was only this day that the danger of that growing friendship had been revealed to her. It was only to-day that she knew what such friendships mean. She slept a feverish sleep, from sheer exhaustion, and dreamt fever-dreams.

Those willows on the bank had recalled Goethe's "Erl König"—the ballad she had learnt by rote in her earliest German studies—and the willows and the ballad were interwoven with her dreams. It was Martin Disney who was riding his charger along a dark road, and she was sitting in front of his saddle, clinging to him, hiding her face upon his breast, and the willows were beckoning—she knew those gaunt arms were beckoning to her, although her eyes were hidden—and *he* was following. He was thundering behind them, on a black horse. Yes, and then the dream changed—the dreamer's wandering thoughts directed by another reminiscence of those girlish studies in German poetry. She was Lenore, and she was in the arms of her dead lover. She felt that bony arm—Death's arm—clutching her round the waist. Her streaming hair mingled with the streaming mane of that unearthly horse. She was with Lostwithiel—in his arms—and they were both dead and both happy—happy in being together. What did they want more than that?

> "Vollbracht, vollbracht ist unser Lauf!
>     Das Hochzeitbette, thut sich auf!
>     Die Todten reiten schnelle!
>     Wir sind, wir sind, zur Stelle."

She woke with the chill of the charnel-house freezing her blood. The fire had gone out. Tim had curled himself at her feet in the folds of her gown. The Persian was staring discontentedly at the ashes in the grate, and Tabitha's sturdy footsteps might be heard in the room above, bustling to and fro, and anon poking the fire, and putting on coals, making all snug and ready for her mistress's toilet.

Isola rang, and Susan, the parlour-maid, brought in the lamp.

"I came twice before, ma'am; but you were fast asleep, so I took the lamp back to the pantry."

Isola looked at the clock. Ten minutes to nine, and she was to meet Mrs. Baynham in the cloak-room at half-past ten. Ten o'clock was the hour on the card, and the fat-faced nieces were feverishly afraid that all the eligible partners would be snapped up by those wise virgins who appeared earliest on the scene.

"You won't keep us waiting in the cloak-room, will you, dear Mrs. Disney?" they pleaded coaxingly.

Was she to put on her finery and go! There would be time yet to send a note to Mrs. Baynham, excusing herself on the score of illness. The doctor's party would not start before half-past nine. What was she to do? Oh, she wanted to see him once more—just once more—in the brightly-lighted rooms, amidst a crowd—in a place where he would have no chance of repeating those wicked, wicked words—of forgetting all that was due to his own honour and to hers. In the crowded ball-room there would be safety—safety even from evil thoughts. Who could think of anything amidst the sound of dance music, the dazzle of lamps and flashing of jewels?

She wanted to go to the ball, to wear her satin gown, to steep herself in light and music; and thus to escape from the dim horrors of that awful dream.

Tabitha seemed like a good angel, when she came in at this juncture with a fresh cup of tea and a plate of dainty little chicken sandwiches.

"Come now, ma'am, I shan't let you go to the ball if you don't take these. What, not a bit of fire—and you asleep here in the cold? What was that addle-pated Susan thinking about, I wonder? I'll take the tray upstairs. There's a lovely fire in your room, and everything ready for you to dress. I want to be able to tell Mr. Martin that his young wife was the belle of the ball."

Isola allowed herself to be led upstairs to the bright, cheerful bedroom, with its pretty chintz-pattern paper, and photographs, and artistic muslin curtains, and glowing fire, and toilet-table, with its glitter of crystal and silver in the pleasant candlelight. She suffered herself to be fed and dressed by Tabitha's skilful hands, almost as if she had been a child; and she came out of her dismal dream into the glad waking world, a radiant figure, with violet eyes and alabaster complexion, flushed by the loveliest hectic. The simply-made, close-fitting bodice, with folded crape veiling the delicate bust, and the pure pearly tint of the satin, set off her fragile beauty, while the long train and massive folds of the rich fabric gave statuesque grace to her tall, slim figure; but the crowning glory of her toilette was the garland of white chrysanthemums, for which Tabitha had ransacked all the neighbouring green-houses; a garland of fluffy, feathery petals, which reached in a diagonal line from her shoulder to the hem of her gown. It was her only ornament, for by some strange caprice she refused to wear the modest pearl necklace and diamond cross which had been her husband's wedding gift.

"Not to-night, Tabbie," she said; and Tabitha saw in this refusal only the coquetry of a lovely woman, who wanted to show the great ladies and squire's wives how poor and common diamonds are by the side of youth and beauty.

"Well, you don't want any jewels, certainly," said Tabitha. "You look as if you were going to be married—all but the veil. Those chrysanthemums are ever so much prettier than orange blossoms. There's the fly. Let me put on your cloak. It's a beautiful night, and almost as mild as May. Everybody will be at the ball. There's nothing to keep folks away. Well, I do wish the major was here to go with you. Wouldn't he be proud?"

The stars were shining when Isola went along the gravel path to the gate where Masters' fly was waiting, with blazing lamps, which seemed to put those luminous worlds yonder to shame. There was no carriage-drive to the hall door of the Angler's Nest. The house retained all its ancient simplicity, and ignored the necessities of carriage people. Tabitha wrapped her mistress's fur-lined cloak close round her, before she stepped into the fly, which was provided with those elaborate steps that seem peculiar to the hired brougham.

"Good night, Tabitha, and thank you for all the pains you've taken in dressing me—and for the lovely wreath. I shall come home early. I shan't wait for Mrs. Baynham's party."

"Don't you hurry," said Tabitha, heartily. "The Hunt Ball only comes once a year, and you'd better make the most of it. I shan't mind sitting up; and perhaps I shan't be half so dull as you think for."

The flyman shut the door, which nobody but himself could shut—another peculiarity of hired broughams. The fly vanished in the darkness, and Tabitha ran back to the house, where she found Susan waiting at the hall door in her jacket and hat, as near a reproduction of Mrs. Disney's jacket and hat as local circumstances—or the difference between Bond Street and Lostwithiel—would allow.

"Have you locked and bolted the back doors?" asked Tabitha; "but, lor, I'll go and look myself; I won't trust to your giddy young brains. Mr. Tinkerly will be here with the cart directly. I've only got to put on my bonnet and dolman, after I've taken a look round, and put away Mrs. Disney's jewel-box."

Tabitha was no light-minded housekeeper, but she had her hours of frivolity, and she loved pleasure with the innocent freshness of a most transparent soul. Tinkerly, the butcher, had offered to drive the two ladies—Tabitha and Susan—into Lostwithiel in his tax cart, and, furthermore, to place them where they would see something of the ball, or at least of the company arriving and departing, and beyond all this to give them a snack of supper, "Just something to bite at and a glass of beer," he told Tabitha deprecatingly, lest he should raise hopes beyond his power of realization.

He meant to do the thing as handsomely as circumstances would permit, certainly to the extent of cold boiled beef and pickles, with Guinness or Bass. He was a family man, of irreproachable respectability, and his meat was supposed to be unmatchable for thirty miles round. He grew it himself, upon those picturesque pastures which sloped skyward, dipping towards the blue of the river, rising towards the blue of the sky.

No precaution of lock, bolt, or bar did Tabitha neglect before she put on her best bonnet, and dignified black cloth dolman, heavy with imitation Astrachan. She and Susan were standing at the gate when

Tinkerly drove up with his skittish mare and spring cart, a cart so springy that it threatened to heel over altogether when Tabitha clambered into the place of honour. Mr. Tinkerly's foreman was sitting behind to take care of Susan, and the foreman was unmarried, and of a greasy black-haired comeliness, and there was none happier than Susan under those wintry stars—not even the great ladies in their family diamonds.

"What are diamonds," said Susan, philosophically, with the foreman's arm sustaining her at a sharp turn in the road, "if you don't care for each other?"

## CHAPTER V.

## "AND THE CHILD-CHEEK BLUSHING SCARLET FOR THE VERY SHAME OF BLISS."

People who were familiar with the Talbot Hotel, Lostwithiel, in its everyday aspect would hardly have recognized the old-fashioned hostelry to-night, under the transforming hand of the Hunt Club, with Lord Lostwithiel and Vansittart Crowther on the committee. The entrance hall, usually remarkable only for various cases of stuffed birds, and a monster salmon—caught in the Lerrin river in some remote period of history—was now a bower of crimson cloth and white azaleas. In the ball-room and ante-room, tea-room and supper-room, were more flowers, and more crimson cloth, while on every side brushes and vizards against the crimson and white panelling testified to the occasion. The dancing-room was very full when Mrs. Baynham's party made their entrance, the matron in her historical black velvet—which had formed part of her trousseau thirteen years before, when she left the family residence in the chief street of Truro, and all those privileges which appertained to her as the only daughter of a provincial banker, to grace Dr. Baynham's lowlier dwelling. The black velvet gown had been "let out" from time to time, as youth expanded into maturity: and there had been a new bodice and a real Maltese lace flounce within the last three years, which constituted a second incarnation; and Mrs. Baynham walked into the Talbot ball-room with the serene demeanour that goes with a contented mind. She was satisfied with herself, and she was proud of her party, the two fresh, rosy-cheeked girls in sky-blue tulle, Isola, looking like a Mary lily in her white satin raiment, and the village surgeon, who always looked his best in his dress clothes, newly-shaven, and, as it were, pulled together in honour of the occasion.

The room was full, and very full; but Lostwithiel was not there. Isola had an instinctive consciousness that he was missing in that brilliant crowd. People came buzzing round her, and she was made room for upon a raised bench opposite the gallery where a military band was playing a polka in which the brasses predominated to an ear-splitting extent.

The Glenaveril party made their entrance ten minutes later. The Crowther girls were not afraid of wanting partners. Most young men are glad to dance with half a million of money. There is always an off chance of a good thing, just as there is a chance of breaking the bank at Monte Carlo. Belinda looked superb in a cloud of tulle, like a goddess. Alicia looked too well on horseback to look well off. Her spare straight figure and sharp elbows were not at their best in evening dress. She wore black, and an infinity of bugles, and flashed and glittered more than any one else in the room, though she wore never a jewel.

"Worth, my dear," said Mrs. Baynham to a blue niece, in a mysterious whisper; "I know his style."

There was a buzz of conversation on that raised divan where the matrons were sitting with those newly arrived maidens who were like ships waiting to slide out of their cradles and float away to sea. Isola and the sky-blue nieces had not long to wait; especially Isola. Men were entreating the stewards to introduce them to that lovely fragile-looking creature in white satin—the best men in the neighbourhood, or those wandering stars from distant counties, or the London galaxy, "men with handles to their names," as Mr. Baynham told Mrs. Crowther, resplendent in salmon brocade, and Venetian point.

"My presentation gown," she informed the doctor's wife; "the Court mantle is ruby velvet, lined with salmon satin. The weight of it almost pulled me backwards when I curtsied to the royalties—such a lot of them, and I'm afraid I curtsied rather too low to one of the Princesses, for I caught her taking me off when she returned my curtsy."

Isola danced through the lancers as one in a dream. When the heart of a man is oppressed with care, "Ta-rarra, ta-rarra, ta-rà, ta-rà!" What foolishness it all seemed. And her husband in Burmah, hemmed round by murderous dacoits!

She went back to her seat among the matrons, after almost curtly refusing either refreshment or a promenade through the rooms. Mrs. Crowther was saying solemnly, "I do believe Lord Lostwithiel is not coming after all, and yet he worked so hard on the committee, my husband said, and took such pains about the flowers, and what not."

The tall, slim figure cut its way through the crowd two or three minutes later, and Lostwithiel was standing in front of Isola, and the two matrons.

He wore a pink coat, as became a member of the Lostwithiel Hunt, and the vivid colour accentuated the pallor of his long thin face. He talked to all the ladies on the divan; to the sky-blue nieces even, hoping that their cards were full.

"If not, I must bring you some men I know," he said. "You mustn't miss a dance."

They blushed and trembled with delight, never before having been thus familiarly addressed by a peer of the realm. He asked Isola for her programme, with well-simulated indifference, yet with that air of profound respect with which he talked to all women.

"I hope you can spare me some waltzes," he said.

"She is only just come," said Mrs. Baynham.

"And yet her card is almost full. People have been very officious. Here is a poor little waltz—number seven. May I have that, and number eleven, and number——"

"Please don't put down your name for anything later than number eleven. I shall be gone long before those late dances."

"Oh, surely, you don't mean to desert us early. Remember this is the one festive occasion of our lives as a sporting community. All our other meetings are given up to carking care, financial difficulties, and squabbling. I shall put down my name in these tempting blanks, and if you disappoint me—well—it will only be like my previous experiences as a fox-hunter."

He gave her back her programme, with all the blanks filled in, and at the bottom a word written, and triply underscored,

ΆΝΑΓΚΗ.

They had talked of Victor Hugo's romantic story—that romance which the great man so despised in after years that he was almost offended if any one presumed to praise it in his hearing, although in the half-century that has gone since Victor Hugo was a young man this story of Notre Dame has been unsurpassed as an example of the romantic novel. Lostwithiel had praised the book, and had talked of the monk Frollo, and his fatal love—and that word Fatality, graven upon the wall of his cell, and burnt into his soul.

Isola knew what those Greek letters meant. She dropped the little white and gold programme as if it had been an adder. He went away to a duty dance with a great lady of the district—a lady whose diamonds made a light about her wherever she moved; and then he waltzed with Belinda Crowther, to the admiration of the young lady's mother, and of two or three other matrons on the divan by the door. Were they not a splendid couple, she so brilliantly fair, he dark and pale, bronzed slightly with exposure to the sun in warmer climates than this—not positively handsome, but with such an interesting countenance. So, and so, and so prosed the matrons, until various middle-aged cavaliers came to invite them to the tea-room, where there was the usual drawback in the shape of a frightful draught from open windows, which the dancers, coming in flushed and heated, voted delicious.

"This will be a good night's work for me," said Dr. Baynham, cheerfully, although he considered it his duty to warn his patients of their danger.

Conscience thus satisfied, he could look on complacently as they eat ices, and selected cool corners of the refreshment-room to flirt in.

"Next to a juvenile party, I don't know anything better—from a professional point of view—than a public ball," he said. "Your canvas corridors, decorated with flowers and bunting, are a fortune to a family practitioner."

Isola danced every dance. She hardly knew who her partners were. She had only a sense of floating in a vortex of light and colour, to some swinging melody. Everything was dream-like—but not horrible, as in her dream by the fireside at home. This was a happy dream, as of a creature with wings, who knew not of care in the present or a soul to be saved in the future. And then came her waltz with Lostwithiel, and that strong arm was round her, bearing her up

60

as a flower is borne upon a rushing tide, so that she had no consciousness of movement on her own part, only of floating, floating, floating, to that languid three-time melody.

It was the last popular waltz they were playing—a waltz that had been last summer's delight in the arid gardens of South Kensington—"Il n'y a que toi;" a waltz with a chorus which the band trolled out merrily, at intervals, in the French of Stratford atte Bow.

"Il n'y a que toi," whispered Lostwithiel, with his lips close to the soft brown hair above the white forehead. "Not a bad name for a waltz when one is waltzing with just one person in the world."

---

Out in the cool night there was a little knot of people as merry after their homelier fashion as town and county in the ball-room. One of the windows had been opened at the top for ventilation, and this opening had been turned to advantage. A large, substantial kitchen table had been placed in front of the window, and upon this improvised platform stood Tabitha, Susan, the head chamber-maid, and the ostler's wife—this last on sufferance, and evidently not in society—looking on at the ball. The window was under a verandah, that sloped above these spectators' heads. They were thus in dense shadow, and unseen by the occupants of the lamp-lit room.

Susan was exuberant in her delight.

"I was never at a ball before," she said. "Oh, ain't it lovely? Don't I wish I could dance like that? Lor, do look at that fat old party, spinning round like a teetotum! Well, I never did! Don't she perspire!" exclaimed Susan, indulging in a running commentary which left much to be desired in the matter of refinement.

This unsophisticated damsel heartily admired youth and beauty, and the smart frocks and flashing gems; but she was cruelly hard upon those dancers whose charms were on the wane, or whose frocks were inferior or ugly.

"Well, I wouldn't," said Susan, "I wouldn't go to a ball like this if I couldn't have everythink nice. Look at that tall girl in yeller. Did you ever see such a scarecrow? I'd ever so much rather stay at home, or stand outside, like this. I should feel it better became me."

Tabitha made no such remarks. She was singularly silent and thoughtful, as she stood looking down at the crowded room from her point of vantage on the kitchen table. She had only eyes for one figure—the willowy form in the glistening white satin gown, with the feathery Japanese chrysanthemums, a little crushed and faded by this time; or perhaps it may be said for two figures, since one followed the other as the shadow follows the substance. She saw them waltzing together, when supper was in full progress, and the room comparatively clear. She saw the graceful head inclining towards his shoulder, the slender waist held in his firm embrace; and it seemed to her that the waltz was an invention of the Arch Enemy. She thought of it very much as people thought seventy years ago when Byron wrote his poetical denunciation of the new dance. She saw those two moving slowly towards an adjacent ante-room, where banks of flowers, and a couple of sofas and low easy-chairs made a retreat which was half boudoir, half conservatory. She saw them moving side by side, talking to each other in tones so confidential that his head bent low over hers each time she spoke; and then she watched them sitting just within the doorway, at an angle where she could see their faces, and attitudes, still in the same confidential converse, she with downcast eyes, and he leaning forward with his elbow on his knee, and looking up at her as he talked.

"It is too bad of him," muttered Tabitha, writhing at that spectacle. "Does he think what a child she is, and what harm he may be doing? It is wicked of him, and he knows it; and other people must notice them—other people must see what I see—and they will be talking of her, blighting her good name. Oh, if I could only get her away at once before people begin to notice her!"

She could see her young mistress's face distinctly in the lamplight. Isola was very pale, and her face was full of trouble; not the face of a woman amusing herself with an idle flirtation, playing with fire without the least intention of burning her fingers. There were plenty of flirtations of that order going on in the Talbot ball-room; but this was not one of them. This meant peril of some kind. This was all evil. That pale face, those heavy eyelids, shrouding eyes which dared not look up. That tremulous, uncertain movement of the snowy ostrich fan! All these were danger signals.

"If I get her safe at home presently, I'll open her eyes for her," thought Tabitha. "I'll talk to her as if I was her mother. God knows I should be almost as sorry as ever her mother could be if she came to any harm."

If she came to any harm. What harm was there to fear for her, as she sat there, with Lostwithiel lounging across the low chair beside the sofa where she sat, leaning forward to look into her downcast face? What harm could come to her except that which meant destruction— death to peace, and gladness, and womanly fame? If there were danger it was a desperate danger, and Tabitha shuddered at the mere thought of that peril.

"But, lor, she's little more than a child," mused Tabitha. "She means no wrong, and she knows no wrong. She's too innocent to come to any harm."

Yet in the landlady's snuggery, by-and-by, seated at the comfortable round table, with its spotless damask and bright glass and silver, Tabitha was quite unable to do justice to that snack which Mr. Tinkerly had ordered in her honour—a chicken and lobster-salad from the supper-room, and three parts of a pine-apple cream. Susan and the foreman fully appreciated these dainties; but Tabitha only munched a crust and sipped a tumbler of beer.

"I'm a little bit out of sorts to-night," she said.

"I hope you haven't taken cold, Mrs. Thomas," said the polite Tinkerly. "Perhaps we ought to have brought another rug?"

"No, it isn't that. I've been quite warm and comfortable. Eat your supper, Mr. Tinkerly, and don't bother about me. I've been interested in looking on, and I'm too much took up with what I've seen to be able to eat."

"Well, it was a pretty sight," exclaimed Tinkerly, enthusiastically; "but I don't think I ever saw such a mort of plain women in my life."

"Lor, Mr. Tinkerly," cried Susan, with a shocked air. "Why, look at our young mistress, and at Miss Crowther, and Miss Spenthrop from Truro, and Mrs. Pencarrow, and Lady Chanderville."

"Well, I don't say they're all ugly. Some of 'em are handsome enough, and there's plenty of thorough-breds among 'em, but there's a sight of plain-headed ones. There's quite as much beauty in your spear as there is among the county folks, Miss Susan. I'll answer for that."

―――――――――――――――――

The night was waning. Isola had ordered her carriage for half-past two: but three o'clock had struck from the church tower of Lostwithiel, and the dance was still at its height—at its best, the dancers said, now that the sensual attractions of the supper-room drew off a good many people, and left the floor so much clearer than before supper, when bulky middle-aged gentlemen, talking to the matrons seated upon the divan, had projected their ponderous persons into the orbit of the waltzers.

Isola and Lostwithiel had danced only two waltzes, but since two o'clock they had sat out several dances, Mrs. Disney having cancelled all her engagements after that hour by declaring that she would dance no more.

"I am dreadfully tired," she told her partners piteously, and her pallor gave force to the assertion. "Please get some one else for our dance, Captain Morshead," and so on, and so on, to half a dozen disappointed suitors.

Perhaps some of those who happened to be experienced in such complications may have divined which way the wind blew, for no one offered to sit out the promised dances, and Isola and Lostwithiel were left pretty much to themselves among the palms and orange-trees in the ante-room. They were not unobserved, however; and among the eyes which marked them with no friendly notice were the fine, steel-blue eyes of Miss Crowther.

"Is that a flirtation?" she asked Captain Morshead, glancing in the direction of the ante-room where those two were sitting, as she and Isola's cast-off partner waltzed past the muslin-draped doorway.

"They seem rather fond of talking to each other, don't they? Who was she? She's uncommonly pretty."

"Oh, her people were army, I believe—as poor as church mice—buried alive in Dinan."

"At Dinan—and now she lives at Trelasco, she tells me. It seems scarcely worth while to have exhumed her in order to bury her again. Such a girl as that ought to be in London enjoying life."

"Oh, but she's a grass widow, don't you know. Her husband is in Burmah. I don't think it's quite nice in her to be here to-night; only as my too good-natured mother sent her a ticket, I suppose I oughtn't to say anything about it. Perhaps if mother sees the way she goes on with Lord Lostwithiel she'll rather regret that ticket."

---

What was Lostwithiel saying all this time in that gentle baritone, which was heard only by one listener? He was asking forgiveness for his indiscretion of the afternoon, and in that prayer for pardon was repeating his offence. Isola was less inclined to be angry, perhaps, now. The magic of the dance was still upon her senses, the dance which had brought them nearer than all the days they had met; than all their long confidential conversations on the heights above the harbour, or on the river path, or dawdling on the bridge. She had felt the beating of his heart against her own, breath mingling with breath, the thrilling touch of his encircling arm; and it was as if he had woven a spell around her which made her his. She had never danced with her husband, who had no love of that heathenish art. In all their brisk, frank courtship there had been no intoxicating hours. She hardly knew what dancing meant till she waltzed with Lostwithiel, who had something of the fiery ardour of a Pagan worshipping his gods in wild gyrations upon moonlit mountain or in secret cave. She let him talk to her to-night—let him pour out the full confession of his unhappy love. He spoke not as one who had hope; not with that implied belief in her frailty which would have startled her into prompt resistance. His accents were the accents of despair, his love was a dark fatality.

ΑΝΑΓΚΗ

"Why did you write that word?" she asked.

"Why? Because I could not give you back that card without some token of my passion—with only commonplace entries which Jones, Brown, and Robinson might write there. I want you to feel that you belong to me, somehow, in some way, as the spirits of the dead and the souls of the living belong to each other sometimes, by links which none can see. When I am at the other end of the earth I want to feel that there is something, if it were only a word, like a masonic sign, between us; if it were only a promise that in such or such a phase of the waning moon we would each look up and breathe the other's name."

"You are going away?"

"What else can I do? Can I stay? You tell me I made you miserable by what I said this afternoon. That means we must meet no more. I can't be sorry for my offence. I cannot answer for myself. My love has passed the point of sanity and self-control. I have no option. I must offend you, or I must leave you."

"You need not leave Trelasco," she said gently. "I am going away to-morrow."

"Going away! Where?"

"To London first, and then to India."

"To Burmah? Impossible!"

"If not to the front, to the nearest convenient station. I am going to my husband; as nearly as I can reach him; and as quickly as I can make the journey."

"You are dreaming."

"No, I have quite made up my mind. I hated to be left behind last year; and now that his return is deferred my only chance of happiness is to go to him. Some one called me a grass widow the other day. What a detestable name!"

"Give me this one waltz?" he asked, without any comment upon her intended journey.

"Impossible. I told them all I shouldn't dance any more."

"Oh, your partners are all in the supper-room, I dare say. The dancing men go in last. Hark! it's the Myosotis. Just one turn—only one."

He had risen from his low seat, and she rose involuntarily at the sound of the opening bars. He put his arm round her gently, and drew her into the ball-room, waltzing slowly as they went, and then, with the sudden impetus of an enthusiastic dancer, he was whirling her round the room, and she know nothing, cared for nothing, in the confusion of light and melody.

"Think of me sometimes when you are far away!" he whispered, with his lips almost touching her forehead.

She did not resent that whisper. Already, within a dozen hours of his first offence, she had grown accustomed to his words of love. It seemed to her as if they had loved each other for years—had loved and had despaired long ago, in some dim half-remembered past. A passion of this kind is like a dream, in which an instant gives the impression of half a lifetime, of long memories and old habit.

The room was much clearer now.

"Is it very late?" asked Isola.

"About four."

"So late—and I told the flyman half-past two. It is dreadful. Let us stop, please."

He obeyed, and went with her towards the cloak-room. The seats were nearly empty now where the matrons had sat in their velvet and brocade, a gorgeous background to the clouds of tulle and sylph-like figures of the dancers. Mrs. Baynham was nowhere to be seen, and the diminished bundles of tabby-cat cloaks and Shetland shawls in the cloak-room indicated that a good many people had left. Isola put on her soft white shawl hurriedly, and went out into the hall, where Lostwithiel had gone to look for her carriage.

People were going away very fast, and through the open doorway there was a sound of voices and wheels; but, in spite of footmen, constables, and hangers-on, there seemed a prodigious difficulty in getting any particular carriage to the door.

It was a mild, misty night, and the moon, which had been counted on for the return home, was hidden behind a mass of black clouds — or in the expressive phraseology of one of the foxhunters, had gone to ground. Mrs. Disney waited near the door while Lostwithiel searched for her fly. There were several departures of other muffled figures, features undistinguishable behind Shetland wraps, or furry hoods, as the men hustled their womenkind into the carriages. It seemed an age to Isola, waiting there alone in the corridor, and seeing no mortal whom she knew among those passersby, before Lostwithiel came, hurried and breathless, to say that her carriage was just coming up to the door.

"Wrap your shawl round your head," he said quickly, as he gave her his arm. "There's a nasty damp fog—so," muffling her, almost to blindness. "Come along."

She looked at the carriage, with its lamps shining red against the grey mistiness like great fiery eyes, and then, glancing at the horse, she cried suddenly, "I'm afraid that's the wrong fly. I think mine had a grey horse."

"No, no, it's all right. Pray don't loiter in this chilling air."

The carriage door was open, the constable standing by, bull's-eye in hand, a pair of horses snorting close behind, another carriage coming up so near that the pole threatened destruction. There was no time for loitering. Everybody was in a hurry to get home. Isola stepped lightly into the brougham, which drove slowly off.

"Next carriage, Mrs. Brune Prideaux," roared the constable. "Mrs. Prideaux' carriage stops all the way."

## CHAPTER VI.

### "A LOVE STILL BURNING UPWARD."

It was early summer, summer in her first youth, when she is frivolous and capricious, laughs and weeps she knows not why; smiling through her tears, and never knowing her own mind for a week together; to-day gracious-tempered and tropical; to-morrow east-windy and morose. In a word, it was June, a season of roses and rains, blue skies and thunder-clouds. It was June, and Martin Disney was looking out of the window with a keen eager face, much bronzed, and somewhat haggard, after a fatiguing campaign, looking out across the vales and woods of his native county, as the Penzance train sped along the high-level line betwixt Plymouth and Par. Those keen, grey eyes of his, accustomed to searching out far-off objects, looked as if they could pierce through the green heart of the Cornish valleys to the sheltered little harbour of Fowey and the blue sea that opened wide to the far-off West.

His labours were over, and he was going to take his rest, going to hang up his sword, that sword which had done such good work, or to transform it into a reaping-hook. He was Colonel Disney now, had given the State his best service, and now, in the very prime and vigour of his manhood, the State had done with him, and he was free to do what he listed with the maturer half of his life. He would have been very sorry to retire from active service had it not been for that tender tie which gave such sweetness to the thought of retirement and tranquil days. He was going home. The word thrilled him like music; home to his fair young wife, his chosen one, his domestic divinity. He had not left off wondering how it had ever come to pass that so young and fair a creature could care for him.

"It isn't as if I were one of your accomplished fellows," he said to himself, "able to sing, or play the flute, or paint in water-colours. Except a very earnest love of a few good books, I have no culture. How can any girl in the present day care for a man without culture? I could never appreciate Keats, for instance; and not to appreciate Keats is to be an outsider in literature."

Yet, in spite of his seven and forty years, in spite of his deficiencies, his homeliness, that young heart had gone out to him. She loved him, and his lot was full. There was nothing more upon God's earth that he could desire, were it not a miracle, and that the mother he had so fondly loved might be given back to him, to share his happiness, to make the third in a trinity of trusting love. Since that could not be, there was nothing left for him to yearn for.

The beating of his heart quickened almost unbearably, as the train drew near Par. Isola would meet him at the Junction, perhaps. He had not announced the actual hour of his arrival, for matters had been a little uncertain when he wrote yesterday, and he had not cared to telegraph this morning before he left Paddington. Yet she would know that this was the only likely train for him to choose; and she would be at the Junction, he thought, smiling her glad welcome, a fair young face, rosy in the sunset; for it was evening as he drew near the end of his journey.

No; there was nobody he knew at the Junction. He walked up and down the platform, and stared about him in rather a forlorn way during the few minutes before the starting of the train for Fowey. She had not come to anticipate their meeting by an hour or so, as he had hoped, as he had felt almost certain, she would come.

It was more natural that she should wait and receive him at the Angler's Nest, he told himself, sitting in the corner of the railway carriage presently, in a train of three coaches, steaming through the pretty picturesque country between Par and Fowey. In the colder light of reason it seemed preposterous to have expected to see her at the Junction. She would like to welcome him amidst her own surroundings, in the home to which she had doubtless given those little beautifying touches in honour of his coming, which are such delight to women, and which sometimes pass altogether unobserved by that pachydermatous animal, man! How slowly the engine moved along that little bit of line! Martin Disney sat with his face to the wind, and snuffed the sea breeze as if it had been the odour of home. He thought of Ulysses, and his return from distant lands. Would Tim, the fox terrier, know him? and Shah, the Persian cat? Perhaps not. Tim was no Argus; vastly affectionate and demonstrative, but not a dog to expire at one's feet, in the rapture of his master's return. Penelope would know him, and welcome him. That was enough for this modern Ulysses, who had no reason to disguise himself in re-entering his home—who had no fear of rival suitors, or interlopers of any kind. Penelope would welcome him, and trusty Tabitha. He thought of the old servant's honest face with delight. She was something left to him out of boyhood and youth. He felt like a young man when he talked to her. She was the one strong link betwixt the present and the past. She was his memory embodied. He could refer to her as to a dictionary of days long gone. When did we do such and such a thing—or go to such a place? What was the name of the bay horse I bought at Plympton? Where did my mother pick up the Sheraton secretaire? Tabitha could answer all such trivial questions: and Tabitha could talk to him for hours of his mother's words and ways—of the things that were only history.

At last! The train crept into the little station, nestling on the edge of a wood, and there was Fowey, homely, friendly little Fowey, so strange and yet so familiar; strange to eyes that had so lately looked upon the cities of the East; familiar to the man who had been reared in the neighbourhood, whose first impressions of God's earth had stamped harbour and hills upon his brain, like an indelible picture. There was Masters's fly, an eminently respectable vehicle that never touted for chance passengers, waiting for him. He was expected, evidently.

"Did Mrs. Disney send you?" he asked the driver.

"Yes, sir."

How thoughtful of the young wife, who might be forgiven if she had left such a small duty unfulfilled. Yet he would have liked to see her sweet self at the station—only, as he had argued with himself just now, it would have discounted the home-welcome. It would have been an anti-climax.

Dearly as he loved that home river, and those fertile hills, and beautiful as they were after their kind, they could but seem small and tame to eyes that had looked upon the glories of the East. Disney contemplated the scene with a touch of sad surprise, wondering at this miniature loveliness; recalling the day when those steep hillsides, where the red cattle were grazing in the mists of eventide, had seemed grand in his sight. Now they had a kind of pitiful prettiness. His heart yearned towards them with compassion for their insignificance.

For nearly two years he had been moving about with his company in the land of jungle and mountain, and in that vast table-land through which the Salween river runs down to the Gulf of Martaban; and after those wider horizons, he found himself in a narrow road, shut in by grassy hills, and hugging the margin of a silver thread that called itself a river.

There is always a tinge of melancholy in that hour after sundown; and Martin Disney's heart saddened a little as he looked at the quiet river, and the shadows on the hillside—that pale mistiness of summer evening which gives a ghostly touch to all things, as if it were a brief revelation of a spirit world. It is an hour at which even a strong man's heart is apt to sink with a vague sense of fear.

The fly drew up at the little wooden gate between high hedges of escalonia, with glossy leaves and bright red blossom. A slender figure in a white gown was visible on the threshold, as Disney sprang out of the fly, and while the flyman was lifting down the luggage, that airy form flitted across the lawn, and Colonel Disney's wife was standing shyly within the open gate, almost as if she had come out to receive a stranger.

He could not clasp her to his breast before a flyman; but he seized both her hands, gripped them convulsively, and then led her towards the house, leaving Masters's man to deal as he pleased with portmanteaux and hat-box, gun-case and umbrella-case, despatch-box, and other chattels; to leave them out in the lane to the dews and the night-birds, if he so listed. Martin Disney had no consciousness of anything in this world except the woman by his side.

"My darling! my darling!" he ejaculated, in a choked voice, "how I have longed for this hour, with a longing that has been almost madness!"

And then he saw for the first time that her face was as white as her gown. Was it the twilight that made her look so pale? Could he wonder if the emotion of this supreme moment blanched that young cheek, when he, soldier and wayfarer upon the world's roughest roads, felt like a child, striving to hold back his tears?

Lamps were burning in dining-room and drawing-room. He saw the table laid for dinner through the open door as he and Isola passed by; but the idea of eating and drinking seemed very far off just now. They went into the drawing-room together, where a solitary lamp was shining upon a table crowded with flowers, and where the scents of the garden came in through the open window. Here he satisfied the longing of his hungry heart, and took that fragile form in his arms, and kissed the pale cold lips. She lay upon his breast unresistingly; helpless, unresponsive, like a dead thing.

"Isola, have you forgotten that you once loved me?"

"Forgotten! No, no, no! There is no one in the world so good and true as you are. I love you with all my heart and soul."

Her face was hidden on his breast, but she lifted up her arms and clasped them round his neck. He seated himself in his accustomed chair—it was standing where it had always stood before he went away—and took her upon his knee, as if she had been a child. Then a great storm of sobs suddenly burst from throat and bosom, a flood of tears streamed upon his breast, and he felt her arms trembling as they clasped his neck.

"My own dear love," he murmured gently, "one would almost think you were sorry I have came back."

She could not answer him at first for her sobs, but she shook her head, and at last the words, "No, no, no," came from her lips; and he kissed and calmed her with almost fatherly gentleness. And then they went into the dining-room, where the soup-tureen was waiting for them on the sideboard, with a neat little parlour-maid—not Susan, but another—ready to minister to them.

The table had been decorated by Isola's own hands. Dark crimson roses were lying on the fair white damask; one tall glass stood in the centre with three slim golden lilies, pale and heavy-headed, which filled the room with perfume. These came from one of the hothouses at Glenaveril, whence good-natured Mrs. Crowther had sent a basket of exotics in honour of the colonel's return. The lamplight, the flowers, the pretty old Wedgwood service of creamy white and dull brown, made up a feast for Martin Disney's eye, after a life spent mostly under canvas. He looked from the gaily adorned table to the face beside him, pallid and pinched, despite its sweetness.

"My dear one, you are looking very ill," he said, with an anxious air.

"What an ungallant speech!" she answered, smiling at him with unexpected gaiety. "I have been fretting at your long, long absence, and you reproach me for my deteriorated appearance. Never mind, Martin, you will see how rosy and bright I shall get now our parting has come to an end."

"Yes, love, we must coax the roses back to your cheeks. I must have a good mount ready for you when the cubbing begins, and a few morning gallops will soon make a change in my fragile wife's appearance. And I'll charter a yacht and steep you in ozone."

"Oh, one gets enough of that on shore, there is no need to go further."

"But I thought you adored yachting? It was one of our grand schemes for the future, to hire a modest little yawl and go round the coast to Clovelly. Have you forgotten?"

"No, no; only I don't want you to waste your money—and, if we start a bigger stable——"

"Ah, you don't know what a Crœsus I have become. You needn't be afraid of ruining me. My poor lonely little wife. Why didn't you send for Allegra?"

"She wouldn't have been of any good to me. She is all that is sweet and lovable, and she is your sister; but she wouldn't have filled your vacant place. I should have only felt lonelier for having to talk every day, and pretend a kind of happiness. Being alone, I could bury myself in a book, and forget my troubles."

"This soup doesn't look up to Tabitha's old form. Do you know that among other delights of this earthly paradise I have been looking forward to Tabitha's little dinners. I don't believe there is a *chef* in Paris who can cook so well as that self-taught genius, who ripened into perfection by a process of gradual evolution, from the early days when my mother discovered that nobody could make arrowroot or cook a mutton cutlet as well as Tabitha. By-the-by, why has not that good soul shown herself? I thought she would have disputed with you for my first kiss."

While he ran on in this fashion, Isola sat looking down at the table-cloth, pallid no longer, but crimson.

"Tabitha has gone!" she said abruptly.

"Tabitha gone—for a holiday?"

"No, she has left me, altogether."

"Left you—altogether?" exclaimed Disney, with the tone of a man who could scarcely believe in his own sense of hearing, so astounding was the statement that met his ears. "Tabitha, my mother's faithful old servant, who was like my own flesh and blood! What in God's name made her leave you? Did you quarrel with her?"

He asked the question almost sternly. For the first time in his life he was angry with this dear fragile creature, the idol of his heart. He had loved Tabitha as servants are not often loved. He had left his young wife in her charge, desiring no better custodian, full of faith in Tabitha's ability both to protect and counsel her girlish mistress.

"No, no; we did not quarrel. I liked Tabitha very much. I was almost as fond of her as you yourself could be."

"And yet you dismissed her!" Disney retorted bitterly. "She was not smart enough for you, perhaps. Those Crowther people may have put it into your head that she was old-fashioned—that you could never have a modish household with such a humdrum old person at the head of it. Was that your motive?"

"Oh, Martin, how can you think me so frivolous? I hate smartness and pretension as much as you do. No, I should never have dismissed Tabitha. She left me of her own accord."

"Why?"

"She wanted rest. She was too old for service, she told me. I tried to keep her. I humiliated myself so far as to beg her to stay with me" —

the tears came into her eyes at the mere memory of that humiliation—"but she had made up her mind. She would not give way."

"Where did she go?"

"To Falmouth—to live with her sister, a shoemaker's widow. They let lodgings, I believe."

"She must have gone mad! A lodging-house must be harder work than anything she had to do here."

"Yes, I think it must."

"When did she go?"

"At the beginning of the year—in January."

"She left you six months ago, and in all that time you never told me she was gone."

"I did not want you to know, for fear you should be worried or vexed."

"I should have been both; but you ought to have told me. I had a right to know. I left you in her charge, Isola. You are much too young and too pretty to be living alone without some kind of dragon—and I knew Tabitha would be a very gentle dragon—a good motherly soul, able to wait upon you and look after your health, and yet grim enough to keep marauders off the premises. Indeed, my pet, you should have let me know of her departure without an hour's delay. She was very wrong to go. It was a breach of faith I could never have expected."

"Pray don't be angry with her, Martin."

"But I am angry. I have a right to be angry. I'll go to Falmouth to-morrow, and have it out with her."

"No, no, pray don't! We parted good friends. She can say nothing to you more than she said to me. Pray don't let there be any bad blood between you. What could be gained by your going? To-morrow, too—our first day together!"

"Well, it shall not be till the day after; but go I must. To-morrow I will revel in the delights of home, and my dear one's society. To-morrow I will be drunken with joy. The day after will do for Tabitha."

"I think it is making a great deal too much of her to go to Falmouth on purpose to see her," said Isola, with a grain of pettiness; and then, after a pause, during which the colonel had been trying to appease a sharp appetite with the muscular leg of an elderly fowl, she said nervously—

"I'm afraid you are not enjoying your dinner."

"What do I care for dinner on such a night as this; but, as a matter of plain truth, I must say that your new cook is a very bad substitute for Tabitha. Her soup was watery, her fish was greasy, her poultry is hardly eatable. If she has talents in any other line she is keeping them in reserve for another day. It may be that she excels in made-dishes—a misfortune for me, as I never eat them."

"I had a splendid character with her," said Isola, piteously, with the helpless feeling of a housewife who sees before her a dark prospect of bad dinners and marital grumblings, or the agonizing wrench involved in changing her cook.

"Yes, my love, people generally give splendid characters to servants they want to get rid of," answered Disney, dryly.

---

These wedded lovers went out very early next morning to explore the gardens and meadows; Isola eager to point out various small improvements which she had made with the help of the old gardener, who would have plunged his hand and arm into a fiery furnace to procure plant or flower which his young mistress desired. Sweet words and sweet looks go very far in this world. They are a mighty revenue, and will often do their owner as good service as gold and silver.

Isola had worked in the garden with her own hands ever since the beginning of spring, the first tender opening of Earth's heavy eyelids, her first pale smile of snowdrops, her broad laughter of daffodils, her joyous peal of bluebells, and riotous mirth of May blossom. She had toiled in the sweat of her brow so that the garden might be beautiful at mid-summer: for early in March there had come a letter full of rejoicing from that distant hill-kingdom, and she knew that the year of absence to which she had looked so hopelessly last November was commuted to half a year.

Martin Disney was full of admiration for his wife's improvements. The old-fashioned borders were brimming over with old-world flowers; the shrubberies had grown out of knowledge; the escalonia hedge by the kitchen garden was a thing to wonder at.

"I remember the hedge at Tregenna Castle before that good old place was an inn," said Martin; and then, having admired everything, he walked up and down the grass beside the laurel hedge with his wife—while the Satan-sent cook was spoiling the food that bounteous Nature had provided for man's enjoyment—and questioned her about the life she had been leading in his absence.

"You used to write me such good letters, dearest, so full of detail, that I knew exactly how your days were spent, and could picture every hour of your life: but of late your descriptive powers have flagged. I dare say you got tired of writing long letters to a dull old fellow in India, who could never write you a clever letter in reply. It must have seemed a one-sided business?"

"Indeed, no, dear. Your letters had only one fault. They were never half long enough; but I knew how busy you were, and I thought it was so good of you never to miss a mail."

"Good of me! Had there been twice as many mails I would not have willingly missed one. But there is no doubt your letters fell off after last autumn. They were sweet, and ever welcome to me—but they told me very little."

"There was very little to tell."

"Ah, but in the old days you used to make it seem so much. You had such a delightful way of describing trifling events. I thought at one time you had the makings of a Jane Austen; but afterwards I began to fear you must be out of health. Your letters had a low-spirited tone. There were no more of those sharp little touches which used to make me laugh, no more of those tiny word-pictures, which brought the faces and figures of my old neighbours before me."

"You can hardly wonder if my spirits sank a little when you had been so long away. And then life seemed so death-like in its monotony. There were days when I felt I might just as well have been dead. There could be very little difference between lying under the earth and crawling listlessly on the top of it."

"You were too much alone, Isola," he answered, distressed at this revelation. "You ought to have sent for Allegra. I begged you to send for her, if you felt dull."

"Do you think she could have cured my dulness?" exclaimed his wife, impatiently. "Life would have seemed still more tiresome if I had been obliged to talk when there was nothing to talk about, and to smile when I felt inclined to cry."

"Ah, you don't know what a companion Allegra is—brimming over with fun! She knows her Dickens by heart; and I never met with anybody who appreciated him as intensely as she does."

"I don't care about Dickens."

"Don't—care—about Dickens!"

He echoed her words as if almost paralyzed by horror.

"Not as I used to care. One's taste changes as life goes on. Lately I have read nothing but Victor Hugo, and Keats, and Shelley."

"Very well in their way, but not half cheery enough for a lonely little woman beside the Fowey river. You ought to have had Allegra. It would have been better for you and better for her. She is tired of the Art school; and the other pupils are tired of her. They are very fond of her; but she has done all the work twice over, and there is nothing more for her to do, unless we meant her to enter the Royal Academy and go in seriously for art, Mrs. Meynell tells me. According to that lady's account my sister must be an Admirable Crichton in petticoats."

"I have no doubt she is very clever and very nice; but, as I could not have you, I preferred being alone," answered Isola.

She was walking slowly by his side along the closely shaven grass, and every now and then she stretched out a hand that looked semi-transparent, and gathered a flower at random, and then plucked off its petals nervously as she walked on. Her eyelids were lowered, and her lips were tightly set. Martin could but think there was a vein of obstinacy in this bewitching wife of his—a gentle resistance which would tend to make him her slave rather than her master in the days to come. He saw with pain that her cheeks were hollow and pinched, and that her complexion had a sickly whiteness. She had fretted evidently in those long months of solitude, and it would take time to bring back the colour and gaiety to her face. As for dulness, well, no doubt Fowey was ever so much duller than Dinan, where there were officers and tennis-parties and afternoon tea-drinkings, and a going and coming of tourists all the summer through, and saints' days, and processions, and *fêtes* and illuminations in the market square, beneath the statue of Duguesclin.

"And how did the world use you, Isola?" he asked presently. "Was everybody kind?"

"Oh yes, people were very kind; especially Mrs. Baynham and Mrs. Crowther. They sent me ever so many invitations, and wanted me to go on their day every week."

"And I hope you accepted their invitations."

"I went to Mrs. Baynham's sometimes on her day; but I didn't care about going to Glenaveril. It is all too grand and too fine—and I don't like Mr. Crowther."

"He was always courteous to you, I hope?"

"Oh yes, he was particularly courteous. I have no reason for disliking him. He is my Dr. Fell—the reason why I cannot tell, but I would walk a mile to avoid meeting him."

"Then we will not cultivate social relations with Glenaveril. We will visit at no house where my dearest does not feel happy and at ease. And as for the finery, I agree with you, there is something too much of it. I like powder and plush when the people they serve are to the manner born, and when powder and plush seem more natural than parlour-maids; but I don't care for the solemn stateliness of a big establishment when it has been newly set up—at least, not by such folks as the Crowthers. There are some men to whom such surroundings seem natural, even though fortune has come late in life. Is the beautiful Belinda married yet?"

"No. I do not think she is as much as engaged."

"I thought Lostwithiel would have married her. She would have been a grand catch for him, and no doubt she would have snapped at a coronet, even without strawberry leaves. But I hear he is in South America orchid-hunting. He was always a capricious individual. There goes the gong for breakfast. I hope your cook can fry a rasher and boil an egg better than she can dress a dinner."

They went in together to the pretty dining-room, so bright with books and flowers, and a life-sized girlish head in water-colours, by Dobson, R.A., over the chimney-piece, and Venetian glass here and there, that all characteristics of the ordinary eating-room were effaced, and only a sense of homeliness and artistic surroundings was left. Isola had been down at six, and her own hands had given the finishing touches to the room, and the flowers were of that morning's gathering, and had the dew and the perfume of morning upon them. The room was so pretty, and Isola was so much prettier than the room, that a husband would have been of very dull clay had he troubled himself about the handiwork of the cook. Martin Disney was not made of dull clay, and he ate an overdone rasher and a hard-boiled egg without a murmur, and then set out for a long ramble with Isola.

They went up to the hill upon whose landward slope stood Lostwithiel's old grey manor-house, with its gardens and park. Isola had not been there since that never-to-be-forgotten November evening when she met Lostwithiel in the rain. She had avoided the spot from that time forward, though she had no especial reason for avoidance, since there was no one there but Mrs. Mayne and her underlings. Lostwithiel and the *Vendetta* had sailed away into space directly after the Hunt Ball, and little had been heard of him save that dim rumour of orchid-hunting on the shores of the Amazon, which had filtered from the society papers down to Fowey, *viâ* the *Western Daily Mercury*.

Isola and her husband lingered for a long time upon the hilltop, he revelling in the familiar beauty of that magnificent stretch of cliff and sea, out to the dim slate colour of the Dodman Point, bay beyond bay, curving away towards Falmouth and the Lizard—while between that hill and the sea lay a world of fertile meadows and bright green cornfields, of hill and hollow, wood and common, copse and garden, a rich and smiling country, a land of summer flowers and plenteous growth.

"I never stand upon this hill without feeling proud of being a Cornishman," said Disney, "and yet, after all, it is a foolish thing to be proud of an accident. My little Breton girl might as well be proud of being a countrywoman of Duguesclin's."

"Perhaps if I had been born anywhere else I should not have been so ready to fall in love with a soldier," answered Isola. "I was brought up to think a knight and a warrior the one ideal: and so I was fascinated by the first soldier who took any notice of me."

"But were you really fascinated, and were you really in love," exclaimed Disney, infinitely delighted at this little speech of his wife's, "in love with a battered campaigner—or did you just think you liked me a little bit, only because you wanted to get away from Dinan?"

"I really—really—really loved you," she answered softly, looking up at him with eyes dimmed by tears, as he drew her nearer to him in his gladness. "I was not tired of Dinan—or my life there—and my heart went out to you at once, because you were good and noble, and seemed to care for me."

"There was no seeming in it, Isola. I was knocked over at once, like a pigeon out of a trap. I had been in love with you three weeks—three centuries it seemed—before I could screw up my courage so far as to think of proposing for you. And then if Hazelrigg hadn't helped me with your father, I don't suppose I should ever have broken the ice. But when he—the colonel—showed himself so frank and willing—and the way was all made smooth for me from a domestic point of view—and when I saw that kind little look in your eyes, and the shy little smile—yes, you are smiling so now—I took heart of grace, and stormed the citadel. Do you remember the evening I asked you to be my wife, Isola; that starlit night when I had been dining with your people, and you and Gwendolen, and Hazelrigg and I went out upon the terrace to look at the stars, and the river, and the twinkling lights of the boats down by the quay, and the diligence driving over the bridge, deep, deep down in the valley below us? Do you remember how I lured you away from the other two, and how we stood under the vine-leaves in the berceau, and I found the words somehow—feeblest, stupidest words, I'm afraid—to make you know that all the happiness of my life to come depended upon winning you for my wife?"

"I remember as if it were last night," she answered gravely. "But oh, how long ago it seems!"

"Why do you sigh as you say that?"

"Oh, one always sighs for the past! How can one help feeling sorry that it should be gone—so much of our lives and of ourselves gone for ever?"

"Oh, but when the future is so fair, when the present is so happy, there should be no more sighing. It is an offence against the Great Father of all, who has been so good to us."

She did not answer, and they remained silent for some minutes, she seated on a bank covered with heather and wild flowers; he stretched on the short, sweet turf at her feet. The heather had not begun to show its purple bloom, but there was the gold of the gorse, and the brightness of innumerable wild flowers around and about them as they basked in the sunshine.

"Dearest, do you believe in dreams?" Disney asked suddenly.

"Sometimes—not much—dreams are often dreadful," she answered, with a startled air.

"I don't believe in them a bit," he said, lifting himself into a sitting position, and addressing himself to her with increasing earnestness, "not now that I have you here safe within reach of my hand—so," taking her hand in his, and keeping it clasped in both his own; "but I had a dream about you in Burmah, which kept me in a fever of anxiety for nearly a month. I should have telegraphed to ask if all was right with you, only I told myself that if anything was wrong Tabitha would instantly telegraph to me. I made her promise that before I left England. It was almost my last injunction. And to think that she left you half a year ago, and that anything might have happened to you after that, and that there was no one—no one——"

"But, you see, I am quite safe. There was no bad news to send you. Besides, if I had been ill, or anything had gone wrong, there was Mrs. Baynham. She has been like a mother to me. I am so sorry you feel vexed about Tabitha's leaving me."

"Doubly vexed, dear, because you left me in ignorance of the fact."

"Pray don't be angry with me, Martin, so soon," she pleaded meekly.

"Angry, no. I am not angry. I don't know how to be angry with you, Isola; but I can't help being distressed. However, let the past be past. I shall never leave you to the care of strangers again till I die."

Her only answer was to bend her head down to kiss the hands that clasped her own.

"Tell me about your dream," she said, after a pause, with her forehead still resting on his hands, and her face hidden. "Was it something very awful?"

"It was all confusion—a wild chaos—a nightmare of strange sounds and sensations—tempest, fire, earthquake—I know not what—but it meant deadly danger for you—death perhaps. I saw you hanging in space—a white figure, with piteous, pain-wrought face. Never have I seen you look like that—your eyes staring wildly as if they were looking at death; your features drawn and rigid, and through all the confusion, and noise, and ceaseless movement, I was trying to follow you—trying, but impotently—to save you. The white figure was always before me—far off—yet visible every now and then across the darkness of a world where everything was shapeless and confused. But the worst of all was that every now and then a black wall rose up between your distant figure and the stony difficult path that I was treading—a wall against which I flung myself, mad with rage and despair, trying to tear the stones asunder with my hands, till the blood ran in streams from my fingers. It was a dream that seemed to last through a long night, holding in it the memory of a painful past; yet I suppose it was like other dreams—momentary, for I had heard three o'clock strike before I fell asleep, and when I sounded my repeater it was only a quarter past."

84

"Rather a meaningless dream," she said, in a sleepy voice, without looking up. "I don't think it ought to have alarmed you."

"Ah, it sounds meaningless to you; but to me it was full of meaning! The idea of danger to you was so intense—so real. The cold sweat of deadly fear was on my face when I awoke, and it was some minutes before I could get my senses clear of that ghastly horror, before I could realize where I was, and that the thing I had seen was a dream. That stone wall seemed still in front of me, and I had still the feeling that you were on the other side of it, in ever-increasing peril."

"It was a horrid dream, certainly; but, you see, it had no meaning."

"There were such strange things mixed up in it—thunder and lightning, a roaring wind, a sound of rushing waters; and then, amidst wind and thunder, there rose the dark barrier that shut out everything."

"Was it long ago that you dreamt this horrid dream?"

"Yes, a long while. It was just before Christmas. I made a note of the dream in my journal—wrote it down in fear and trembling, lest there should be some kind of fulfilment. But then came your letter—written at the beginning of January, with your description of the ball—and I laughed at my folly in brooding so long upon that phantasmal picture. I remember, by the way, it was two or three nights after your ball that I dreamt my dream, while you no doubt were sleeping just a little sounder than usual after your gaieties."

"Dreams are very strange," said Isola, absently. "I wonder whether there is any good in them to counterbalance so much pain?"

## CHAPTER VII.

### "LOOK THROUGH MINE EYES WITH THINE, TRUE WIFE."

There were steamers plying between Fowey and Falmouth in this summer weather, and Colonel Disney suggested next morning that Isola should go with him on his journey in search of Tabitha. They would go by water and return in the afternoon by rail. The morning was lovely, and the trip round the coast would be delightful.

"I don't want to see Tabitha," Isola answered, with a touch of impatience. "If you are so bent upon seeing her I had rather you went alone."

"But I had rather not spend a whole day away from you. As for Tabitha, a visit of ten minutes will be quite enough for me. I have brought her a Rhampoor Chuddah—a warm red one. I have only to make her my little gift, and to say a few words—without any anger—about her breach of faith."

"It was really not a breach of faith. I gave her full permission to go. I was getting just a little tired of her fussiness. She was not *my* old servant, you know, Martin. I had not been used to her all my life, as you have."

"Ah, but she is so good—such a thoroughly good woman."

"Yes, she is good, no doubt."

"Well, we'll go to Falmouth together, and you can stop at the Green Bank, where we can lunch, while I go and find Tabitha. You know her address, I suppose?"

"Yes. She lives at No. 5, Crown Terrace, overlooking the harbour."

This conversation took place in the garden, where they breakfasted, under a square striped awning, an apology for a tent, set up on the lawn by the river. A badly cooked breakfast seemed less offensive in the garden, where the summer air, and the perfume of the roses eked out the meal. After breakfast Disney called his wife to the drawing-room, where he had brought his spoil from the East, and laid his offerings, as it were, at the feet of his idol.

86

"See, love, here is a shawl which you can use as a *couvre-pied*," he said, flinging a fine cashmere over a chair, "since Fashion decrees that women shall wear shawls no more. And here are some ivory chessmen to assist you in puzzling your brains over the game of Eastern antiquity; and here are vases and things for odd corners. And I have brought you a carved Persian screen, and some Peshawur curtains for your door-ways, and a lamp from Cairo, to make your drawing-room a little more fantastically pretty. I know you love these things."

She was enraptured with his gifts. Her face lighted up like the face of a child, and she ran from one object to the other in a confused gladness, scarcely able to look at one thing at a time.

"They will make the room too lovely," she cried; "and they will tell everybody of your far-away travels. I can never thank you half enough for all these treasures."

"Love me a little, and that will be more than enough."

"A little. Ah, Martin, I love you so much."

"Then why do you sigh as you say it? There need be no sighing over our love now. I never shall leave you again."

He caught her to his breast as he spoke, and kissed the pale sweet face, with a kind of defiant rapture, as if he challenged Fate to do him any harm. The pain of separation from that fair young wife had been so keen an agony that there was a touch of savage exultancy in the joy of re-union—some such fierce gladness as a knight-crusader might have felt in days of old, coming back to his beloved after years of war and travel.

God help the crusader's wife of those rough days if she had turned from the path of virtue during his exile. There would be a short shrift and a bloody shroud for such a sinner!

They walked into Fowey by that pathway which Isola had trodden so often in the year that was gone—not always alone. The pleasure steamer was waiting in the little haven, where the two rivers part under the cloven hills. Out seaward the air blew fresh and free, and the spray was dashing up against the rocks, and Polruan's grey roofs were wrapped in morning shadows while Fowey laughed in the sunshine.

That water journey to Falmouth was delicious upon such a morning, and it needed not a brass band of three men and a boy, blaring out the new and popular music-hall song of the year before last, to enliven the voyage. Those arable lands yonder, undulating with every curve of the ever-varying coast-line, the emerald green of young corn shining in the sunlight, copse and spinney here and there in the clefts and hollows, the Gribbin Head standing up stony and grim on the crest of the topmost hill, and, anon, Par harbour lying low upon the level sands, and then this point and that, till they meet the gallant fleet of fishing-boats sailing out from Mevagissey, like a peaceful Armada, and skim past the haven, and the little town and quay crowded at the foot of the hill, and the coastguard's stronghold yonder, high up against the bright blue sky, whiter than any other mortal habitation ever was or will be. And so to Falmouth, with porpoises playing under their bows, like sportive dolphins, as if they carried Dionysius or Arion on their deck—a brief summer sail, in the keen sweet air of an English summer. To Martin Disney's British nostrils that atmosphere seemed soul-inspiring, the very breath of life and gladness, after the experiences of a hot-weather campaign.

And here was Falmouth, with proud Pendennis on a sunny height, and bay and harbour, town and hill, terrace above terrace, tower and steeple—the town and streets all crowded and clustered in the foreground, where the river winds inward to the heart of the land.

The Green Bank gave them cordial welcome, and luncheon was speedily spread in a private sitting-room, at a snug round table by a window overlooking the harbour—luncheon, and of the best, tongue and chicken, and salad, cherry pasty, junket and cream.

Colonel Disney applied himself to the meal with a hearty relish.

"There is just this one advantage in bad cooking at home that it makes one so thoroughly enjoy everything one gets abroad," he said, laughing at his own prowess.

"I'll try and get a better cook, if you like, Martin," Isola said, with rather a helpless air.

To a wife of one and twenty there seems such futility in worrying about a cook.

"You couldn't possibly get a worse. How long have you put up with this one?"

"Ever since Tabitha left."

"Good heavens! You have been starving upon ill-cooked food for six months. No wonder you look thin and out of health."

"I am really very well. There is nothing the matter with me."

"Yes, yes, there is a great deal the matter. A bad cook, solitude, no one to watch over you and care for you. But that is all over now. You are eating no lunch—not even that superb cherry pasty. I'll be off to find Tabitha. I shan't be more than half an hour, unless Crown Terrace is at the extremity of Falmouth. Have you brought a book to read while I am away? No, foolish child. Never mind. There is the county paper, and there is the harbour, with all its life, for you to look at."

He started on his voyage of discovery, with the warm, comfortable shawl which he had bought for his mother's old servant hanging over his arm. It was a small disappointment amidst the infinite delight of his home-coming, but when he bought the shawl he had fancied himself putting it round Tabitha's ample shoulders in the little housekeeper's room at the Angler's Nest, a room that was just large enough to hold a linen cupboard, a Pembroke table, a comfortable armchair, and Tabitha, who seemed bigger than all the furniture put together.

He was a man of warm affections, and of that constancy of mind and temper to which forgetfulness of old ties or indifference to past associations is impossible. Tabitha's image was associated with all the tenderest memories of his youth; with his mother's widowhood, and with her second marriage—a foolish marriage. At seven and thirty years of age she had taken to herself a second husband, some years her junior, in the person of George Leland, a well-meaning and highly intellectual curate with weak lungs, a union entered upon while her only son was a cadet, and which left her four years later again a widow, with an infant daughter, a child born amidst sickness and sorrow, and christened at the father's desire Allegra, as if she had entered a world of joy. Through that Indian summer of his mother's second love, in all the cares and griefs of her second marriage, Tabitha had been trusty and devoted, nursing the frail husband through that last year of fading life which was one long illness, comforting the widow, and rearing the sickly baby until it blossomed into a fine healthy child, whose strength and beauty took every one by surprise.

With all the joys and sorrows of his mother's life Tabitha had been associated for five and thirty years of conscientious service; and to have lost the good soul now from his fireside was a positive affliction to Martin Disney. Her loss gave an air of instability to his domestic life. Who would ever care for his property as Tabitha had cared—Tabitha who had seen the china and the pictures and drawings collected piece by piece, who had seen the old family silver drop in by way of legacy from this and that aunt or uncle, till the safe was full of treasures, every one of which had its distinct history? What would a new housekeeper care for General Disney's coffee-pot, for the George the Second urn that had belonged to his uncle the Indian judge, for his grandmother's decanter stands? A modern servant would scoff at decanter stands; would wonder they were not melted down. No, rejoiced as he was to be at home once more, home without Tabitha would be something less than home to Martin Disney.

He found Crown Terrace, a row of neat little houses high above the harbour on the Helston road. He had no need to look at the numbers on the doors. He knew Tabitha's house at a glance, four or five doors off. Who else would have devised such pretty window-boxes, so simple and so artistic; or who else would have hit upon so perfect a harmony of colour in the flowering plants? Who else, of that lowly status, would have chosen such curtains or draped them so gracefully? The little bow-windowed band-box of a house was as pretty as a Parisian toy.

Tabitha was in the window, working with scissors and sponge at one of the flower-boxes. Never an aphid was allowed to rest on Tabitha's roses or geraniums. She gave a little cry of mixed alarm and delight as she saw that stalwart figure come between her and the sunshine.

"Lor' sakes, Captain Martin, is it you?" she cried.

"Yes, Tabby, it is I—and I want to know what you've got to say to me. Do you know how a deserter feels when he suddenly finds himself face to face with his commanding officer? I never had such a knock-down blow as when I came home the day before yesterday and found you had deserted your post—you whom I trusted so implicitly."

Tabitha looked at him dumbly—entreatingly—as if she were mutely supplicating him not to be angry. She took this reproof with an air of having thoroughly deserved it, of not having any plea to offer in her defence.

"You'll come in and sit down a bit, won't you, Captain Martin?" she said deprecatingly; and then, without waiting for an answer, she bustled out of the parlour, and anon appeared at the open door.

"Yes, of course I am coming in. I have a great deal to say to you— much more than can be said in the open street."

Tabitha ushered him into the little parlour; so neat, so cool and dainty a bower, albeit the whole of its contents would scarcely have realized ten pounds at an auction. She offered him her most luxurious easy-chair—a large Madeira chair, with pale chintz cushions and artistic draping; and then, when he had seated himself, she stood before him like a prisoner at the bar, and with unmistakable guilt disturbing the broad placidity of her countenance.

"Tabby, there is my offering from the Indies. May it keep you warm when you run out upon your mysterious errands on autumn evenings, as you used to do in my mother's time. Sit down, pray; I have lots to say to you."

Tabitha received the comfortable gift with rapturous thanks. That Captain Martin should have thought of her, so far away, with his head full of fighting, and with death looking him in the face! It was too much, and the tears rolled down her honest cheeks as she thanked him.

"And now, Tabitha, I want a candid answer to a straight question. Why did you leave my wife last January?"

"That's easily explained, sir. I'm getting old, and I was tired of service. Mrs. Disney was very well able to spare me. Perhaps she didn't set the same value on me as you did. Young people like young faces about them."

"All that I can understand; but it didn't exonerate you from your duty to me. You promised me to take care of my young wife."

"I did my best, Captain Martin, as long as I could give satisfaction," faltered Tabitha, growing very pale under this reproof.

"Had you any misunderstanding with Mrs. Disney? Did she find fault with you?"

"Oh no, sir. Mrs. Disney is not one to find fault. She's too easy, if anything. No one could be sweeter than she was to me. God knows, if she had been my own daughter I could not have loved her better than I did."

Here Tabitha broke down altogether, and sobbed aloud.

"Come, come, my good soul, don't distress yourself," cried Disney, touched by this emotion. "You loved her; you could not help loving her, could you? And yet you left her."

"I was getting tired and old, sir; and I had saved enough money to furnish a small house; and my sister, Mrs. David, being a widow without chick or child, wanted me to join her in a lodging-house at the seaside. She's a beautiful cook, is my sister, much better than ever I was. So perhaps I was over-persuaded: and here I am. What's done cannot be undone, Captain Martin; but if ever Mrs. Disney should be ill or in grief or trouble, and she should want me, I'll go to her without an hour's loss of time. I can never forget that she is your wife, and that she was a kind mistress to me."

Martin Disney breathed more freely after this speech. He had been curiously disturbed at the idea of a breach between his wife and the old and faithful servant.

"Well, Tabby, I'm glad at least you and my wife are not ill friends," he said. "I do not care for the loosening of old ties. And now I must be off. Mrs. Disney is waiting for me at the Green Bank."

Tabitha seemed a little startled on hearing that her late mistress was in Falmouth, but she made no remark upon the fact.

"Good-bye, Tabby. Stay, there's one favour you can do me. Get me a good cook. The woman we have at present would be a blight upon the happiest home in Christendom."

"I'll find you a better one, sir. I'll set about hunting for a good one this afternoon."

Martin shook hands with her on the door-step, and she stood watching him till he disappeared at the turn of the road. She watched him with a countenance full of sorrow.

## CHAPTER VIII.

### MY FROLIC FALCON, WITH BRIGHT EYES.

Everybody in Trelasco and in the neighbourhood seemed glad to see Colonel Disney again. All the best people within a six-mile drive came bearing down upon the Angler's Nest in the week that followed his return; and there were cosy little afternoon tea-drinkings in the drawing-room, or on the lawn, and Isola had her hands full in receiving visitors. Everybody congratulated her upon having her hero back from the wars.

"You ought to be very proud of your husband, Mrs. Disney," said Vansittart Crowther, with his air of taking all the world under his protection.

"I have always been proud of him," Isola answered gently. "I was proud of him before the Burmese War."

"Your poor wife has been looking very unhappy for the last few months," Mrs. Crowther said to the colonel, with a motherly glance at Isola. "I really had a good mind to write to you and beg you to hurry home if you didn't want to find the poor thing far gone in a decline when you came back."

"My dear Mrs. Crowther, what nonsense," cried Isola, growing crimson at this motherly officiousness. "I have never been out of health, or in the least likely to go into a decline. One cannot always look like a dairy-maid."

"My dear, there's no use talking, you looked very bad. Had one of my girls looked as ill, I should have taken her off to Buxton to drink the waters, without an hour's delay."

That visit of the Crowthers seemed much longer than any other afternoon call. The Crowthers, husband, and wife, and elder daughter, had an inquisitorial air, Isola fancied, an air of scrutinizing her house and herself and her surroundings, which was intolerable to her; although on Mrs. Crowther's part she knew the scrutiny was made in the utmost benevolence, and the officiousness was the outcome of a nature overflowing with the milk of human kindness.

"I wish you had written to me, Mrs. Crowther," said Disney. "I couldn't have come home any sooner, but I could have telegraphed to my sister Allegra to look after my wife, and cheer her solitude. I was a fool not to have had her here all along."

"Hadn't I better go out of the room while you are holding your consultation about me?" exclaimed Isola, fretfully. "It's rather hard upon the patient to hear her case discussed in cold blood. I am tired of declaring that I have not been ill, and that it is my misfortune and not my fault to have a pale complexion."

"You were not always so pallid, my dear," said Mrs. Crowther, persistently. "You were one of the beauties of the Hunt Ball, and you had colour enough that night."

---

Dr. and Mrs. Baynham came the following afternoon, and these two told the same story, though with less obtrusive concern.

"I looked after the young lady now and then," said the worthy doctor, "and as I found there was nothing radically wrong, I didn't worry you with any low-spirited reports; but I expect to see her pick up wonderfully now you have come home. She didn't take enough outdoor exercise, that's where the harm was. She used to be so fond of her boat last year, but this year I fancy she didn't feel herself up to handling the sculls. You didn't now, did you, Mrs. Disney?"

"I don't know about that, but I am ready to row to the Land's End, now Martin is back," said Isola, and those few words seemed the sweetest Martin Disney had heard since Colonel Manwaring's daughter promised to be his wife.

Mrs. Baynham sat on the lawn, sipping her tea, and basking in the afternoon sunshine.

"You should have seen your wife in her wedding-gown at the Lostwithiel dance," she said. "You would have been proud of her. She didn't want to go—refused Mrs. Crowther and me again and again. She thought it wasn't right to be at any merry-making while your life was in danger."

"Yes, I know—I know. My tender-hearted Isola!"

"But at last we got the better of her objections; and though there were a good many pretty women there, and though Miss Crowther, perhaps, pleased most tastes, being a more showy style of beauty, to my thinking there wasn't one came up to Mrs. Disney."

"Her partners seemed of the same opinion," put in the doctor, cheerily. "Why, how often did Lord Lostwithiel dance with you, Mrs. Disney? Oftener than with anybody else, I'll be bound."

Mrs. Baynham nodded approvingly.

"I was very proud of my party that evening, I can tell you, Colonel Disney," she said. "It isn't often that one has to chaperon three attractive young women. Do you know that my youngest niece, Maria, has had two offers since that night, Isola, and when I last heard from her she was on the brink of an engagement? Ah, well, I hope we shall have another ball next December, now that the neighbourhood has begun to wake up a bit. We have been thinking of getting up a water picnic this summer—just a little excursion to Mevagissey, and a little fishing for those who might care for it."

"Very pleasant, indeed, of you," answered the colonel, cheerily. "We will be there."

"The Crowthers are rather grand in their ideas," said the doctor, "but Alicia is very keen upon all kind of sport, so I know she'll want to come, whatever Belinda may say to it."

Mrs. Baynham made a wry face at the name of the elder sister. It was an involuntary and unconscious contortion; but Belinda had tried to snub Mrs. Baynham, who never could forget that her father was a banker at Truro, and held the fortunes—the mortgages and encumbrances of the landed gentry—in the hollow of his hand.

"You don't like the elder Miss Crowther?" speculated the colonel.

"Well, if I am to be candid, I must confess that I have a positive aversion to that young lady. The airs she gives herself on the strength of her father's wool are really insupportable, and since Lord Lostwithiel disappointed her she has been more odious than she was before."

"What do you mean by Lostwithiel disappointing her? Did he jilt her?"

"Well, it could scarcely be called jilting, and I really don't know that there was anything between them; but people had coupled their names—and he dined at Glenaveril at least once a week all the time he was at the Mount—and people had quite made up their minds it was to be a match. Mr. Crowther went about talking of Lord Lostwithiel and his affairs as if he was his father-in-law—the neglected condition of the land, and what ought to be done at the Mount, and that the estate wanted judicious nursing, and all that sort of thing. And then one December morning his lordship sailed off in his yacht before it was light, and there was no more heard of him. It was quite in his way to go off suddenly like that, but the Crowthers were evidently taken by surprise, and we heard no more about Lord Lostwithiel and the Mount."

"They dropped him like a hot potato," said the doctor. "Well, we shall depend upon you both for our water-party. It will not be till the middle of July, when an old chum of mine, a sailor, will be coming this way."

This was a sample of many such visits. In the country, and even in London upon occasion, people are given to discussing the same subjects. Martin Disney heard a good deal about the Crowthers and their supposed disappointment. People liked Mrs. Crowther for her simple, unaffected ways, and thorough-going kindliness; but Vansittart and his daughters had made a good many enemies. He was too coarse; they were too fine; only the mother's simple nature had caught the golden mean between blunt vulgarity and artificial smartness.

Colonel Disney heard all this village gossip with an unheeding ear. He was secure in his own position as a son of the soil, a man whose pedigree could pass muster with that of the Rashleighs and the Treffrys, a man of means that were ample for his own unpretending tastes and requirements. He cared not a jot how many guineas a year the Crowthers might give to their cook, or how much Mr. Crowther had paid for the furnishing and decoration of his house, a theme upon which the gossips of the neighbourhood loved to enlarge. That Mrs. Crowther had gowns from Worth, and that her daughters employed Mrs. Mason, irked not this simple soldier. The only point in all the stream of talk that had affected him was the unanimous opinion that Trelasco in the spring had been too relaxing for Mrs. Disney, or else that her solitude had preyed upon her mind, inasmuch as she had looked so ill as to afford an interesting subject of conversation to a good many friendly people who suffered from the chronic malady of not having enough to talk about, a form of starvation almost as bad as not having enough to eat.

The colonel listened, and made his own conclusions. He did not believe that Trelasco was "relaxing." Ho loved the district too well to believe any evil thing about it. Those fresh breezes that blew up from the sea, those balmy airs that breathed across the heather-clad hills, must bring health with them. What could one have better than that mingling of sea and hill, brine and honey, gorse-bloom and seaweed? No, Trelasco was not to blame. His young wife had suffered for lack of youthful company. He made up his mind accordingly.

"I suppose you won't object to our having Allegra here for a summer visit, will you, love?" he asked at breakfast the day after Mrs. Baynham's call. "London must be hot, and dusty, and dreary in July, and she must want rest and country air, I fancy, after having worked so hard in her art school."

Isola gave a scarcely perceptible sigh as she bent to caress Tim, a privileged attendant of the breakfast-table.

"Object! Of course not, Martin. I shall be very pleased for your sister to come here."

"I feel very sure you will be pleased with her when you and she get upon intimate terms. You could know so little of her from that one evening in the Cavendish Road."

The occasion in question was an evening in which Isola and her husband had been bidden to a friendly dinner, on their way through London, by the clergyman's widow with whom Allegra lived while she pursued her study of art at a famous school in St. John's Wood. The clergyman's widow, Mrs. Meynell, was a distant cousin of the Disneys, and Allegra's home had been with her from the time she left school. The extent of her wanderings after she was old enough to be sent to a boarding-school had been from Falmouth to Kensington, and from Kensington to St. John's Wood, with occasional holidays in the Isle of Thanet.

"I thought she was very fresh and bright and loving," answered Isola, "and I could see even in that one evening that she was very fond of you."

"Yes, God bless her, there is no doubt about that. I have been brother and father too for her. She has had no one but me since our mother's death."

"Shall I write and ask her to come to us, Martin, or will you?"

"I fancy she would take it more as a compliment if the invitation went straight from you. She would know that I would be glad to have her, but she might feel a little doubtful about you."

"Then I'll write to her to-day, Martin, and beg her to come at once—as soon as ever she can pack her boxes."

"That's my darling! I hope she won't bore you when she is here. I have a shrewd idea she'll make your life happier. She'll awaken you from that languor which has grown upon you in your loneliness."

"At least I'll try to make her happy, Martin, if it is only for your sake."

"Ah, and you will soon love her for her own sake."

"I'll get the boat looked to at once, and I'll see about making the spare room pretty for her," said Isola.

A week later Allegra was with them, breakfasting on the lawn in the balmy atmosphere of July. There were two girls, in white gowns, under the tulip tree, instead of one; and Martin Disney felt as if his domestic happiness were doubled, as he looked at those two graceful figures in the flickering light below that canopy of broad bright leaves. Another element of comfort, too, had entered the Angler's Nest; for the incompetent cook had taken her incompetency and a month's wages to her native city of Truro; and a buxom damsel from Falmouth, recommended by Tabitha, had already proved herself a treasure in the culinary art.

Never was there a fairer picture than that domestic group under the tulip tree. The two girlish figures in white muslin, with palest salmon and palest azure ribbons fluttering and glancing in the light and deepening in the shadow; the white fox-terrier, alert, muscular, mercurial; the tortoise-shell cat, long-haired, aristocratic, and demure; the pretty Moorish plateau on bamboo legs, the purple and crimson breakfast service and rare old silver urn, the fruit and flowers, and amber-hued butter, and rustic luxury of preserved fruit and clotted cream.

"How lovely it all is after Cavendish Road!" cried Allegra, rapturously. "When I see the lights and shadows upon those hills, I despair of ever being able to paint a landscape as long as I live. Nature is maddeningly beautiful."

"What is your particular line, Allegra?" asked her brother. "Is it landscape?"

"No; I only care for landscape as a background for humanity. I want to paint genre pictures in water-colour—women and children—beautiful women amidst beautiful surroundings—picturesque poverty—interesting bits of daily life. Mrs. Allingham is the ideal after which I strive, but I am only at the bottom of the ladder. It is a long climb to the top; but one does not mind that in a profession where labour is delight."

"You are fond of art, then?" said Isola, watching the earnest face of the speaker.

"Fond of it! Why, I live for it! The dream of my life from the time I was seven years old has been one long dream of the bliss that was to be mine when I could feel myself able to paint. I have toiled with all my might. Martin disliked the idea of my being an Academy student—poor, foolish, ignorant Martin—so I have been obliged to plod on at St. John's Wood, without hope of prizes or medals; but on the whole I have been very lucky, for I have made friends among the Academicians. They are very kind to any student who seems in rightdown earnest; and they have been ever so good to me. I hope, Martin, you will find some day that I am something better than an amateur," she concluded, resting her two hands caressingly upon her brother's shoulder.

"My dearest, I have not the least doubt you will astonish me. I am very ignorant of everything connected with art. I set my face against the Academy because I thought the training and the life would be too public for my sister."

"As if Burlington House were any more public than that big school at St. John's Wood, my dear illogical brother: and yet we women are the only people who are said to be wanting in the logical faculty."

She leant back in her basket-chair, revelling in the rural atmosphere, and in that new sense of being in the bosom of her family. Tim leapt upon her lap and licked her face, in token of his acceptance of her into the home-circle. Nobody had ever called Miss Leland a beauty, nor had she ever received those disquieting attentions which follow the footsteps of exceptional loveliness. She was sometimes described as a girl who grew upon one; and people who knew her well generally ended by thinking her distractingly pretty. She had a brilliant complexion, of the true English type, fair and blooming—a complexion which indicated perfect health and an active, orderly life; no late hours or novel-reading over the fire—an out-of-door complexion, which would have looked its best under a neat little felt hat in the hunting-field, or under a coquettish straw sailor hat on board a yacht. Her eyes were blue-grey, with long, brown lashes and boldly marked eyebrows; her nose was firmly modelled, inclining a little to the aquiline order. Her mouth was the prettiest feature in her face, and yet it was a shade larger than accepted perfection in mouths. It was a mouth chiefly remarkable for character and expression; and, indeed, it was the individuality and variety of expression in the fair young face which constituted Miss Leland's chief claim to distinction.

She started up from the nest of basket-work and flowered chintz, and stood tall and erect, a Juno-like young woman, with heavy plaits of reddish-brown hair rolled in a great knot at the back of her head. She might have answered one of those harsh advertisements for parlour-maids, in which the words, "No fringe," figure with curt cruelty; for her hair was brushed smoothly back from the fair forehead, and the severity of the style became that wide sagacious brow. It was just the kind of forehead which can endure exposure without conveying an idea of bald ugliness.

She was tall and strongly made, fashioned after the semblance of Diana or Atalanta rather than Venus or Psyche. Her every movement had the bold, free grace of vigorous, unspoiled youth. She had always been active—fond of walking, riding, rowing, swimming, as well as of art, and with an ardent passion for the country, which had made existence in a London suburb one long sacrifice.

"I used to take the train for Hampstead Heath or Willesden," she told her brother, "and go off for long, lonely tramps to Finchley or Hendon. I have watched the builder's progress along roads and lanes I loved. I have seen horrid brick boxes creeping along like some new kind of noxious insect, eating up fields and hedgerows, old hawthorns and old hollies. I could have sat down in the muddy road and cried sometimes, at the thought that soon there would be no country walk left within reach of a Londoner. Once I went off to the north-east, to look for the rural lanes Charles Lamb and his sister loved—the lanes and meadows where they carried their little picnic basket, till they took shelter at a homely inn. Oh, Martin, all those fields and lanes, Charles Lamb's country—are going, going, or gone! It is heartbreaking! And they are building at Fowey, too, I see. Positively there will be no country anywhere soon. There will be crescents and terraces and little ugly streets at the very Land's End, and the Logan Rock will be the sign of a public-house."

"Don't be down-hearted, Chatterbox! I think Cornwall may last our time," said Disney, laughing at her vehemence.

Allegra was a great talker. It seemed as if she had a well-spring of joy and life within her which must find an outlet. When people ventured to hint at her loquacity she declared that her name was in fault.

"I have grown up to match my name," she said; "if I had been christened Penserosa I might have been quite a different person."

Her vivacity gave a new element of brightness to the Angler's Rest, where Disney had been somewhat oppressed by the sensation of intense repose which had pervaded his *tête-à-tête* life with Isola. He loved his wife so entirely, so unselfishly, and devotedly, that it was happiness to him to be with her; yet in the three or four weeks that had gone by since his return he had struggled in vain against the feeling that there was something wanting in his home. Isola waited upon him and deferred to him with more than wifely submissiveness. He would have liked a spurt of rebellion once in a way, a little burst of girlish temper, just to show that she was human; but none ever came. His every desire was anticipated. Whatever plan he suggested—to walk, to drive, to visit, or not to visit—the river or the sea—was always the plan that pleased her best, or at least she said so.

"I think I shall call you Griselda instead of Isola," he said one day, taking the fair pale face between his hands and gazing into the mournful depths of the dark violet eyes—inscrutable eyes they seemed to him, when the pupils dilated under his gaze, as if the eyes made a darkness to hide their meaning.

"Why?" she asked.

A flood of crimson passed over her face like a fire, and left her paler than before.

"Because you are only too dutiful. Would you resist if I were to turn tyrant, I wonder?"

"I have no fear of your turning tyrant," she answered, with a sad little smile; "you are only too good to me."

"Good! There can be no question of goodness. If a man picked up a diamond as precious as the Koh-i-noor, could he be good to it? How can I be good to my gem? I have but one thing left in the world to desire, or to pray for."

"What is that, Martin?"

"To see you happy."

Again the sudden flame crimsoned her face, that sensitive spiritual face which reflected every change of feeling.

"I am happy, Martin, quite happy, happier than I ever thought to be, now that you are home again. What have I more to desire?"

"Is that really so? Was my long absence your greatest trouble?"

"Yes," she answered slowly, looking at him with a curiously steady look, "that was the beginning and end of my trouble."

"Thank God!" he said, drawing a deep breath. "There have been moments—just of late—when I have puzzled my brains about you—until I thought—" very slowly, "there might have been something else."

He clasped her in his arms, and hid her face upon his breast, as if—fearing that he might have wounded her by those last words—he wanted to make amends before she had time to feel his unkindness. His tenderness for her had so much of that pitying love which a strong man feels for a child.

This conversation occurred the day before Allegra's arrival; but with that young lady's appearance on the scene, new life and gladness came into the little household. Allegra sang, Allegra played, Allegra ran out into the garden twenty times a day, and called through the open window to Isola, sitting quietly in the drawing-room, to come out and look at this or that—a rose finer than all other roses—a suggested alteration—an atmospheric effect—anything and everything. She was a keen observer of Nature, full of vivid interest in every creature that lived, and in every flower that grew. Tim followed her everywhere as she danced along the gravel walks, or across the short springy turf. Tim adored her, and grinned at her, and threw himself into all manner of wriggling attitudes upon the grass to express his delight in her company, and fawned at her feet, and talked to her after his guttural fashion, snorting his friendly feelings. Tim had long languished for such a companion, having found his young mistress's society very heavy of late. No more runs in the meadow, no more rambles in the neighbouring spinney, and very little boating. But now that Allegra had come the skiff was seldom idle. Isola had to go on the river whether she liked or not. There were strong young arms ready to pull her—round young arms, of a lovely roseate fairness, which looked their best, stretched to the motion of the sculls, with the white cambric shirt rolled up above the elbow.

"You can read Shelley while I scull the boat," said Allegra. "I don't want any help. If you knew what rapture it is to me to feel the breath of Seagods and Tritons after St. John's Wood, and the smoke from the Metropolitan Railway, you wouldn't pity me."

Isola submitted, and sat at her ease upon bright-coloured cushions with an Indian rug spread round her, as idle as if she had been the belle of a Zenana, and read Alastor while the boat sped seaward in the sunshine.

Sometimes they moored their boat at the landing stage at Polruan, and walked up the hill to the Point, and sat there for an hour or two in the summer wind with their books and picnic basket, seeing great ships go out towards the Lizard and the big distant world, or sail merrily homeward towards Plymouth and the Start. Isola looked at those outward-bound ships with a strange longing in her eyes—a longing to flee away upon those broad wings that flashed whitely in the sunlit distance. Were people happy on board those ships, she wondered, happy at escaping from the fetters of an old life and a beaten path, happy going away to strange lands and freedom? She had been reading many books of travel of late, and a kind of passion for remote uncivilized countries had come upon her; as if that untrammelled life meant release from memory and saddening cares—a new birth almost. It seemed from some of those books as if there could be no greater happiness upon this earth than to tramp across sandy deserts and stalk occasional lions; while in others the supreme good seemed to be found in the attempt to scale impossible mountains. What was it that made the rapture of these things? Isola wondered. Was it that perils and wild solitudes offered the only possible escape out of a past existence, on this side the grave? Allegra had never so much as crossed the Channel. She had been brought up in the most humdrum fashion. First a school at Falmouth, and then a smarter school at Kensington, and then St. John's Wood and the Art School. Her mother had died when she was fourteen years of age, and since that time her brother had been her only guardian and almost her only friend. Her life had seen but little variety, and very little of the dancing and gaiety which for most girls is the only form of pleasure. She and Isola talked about the ships as they sat upon the grassy hill at Polruan, and speculated about the lands of which they knew only what they had read in books of travel.

"You, at least, know what France is like," said Allegra, "and that is something."

"Only one little corner of France."

"And to think that you were born in an old French city! It seems strange. Do you feel at all French?"

"I don't think so; only sometimes a longing comes upon me to see the old grey walls, and to hear the old voices, and see the curious old women in their white caps and bright-coloured handkerchiefs, clattering along to the Cathedral. There must be more old women in Brittany than in Cornwall, I think. Fowey does not swarm with old women as Dinan did. And sometimes I long to see mother, and the good old Brittany servants, and the garden where the hours went by so slowly—almost as slowly as they go here"—with a sigh.

"Does time go so very slowly here?" asked Allegra, quickly. "That sounds as if you were unhappy."

"What nonsense you talk!" cried Isola, with a flash of sudden anger. "Cannot one be dull and bored sometimes—from very idleness— without being unhappy?"

"I don't know; but, for my own part, when I am happy I am never dull."

"You have more of what people call animal spirits than I have."

"I'm glad you apologize in a manner for that odious phrase—animal spirits. I would not apply such a phrase to Tim. It suggests nothing but Audrey at a statute fair. Heaven gave me a capacity for happiness, and I thank God every night in my prayers for another happy day. Even at school I contrived to be happy, somehow; and think what it must be after seven years of dull routine to feel that I have done with sitting at a stranger's table and that I am here in a home, my own home, with my brother and sister."

The two women clasped hands, and kissed each other upon this. Only the night before Isola, of her own free will, had asked her sister-in-law to make her home at the Angler's Nest always, always, till she should be led out of it as a bride; and Martin had shown himself supremely happy in the knowledge that his sister had won his wife's love and confidence.

When Isola and he were alone together after the sealing of that family bond, he kissed and thanked her for this boon which she had bestowed upon him.

"I never could have felt quite at ease while Allegra was living with strangers," he told her. "And now my cup is full. But are you sure, dearest, that you will never find her in the way, never fancy yourself any the less mistress of your house, and of my life, because she is here?"

"Never, never, never! I am gladder than I can say to have her. She is a delightful companion. She helps me in a hundred ways. But even if she were less charming it would be my duty to have her here since you like her to be with us."

"But it must not be done as a duty. I will not have you sacrifice your inclination in the slightest degree."

"What an obtuse person you are! Don't I tell you that I am enchanted to have her? She is as much my sister as ever Gwendolen was; indeed, she is much more sympathetic than Gwen ever was."

"Then I am perfectly content."

Allegra wrote to Mrs. Meynell next day, announcing the decision that had been arrived at, not without grateful acknowledgments of that lady's kindness. The rest of her belongings were to be sent to her forthwith, easels, and colour-boxes, books and knickknacks; her brother's gifts, most of them from the romantic East; things which made her few little Kensingtonian keepsakes look very trivial and Philistine. Allegra's possessions gave a new individuality to the large, airy bedroom, and the tiny boudoir at the corner of the house, looking seaward, which Isola had arranged for her.

While these things were doing Martin Disney was buying horses and buying land—a farm of over two hundred acres which would make his property better worth holding—and he had further employed a Plymouth architect to plan an enlargement of the old-fashioned cottage—a new and much more spacious drawing-room, two bedrooms over, a verandah below, and a loggia above. In that mild climate the loggia would afford a pleasant lounge even in winter, and myrtle and roses would speedily cover the wooden columns which sustained the tiled roof. It was to be a homely Italian loggia—unpretentious, and not particularly architectural; but Isola and her sister-in-law were delighted at the idea.

The stables were to be enlarged as well as the house.

"You have no idea how I have hoarded and scraped to lay by money ever since I bought the Nest," said Disney. "I believe I was the greatest screw in the service all through my last campaign."

He laughed aloud in amused remembrance of many small sacrifices, while the three heads clustered over the architect's plan, which had that factitious prettiness of delicate drawing and colour which makes every house so much nearer perfection upon paper than it ever can be in brick and stone.

## CHAPTER IX.

### "LIES NOTHING BURIED LONG AGO?"

Like most small country settlements, little fraternities of well-to-do people who think themselves the beginning and end of the world, Trelasco was slow to rise to any festivity in the way of party-giving. So it was about two months after Colonel Disney's return before the friendly calls and interchange of small civilities culminated in a dinner-party at Glenaveril. It seemed, indeed, only right and natural that the great house of the district, great by reason of Lord Lostwithiel's non-residence, should be the first to open its doors in a ceremonial manner to the colonel and his womankind. The invitation to his sister might be taken as an especial compliment, arms outstretched to receive one who was a stranger in the land.

"We want to know that nice, young sister of yours," Mr. Crowther said to Colonel Disney, in his patronizing way, as they all came out of church the Sunday before the dinner-party. "A remarkably fine girl."

The colonel did not thank him for this compliment, which was pronounced in a loud voice, amidst the little knot of acquaintances taking leave of each other on the dip of the hill, where there was a sign-post on a patch of waste grass, and where road and lanes divided, one up the hill to Tywardreath, another to Fowey, and a narrow-wooded lane leading down to Glenaveril and the Angler's Nest. Short as the distance was, there were carriages waiting for the Crowthers, who never walked to church, however fine the weather. Mrs. Crowther came to the morning service resplendent in a brocade gown and a Parisian bonnet, on pain of being condemned as dowdy by her husband, who liked to put the stamp of his wealth upon every detail. His wife obeyed him with wifely meekness, but the daughters were not so easily ruled. Both were keen-witted enough to feel the vulgarity of Sunday morning splendour. So Belinda worshipped in the exaggerated simplicity of an unstarched jaconet muslin, a yellow Liberty sash, a flopping Gainsborough hat, and a necklace of Indian beads, an attire which attracted every eye, and was a source of wonder to the whole congregation, while Alicia's neat grey cashmere frock, and smart little toque to match, grey gloves, grey Prayer-book and sunshade, challenged criticism as a study in monochrome.

Mr. Crowther would have lingered for farther conversation before getting into the family landau, but Colonel Disney bade a rather abrupt good morning to the whole group, and hurried his wife and sister down the hill.

"I'm rather sorry we accepted the Glenaveril invitation," he said to Isola. "The man is such an unmitigated cad."

"Mrs. Crowther is very kind and good," replied his wife; "but I have never cared much about going to Glenaveril. I don't feel that I get on particularly well with the girls. They are both too fine for me. But I should be sorry to offend Mrs. Crowther."

"Yes, she seems a kindly creature. It was thoughtful of her sending you a ticket for the ball. A woman with daughters is seldom over-kind to outsiders."

"Oh, I believe Mrs. Crowther's heart is big enough to be kind to a whole parish."

"Well, on her account, perhaps it was best to accept the invitation."

"Don't be so grand about it, Martin," said Allegra. "You forget that I am pining to see what a dinner-party in a very rich house is like. I have seen nothing in London but literary and artistic dinners, third-rate literary and third-rate artistic, I'm afraid—but they were very nice, all the same. Glenaveril is a place that takes my breath away; and I am curious to see what a dinner-party can be like there."

"Then for your sake, Allegra, I'm glad we said yes. Only I couldn't stand that fellow patronizing you. Calling you a fine girl, forsooth!"

"Yes, it is an odious phrase, is it not? I'm afraid I shall have to live through it, because, like Rosalind, 'I am more than common tall.'"

She drew herself up to her full height, straight as a reed, but with fully developed bust and shoulders which showed to advantage in her pale tussore gown—silk that her brother had sent her from India. She looked the incarnation of girlish innocence and girlish happiness—a brow without a cloud, a step light as a fawn's—a fearless, joyous nature. Her more commonplace features and finer figure were in curious contrast with Isola's pensive beauty and too fragile form. Disney glanced from one to the other as he walked along the rustic lane between them; and, though he thought his wife the lovelier, he regretted that she was not more like his sister.

---

A man who is very fond of home and who has no professional cares and occupations is apt to degenerate into a molly-coddle. Martin Disney gave an indication of this weakness on the day before the dinner at Glenaveril.

"What are you two girls going to wear?" he asked. "At least, I don't think I need ask Isola that question. You'll wear your wedding-gown, of course, love?" he added, turning to his wife.

"No, Martin, I am going to wear my grey silk."

"Grey! A dowager's colour, a soured spinster's colour—a Quaker's no colour. I detest grey."

"Oh, but this is a very pretty gown—the palest shade of pearl colour—and I wear pink roses with it. It was made in Paris. I feel sure you will like me in it, Martin," Isola said hurriedly, as if even this small matter fluttered her nerves.

"Not as well as I like you in your wedding-gown. That was made in Paris, and it fitted you like a glove. I never saw such a pretty gown—so simple, yet so elegant."

"I have been married much too long to dress as a bride."

"You shall not seem as a bride—except to me. For my eyes only shall you shine in bridal loveliness. Bride or no bride, what can be prettier for a young woman than a white satin gown with a long train? You can wear some touch of colour to show you have not got yourself up as a bride. What do you say, Allegra? Give us your opinion. Of course you are an authority upon dress."

"Oh, the white satin, by all means. Isola looks ethereal in white. She ought hardly ever to wear anything else."

"You hear, Isa. Two to one against you."

"I'm sorry I can't be governed by your opinions in this instance. You forget that I last wore my gown at a ball. I danced a good deal—the floor was dirty—the gown was spoilt. I shall never wear it again. I hope that will satisfy you, Martin."

She spoke with a touch of temper, her cheeks flushed crimson, and her eyes filled with sudden tears as she looked deprecatingly at her husband. Martin Disney felt himself a brute.

"My dearest, I didn't mean to tease you," he said; "wear anything you like. You are sure to be the prettiest woman in the room. I am sorry the gown was spoilt; but it can't be helped. I'll buy you another white satin gown the first time you and I are in Plymouth together. And, pray, Miss Allegra, what bravery will you sport?"

"I have only a white lace frock that has seen some service," replied his sister, meekly. "I dare say I shall look like somebody's poor relation at such a place as Glenaveril."

"Oh, it's not to be a grand party, by any means. Mrs. Crowther told me she had asked the Baynhams and the Vicarage people to meet us, just in a friendly way."

The party was decidedly small, for on arriving with reasonable punctuality the Disneys found only one guest on the scene, in the person of Mr. Colfox, the curate, who was sitting by one of the little tables, showing a new puzzle of two pieces of interlinked iron to the two Misses Crowther. These young ladies were so interested in the trick of disentanglement that they scarcely noticed the entrance of their mother's guests, and only rose and came over to greet the party three minutes later, as an afterthought.

Mr. and Mrs. Crowther, however, were both upon the alert to receive their friends, the lady frankly cordial, the gentleman swelling with pompous friendliness, as if his manly breast were trying to emerge from the moderate restriction of a very open waistcoat. He protested that he was charmed to welcome Colonel Disney to Glenaveril, and he glanced round the splendid walls as who should say, "It is no light thing to invite people to such a house as this."

Vansittart Crowther was a man of short, squat figure, who tried to make up for the want of inches by extreme uprightness, and had cultivated this carriage until he seemed incapable of bending. He had a bald head, disguised by one dappled streak of grey and sandy hair, which was plastered into a curl on each side of his brow — curls faintly suggestive of a cat's ears. He had blunt features, a sensual lip, and dull, fishy eyes, large and protuberant, with an expression in perfect harmony with the heavy, sensual mouth.

Mr. and Mrs. Baynham were the next arrivals; the lady wearing the family amethysts and the well-known black velvet, under whose weighty splendour she arrived short of breath; the gentleman expansive of shirt front, and genial of aspect, jovial at the prospect of a good dinner and choice wines, and not hypercritical as to the company in which he ate the feast. He shook hands with his host and hostess, and then went over to the Misses Crowther, who had not thought it necessary to suspend their absorbing occupation in order to welcome the village doctor's wife — a fact which Mrs. Baynham observed and inwardly resented.

Mr. Colfox deserted the young ladies, still puzzling over the two bits of iron, and went across the room to greet the Disneys. He was an intelligent young man, steeped to the lips in the opinions and the prejudices of university life — Oxford life, that is to say. He ranked as a literary man in Trelasco, on the strength of having had an article almost published in Blackwood. "The editor had accepted my paper," he told people modestly; "but on further consideration he found it was a little too long, and so, in point of fact, he sent it back to me in the most courteous manner. He couldn't have acted more kindly — but I was disappointed. It would have been such an opening, you see."

All Mr. Colfox's friends agreed that with such an opening the high road to literary fame and fortune would have been made smooth for his feet. They respected him even for this disappointment. To have been accepted by Blackwood made him almost a colleague of George Eliot.

He was a tall and rather lean young man, who wore an eye-glass, and seemed to live upon books. It was irritating to Vansittart Crowther, who prided himself on his cellar and his cook, to note how little impression food and drink made upon Francis Colfox.

"He takes my Château Yquem as if it were Devonshire cider," said the aggrieved parvenu, "and he hardly seems to know that this is the only house where he ever sees clear turtle. The man's people must have lived in a very poor way."

In spite of this contemptuous opinion, Mr. Crowther was always polite to Francis Colfox, and had even thought of him as a *pis-aller* for one of his daughters. There is hardly anything in this life which a self-made man respects so much as race, and Francis Colfox belonged to an old county family, had a cousin who was an earl, and another cousin who was talked of as a probable bishop. He was, therefore, allowed to make himself very much at home at Glenaveril, and to speak his mind in a somewhat audacious way to the whole family.

Captain Pentreath, an army man of uncertain age, a bachelor, and one of a territorial family of many brothers, came next; and then appeared the vicar and his wife and one daughter, who made up the party. The vicar was deaf, but amiable, and beamed benevolently upon a world about whose spoken opinions he knew so little that he might naturally have taken it for a much better world than it is. The vicar's wife spent her existence in interpreting and explaining people's speech to the vicar, and had no time to spare for opinions of her own. The daughter was characterized by a gentle nullity, tempered by a somewhat enthusiastic and evangelical piety. The chief desire of her life was to keep the Church as it had been in the days of her childhood, nearly thirty years before.

It was the first time the Disneys had dined together at Glenaveril, so it seemed only proper that Mr. Crowther should give his arm to Isola, which he did with an air of conferring an honour. The colonel had been ordered to take the vicar's wife, and the doctor was given to Allegra; Captain Pentreath took Miss Trequite, the vicar's daughter; Mr. Colfox followed with Mrs. Baynham, and the daughters of the house went modestly to the dining-room after the vicar and Mrs. Crowther.

The dinner-table was as pretty as roses and Venetian glass could make it. There was no pompous display of ponderous plate, as there might have been thirty years ago on a parvenu's board. Everybody is enlightened nowadays. The great "culture" movement has been as widespread among the middle class as compulsory education among the proletariat, and everybody has "a taste." Scarcely were they seated, when Mr. Crowther informed Mrs. Disney that he hated a display of silver, but at the same time took care to let her know that the Venetian glass she admired was rather more valuable than that precious metal. "And if it's broken, there's nothing left you for your outlay," he said; "but it's a fancy of my wife and girls. Those decanters are better than anything Salviati ever made for Royalty."

The table was oval, lighted by one large lamp, under an umbrella-shaped amber shade, a lamp which diffused a faint golden glow through the dusky room; and through this dreamy dimness the footmen moved like ghosts, while the table and the faces of the diners shone and sparkled in the brilliant light. It was as picturesque a dining-room and table as one need care to see; and if the Gainsboroughs and Reynoldses, which here and there relieved the sombre russet of the Cordovan leather hangings, were not the portraits of Mr. and Mrs. Crowther's ancestors, they were not the less lovely or interesting as works of art.

Isola sat by her host's side, with a silent and somewhat embarrassed air, which her husband noted as he watched her from the other side of the table.

All the decorations were low, so that no pyramid of fruit or flowers intervened to prevent a man watching the face opposite to him. Disney saw that while Allegra, in her place between Mr. Baynham and Alicia Crowther, was full of talk and animation, Isola sat with downcast eyes, and replied with a troubled look to her host's remarks. There was something in that gentleman's manner which was particularly obnoxious to the colonel—a protecting air, a fatherly familiarity, which brought the bald, shining forehead almost in contact with Isola's shoulder, as the man bent to whisper and to titter in the very ear of his neighbour.

The colonel got through a little duty talk with Mrs. Trequite, whose attention was frequently distracted by the necessity of explaining Mrs. Crowther's polite murmurs to the vicar on the other side of the table; and this duty done he gave himself up to watching Isola and her host. Why did she blush so when the man talked to her? Was it the bold admiration of those fishy eyes which annoyed her, or the man's manner altogether; or was it anything that he said? Disney strained his ears to hear their conversation, if that could be called conversation which was for the most part monologue.

The man was talking of the Hunt Ball of last winter. Disney heard such snatches of speech as "the prettiest woman in the room," "everybody said so," "Lostwithiel was evidently *épris*."

Mr. Crowther had a penchant for scraps of French, which decorated his speech as truffles adorn a boned turkey.

"Isn't it odd that he should be such a rover?" he asked, in a less confidential tone than before.

Isola looked up at him, as if hardly understanding the question.

"I mean Lostwithiel. With such a nice place as he has here, it seems a pity to be broiling himself in Peru. I never could understand the taste for orchids; and in his case—well, I hardly believe in it. He is the last man to emulate a Hooker or a Lawrence. Orchid-hunting must be an excuse for keeping away from England, I take it. Don't you think so, now, Mrs. Disney?"

"I really don't know."

"You don't know why he should want to keep away? No, no more does anybody else. Only we all wonder, don't you know. He talked to me of settling down in the county—looking after the estate a little. He even hinted that he might, in due course, cast about for a nice young wife—with a little money. And then all of a sudden off he sails in that rakish yacht of his, and roves from port to port like the Flying Dutchman in the Opera, till at last we hear of him on the coast of Peru. Curious, ain't it, Mrs. Disney?"

"Why curious?" asked Isola, coldly. "Was not Lord Lostwithiel always fond of yachting?"

"No doubt; but when a man talks of settling down in his native place—and then doesn't do it—there must be a reason, mustn't there?"

"I don't know. People act as often from caprice as from reason."

"Ah, that is a lady's idea. No man who is worthy the name ever acts from caprice," said Mr. Crowther, with his insinuating air, as if some hidden meaning were in the words, and then looking across the table and seeing the colonel's watchful face, he altered both tone and manner as he added, "Of course you know Lostwithiel, Colonel Disney?"

"I saw a good deal of Lord Lostwithiel when he was a small boy," answered the colonel, coldly. "His father was one of my early friends. But that is a long time ago."

"How old is he, do you say?"

"Debrett will answer that question better than I can. I have never reckoned the years that have gone by since I saw him in an Eton collar."

The men did not sit long over their wine. The doctor and his host talked agriculture, Mr. Crowther discussing all farming operations upon a large scale as became a man of territorial magnitude. The vicar prosed about an approaching lecture at the schoolroom, and utterly failed in hearing anything that was said in reply to his observations. Colonel Disney smoked a cigarette in silence, and with a moody brow.

Later, in the drawing-room, while the Crowther girls were playing a clamorous duet, by the last fashionable Sclavonic composer, Vansittart Crowther directed his conversation almost wholly to Mrs. Disney, as if she were the only person worthy of his attention. He was full of suggestions for future gaieties in which the Disneys were to share—picnics, boating parties.

"You must help us to wake up the neighbourhood, colonel," he said, addressing Disney, with easy friendliness.

"We are not very likely to be of much assistance to you in that line," Disney answered coldly. "We are quiet stay-at-home people, my wife and I, and take our pleasures on a very small scale."

Colonel Disney's carriage was announced at this moment. He gave his wife a look which plainly indicated his wish to depart, and she rose quickly from the low, deep chair in which she had been sitting, in some manner a captive, while Mr. Crowther lolled across the broad, plush-cushioned arm to talk to her. Allegra was engrossed in a talk about William Morris's last poem with Mr. Colfox, who was delighted to converse with any one fresh from the far-away world of art and literature—delighted altogether with Allegra, whose whole being presented a piquant contrast to the Miss Crowthers. But the colonel's sister saw the movement towards departure, and hastened to her brother's side. Briefest adieux followed, and the first of the guests being gone, left behind them a feeling of uneasiness in those whose carriages had been ordered half an hour later. One premature departure will cast a blight upon your small dull party; whereas from a scene of real mirth the nine Muses and three Graces might all slip away unmissed and unobserved.

## CHAPTER X.

### "OF THE WEAK MY HEART IS WEAKEST."

"You had better send cards to Mrs. Crowther, Isola," said Martin Disney, two days afterwards, when his wife was sitting at her Davenport writing her family letters.

"Cards! Oh, Martin, she would think that so very formal. I can call upon her. She is always at home on Thursday afternoons, and she likes me to go."

"I am sorry for that, since I had rather you should never enter her house again."

"Martin!"

"I have nothing to say against Mrs. Crowther, my dear Isola. But the man is more detestable than I could have believed low birth and unlimited money could make any man. Guileless and inexperienced as you are, I think you must have felt that his manner to you the other night was familiar to the point of being insulting."

Isola had felt both embarrassed and distressed by her host's attentions—the insinuating inflections of his fat, pompous voice; his air of being upon a confidential footing with her. It had seemed to her on that evening as if for the first time in her life, before the eyes of men and women, she drank the cup of shame. She had said no word to her husband of Mr. Crowther's oppressive familiarity, and she had fondly hoped that the matter had escaped his notice.

She sat before him now, flushed and agitated, with lowered eyelids, and one hand restlessly moving about the papers on her blotting-pad.

"My dearest, there is nothing in all this to distress you," said Disney, with infinite gentleness. "It is not your fault that the man is a cad; but it would be my fault if I were to allow you or Allegra to go to his house again."

"He was not rude to Allegra."

"No; it would be her turn next, perhaps. He did not mean to be rude to you. He only wanted to be especially polite in his own odious fashion. There are men in that class who cannot behave decently to a pretty woman, or civilly to a plain one. He meant no doubt to gratify you by his compliments. What a stress he laid upon Lostwithiel's attention to you at the ball. Were his attentions so very marked?"

"Oh no; not more to me than to others," Isola answered quickly. "He danced a good many times—twice or three times—with Belinda Crowther. Everybody noticed them as the handsomest couple in the room; not that he is handsome, of course—only tall and distinguished-looking."

Allegra came running in from the garden, and broke the thread of the conversation. Isola put the visiting-cards into an envelope and addressed it to Mrs. Vansittart Crowther. She felt that the kindly matron would be puzzled and vexed at this ceremony, from a young person towards whom she had assumed so motherly a tone, urging her to run over to Glenaveril at any hour of the day—asking her to lunch or to tea at least once a week—wanting to take her for drives to Lostwithiel, or railway jaunts to Plymouth.

Isola was not mistaken, for Mrs. Crowther called three or four days afterwards and upbraided her for sending the cards.

"You might have all come to tea on Thursday, if you had been good-natured," she said. "Mr. Colfox read us a poem by Swinburne, out of one of the new magazines—there are so many nowadays that I never remember which is which. Belinda was delighted with it—but Alicia and I can't rise to her height. Mr. Colfox reads poetry beautifully. You can't judge of his powers by only hearing him read the lessons," added Mrs. Crowther, as if the English Bible were a poor thing.

She stopped an hour, praised Isola's tea-making and the new cook's tea-cakes, asked a great many questions about Allegra's ideas and occupations, and was as hearty, and simple, and friendly, and natural as if she had been a duchess.

It grieved Isola to be obliged to refuse an invitation to luncheon, most cordially pressed upon her and Allegra.

"I would drive you both to Lostwithiel after lunch, and we could do our little bit of shopping and then have a cup of tea at the Talbot while the horses had their mouths washed out, and I'd show you the room where your brother's wife was so much admired last year, Miss Leland, and where I hope you'll have many a good dance next winter. Now the ice is broken we mean to go on with our balls, I can tell you. Indeed, my girls are thinking of trying to get up a tennis-club ball about the end of September."

This was the last time Mrs. Vansittart Crowther appeared in a friendly manner at the Angler's Nest, for after two or three further invitations—to a picnic—to tea—to lunch—had been declined, in most gracious little notes from Isola, that good lady perceived that there was some kind of barrier to friendly intercourse between her and Colonel Disney's wife, and she told herself with some touch of honest middle-class dignity that if Martin Disney was proud she could be proud too, and that she would make no further offer of friendship which was undesired.

"I suppose he thinks because he comes of a good old family, while we have made our money in trade, that we are not quite good enough to associate with his wife and sister," she said to her daughters. "I thought he was too much of a gentleman to have such a petty feeling."

"How innocent you are, mother," cried Alicia, contemptuously; "can't you see that they are all bursting with envy? That was what made the colonel so gloomy and disagreeable the night of our little dinner. He was vexed to see things done with as good taste as in a nobleman's house. It cuts these poor gentilities to the quick to see that. They don't much mind our being rich, if we will only be vulgar and uneducated. But when we have the impertinence to be as well up in the ways of good society as they are themselves, they can't forgive us. Good taste in a parvenu is the unforgivable sin."

"Well, I don't know," mused Mrs. Crowther, sadly. "I'm sure there's neither pride nor envy in Isola, and Miss Leland looks a frank, straightforward girl, above all foolish nonsense; so it must be the colonel's fault that they've cut us."

"Cut us!" echoed Belinda; "the Angler's Nest cutting Glenaveril is rather too absurd an idea."

"My dear, you don't know the importance Cornish people attach to old family—and the Disneys are a very old family—and no one can deny that he is a gentleman, though we don't like him."

"Oh, no doubt he considers that he belongs to the landed gentry. He has bought Rowe's farm, two hundred and sixty acres. He had forty to begin with, so he is now lord of three hundred acres, just half our home farm."

"His cousin, Sir Luke Disney, has a large estate near Marazion," said Mrs. Crowther, meekly.

"Yes, but we don't reckon a man's importance by his cousin's estate. Colonel Disney is only a squatter in this part of the country."

Alicia pronounced the word with gusto. It had been whispered to her that the squire of Fowey had spoken of her father—who counted his acres by thousands—as a squatter. That unimpeachable importance, founded upon the established respectability of bygone centuries—centuries in which men wore armour and women breakfasted on beef and ale—was not to be bought with gold and silver, and the want of it often made the Miss Crowthers angry. Diamonds they could have, and land, art, and beauty, even the ways and manners of good society, but they could not buy themselves a history. Everybody knew that their splendours had all come out of a cloth mill, that their ingots had been in some part transmuted from pestiferous woollen rags gathered in the Jewish quarters of far-off cities, ground into shoddy, and anon issued to the world as sleek superfine cloth. The more shoddy the higher interest upon capital; and Vansittart Crowther's daughters knew too many of the secrets of the mills to be proud of the source of their prosperity.

Mrs. Crowther was sorry to lose Isola as a friend and *protégée*. Her daughters were furious at the slight implied in this gradual dropping away. They passed Mrs. Disney and her sister-in-law with their noses in the air, as they went from the church-porch to their carriage. They cut them ostentatiously if they met on the quiet country roads. Mrs. Crowther would still stop to speak and shake hands, albeit she urged no further invitations.

And while the gulf widened between the great house and the small one the glorious Cornish summer waned, and slowly, slowly, melted away, lingering very late in that fair western land, which was full of flowers even when the home counties were being withered and blackened by the first frosts. At last came winter, and the gradual turn of the year; short days slowly lengthening out by leisurely sunsets; pale snowdrops glimmering in the borders; and then the gold of crocuses and the bright blue of the Siberian bell-flower in patches of vivid colour; and then hyacinths and tulips, primroses on every bank, narcissus and jonquil in every garden; and by-and-by the full glory of bluebell and hawthorn blossom. And anon in the middle of May came an event in which all the interests of Colonel Disney's life seemed to culminate. In that balmy Maytime Isola's firstborn son came into the world, and Isola's young life hovered at the gate of death, in so terrible an uncertainty that Martin Disney's hair grew grey while he awaited the issue of the contest between youth and weakness.

For more than a week after the birth of her baby Isola's condition had satisfied the trained nurse and the kindly doctor. She was very white and weak, and she showed less interest in her baby than most young mothers—a fact which Mr. Baynham ascribed to over-education.

"The young women of the present day aren't half such good mothers as those I used to attend when I began practice," he said discontentedly. "Their heads are stuffed with poetry, and such-like. They're nervous and fanciful—and the upshot of it all is that babies have to be wet-nursed or brought up by hand. If I had the government of a model state I wouldn't allow any married woman the run of a library until she had reared the last of her babies. What does a young married woman want with book-learning? She ought to have enough to do to look after her husband and her nursery."

Before the baby son was a fortnight old, fever supervened, and Isola's state gave poor Mr. Baynham the keenest anxiety. A hospital nurse was sent for to assist the established custodian; and a great authority was brought over from Plymouth to approve the village doctor's treatment, and to make a trifling alteration in a prescription, substituting bromide of sodium for bromide of potassium.

Many days and nights of delirium followed the physician's visit, a period in which the patient was watched at every hour of the day and night; and one of the most constant watchers through all that dreary time was Martin Disney. It was in vain that Allegra and the nurses urged him to consider his own health. He would consent only to leave the sick-room for briefest intervals of rest. Day after day, night after night, he sat in the same chair—an old-fashioned armchair, with projecting sides, which almost hid him from the patient—beside the bed. He was never in the way of the nurse. He was always helpful when a man's help was needed. He was so quiet that it was impossible to object to his presence. He sat there like a statue of patience. No moan escaped his pallid lips; no tear stole down his haggard cheek. He sat and watched and waited for the issue, which was to make him happy, or desolate for ever.

All his future was involved in that issue. He looked with a faint smile upon the pink little baby face, when they brought his son to him. No one would have dared to suggest that he should take care of himself and be comforted for that little one's sake. They all knew that his firstborn was as nothing to him. All his hopes and all his fears were centred in the wife who lay upon yonder bed, with glassy eyes and babbling lips, a wanderer in a world full of torturing images— fountains of bubbling water which she longed to drink—great black serpents, which came crawling in at the window, and creeping nearer, nearer to her bed—wriggling, hideous forms that hemmed her in on every side—giant staircases that she was always trying to climb—mammoth caves in which she lost herself, fifty times bigger and more awful than those serpentine caverns near the Lizard, which she and Allegra had explored in the previous autumn— steeper, stonier than the tall cliffs and pinnacled rocks above Bedruthan sands.

Day after day, night after night, Martin Disney sat in his place and listened to those ravings of a mind distraught. He could not keep himself from trying to follow her in that labyrinth of disconnected fancies—visions of shapeless horror, trouble, confusion—a wild babbling of numbers, prattling of millions, billions, trillions—as if her days of health and sense had been spent in the calculations of a

Rothschild, she who could scarcely reckon the simplest account in a tradesman's book.

What had she to do with this torturing recital of thousands and millions, this everlasting heaping up of figures?

Then at another period of that long struggle between life and death, reason and unreason, she had a ghastly vision of two children, squatting on each side of her bed, one living, the other dead, a grisly child with throat cut from ear to ear. Again and again she implored them to take away those babies—the dead child whose horrid aspect froze her blood—the living child that grinned and made faces at her.

Once and once only during that season of delirium the elder of her nurses carried the baby to her bedside, the tiny form in snowy cambric and lace, a little roseate face, on which the first glimmer of intelligence was already dawning, sweet blue eyes that smiled at the light, rosebud lips that invited kisses. The nurse took the infant to the side of the bed, and asked the young mother to look at him. Those fever-bright eyes stared at the sweet small face with a gaze of ever-growing horror, and then with a wild shriek Isola clasped her hands before her eyes, and drew herself cowering to the further side of the bed.

"The dead child!" she cried. "Why do you show me that dead child? Don't you see his throat streaming with blood?"

---

It was a case in which the nurses had no easy duty by day or night; and there were times when Disney insisted that the night-nurse should have extra rest, while he kept guard.

"But if she should be very bad, sir, you might not be able to manage."

"Oh yes, I should. My sister is a very light sleeper. She would come to me in a moment, and she has a great deal of influence with my wife."

This was true. From the beginning of evil Allegra's presence had exercised a soothing power. She had been able to lull the patient to sleep sometimes, when opiates had failed to produce even fitful slumber. Isola was calmer and less restless when her sister-in-law was by her side.

In those long night watches, sometimes in solitude, Martin Disney had ample leisure in which to ponder upon his wedded life, and to consider how far the hopes with which he had entered upon that life had been realized. The retrospect left him melancholy, and with a latent sense of loss and disappointment; and yet he told himself again and again that he did ill to be dissatisfied, that Providence had dealt kindly with him.

At five and forty years of age, he, Martin Disney, of modest fortune and social status, and of no especial claim to be admired, intellectual or physical, had won the hand of a lovely and interesting girl. He had been so bewildered and overcome by the delight of his conquest, that he had entered upon no laborious process of self-examination before he took to himself this fair and winning partner. It had been enough for him that she came to him willingly, lovingly, in all truth and girlish simplicity, loyal as she was pure. He had never asked himself could such an attachment last—on her side? It had been enough for him that the love existed. It would be his duty and his delight to strengthen the bond, to draw that fair spirit into closer union with his own. He had felt no shadow of fear for the future. Once having won her, it must be easy to keep his treasure—easy for him who would so faithfully guard and cherish this priceless gift of a benign Providence. He was a man of deep religious feeling—a man who recognized in good and evil, in joy and in sorrow, the dealings of an Almighty God with His short-sighted creatures. He accepted his happiness in fear and trembling, knowing the instability of all mortal joys; but he had never feared the loss of Isola's love.

Yet now, sitting in the deep of night beside that bed which might be the bed of death, he told himself that his wife's love was lost to him, had been lost from the hour of his return to Trelasco, when he went back to her with all the enthusiasm of a lover, forgetful of his mature years, of his long experience of life—hard fighting, hard knocks of all kinds in the great life-battle.

He had gone back to her as Leander to Hero, a boy in heart and hopefulness; and what had he found in her? A placid, obedient wife, gentle almost to apathy, but with a strain of melancholy underlying all their relations which his devoted love could not conquer.

To all his interrogations her answer had been the same. She was not unhappy. She had everything in life that she desired. There was nothing that he could give her, no possible change in their existence which could add to her content. All this should mean domestic peace, a heart at ease; yet all this was unsatisfying to Martin Disney; for his instinct told him that his wife was not happy—that the element of gladness was, for some inscrutable reason, banished from her life.

She had seemed happier, or at least the little home had been brighter and gayer after Allegra's coming; but as the time wore on it became clear to him that the life and gaiety were all in Allegra herself, and that Isola was spiritless and depressed. It was as if the spring of her life had snapped suddenly, and left her nerveless and joyless, a submissive, unhopeful creature. That sense of disappointment and loss which he had dimly felt, even when his home-coming had been a new thing, had grown and deepened with the passage of time. He had bought his land; he had added to the space and comfort of his house; he had enlarged the stables, and bought a couple of hunters, and a cob for harness; and while these things had been doing, the activity of his days, the fuss and labour of arrangement and supervision, had occupied his mind so pleasantly as to stifle those growing doubts for the time being. But when all was done; when the vine and the figtree had been planted, and he sat down to take his ease in their shade, then he began to feel very keenly that his wife's part in all that he had done was the part of submission only. She liked this or that because he liked it. She was content, and that was all. And the line between contentment and resignation is so faint a demarcation that it seemed to him sometimes as if she were only resigned, as if she suffered life rather than lived—suffered life as holy women suffer some slow, wasting disease, in meek subjection to a mysterious decree.

He sat beside her bed, while she battled with all the demons of delirium; and he wondered whether—when she had been at her best, when her mind had been brightest and clearest—she had been any nearer to him than she was now in her madness; whether he had known any more of her inner self—the mystery of her heart and conscience—than he knew now, while those wild eyes stared at him without sight or knowledge.

One summer morning, as he sat alone in his watch in that dull interval between darkness and dawn, the visions of the wandering mind took a more consecutive form than usual. She fancied herself in a storm at sea. The waves were rolling mountains high—were bearing down upon her with threatenings of instant death. She feared, and yet she courted the danger. In one minute she was recoiling from the wild rush of waters, clinging distractedly to the brass rail at the head of her bed, crouching against the wall as if to save herself from an advancing wave; and in the next minute she sprang out of bed, and rushed to the open window, wanting to throw herself out of it. Disney was only just quick enough to seize her in his arms, and carry her back to bed. He held her there, battling with him in a vehement effort to escape from his restraining arms.

"Why do you stop me?" she cried, looking at him fiercely with her distracted eyes. "What else is there for me? What other refuge? what other hope? Let me go! let me go! Cruel! cruel! cruel! Let me throw myself into the sea! Don't you understand? Oh, cruel! cruel! Cold and wicked, shameless and cruel! There is nothing else—only that refuge left! Let me hide myself in death! let me hide—hide!"

Her voice rose to a shriek; and both the nurse and Allegra came hurrying in. The faint white dawn shone upon her livid face and on the scarlet spot upon each hollow cheek. Her eyes stared wildly, starting from their sockets in that paroxysm of her madness.

Only a few days after that night of terror Isola was lying calm as a child. The fever had gone down—the enfeebled constitution had at last answered to the influence of medicine; and gradually, like the slow lifting of the darkness after a long night of cloud and fog, consciousness and reason came back. Sleep soothed the strained and weary nerves, and the exhausted frame, which a few days before had seemed endowed with a superhuman strength, lay like a log upon the bed of sickness.

Recovery was slow, but there was no relapse. Slow as the dawning of day to the tired watcher, after the long, blank night, there came the dawn of maternal love. The young mother began to take delight in her child; and it was rapture to Martin Disney to see her sitting opposite him under the tulip-tree, in the low Madeira chair, with her baby in her lap. Allegra vied with her in her devotion to that over-praised infant; while the Shah and Tim, of the same opinion for the first time in their lives, were almost rabid with jealousy.

They all lived in the garden in that happy summer season, as they had done the year before, when Allegra first came among them. It was in the garden they received their visitors, and it was there that Mr. Colfox came at least thrice a week, upon the flimsiest pretexts of parish business, to drink tea poured out for him by Allegra's helpful hands, while Isola sat quietly by, listening to their talk, and watching every change in her child's face; from smiles to frowns, from slumber to waking.

Allegra had taken kindly to parish work, and, in Mr. Colfox's own phraseology, was a tower of strength to him in his labours among the poor of Trelasco. She had started a series of mothers' meetings in the winter afternoons, and had read to the women and girls while they worked, helping them a good deal with their work into the bargain. She had done wonders at penny readings, singing, reciting, drawing lightning caricatures of local celebrities with bits of coloured chalk on rough white paper. Her portrait of Vansittart Crowther had been applauded to the echo, although it was not a flattering portrait. She had visited the sick; she had taught in the night school. The curate had been enthusiastic in his appreciation of her, and his praises had been listened to contemptuously by the two Miss Crowthers, each of whom at different periods had taken up these good works, only to drop them again after the briefest effort.

"She will get tired as soon as we did," said Alicia, "when she finds out how impossible these creatures are—unless she has an ulterior motive."

"What ulterior motive should she have?" asked Colfox, bluntly.

"Who can tell? She may want to get herself talked about. As Miss Leland, of the Angler's Nest, a sort of useful companion to her brother's wife, she is a nobody. If she can get a reputation for piety and philanthropy, that will be better than nothing. Or she may be only angling for a husband."

"If you knew her as well as I do you would know that she is above all trivial and selfish motives, and that she is good to these people because her heart has gone out to them."

"Ah, but you see we don't know her. Her brother has chosen to hold himself aloof from Glenaveril; and I must say I am very glad he has taken that line—for more than one reason."

"If any of your reasons concern Miss Leland you are very much mistaken in under-rating her. You could not have had a more delightful companion," said Mr. Colfox, with some warmth.

"Oh, we all know that you have exalted her into a heroine—a St. John's Wood St. Helena. But she is a little too unconventional for my taste; though I certainly would rather be intimate with her than with her sister-in-law."

"Surely you have no fault to find with that most gentle creature?"

"She is just a little too gentle for my taste," replied Alicia, who usually took upon herself all expression of opinion, while Belinda fanned herself languidly, in an æsthetic attitude, feeling that her chief mission in this life was to sit still and look like *la belle dame sans merci*. "She is just as much too quiet as Miss Leland is too boisterous. I have no liking for pensive young women who cast down their eyelids at the slightest provocation, and are only animated when they are flirting."

"The tongue is a little member," quoted Mr. Colfox, taking up his hat, and holding out his hand in adieu.

He was very unceremonious to these fair parishioners of his, and talked to them as freely as if he had been an old French Abbé in a country village. It is needless to say that they valued his opinion so much the more because he was entirely unaffected by their wealth or their good looks. They were naturally aggrieved at his marked admiration for Miss Leland.

Those ripe months of harvest and vintage, July, August, and September, passed like a blissful dream for Martin Disney. He had snatched his darling from the jaws of death. He had her once more—fair to look upon, with sweet, smiling mouth and pensive eyes; and she was so tender and so loving to him, in fond gratitude for his devotion during her illness, so seemingly happy in their mutual love for their child, that he forgot all those aching fears which had gnawed his heart while he sat by her pillow through the long anxious nights—forgot that he had ever doubted her, or remembered his doubts only to scorn himself as a morbid, jealous fool. Could he doubt her, who was candour and innocence personified? Could he think for an instant that all those sweet, loving ways and looks of hers which beautified his commonplace existence, were so much acting—and that her heart was not his? No! True love has an unmistakable language; and true love spoke to him in every word and tone of his wife's.

The child made so close a bond between them. Both lives were seemingly bound and entwined about this fragile life of Isola's firstborn. Mr. Baynham had no reason now to complain of his patient's want of the maternal instinct. He had rather to restrain her in her devotion to the child. He had to reprove her for her sleepless nights and morbid anxieties.

"Do you think your baby will grow any the faster or stronger for your lying awake half the night worrying yourself about him?" said the doctor, with his cheery bluntness. "He has a capital nurse—one of those excellent cow-women, who are specially created to rear other people's babies; and he has a doctor who is not quite a fool about infant maladies. Read your novels, Mrs. Disney, and keep up your good looks; or else twenty years hence you will see your son blushing when he hears his mother mistaken for his grandmother."

After giving his patient this advice, Mr. Baynham told his wife, in confidence, that were anything to happen to the little one, Isola Disney would go off her head.

"I'm afraid she is sadly hysterical," replied Mrs. Baynham. "I am very fond of her, you know, Tom; but I have never been able to understand her. I can't make out a young woman who has a pretty house and an indulgent husband, and who never seems quite happy."

"Every woman can't have your genial disposition, Belle," answered the doctor, admiringly. "Perpetual sunshine is the rarest thing in Nature."

---

The early western harvest had been gathered in. Upland and valley in that undulating land were clothed with the tawny hue of the stubble. Here and there the plough horses were moving slowly along the red ridges on the steep hillside. No touch of frost had dulled the rich hues of the autumnal flowers, and the red carnations still glowed in every cottage garden, while the pale pink trusses of hydrangea filled all the shrubberies with beauty. A keener breath came up at eventide from the salt sea beyond Point Neptune, and wilder winds crept across the inland valleys with the on-coming of night. Summer and the swallows were gone. October, a balmy season for the most part, was at hand; and there were no more tea-drinkings and afternoon gossipings in the garden at the Angler's Nest. The lamps were lighted before dinner. The evenings were spent in the old library and the new drawing-room, the new room communicating with the old one by a curtained archway, so that of a night the curtains could be drawn back and Martin Disney could sit among his books by the fireplace in the library, and yet be within conversational reach of Isola and Allegra in the drawing-room, where they had piano and table-easel, work-baskets, and occupations of all kinds.

Mr. Colfox sometimes dropped in of an evening, on parish business of course, took a cup of coffee, listened while Allegra played one of Mozart's sonatas or sang a song by Gluck or Haydn or Handel. Mr. Colfox was not one of the advanced people who despise Mozart or Handel. Nor did he look down upon Haydn. Indeed, he sat and stroked his thin legs with a sheepish appreciation, wrinkling up his loose trousers, and showing a large amount of stocking, while Allegra sang "My mother bids me bind my hair," in her clear, strong mezzo-soprano, which was of infinite use to him in his choir.

He told everybody that Martin Disney's was an ideal household — a home into which it was a privilege to be admitted.

"I feel as if I never knew the beauty of domestic life till I knew the Angler's Nest," he said one evening after dinner at Glenaveril, when he and the village doctor had accepted one of Mr. Crowther's pressing invitations to what he called "pot-luck," the pot-luck of the man whose spirit burns within him at the thought of his hundred-guinea cook, and whose pride is most intolerable when it apes humility.

"Really, now," said Mr. Crowther, "you surprise me, for I have always fancied there was a screw loose there."

"What does that expression imply, Mr. Crowther?" asked the curate, coldly.

"Oh, I don't know! Nothing specific: only one's notion of an ideal home doesn't generally take the shape of a beautiful girl of twenty married to a man of forty-five. The disparity is just twice as much as it ought to be."

"Upon my soul," cried the curate, "I don't believe that wedded love is affected by any difference of years. Desdemona loved Othello, who was a man of mature age— —"

"And black," interrupted Mr. Crowther, with a coarse laugh. "Well, let us be thankful that Colonel Disney is not a nigger; and that there is so much the less danger of a burst-up at the Angler's Nest. And now, Baynham, with regard to this footpath across the wood, who the deuce will be injured if I shut it up?"

"A good many people, and the people I think you would least like to injure," answered the doctor, sturdily. "Old people, and feeble, ailing people, who find the walk to church quite far enough even with the help of that short cut."

"Short cut be hanged!" cried Mr. Crowther, helping himself to a bumper of port, and passing on the decanter with hospitable emphasis. "It can't make a difference of a hundred yards."

"It does make a difference of over a quarter of a mile—and the proof is that everybody uses it, and that it goes by the name of the Church path. I wouldn't try to stop it, if I were you, Mr. Crowther. You are a popular man in the parish, for you—well, you have spent a heap of money in this place, and you subscribe liberally to all our charities and what not; but, I don't mind telling you, if you were to try and shut off that old footpath across your wood, you'd be about the most unpopular man within a radius of ten miles."

"Don't talk about trying to shut it off, man," said Mr. Crowther, arrogantly. "If I choose to lock the gates to-morrow, I shall do it, and ask nobody's leave. The wood is my wood, and there's no clause in my title-deeds as to any right of way through it; and I don't see why I am to have my hazel bushes pulled about, and my chestnut trees damaged by a pack of idle boys, under the pretence of church-going. There's the Queen's highway for 'em, d—n 'em!" cried Mr. Crowther, growing more insolent, as he gulped his fifth glass of Sandemann. "If that ain't good enough, let 'em go to the Ranters' Chapel at the other end of the village."

"I thought you were a staunch Conservative, Mr. Crowther, and an upholder of Church and State," said Mr. Colfox. "Am I to believe my ears when I hear you advocating the Ranters' Chapel?"

"It's good enough for such rabble as that, sir. What does it matter where they go?"

"Prosecute the boys for trespass, if you like," said the doctor; "though I doubt if you'll get a magistrate to impose more than a nominal fine for the offence of taking a handful of nuts in a wood that has been open ever since I began to walk, and heaven knows how many years before; but let the old gaffers and goodies creep to church by the shortest path that can take them there. They'll have to travel by the Queen's highway later, when they go to the churchyard—but then they'll be carried. Don't interfere with the privileges of the poor, Mr. Crowther. No one ever did that yet and went scot free. There's always somebody to take up the cudgels for them."

"I don't care a doit for anybody's cudgels, Baynham. I shall have a look at my title-deeds to-morrow; and if there's no stipulation about the right of way, you'll find the gates locked next Sunday morning."

Sunday morning came, and the gates at each end of the old footpath were still open, and nothing had come of Mr. Crowther's threat. The gates had stood open so long, and were so old and rotten, their lower timbers so embedded in the soft, oozy soil, so entangled and overgrown with foxglove and fern, so encrusted with moss and lichen, that it is doubtful if anybody could have closed them. They seemed as much rooted in the ground as the great brown fir trunks which rose in rugged majesty beside them.

## CHAPTER XI.

### "WHERE THE COLD SEA RAVES."

In the keen, fresh October afternoons, there was no walk Allegra loved better than the walk to Neptune Point, and higher up by winding footpaths to the Rashleigh Mausoleum, fitting sepulchre for a race born and bred in the breath of the sea; a stately tomb perched on a rocky pinnacle at the end of a promontory, like a sea-bird's nest overhanging the wave.

Allegra was in raptures with that strange resting-place.

"I like it ever so much better than your Cockneyfied cemetery," she exclaimed. "Think how grand it must be to lie for ever within the sound of the sea—the terrible, inscrutable sea, whose anger means death—the calm, summer sea, whose waves come dancing up the sands like laughing water. I wonder whether the Rashleighs would let me have a little grave of my own somewhere among these crags and hillocks—a modest little grave, hidden under wild foliage, which nobody would ever notice? Only I should hear the sea just as well as they do in their marble tomb."

"Oh, Allegra, how can you talk so lightly of death?" said Isola, shocked at this levity. "To me it is always dreadful to think of—and yet it must come."

"Poor child!" said Allegra, with infinite pity, putting her arm round her sister-in-law's slighter figure, as they stood by the railing of the Mausoleum, in the loveliness of an October sunset.

The sun had just gone down, veiled in autumnal haze, and behind the long ridge of waters beyond the Dodman there glowed the deep crimson of the western sky. Eastward above the Polruan hills the moon moved slowly upward, amidst dark masses of cloud which melted and rolled away before her on-coming, till all the sky became of one dark azure. The two girls went down the hill in silence, Allegra holding Isola's arm, linked with her own, steadying those weaker footsteps with the strength of her own firm movements. The difference between the two in physical force was no less marked than the difference in their mental characteristics, and Allegra's love for her sister-in-law was tempered with a tender compassion for something so much weaker than herself.

"Poor child!" she repeated, as they moved slowly down the steep, narrow path, "and do you really shudder at the thought of death? I don't. I have only a vast curiosity. Do you remember that definition of Sir Thomas Browne's which Martin read to us once—'Death is the Lucina of life.' Death only opens the door of the hidden worlds which are waiting for all of us to discover. It is only an appalling name for a new birth. I love to dream about the infinite possibilities of the future—just as a boy might dream of the time when he should become a man. Look, look, Isa, there's a yacht coming in! Isn't it a lovely sight?"

It was a long, narrow vessel, with all her canvas spread, gleaming with a silvery whiteness in the moonlight. Slowly and with majestic motion she swept round towards Neptune Point and the mouth of the harbour. There was only the lightest wind, and the waves were breaking gently on the rocks at the base of the promontory—a night as calm and fair as June.

"Look!" repeated Allegra, "isn't she lovely? like a fairy boat. Whose yacht can she be, I wonder? She looks like a racer, doesn't she?"

Isola did not answer. She had seen such a yacht two years ago; had seen such a long, narrow hull lying in the harbour under repairs; had seen the same craft sailing out to Mevagissey on a trial trip in the wintry sunlight. Doubtless there were many yachts in this world of just the same build and character.

They stood at an angle of the hill-path looking up the river, and saw the yacht take in her canvas as she came into the haven under the hill; that sheltered harbour, with its two rivers cleaving the hills asunder, one winding away to the right towards Lerrin, the other to the left towards Trelasco and Lostwithiel. It looked so perfect a place of shelter, so utterly safe from tempest or foul weather; and yet there were seasons when a fierce wind from the great Atlantic came sweeping up the deep valleys, and all the angry spirits of the ocean seemed at war in that narrow gorge. To-night the atmosphere was unusually calm, and Isola could hear the sailors singing at their work.

Slowly, slowly the two young women went down the hill, Allegra full of speculation and wonderment about the unknown vessel, Isola curiously silent. As they neared the hotel a man landed from a dinghy, and came briskly up the slippery causeway—a tall, slim figure in the vivid moonlight, loose limbed, loosely clad, moving with easiest motion.

Isola turned sick at the sight of him. She stopped, helplessly, hopelessly, and stood staring straight before her, watching him as he came nearer and nearer, nearer and nearer—like some awful figure in a nightmare dream, when the feet of the dreamer seem frozen to the ground, and flesh and blood seem changed to ice and stone.

He came nearer, looked at them, and passed them by—passed as one who knew them not, and was but faintly curious about them. He passed and walked quickly up towards the Point, with the rapid swinging movements of one who was glad to tread the solid earth.

No, it was not Lostwithiel. She had thought at first that no one else could look so like him at so short a distance; no one else could have that tall, slender figure, and easy, buoyant walk. But the face she saw in the moonlight was not his. It was like, but not the same: darker, with larger features, a face of less delicacy and distinction; but oh, God! how like the eyes that had looked at her, with that brief glance of casual inspection, were to those other eyes that had poured their passionate story into her own that unforgotten night when she sat out the after-supper waltzes in the ante-room at the Talbot. She could not have believed that any man living could so recall the man whose name she never spoke of her own free will.

There were some sailors standing about at the top of the steep little bit of road leading down to the granite causeway, and their voices sounded fresh and clear in the still evening, mixed with the rippling rush of the water as it came running up the stones. The moonlight shone full upon one of the men as he stood with his face towards the sea, and Isola read the name upon the front of his jersey.

"*Vendetta.*"

"*Vendetta,*" cried Allegra, quick to observe the name. "Why, is not that Lord Lostwithiel's yacht?"

"Yes—I think so," faltered Isola.

"Then that must have been Lord Lostwithiel who passed as just now; and yet you would have known him, wouldn't you?"

"That was not Lord Lostwithiel."

"A friend of his, I suppose; such a nice-looking man, too. There was something so frank and cheery in his look as he just glanced at us both and marched briskly on. He did not pay us the compliment of seeming curious. I wonder who he is?"

Isola was wondering about something else. She was looking with a frightened gaze across the harbour, towards that one break in the long golden trail of the moonbeams where the *Vendetta* cast her shadow on the water. There were lamps gleaming brightly here and there upon the vessel—a look of occupation.

"Is Lord Lostwithiel on board his yacht?" Allegra asked of one of the sailors, not ashamed to appear inquisitive.

"No, ma'am; Mr. Hulbert is skipper."

"Who is Mr. Hulbert?"

"His lordship's brother."

"Was that he who went up towards the Point just now?"

"Yes, ma'am."

"Is he going to stop here long, do you know?"

"I don't think he knows himself, ma'am. It'll depend upon the weather most likely. If we get a fair wind we may be off to the Lizard at an hour's notice, and away up north to the Hebrides."

"Doesn't that seem inconsistent?" exclaimed Allegra, as they walked homewards. "What is the good of coming to Cornwall if he wants to go to the Hebrides? It must be very much out of his way."

"He may want to see his old home, perhaps. He was born at the Mount, you know."

"Indeed! I don't know anything about him, but I want to know ever so much. I call it an interesting face."

Allegra was full of animation during the homeward walk. A stranger of any kind must needs be a God-send, as affording a subject for conversation; but such a stranger as Lostwithiel's brother afforded a theme of strongest interest. She had heard so much about Lord Lostwithiel and all his works and ways—the pity of it that he did not marry; the still greater pity that he did not live at the Mount, and give shooting parties and spend money in the neighbourhood. She had heard in a less exalted key of his lordship's younger brother, who had fought under Beresford in Egypt, and who had only lately left the navy. What more natural than that such a man should sail his brother's yacht?

Captain Hulbert was still unmarried; but no one talked about the pity of that. People took a severely sensible view of his case, and were unanimous in the opinion that he could not afford to marry, and that any inspiration in that line would be criminal on his part. There was an idea at Trelasco that the younger sons of peers of moderate fortune have been specially designed by Providence to keep up the race of confirmed bachelors. There must be bachelors; the world cannot get on without them; society requires them as a distinct element in social existence; and it would ill become the offshoots of the peerage to shrink from fulfilling their destiny.

Allegra was not the less curious about Captain Hulbert, although his celibate mission had been frequently expounded to her. She was interested in him because she liked his face, because he was Lostwithiel's brother, because he was sailing a very beautiful yacht, because he had appeared in her life with a romantic suddenness, sailing out of the sea unheralded and unexpected, like a man who had dropped from the moon.

She fell asleep that night wondering if she would ever see him again—if the *Vendetta* would have vanished from the harbour to-morrow at noontide, like a boat that had only lived in her dreams; or whether the yacht would still be anchored there in the haven under the hill. And, if so, whether Captain Hulbert would call at the Angler's Nest, and tell them about Lostwithiel's South American adventures, and how he came to be skipper of his brother's yacht.

At breakfast next morning, Colonel Disney's talk was chiefly about Captain Hulbert. The colonel had been for an early walk, and had seen the *Vendetta* from the little Quay at Fowey, by the Mechanics' Institute, and had heard who was the skipper.

"I remember him when he and his brother were at Eton together—nice boys—capital boys, both of them—but I liked Jack Hulbert better than Lostwithiel. He was franker, more spontaneous and impulsive. Yes, Jack was my favourite, and everybody else's favourite, I think, when the two were boys. I saw very little of them after they grew up. I was away with my regiment, and Jack was away with his ship, and Lostwithiel was wandering up and down the earth, like Satan. I left a card for Captain Hulbert at the club, asking him to dinner this evening. You don't mind, do you, Isola?"

Isola had no objection to offer, and Allegra was delighted at the prospect of seeing more of the man with the nice frank countenance, and that seafaring air which most women like.

"I am a dreadful person for being influenced by first impressions," she said, "and that one glance at Captain Hulbert in the moonlight assures me that I shall like him."

"Don't like him too well," said Martin, laughingly, "for I'm afraid he's a detrimental, and would make even a worse match than Colfox, who may be a bishop one day, while Hulbert has left the navy, and is never likely to be anything."

"Match! detrimental!" cried Allegra, indignantly. "Can it be my brother who talks in such a vulgar strain? As if a woman could not look at a man without thinking of marrying him!"

"Some women can't," answered Martin. "With them every free man is a possible husband—indeed, I believe there are some who cannot look at a married man without estimating the chances of the divorce court—if the man is what they call a catch."

"That is your Indian experience!" exclaimed Allegra, scornfully. "I have heard that India is a sink of iniquity."

She went about her day's varied work as usual—curious to see the new acquaintance—yet in no wise excited. Vivid and animated, enthusiastic and energetic as she was in all her thoughts and ways, gushing sentimentality made no part of Miss Leland's character. Life at Trelasco flowed with such an even monotony, there was such a dearth of new interests, that it was only natural that a girl of vivacious temper should be curious about new-comers. At St. John's Wood every day had brought some new element into the lives of the students, and almost every day had brought a new pupil, drawn thither by the growing renown of the school, pupils from the uttermost ends of the earth sometimes, pupils of swart complexion speaking unknown tongues, pupils patrician and pupils plebeian, each and all conforming to the same stringent rules of art, spending patient months in the shading of a brace of plums or a bunch of grapes, from a plaster cast, and toiling slowly up the gradual ascent which leads to the Royal Academy and the gold medal. Many there were who sickened at the slow rate of progress and who fell away. Only the faithful remained. And this going and coming, this strife between faith and unfaith, patience and impatience, had made a perpetual movement in the life of the great school—to say nothing of such bodily activities as lawn tennis, for which the master had provided a court—a court for his girl-pupils, be it noted, where they played among themselves, as if they had been so many collegians in the college of Tennyson's "Princess."

Allegra had liked her life at the great art school, but she had never regretted its abandonment. She loved her brother, and her brother's wife, better even than she loved art. It was only now and then that she felt that existence at Trelasco was as monotonous as the flow of the river going up and coming down day by day between Lostwithiel and the sea.

She spent the hours between breakfast and luncheon hard at work in her painting-room—a little room with a large window facing northward. She had the coachman's girl and boy for her models, and was engaged upon a little water-colour picture after the school of Mrs. Allingham, a little picture which told its story with touching simplicity.

It was not the first picture of the kind she had painted. Several of her works had been exhibited at the minor galleries which are hospitable to the new-comer in the world of art; and two small pictures had been bought at prices which seemed to promise her an easy road to fortune.

The coachman's children profited greatly by this new profession which had been devised for them. Allegra made their frocks in her leisure hours, when the active fingers must have something to do, while the active tongue ran on gaily in happy talk with Martin and Isola. Allegra made up to her little models for their hours of enforced idleness by extra tuition which kept them ahead of most of the other pupils in the village school; and Allegra supplied them with pocket-money.

"I don't know however the children got on before Miss Leland came," said the coachman's wife. "They seem to look to her for everything."

Allegra had other models, village children, and village girls—her beauty-girl, a baker's daughter with a splendid semi-Greek face, like Mrs. Langtry's, whom she dressed up in certain cast-off finery of her own, and painted in her genre pictures, now in this attitude, and now in that, imparting an air of distinction which elevated the Cornish peasant into a patrician. She it was, this baker's fair-haired daughter, who stood for Allegra's successful picture—"A daughter of the gods, divinely tall," a little bit of finished painting which had brought the painter five and thirty guineas—boundless wealth as it seemed to her—and ever so many commissions.

Art, even in despondency and failure, is a consolation; art successful is an intoxicating delight. Allegra was as happy a young woman as could be found in Cornwall that day, when she shut her colour-box, dismissed her little maiden, and ran down to lunch, where she found Isola more silent than usual, and made amends by her own light-hearted chatter for the morning's absorption over the easel. After lunch she ran off to the village to pay her parish visits to the sick and old, and on her way to an outlying cottage she met Mr. Colfox, who immediately turned to accompany her, a way he had, but a way to which she had never attached any significance. He was a clever, well-read man, of somewhat original temper, who had to pass most of his life among unlettered or dull people; therefore it surprised Allegra in no wise that he should like to talk to her. A bright, attractive girl of three and twenty is very unsuspicious about the feelings of a homely looking man at least a dozen years her senior.

"Your brother has been good enough to ask me to dinner," he said, after a little talk about the Goodies and their ailments. "I met him at the club this morning."

"He wants you to meet Captain Hulbert. Perhaps you know him already?"

"No, he has not been here within my time. He only left the navy a year ago, and he was generally stationed at the utmost ends of the earth, keeping guard over our remote possessions. Have you seen him?"

"Only for an instant. He passed my sister and me yesterday evening in the moonlight. I thought he looked a nice person—but I think women have a natural leaning towards sailors. I could never imagine a seaman telling a falsehood or doing a mean action."

"There is a kind of open-air manner which suggests truthfulness," admitted Mr. Colfox. "Yet there have been dark deeds done by sailors; there have been black sheep even in the Queen's Navee. However, I believe Captain Hulbert is worthy of your good opinion. I have never heard anybody speak against him, and the old people who knew him as a lad seem to have liked him better than Lord Lostwithiel."

"Do tell me your opinion of Lord Lostwithiel. I am very curious about him. Mr. Crowther talked of him so much the night we were at Glenaveril."

"Mr. Crowther loves a lord."

"Please satisfy my curiosity. Is he really such a fascinating personage?"

"He has very pleasant manners. I don't know what constitutes fascination in a man, though I know pretty well what it means in a woman. Lord Lostwithiel's manners are chiefly distinguished by repose without languor or affectation—and by an interest in other people so cleverly simulated that it deceives everybody. One finds him out by the way in which people boast of his friendship. He cannot be so attached to all the world. He has a manner which is generally described as sympathetic."

"Mr. Crowther enlarged a good deal upon his lordship's admiration for my sister at the Hunt Ball. Was that so very marked?"

Mr. Colfox coloured violently at this direct question—assuredly not easy to answer truthfully without hazard of offence.

"I was not at the ball—I—I heard people talk a little—in the way people talk of everything—about Lostwithiel's attention to Mrs. Disney, and about her prettiness—they all agreed that if not the loveliest woman in the room, she was at least the most interesting."

"It was very natural that he should admire her; but I don't think Martin liked Mr. Crowther's talking about it in that way, at the dinner-table. The man is horridly underbred. Has Lord Lostwithiel what you call—" she hesitated a little—"a good character?"

"I don't know about the present. I have heard that in the past his reputation was not altogether good."

"I understand," said Allegra, quickly. "The admiration of such a man is an insult; and that is why Mr. Crowther harped upon the fact. I am sure he is a malevolent man."

"Don't be hard upon him, Miss Leland. I believe he has only the misfortune to be a cad—a cad by birth, education, and associations. Don't fling your stone at such a man—consider what an unhappy fate it is."

"Oh, but he does not think himself unhappy. He is bursting with self-importance and the pride of riches. He is the typical rich man of the Psalmist. He must be the happiest man in Trelasco, a thick-skinned man whom nothing can hurt."

"I am sorry you think so badly of poor Mr. Crowther, because I am really attached to his wife. She is one of the best women I know."

"So my sister tells me, and I was very much taken with her myself, but one cannot afford to be friendly with Mrs. Crowther at the cost of knowing her husband."

She spoke with some touch of the insolence of youth, which sets so high a value upon its own opinions and its own independence, and looks upon all the rest of humanity as upon a lower plane. And this arrogant youth, which thinks so meanly of the multitude, will make its own exceptions, and reverence its chosen ideals with a blind hero-worship—for its love is always an upward-looking love, "the desire of the moth for the star."

Mr. Colfox sighed, and smiled at the same moment, a sad little half-cynical smile. He was thinking how impossible it was to refrain from admiring this bright out-spoken girl, with her quick intellect, and her artistic instincts, so spiritual, so unworldly, and fresh as an April morning—how impossible not to admire, how difficult not to love her, and how hopeless to love.

He thought of himself with scathing self-contempt—middle-aged, homely of feature and of figure, with nothing to recommend him except good birth, a small independence—just so much as enabled him to live where he pleased and serve whom he would, without reference to the stipend attached to the cure; and a little rusty, dry-as-dust learning. Nothing more than this; and he wanted to win and wed a girl whose image never recurred to his mind without the suggestion of a rose garden, or a summer morning. Yes, she reminded him of morning and dewy red roses, those old-fashioned heavy red roses, round as a cup, and breathing sweetest, purest perfume.

He jogged on by her side in silence, and only awoke from his reverie to bid her good-bye at the gate of a cottage garden, in the lane that led up the hill to Tywardreath.

## CHAPTER XII.

### "FAR, TOO FAR OFF FOR THOUGHT OR ANY PRAYER."

Mr. Colfox and Allegra met again in the drawing-room of the Angler's Nest at a quarter to eight. He was the first to arrive, and Isola had not yet appeared. Martin Disney was at his post in front of the library fireplace, library and drawing-room making one spacious room, lighted with candles here and there, and with one large shaded lamp on a table near the piano. Isola had been suffering from headache, and had been late in dressing. Captain Hulbert had been in the room nearly ten minutes before his hostess appeared, looking pale and ill in her black lace gown, and with an anxious expression in her eyes. He had been introduced to Allegra, and was talking to her as if he had known her for years, when his attention was called off by Isola's appearance, and his introduction to her.

Was this Martin Disney's wife, he thought wonderingly—such a girlish fragile creature—so unlike the woman he had pictured to himself? Strange that Lostwithiel should not have told him of her delicate prettiness, seeing that he was a connoisseur in beauty, and hypercritical.

"This is just the kind of beauty he would admire," thought Hulbert, "something out of the common—a pale, spiritual beauty—not dependent upon colouring, or even upon regularity of feature—the kind of thing one calls soul, not having found a better name for it."

They went in to dinner presently, Captain Hulbert and Isola, Mr. Colfox and Allegra. The table was a small oval, at which five people made a snug little party. There was a central mass of white chrysanthemums, a cheerful glow of coloured Venetian glass, delicatest pink and jade-green, under the light of a hanging lamp. John Hulbert looked round him with a pleased expression, taking in the flowers, the glass, the cream-white china, the lamplight, everything; and then the two fair young faces, one pale and pensive, the other aglow with the delight of life, eagerly expectant of new ideas.

They talked of the *Vendetta* and the places at which she had touched lately. Captain Hulbert had spent his summer on the Eastern Liguria, between Genoa and Civita Vecchia.

"Wasn't it the wrong time of year for Italy?" asked Mr. Colfox.

"No, it is the season of seasons in the land of the sun. If you want to enjoy a southern country, go there in the summer. The south is made for summer, her houses are built for hot weather, her streets are planned for shade; her wines, her food, her manners and customs have all been made for summer-time—not for winter. If you want to know Italy at her worst go there in cold weather."

"Where did you leave Lord Lostwithiel?" Disney asked presently.

"I left him nowhere. He left me to rove about Southern Europe—left me on his way to Carinthia. He is like the wandering Jew. He used to be mad about yachting; but he got sick of the *Vendetta* all of a sudden, and handed her over to me. Very generous on his part; but the boat is something of a white elephant for a man of my small means. I wanted him to sell her. Wouldn't hear of it. To let her. Not to be thought of. 'I'll lend her to you,' he said, 'and you shall keep her as long as you like—sink her, if you like—provided you don't go down in her. She is not a lucky boat.'"

"Have you sailed her long?"

"Nearly a year, and I love her as if she were bone of my bone, and flesh of my flesh. Let us all go for a sail to-morrow, Mrs. Disney—to Mevagissey or thereabouts. We could do a little fishing. It will be capital fun. What do you say, Miss Leland?"

"I should adore it," said Allegra, beaming at him. "The sea is my passion—and I think it is my sister's passion too. We are a kind of amphibious creatures, living more on water than on land. We venture as far as we dare in a row-boat—but oh, that is such a little way."

"I'm afraid that some day you will venture so far that you won't be able to get back again, and will find yourselves drifting away to America," said her brother.

Isola answered never a word, until Captain Hulbert addressed her pointedly for the second time.

"Will you go, Mrs. Disney—may we make up the party?"

"I would rather not," she answered, without looking at him.

"But why not? Are you such a bad sailor—in spite of all Miss Leland says of you?"

"I am a pretty good sailor in a row-boat—but not in a yacht. And I hate fishing—such a slow weary business. I would rather not go."

"I am so sorry; but you must not be worried about it," said Hulbert, kindly, seeing the growing distress in her countenance. "We will not go in for fishing—or excursions—but you and Miss Leland will at least come to afternoon tea on the *Vendetta*—to afternoon tea in the harbour. There used to be a comic song when I was a boy—'Come and drink tea in the arbour.' You must come to the arbour with an aspirate. It is not so rustic or sentimental—but there will be no earwigs or creeping things to drop into your tea-cup. Mr. Colfox, you will come, won't you?"

"I shall be delighted," answered the curate. "I have a sneaking kindness for all yachts."

The conversation drifted back to Lostwithiel and his works and ways, presently.

"When he went home two years ago he gave me to understand he was going to settle down at the Mount, and spend the rest of his days in peace and respectability," said Captain Hulbert. "Yet, very soon afterwards, he and his yacht were off again like the *Flying Dutchman*, and the next I heard of him was at Leghorn, and six months later he was coasting off Algiers; and the following spring he was in South America; and the *Vendetta* was laid up at Marseilles, where he begged me to go and look after her, and take her to myself until such time as he should want her again. I was with him for a few days at Leghorn, where he seemed ill and out of spirits. I don't think you can have used him over well in this part of the world, Mrs. Disney," he added, half in jest. "I fancy some of you must have snubbed him severely, or his tenants must have worried him by their complaints and exactions. I could not get him to talk about his life at the Mount. He seemed to have taken a disgust for the old home."

"You must put that down to his roving temper," said Disney, "for although I was away at the time, I can answer for it there was no such thing as snubbing in the case. Your brother is the only peer in these parts, and from the way people talk about him he might be the only peer in Great Britain—the Alpha and Omega of Debrett. Our parvenu neighbour, Mr. Crowther, talked of him one night with a slavish rapture which made me sick. I am a Tory by association and instinct, but I can't stand the vulgarian's worship of a lord."

Isola looked at her sister-in-law, and they both rose at this moment, the Church almost tumbling over the Navy in eagerness to open the door; Navy winning by a neck.

They were not long alone in the drawing-room, not more than the space of a single cigarette, before the men followed. Then came music, and a good deal of talk, in the long, low, spacious room, which looked so bright and homely by candlelight, with all its tokens of domestic and intellectual life.

"What a capital quarter-deck this is," cried John Hulbert, after pacing up and down while he listened, and talked, and laughed at Allegra's little jokes about the narrowness of village life. "It is delightful to stretch one's legs in such a room as this, after six months upon a yacht."

"You will have room enough to stretch your legs at the Mount," said Disney.

Captain Hulbert had announced his intention of spending a week or two under the family roof-tree while the *Vendetta* underwent some slight repairs and renovations.

"Room enough and to spare," he said. "I shan't feel half so jovial walking up and down those grim old rooms as I feel here. I shall fancy a ghost pacing behind me, clump, clump, clump—a slow, solemn footstep—only the echo of my own tread perhaps; but I shall never know, for I shall be afraid to look round."

"You ought not to make sport of weak people's fancies, for I am sure you don't believe in ghosts," said Allegra, leaning with one elbow on the piano, turning over pieces of music absently, a graceful figure in a dark green velvet gown, cut just low enough to show the fine curves of a full, round throat, white and smooth as ivory.

"Not believe in ghosts? Did you ever know a sailor who wasn't superstitious? We are too often alone with the sea and the stars to be quite free from spectral fancies, Miss Leland. I can see in your eyes as you look at me this moment that you believe in ghosts—believe and tremble. Tell me now, candidly—When do you most fear them? At what hour of the day or night does the unreal seem nearest to you?"

"I don't know," she faltered, turning over the loose music with a faintly tremulous gesture, while Isola sat by the piano, touching the notes dumbly now and then.

"Is it at midnight—in the gloaming—in the chill, mysterious dawn? You won't answer! Shall I guess? If you are like me, it is in broad daylight—between two and three in the afternoon—when the servants are all idling after their dinner, and the house is silent. You are alone in a big, bright room, perhaps, with another room opening out of it, and a door a long way off. You sit writing at your table, and you feel all at once that the room is haunted—there must be something or some one stealing in at that remotest door. You daren't look round. You go to the window and look out into garden or street—for a town house may be just as ghastly as a country one—and then with a great effort you turn slowly round and face your terror, in the broad, garish sunlight, in the business hours of the day. There is nothing there, of course; but the feeling has not been the less vivid. I know I shall be spectre-haunted at the Mount. You must all come and scare away the shadows. Mr. Colfox, are you fond of billiards?"

"I own to a liking for the game. I play with Mr. Crowther and his youngest daughter whenever I dine at Glenaveril. Alicia is a very fine player, for a girl, and her father plays a good game."

"Then you will come up to the Mount two or three times a week and play with me, I hope. There's a decent table—cushions as hard as bricks, I dare say, but we must make the best of it—and there's plenty of sound claret in the cellars to say nothing of a keg or two of Schiedam that I sent home from the Hague."

"Mr. Colfox will not make much impression either on your claret or your schnapps," said Disney, laughing. "He is almost as temperate as one of those terrible anchorites in the novel we were reading the other day—'Homo Sum.'"

"I am glad you put in the qualifying 'almost,'" said the curate, "for I hope to taste Captain Hulbert's Schiedam."

The captain expatiated upon what his three new friends—and his one old friend, Martin Disney—were to do to cheer him in his solitude at the Mount.

"There is nothing of the anchorite about me," he said. "I love society, I love life and movement, I love bright faces."

He would not leave until they had all promised to take tea on board the yacht on the following afternoon, an engagement which was kept by Allegra and the colonel; but not by Isola, whose headache was worse after the little dinner-party; nor by the curate, who had parish business to detain him on shore.

## CHAPTER XIII.

### "UNDER THE PINE-WOOD, BLIND WITH BOUGHS."

If Isola had any disinclination to visit Captain Hulbert's yacht, her headache only served to defer the evil day, for after that first tea-drinking came other invitations and other arrangements, fishing-parties, luncheons off Mevagissey, entertainments in which Isola must needs share when she saw her husband and his sister bent upon the enjoyment of the hour, delighted with the *Vendetta* and her warm-hearted skipper.

They were not John Hulbert's only friends in the neighbourhood. Everybody seemed glad to welcome the rover to his native village. Almost everybody had known him in his boyhood; and there was a general consensus of opinion that he was a much better fellow than his brother. He was less courted; but he was better liked. There had been a touch of cynicism about Lostwithiel which frightened matter-of-fact country people.

"One could never feel sure he wasn't laughing in his sleeve at our rustic ignorance," said Mrs. Baynham. "I am more at my ease with Captain Hulbert, and my husband and he were great friends when he was a boy. They used to go fishing together, when Baynham's practice wasn't as good as it is now."

So the brief Indian summer passed in pleasant idlesse on a tranquil sea. The equinoctial gales had not begun to rage yet. There was a lull before the coming of the great winds which were to blow good ships on shore, and startle sleepers in the dead of night. All now was fair and placid—sunlit waters, golden evenings. They spent one bright, balmy day off Mevagissey, a day which was like a long dream to Isola, as she sat on deck in a low folding-chair, wrapped in a great feathery rug from the South Sea Islands, with her languid head reclining against a plush-covered cushion, one of the many effeminate luxuries which abounded in the cabins below. Everybody else was intent upon the nets. Everybody else was full of interest and movement and expectation; but she sat apart from all, with her ivory knitting-needles lying idle in her lap, amidst a soft mass of white wool, which her industry was to convert into a garment for the baby.

Allegra was enraptured with the yacht. She would fain have taken Isola down to the cabins, to explore their wonders of luxury and contrivance, so much comfort and elegance in so restricted an area; but Isola refused to leave the deck.

"I hate all cabins," she said. "They are always suffocatingly hot."

So Mrs. Baynham went below with Allegra, and they two explored the two principal cabins with wondering admiration, and even peeped into the cook's galley, and the odd little places where steward and sailors contrived to bestow themselves.

The chief cabin, saloon, or whatever one liked to call it, was as daintily decorated as a lady's boudoir. There were nests of richly bound books, Oriental bronzes, and all kinds of continental pottery, Japanese and Indian embroideries, Venetian mirrors, quaint little carved cupboards for wine or cigars. Every corner and cranny was utilized.

"What a delicious drawing-room!" cried Allegra. "I could live here all my life. Fancy, how delightful! A floating life. No such thing as satiety. One might open one's eyes every morning on a fresh coast, glorified, as one sees it across the bright, blue water. To explore the Mediterranean, for instance, floating from city to city—the cities of the past, the cities of the Gospel, the shores that were trodden by the feet of St. Paul and his companions—the cities of the Christian saints and martyrs, the island birthplaces of Greek gods and heroes. Think, Mrs. Baynham! A yacht like this is a master-key to open all the gateways of the world."

"I would rather have my own cosy little cottage on terra firma," answered the doctor's wife in a matter-of-fact mood; but this speech of Allegra's set the good lady pondering upon the possibility of John Hulbert falling in love with this nice, clever girl, and making her mistress of his brother's yacht.

Her friendly fancy depicted the village wedding, and those two going forth over the great waters to spend their honeymoon amidst the wonder-world of the Mediterranean, which the banker's daughter knew only in her Atlas.

"He can't be rich," she thought, "but he must have a comfortable income. I know his mother had money. And Allegra can earn a good deal by her painting. She wouldn't be an expensive wife. We ought all to do our best to bring it about. A girl has so few chances in such a place as Trelasco. She might almost as well be in a convent."

Mrs. Baynham was at heart a matchmaker, like most motherly women whom fate has left childless. She was very fond of Allegra, who was so much more companionable than Isola, so much more responsive to kindness and affection. As she sat on deck in the westering sunlight, somewhat comatose after a copious luncheon, Mrs. Baynham's idea of helping Allegra took the form of a dinner-party which she had long been meditating, her modest return for numerous dinners which she had eaten at Glenaveril and at the Angler's Nest. She considered that three or four times a year it behoved her to make a serious effort in the way of hospitality—a substantial and elaborate dinner, in which no good things in season should be spared, and which should be served with all due ceremony. The time was at hand when such a dinner would in a manner fall due; and she determined to hasten the date with a view to Allegra's interests.

"Captain Hulbert is sure to be off again before long," she told herself, "so every evening they can spend together is of importance. I'm sure he is inclined to fall in love with her already."

There was not much doubt about his feelings as he stood by Allegra in the stern, directing the movements of her bare active hands while she hauled in the net; not much doubt that he was as deep in love as a man well can be after a fortnight's acquaintance. He did not make any secret of his bondage, but let his eyes tell all the world that this girl was for him "the world's one woman."

The invitation from Mrs. Baynham was delivered by post next morning, as ceremonious a card as if the place were Mayfair, and the inviter and invitees had not met since last season. A copper-plate card, with name and address filled in by the lady's pen, a detail which distinguished her modest invitation from the Glenaveril cards, of which there were a variety, for at homes, tennis, dinner, luncheon, to accept, and to decline. A fortnight's notice marked the dignity of the occasion—the hour the orthodox quarter to eight.

"We can't refuse, Isola," said Disney, when his wife handed him the card, "although my past experience assures me that the evening will be a trifle heavy. Why will people in small houses insist upon giving dinner-parties, instead of having their friends in instalments? When we go to dine with the Baynhams we go for love of them, not the people they bring together; and yet they insist upon seating twelve in a room that will just comfortably hold eight. It is all vanity and vexation of spirit."

"But Mrs. Baynham is so happy when she is giving a real dinner-party. I don't think we can refuse, can we, Allegra?" asked Isola.

"Mrs. Baynham is a darling, and I wouldn't vex her for worlds," replied her sister-in law. "And in a place like this one can't pretend a prior engagement, unless it were in the moon."

The invitation was accepted forthwith, and when Captain Hulbert dropped in at teatime it was discovered that he, too, had been asked, and that he meant to accept, if his friends at the Angler's Nest were to be there.

---

A thunderbolt fell upon the little village on the following Sunday. When the old men and women, creeping to church a little in advance of younger legs, came to the church-path, they found the gate locked against them, locked and barricaded with bars which looked as if they were meant to last till the final cataclysm. The poor old creatures looked up wonderingly at a newly-painted board, on which the more intelligent among them spelt out the following legend—

"This wood is the private property of J. Vansittart Crowther, Esq. Trespassers will be prosecuted."

Martin Disney and his wife and sister came up when a little crowd of men, women, and children, numbering about thirty, had assembled round the gate, all in their Sunday best.

"What's the meaning of this?" asked Disney.

"Ah, colonel, that's what we all want to know," replied old Manley, the village carpenter, a bent and venerable figure, long past work.

156

"I'm over eighty, but I never remember that gate being locked as long as I have lived at Trelasco, and that's all my life, colonel. There's always been a right of way through that wood."

"And there always shall be," answered Martin Disney. "We won't take any violent measures to-day, my friends—first because it is Sunday, and next because one should always try fair means before one tries foul. I shall write to Mr. Crowther to-morrow, asking him civilly to open that gate. If he refuses, I'll have it opened for him, and I'll take the consequences of the act. Now, my good friends, you'd better go to church by the road. You'll get there after the service has begun. Wait till the congregation are standing up, and then go into church all together, so that everybody may understand why and by whose fault it is that you are late."

The appearance of this large contingent after the first lesson created considerable surprise, and much turning of heads and rustling of bonnet-strings in the echoing old stone church. Mr. Crowther stood in his pew of state on one side of the chancel, and felt that the war had begun. Everybody was against him in the matter, he knew; but he wanted to demonstrate the rich man's right to do what he liked with the things which he had bought. The wood was his, and he did not mean to let the whole parish tramp across it.

He received a stiffly polite letter from Colonel Disney, requesting him to re-open the church-path without loss of time, and informing him of the great inconvenience caused to the older and weaker members of the congregation by the illegal closing of the path during church hours.

Mr. Crowther sent his reply by the colonel's messenger. He asserted his right to shut up the wood which formed a part of his estate, and positively refused to re-open the gate at either end of the footpath in question.

Captain Hulbert dropped in at his usual hour, eager to know the progress of the fight. Fight there must be, he was assured, having seen something of Mr. Crowther's bulldog temper. Then, in the drawing-room of the Angler's Nest, there was hatched a terrible plot—a Catiline conspiracy in a tea-cup—Allegra listening and applauding while the two men plotted.

That night, when the village was hushed in sleep, a boatful of sailors landed at the little hard near the railway station at Fowey, and half a dozen stalwart blue-jackets might have been seen tramping along the old railway track to Trelasco, one carrying a crowbar, another a carpenter's basket. And under the autumn stars that night in the woods of Glenaveril, while Vansittart Crowther slept the sleep of the just man who payeth his twenty shillings in the pound, there rose the sound of a sea-song and the cheery chorus of the sailors, with a rhythmic accompaniment of hammering; and lo, when the October morning visited those yellowing woods, and when Mr. Crowther's gamekeeper went on his morning round, the gate at either end of the church path was wrenched off its hinges, and was lying on the ground. Staple and bolt, padlock and iron hinges, were lying among the dewy dock-leaves and the yellowing fern; and there was free passage between the village of Trelasco and the House of God.

Vansittart Crowther went to Plymouth by the first train that could convey him, and there consulted the lawyer most in renown among the citizens; and that gentleman, after due thought and consideration, informed him that the closing of such an old-established right of way as that of the church-path was more than any landowner durst attempt. Whatever omission there might be in the title-deeds, he had bought the estate subject to that old right of way, which had been enjoyed by the parish from time immemorial. He could no more shut it off than he could wall out the sky.

"But I can punish the person who pulled the locks off my gates, I conclude?" said Mr. Crowther, swelling with indignation.

"That, of course, is a distinct outrage, for which you may obtain redress, if you can find out who did it."

"There can be no difficulty about that. The act must have been instigated by the writer of that impertinent letter."

He pointed to Martin Disney's letter, lying open on the solicitor's table.

"Very probably. But you will have to be sure of proving his share in the act if you mean to take proceedings against him."

Vansittart Crowther was furious. How was he to bring the responsibility of this outrage home to anybody, when the deed had been done in the dead of night, and no mortal eye had seen the depredators at their felonious work? His locks and bolts and hinges, the best of their kind that Sheffield could supply, had been mocked at and made as naught; and all his dumb dogs of serving men and women had been lying in their too comfortable beds, and had heard never a sound of hammer clinking or crowbar striking on iron. There had not been so much as a kitchen-maid afflicted with the tooth-ache, and lying wakeful, to hear the far-off noise of that villainous deed.

Mr. Crowther sent for the police authorities of Fowey, and set his wrongs before them.

"I will give fifty pounds reward to the man who will get me credible evidence as to the person who planned that outrage," he said. And next day there were bills pasted against divers doors at Fowey and Trelasco, against the Mechanics' Institute, and against that curious old oaken door of a mediæval building opposite the club, which may once have been a donjon, and in sundry other conspicuous places, beginning with "Whereas," and ending with Vansittart Crowther's signature.

Nothing came of this splendid offer, though there were plenty of people in the district to whom fifty pounds would have seemed a fortune. Whether no one had seen the crew of the *Vendetta* landing or re-embarking in the night-time, or whether some wakeful eyes had seen, whose owners would not betray the doers of a deed done in a good cause, still remains unknown. Captain Hulbert was enchanted at the success of the conspiracy, and went to church next Sunday by the now notorious footpath, along which an unusual procession of villagers came streaming in the crisp, clear air, proud to assert a right that had been so boldly maintained by their unnamed but not unknown champion. Every one felt very sure that the flinging open of the gates had been somehow brought about by Martin Disney — Martin, whose grandfather they could some of them remember, when he came home after the long war with the French, and took up his abode in an old house among the hills, and married a fair young wife. That had happened sixty-five years ago; but there were those in the village who could remember handsome Major Disney, with only one arm, and a face bronzed by the sun that shines on the banks of the Douro.

Captain Hulbert went by the church-path that morning, although it took him ever so far out of his way. He wanted to walk to church with the Disney family, in order to talk over their victory; and the Disneys seemed to-day to resolve themselves into one; and that one was Allegra Leland; for she and the captain walked ahead and discoursed gaily, perhaps in too exultant and worldly a vein for pious church people; but at worst their exultation was in a good cause; for the horn of the lowly was exalted, and the pride of the rich man was brought low.

"Do you think he will be at church?" asked Allegra, the pronoun standing for Mr. Crowther.

"Of course he will. He must brazen out the position. He will be there, no doubt, gnashing his teeth behind his prayer-book. If angry looks could kill, you and I would be as dead as Ananias and Sapphira before the end of the service."

"Poor, silly man, why did he want to shut up the footpath?" speculated Allegra.

"Only to show his importance—to make himself felt in the neighbourhood. They wouldn't have him for their representative, in spite of his money, and his grand Church and State principles, and all the Primrose Leaguing of his womankind; and so he turns savage and wants to make himself disagreeable."

Yes, it was true that Mr. Crowther had stood for Lostwithiel on three separate occasions, and with equal unsuccess on each. This may have embittered him. If the anger of slighted beauty is a furious thing, no less bitter is the sting of wounded vanity in the rejected candidate.

And then the parson and the doctor had told Mr. Crowther that he could not close his wood against the public; an all-sufficient reason why he should make the attempt.

The Crowther family were in the chancel pew in full force. Allegra thought she detected signs of distress in Mrs. Crowther's countenance; but the daughters went through the service with their noses in the air, and were more than usually vivacious and conversational among their friends between the church-porch and the landau which bore them away to Glenaveril, and the sumptuous boredom of Sunday luncheon.

Merrily went the short autumn days on board the *Vendetta*, and merrily went the tea-drinkings and talk in the drawing-room at the Angler's Nest. Mrs. Disney did not often join the yachting expeditions east or west. The sea made her head ache, she told them; but Mrs. Baynham, who loved pleasure of any kind, was always ready to chaperon Allegra, and Isola welcomed the wanderers to the cheery fireside and the friendly five-o'clock tea. She spent her own days mostly in the society of her baby, with whom she seemed to hold a kind of mysterious commune. She had no idea of amusing him as the nurse had, none of those conventional tricks and movements which are offered to generation after generation of infants; but the child would lie in her lap for hours while she sang to him in her low sweet voice the songs she had learnt in her early girlhood—songs that the peasants of Brittany sing, some of them—and others of a somewhat loftier strain. She would sing him little bits of Mozart, those immortal melodies, of inexhaustible sweetness and ineffable pathos, music mixed with smiles and tears, melody interwoven with such melting tenderness as thrills the coldest heart. There was a gentle happiness in these solitary hours which the young mother spent with her child; and Martin Disney, coming into the room unawares, sometimes stood for a minute or so in loving contemplation of that domestic picture—the young fair face with its long oval form and delicate features; the pensive gravity of the large violet eyes, and mournful droop of the thin, flower-like lips. He had seen such a face on canvas, the ideal Madonna of Raffaelle, with just that subdued blonde colouring and pale auburn hair, and just that thoughtful expression.

His heart swelled with gladness and gratitude as he contemplated mother and son. Yes, the child had made all things well in his home.

Those aching doubts which he felt as he watched beside his wife's sick-bed had vanished like clouds before the sun. Who could doubt the happiness of the mother, absorbed in her firstborn? Who could doubt the love of the wife, looking up at her husband with such tender welcome as he bent over her shoulder to take the little curled-up fist in his, unfold the crumpled fingers, and press them to his lips?

"You are very fond of him, Martin?" she asked, with an often repeated inquiry, knowing what the answer would be.

"Fond of him! After you he is all that I have in this world — except Allegra, who will float away into a world of her own by-and-by, and belong to us no more."

"After me! He ought to be first, Martin — your son, your heir, your second self in the days to come. He ought to have the first place in your heart, Martin, for he is your future."

"No one is first but you."

He dropped the baby hand, and took his wife's head between his hands, and lifted the fair young forehead, looking down at it fondly before he stooped to kiss the soft clustering hair and pencilled brows and ivory temples, with more than a lover's passion.

## CHAPTER XIV.

## "SAY THE FALSE CHARGE WAS TRUE."

The Baynhams' dinner-party was a function to be anticipated with horror, and undergone with resignation. For the first week after the acceptance of the invitation the ceremony had seemed so far off that it could be talked about lightly, and even made an occasion for mirth—Allegra giving her own little sketch of what a dinner at Myrtle Lodge would be like—the drawing-room with its wealth of chair-backs and photograph albums, and the water-colour landscapes which Mrs. Baynham had painted while she was at a finishing school at Plymouth, never having touched brush or pencil since—and Mrs. Baynham's rosy-cheeked nieces from Truro, who always appeared on the scene of any festivity. Yes, one could tell beforehand what the entertainment would be like.

One thing they did not know, however, Mrs. Baynham having been discreetly silent on the subject. They did not know that they were to meet the Glenaveril family in full force, the doctor's wife being of opinion that a friendly dinner-party was the panacea for all parish quarrels and small antagonisms, and that by judiciously bringing the Crowthers and the Disneys together at a well-spread board, and in the genial atmosphere of her unspacious drawing-room, she could bring about an end of the feud, or tacit coldness, which had divided the Angler's Nest and Glenaveril since Colonel Disney's home-coming. It was a disappointment to this worthy woman to see Vansittart Crowther, when Colonel and Mrs. Disney were announced, start and glare as if a mad dog had been brought into the room; but she was relieved at seeing the easy nod which the colonel bestowed upon his vanquished foe, and the friendly hand which good Mrs. Crowther held out to Isola, who paled and blushed, and all but wept at meeting with that cordial matron.

"I don't know why you never come to see me," said Mrs. Crowther, confidentially, having made room for Isola upon a very pretentious and uncomfortable sofa of the cabriole period, a sofa with a sloping seat and a stately back in three oval divisions, heavily framed in carved walnut, a back against which it was agony to lean, a seat upon which it was martyrdom to sit. "But I don't see why we shouldn't be friends when we do happen to meet."

"Dear Mrs. Crowther, we are always friends. I shall never forget your kindness to me."

"There, there; you're a tender-hearted soul, I know. It grieved me so not to go and see you when you were ill; and not to pay attention to your baby. Such a sweet little fellow, too. I've given him many a kiss on the sly when I've met him and his nurse in the lanes. I suppose Mr. Crowther and the colonel don't hitch their horses very well together. That's at the bottom of it all, no doubt. But as for you and me, Isola, I hope we shall always be good friends."

This confidential talk between the two women, observed by Mrs. Baynham out of the corner of her eye, augured well; but Mr. Crowther had not left off glaring, and a glare in those protruding eyeballs was awful. He usurped the hearthrug, as he laid down the law about the political situation and the impending ruin of the country.

"A feeble policy never maintained the prestige of any country, sir," he told Captain Pentreath, the half-pay bachelor, who was devoted to fishing, and cared very little whether his country had prestige or shuffled on without it—so long as fish would bite. "We lost our prestige when we lost Beaconsfield, and with our prestige we are losing our influence. The Continental powers leave us out of their calculations. The neutral policy of the last ten years has stultified the triumph of British arms from Marlborough to Wellington. The day will come, sir, when the world will cease to believe in the history of those magnificent campaigns. People will say, 'These are idle traditions. England could never have been a warlike nation.'"

Captain Pentreath tried to look interested, but was obviously indifferent to the opinion of future ages, and intent upon watching Allegra, looking her handsomest in a yellow silk gown, and deep in talk with Captain Hulbert, who leant his tall form against Mrs. Baynham's cottage piano, which, with a view to artistic effect, had been disguised in Algerian drapery, and wheeled into a position that made the room more difficult of navigation.

One only of the rosy-cheeked nieces was allowed to appear at the dinner-table; firstly because the table was a tight fit for twelve, and secondly because a thirteenth would have excited superstitious fears. The younger sister, whom people asked about with tender solicitude, was to be on view afterwards, when she would perform the bass to her sister's treble in the famous overture to Zampa, which, although not exactly a novelty, may be relied upon to open a musical evening with *éclat*.

Every one had arrived, and after a chilling delay, Potts, the local fishmonger, who had been a butler, and who went out to wait at dinner-parties, and was as familiar a figure as a saddle of mutton or a cod's head and shoulders, made his solemn announcement, and with an anxious mind, Mrs. Baynham saw her guests parade across the narrow hall somewhat overfurnished with stags' heads, barometers, gig-whips and umbrella-stands, to the dining-room, while a hot blast of roast meat burst fiercely from the adjacent kitchen.

Mrs. Baynham had allotted Isola to Mr. Crowther, determined to carry out her idea of bringing about a friendly feeling. Mr. Baynham took Mrs. Crowther, and Captain Pentreath had the privilege of escorting Belinda, whose sentiments and airs and graces of every kind he knew by heart. There was no more excitement in such companionship than in going in to dinner with his grandmother. What is the use of being brought in continual association with a handsome heiress if you know yourself a detrimental?

"She would no more look at me as a lover than she would at a Pariah dog," said the captain, when some officious boon companion at the club suggested that he should enter himself for the Crowther Stakes.

Captain Hulbert was made happy with Allegra, and Colonel Disney was honoured by his hostess, to whom strict etiquette would have prescribed the peer's son. There was surplus female population in the persons of Alicia Crowther and Mary Baynham, who agreeably adorned each side of the table with a little extra sweetness and light; Miss Baynham, buxom and rosy in a white cashmere frock which she had grown out of since her last dinner-party; Miss Crowther, square shouldered and bony, in a black confection by Worth, with a bloated diamond heart making a mirage upon a desert waste of chest, it being a point of honour with thin girls to be more *décoletées* than their plumper sisters.

Mrs. Baynham's conversation at one of her own dinners was apt to be somewhat distracted and inconsecutive in substance, although she maintained a smiling and delighted air all the time, whatever anxieties might be wearing her spirit—anxieties about the cooking and the attendance—angry wonder at the prolonged absence of the parlour-maid—distress at seeing the lobster sauce dragging its slow length along when people had nearly finished the turbot—agonizing fears lest the *vol au vent* should not last out after that enormous help taken by Captain Pentreath, in sheer absence of mind, perhaps, since he only messed it about on his plate, while he bored Miss Crowther with a prosy account of his latest victory over an obstinate demon of the Jack family—"such a devil of a fellow, three feet long, and with jaws like a crocodile."

Colonel Disney was almost as inconsecutive and fragmentary in his conversation as his hostess, and did not imitate her smiling aspect. He was silent and moody, as he had been at the Glenaveril dinner, more than a year ago. That Silenus face bending towards his wife's ear—that confidential air assumed in every look and tone—made him furious. He could scarcely sit through the dinner. He wounded Mrs. Baynham in her pride of heart as a housekeeper by hardly touching her choicest dishes.

"Oh, come now, Colonel Disney," she pleaded, "you must take one of my lobster cromskys. I don't mind owning that I made them myself. It is an *entrée* I learnt from the cook at my own home. My father was always particular about his table, and we had a professed cook. Please don't refuse a cromsky."

Colonel Disney took the thing on his plate, and sat frowning at it, while a bustle at the door and a marked rise in the temperature indicated the entrance of the *pièce de resistance*, in the shape of a well-kept saddle of mutton.

"Oh, but you had seen the *Vendetta* before, hadn't you?" asked the oily voice on the other side of the table. "You knew all about her. Really, now, Mrs. Disney, was that your first visit to Lostwithiel's yacht?"

Isola looked at the speaker as if he had struck her. Great God, how pale she was! Or was it the reflection of the apple-green shade upon the candle in front of her which gave her that ghastly look?

"Yes," she said. "I saw the yacht from the harbour years ago."

"But you were never on board her? How odd, now. I had a notion that you must have seen that pretty cabin, and all Lostwithiel's finical arrangements. He was so proud of the *Vendetta* when he was here. He was always asking my girls on board. You remember, Alicia, how Lord Lostwithiel used to ask you two girls to tea?"

"Yes," answered his daughter, in her hard voice. "He asked us often enough, but mother would not let us go."

"How very severe!" said Captain Hulbert, attracted by the sound of his brother's name. "Why do you object to a tea-party on the *Vendetta*, Mrs. Crowther? Have you a prejudice against yachts? Do you think they are likely to go down in harbour, like the poor old *Royal George*?"

"Oh no, I am not afraid of that. Only I liked Lord Lostwithiel to come to tea with us at Glenaveril; and I did not think it would be quite the thing for my girls to visit a bachelor's yacht, even if I went with them. People at Trelasco are only too ready to make unpleasant remarks. They would have said we were running after Lord Lostwithiel."

"Oh, but it isn't the single girls who run after the men nowadays," said Mr. Crowther, with his Silenus grin; "it's the young married women. They are the sirens."

Nobody took any notice of this remark; and the conversation which had become general for a minute or two resumed its duologue form.

Captain Hulbert and Allegra went on with their animated discussion as to the author of "Macbeth" and "Hamlet;" and Captain Pentreath took up the thread of his story about the obstinate pike; Alicia talked to the doctor about her last day with the hounds; and Mary Baynham told Mrs. Crowther about a church bazaar, which had electrified Truro, and at which she had "helped" at somebody else's stall.

"It was hard work standing about and trying to sell things all day, and persuading stingy old gentlemen to put into raffles for talking dolls," said Miss Baynham. "I have pitied shop-girls ever since."

Mrs. Baynham gave the signal for departure, feeling that her dinner, from a material point of view, had been a success. The lobster sauce had been backward, and the three last people to whom the *vol au vent* was offered had got very little except pie-crust and white sauce, but those were small blemishes. The mutton and the pheasants had been unimpeachable; and on those substantial elements Mrs. Baynham took her stand. She had spared neither pains nor money. Her Italian cream was cream, and not cornflour. Her cabinet-pudding was a work of art. She felt satisfied with herself, and knew that the doctor would approve; and yet she felt somehow that the moral atmosphere had not been altogether free from storm-cloud. Colonel Disney had looked on at the feast with a gloomy countenance; Mr. Crowther had talked in an unpleasant tone.

"I am afraid those two will never forget the church path," she thought, as she set her nieces down to Zampa, and then went to inspect the card-table in a snug corner near the fire, with its freshly lighted wax candles, and new cards placed ready for the good old English game which our ancestors called whist.

Zampa once started meant a noisy evening. Captain Pentreath would sing "The Maid of Llangollen," and "Drink, puppy, drink." Mary Baynham would murder "It was a dream," and scream the higher notes in "Ruby." Duet would follow solo, and fantasia succeed ballad, Mrs. Baynham's idea of a social gathering being the nearest attainable approach to a penny reading. She would have had recitations, and imitations of popular actors, had there been any one capable of providing that form of amusement.

This evening, however, she failed in getting a quartette for whist. Neither Mr. Crowther nor his wife was disposed for cards; Colonel Disney coldly declined; and it was useless to ask the young people to leave the attractions of that woody piano. While she was lamenting this state of things, the whist-table being usually a feature in her drawing-room, the Disneys and Allegra bade her good night, and were gone before she had time to remonstrate with them for so early a departure.

It seemed earlier than it really was, for the dinner had been late. Disney's quick ear had heard the step of his favourite horse, punctual as the church clock. He had ordered his carriage at half-past ten, and at half-past ten he and his party left the drawing-room, the doctor following to hand the ladies to their carriage, while the colonel lighted a cigar on the door-step, preparatory to walking home.

"It's a fine night; I'd rather walk," he said.

He walked further than the Angler's Nest. He walked up to the hill where he and Isola had sat in the summer sunshine on the day after his home-coming. He roamed about that wild height for two hours, and the church clock struck one while he was in the lane leading down to Trelasco.

"If that man has any motive for his insolence—if there is any secret between him and my wife, I'll wring the truth out of him before he is a day older," the colonel said to himself, as he tramped homewards.

He wrote to Mr. Crowther next morning, requesting the favour of half an hour's private conversation upon a very serious matter. He proposed to call upon Mr. Crowther at twelve o'clock, if that hour would be convenient. The bearer of the note would wait for an answer.

Mr. Crowther replied that he would be happy to see Colonel Disney at the hour named.

The colonel arrived at Glenaveril with military punctuality, and was forthwith shown into that grandiose apartment, where all those time-honoured works which the respectable family bookseller considers needful to the culture of the country gentleman were arranged in old oak bookcases, newly carved out of soft chestnut wood in the workshops of Venice. It was an imposing apartment, with panelled dado, gilded Japanese paper, heavy cornice and ceiling, in *carton pierre*—such a room as makes the joy of architect, builder, and furniture-maker. So far as dignity and social position can be bought for money, those attributes had been bought by Vansittart Crowther; and yet this morning, standing before his mediæval fireplace, with his hands in the pockets of his velvet lounge coat, he looked a craven. He advanced a step or two to meet his visitor, and offered his hand, which the colonel overlooked, fixing him at once with a gaze that went straight to the heart of his mystery. He felt that an accuser was before him—that he, Vansittart Crowther, was called to account.

"Mr. Crowther, I have come to ask what you mean by your insolent manner to my wife?"

"Insolent! My dear Colonel Disney, I admire the lady in question more than any other woman within twenty miles. Surely it is not insolent to admire a pretty woman?"

"It is insolent to adopt the tone you have adopted to Mrs. Disney— first in your own house—on the solitary occasion when my wife and I were your guests—and next at the dinner-table last night. I took no notice of your manner on the first occasion—for though I considered your conduct offensive, I thought it might be your ordinary manner to a pretty woman, and I considered I did enough in forbidding my wife ever to re-enter your house. But last night the offence was repeated—was grosser—and more distinctly marked. What do you mean by talking to my wife of Lord Lostwithiel with a peculiar emphasis? What do you mean by your affectation of a secret understanding with my wife whenever you pronounce Lord Lostwithiel's name?"

"I am not aware that there has been anything peculiar in my pronunciation of that name—or in my manner to Mrs. Disney," said Mr. Crowther, looking at his boots, but with a malignant smile lurking at the corners of his heavy lips.

"Oh, but you are aware of both facts. You meant to be insolent, and meant other people to notice your insolence. It was your way of being even with me for defying you to shut up the wood yonder, and cut off the people's favourite walk to church. You dared not attack me; but you thought you could wreak your petty spite upon my wife—and you thought I should be too dull to observe, or too much of a poltroon to resent your impertinence. That's what you thought, Mr. Crowther: and I am here to undeceive you, and to tell you that you are a coward and a liar, and that if you don't like those words you may send any friend you please to my friend, Captain

Hulbert, to arrange a meeting in the nearest and most convenient place on the other side of the channel."

Mr. Crowther turned very red, and then very pale. It was the first time he had been invited to venture his life in defence of his honour; and for the moment it seemed to him that honour was a small thing, a shadowy possession exaggerated into importance by the out-at-elbows and penniless among mankind, who had nothing else to boast of. As if a man who always kept fifty thousand pounds at his bankers, and who had money invested all over the world, would go and risk his life upon the sands of Blankenburgh against a soldier whose retiring allowance was something less than three hundred a year, and who was perhaps a dead shot. The idea was preposterous!

No, Mr. Crowther was not going to fight; and though he quailed before those steady eyes of Martin Disney's, calm in their deep indignation, this explanation was not unwelcome to him. He had a dagger ready to plunge into his enemy's heart, and he did not mean to hold his hand.

"I'm not a fighting man, Colonel Disney," he said; "and if I were I should hardly care to fight for a grass widow who made herself common talk by her flirtation with a man of most notorious antecedents. We will say that it never was any more than a flirtation—in spite of Mrs. Disney's mysterious disappearance after the Hunt Ball, which happened to correspond with Lord Lostwithiel's sudden departure. The two events might have no connection—more especially as Mrs. Disney came back ten days after, and Lord Lostwithiel hasn't come back yet."

"I can answer for my wife's conduct, sir, under all circumstances, and amidst all surroundings. You are the first person who has ever dared to cast a slur upon her, and it shall not be my fault if you are not the last. I tell you again, to your face, that you are a coward and a liar—a coward because you are insolent to a young and lovely woman, and a liar because you insinuate evil against her which you are not able to substantiate."

"Ask your wife where she was at the end of December, the year before last—the year you were in India. Ask her what she had been doing in London when she came back to Fowey on the last day of the

171

year, and travelled in the same train with my lawyer, Mr. MacAllister, who was struck by her appearance, first because she was so pretty, and next because she looked the picture of misery — got into conversation with her, and found out who she was. If you think that is a lie you can go to MacAllister, in the Old Jewry, and ask him to convince you that it is a fact."

"There is no occasion. My wife has no secrets from me."

"I am glad to hear it. Then there is really nothing to fight about except a good deal of vulgar abuse on your part, which I am willing to overlook. A man of your mature age, married to a beautiful girl, has some excuse for being jealous."

"More excuse, perhaps, than a man of your age has for acting like a cad," said the colonel, turning upon his heel, and leaving Mr. Crowther to his reflections.

Those reflections were not altogether bitter. Mr. Crowther felt assured that he had sown the seeds of future misery. He did not believe in the colonel's assertion that there were no secrets between him and his wife. He had cherished the knowledge of that mysterious journey from London on the last day of the year. He had warned his confidential friend and solicitor to mention the fact to no one else. He had pried and questioned, and by various crooked ways had found out that Isola had been absent from the Angler's Nest for some days after the Hunt Ball, and he had told himself that she was a false wife, and that Martin Disney was a fool to trust her.

As for being called by harsh names, he was too much a man of the world to attach any importance to an angry husband's abuse. It made him not a sixpence the poorer; and as there had been no witness to the interview it scarcely diminished his dignity. The thing rested between him and his enemy.

"He took down my gates, but I think I have given him something to think about that will spoil his rest for many a night, before he has thought it out," mused Mr. Crowther.

---

It was after the usual luncheon hour before Martin Disney went back to the Angler's Nest. He had been for a long walk by the river, trying to walk down the devil that raged within him, before he could trust himself to go home. His wife was alone in the drawing-room, sitting by the fire with her baby in her lap; but this time he did not pause on the threshold to contemplate that domestic picture. There was no tenderness in the eyes which looked at his wife—only a stern determination. Every feature in the familiar face looked strange and rigid, as in the face of an accuser and judge.

"Send the child away, Isola. I want some serious talk with you."

She stretched out a faltering hand to the bell, looking at him, pale and scared, but saying no word. She gave the baby to his nurse presently in the same pallid dumbness, never taking her eyes from her husband's face.

"Martin," she gasped at last, frozen by his angry gaze, "is there anything wrong?"

"Yes, there is something horribly wrong—something that means destruction. What were you doing in London the winter before last, while I was away? What was the motive of your secret departure— your stealthy return? What were you doing on the last day of the year? Where had you been? With whom?"

She looked at him breathless with horror; whether at the accusation implied in his words, or at his withering manner, it would have been difficult for the looker-on to decide. His manner was terrible enough to have scared any woman, as he stood before her, waiting for her answer.

"Where had you been—with whom?" he repeated, while her lips moved mutely, quivering as in abject fear. "Great God! why can't you answer? Why do you look such a miserable, degraded creature—self-convicted—not able to speak one word in your own defence?"

"On the last day of the year?" she faltered, with those tremulous lips.

"On the last day of the year before last—the winter I spent in Burmah. What were you doing—where were you—where had you been? Is it so difficult to remember?"

"No, no; of course not," she cried, with a half-hysterical laugh. "You frighten me out of my senses, Martin. I don't know what you are aiming at. I was coming home from London on that day—of course—the 31st of Jan—no, December. Coming home from Hans Place, where I had been spending a few days with Gwendolen."

"You never told me of that visit to Gwendolen."

"Oh yes; I'm sure I told you all about it in one of my letters. Perhaps you did not get that letter—I remember you never noticed it in yours. Martin, for God's sake, don't look at me like that!"

"I am looking at you to see if you are the woman I have loved and believed in, or if you are as false as hell," he said, with his strong hand grasping her shoulder, her face turned to his, so that those frightened eyes of hers could not escape his scrutiny.

"Who has put this nonsense in your head?"

"Your neighbour—your good Mrs. Crowther's husband—told me that his lawyer travelled with you from Paddington—on the 31st of December—the year before last. He got into conversation with you— you remember, perhaps?"

"No," she cried, with a sudden piteous change in her face, "I can't remember."

"But you came from London on that day. You remember that?"

"Yes, yes. I came from Gwendolen's house on that day. I told you so in my letter."

"That letter which I never received—telling me of that visit to which you made no allusion in any of your later letters. It was about that time, I think, that you fell off as a correspondent—left off telling me all the little details of your life—which in your earlier letters seemed to shorten the distance between us."

She was silent, listening to his reproaches with a sullen dumbness, as it seemed to him, while he stood there in his agony of doubt—in his despairing love. He turned from her with a heart-broken sigh, and slowly left the room, going away he scarce knew whither, only to put himself beyond the possibility of saying hard things to her, of letting burning, branding words flash out of the devouring fire in his heart.

She stood for a few moments after he had gone, hesitating, breathless, and frightened, like a hunted animal at bay—then ran to the door, opened it softly, and listened. She could hear him pacing the room above. Again she stood still and hesitated, her lips tightly set, her hands clenched, her brow bent in painful thought. Then she snatched hat and jacket from a corner of the hall where such things were kept, and put them on hurriedly, with trembling hands, as if her fate depended upon the speed with which she got herself ready to go out, looking up at the great, dim, brazen face of the eight-day clock all the while. And then she let herself out at a half-glass door into the garden, and walked quickly to a side gate that opened in to the lane—the gate at which the baker and the butcher stopped to gossip with the maids on fine mornings.

There was a cold bracing wind, and the sun was declining in a sky barred with dense black clouds—an ominous sky, prophetic of storm or rain. Isola walked up the hill towards Tywardreath as if she were going on an errand of deadliest moment, skirted and passed the village, with no slackening of her pace, and so by hill and valley to Par, a long and weary walk under ordinary circumstances for a delicate young woman, although accustomed to long country walks. But Isola went upon her lonely journey with a feverish determination which seemed to make her unconscious of distance. Her steps never faltered upon the hard, dusty road. The autumn wind that swept the dead leaves round her feet seemed to hold her up and carry her along without effort upon her part. Past copse and meadow, common land and stubble, she walked steadily onward, looking neither to right nor left of her path, only straight forward to the signal lights that showed fiery red in the grey dusk at Par Junction. She watched the lights growing larger and more distinct as she neared the end of her journey. She saw the fainter lights of the village scattered thinly beyond the station lamps, low down towards the sandy shore. She heard the distant rush of a train, and the dull sob of the sea creeping up along the level shore, between the great cliffs that screened the bay. A clock struck six as she waited at the level crossing, in an agony of impatience, while truck after truck of china clay crept slowly by, in a procession that seemed endless; and then for the first time she felt that the wind was cold, and that her thin serge jacket did not protect her from that biting blast. Finally the line was clear, and she was able to cross and make her way to the village post-office.

Her business at the post-office occupied about a quarter of an hour, and when she came out into the village street the sky had darkened, and there were heavy rain-drops making black spots upon the grey dust of the road; but she hurried back by the way she had come, recrossed the line, and set out on the long journey home. The shower did not last long, but it was not the only one she encountered on her way back, and the poor little jacket was wet through when she re-entered by the servant's gate, and by the half-glass door, creeping stealthily into her own house and running upstairs to her own room to get rid of her wet garments before any one could surprise her with questions and sympathy. It was past eight o'clock, though she had walked so fast all the way as to feel neither cold nor damp. She took off her wet clothes and dressed herself for dinner in fear and trembling, imagining that her absence would have been wondered at, and her errand would be questioned. It was an infinite relief when she went down to the drawing-room to find only Allegra sitting at her easel, working at a sepia sketch by lamplight.

"Martin is very late," she said, looking up as Isola entered, "and he is generally a model of punctuality. I hope there is nothing wrong. Where have you been hiding yourself since lunch, Isa? Have you been lying down?"

"Yes, part of the time" —hesitatingly. "It is very late."

"Twenty minutes to nine. Dale has been in twice in the last quarter of an hour to say that the dinner is being spoilt. Hark! There's the door, and Martin's step. Thank God, there is nothing wrong!" cried Allegra, getting up and going out to meet her brother.

Colonel Disney's countenance as he stood in the lamplight was not so reassuring as the substantial fact of his return. It was something to know that he was not dead, or hurt in any desperate way —victim of any of those various accidents which the morbid mind of woman can imagine if husband or kinsman be unusually late for dinner; but that things were all right with him was open to question. He was ghastly pale, and had a troubled, half-distracted expression which seared Allegra almost as much as his prolonged absence had done.

"I am sure there is something wrong!" she said, when they were seated at dinner, and the parlour-maid had withdrawn for a minute or two in pursuance of her duties, having started them fairly with the fish.

"Oh no, there is nothing particularly amiss; I have been worried a little, that's all. I am very sorry to be so unconscionably late for dinner, and to sit down in this unkempt condition. But I loitered at the club looking at the London papers. I shall have to go to London to-morrow, Isola—on business—and I want you to go with me. Have you any objection?"

She started at the word London, and looked at him curiously—surprised, yet resolute—as if she were not altogether unprepared for some startling proposition on his part.

"Of course not. I would rather go with you if you really have occasion to go."

"I really have. It is very important. You won't mind our deserting you for two or three days, will you, Allegra?" asked Disney, turning to his sister. "Mrs. Baynham will be at your service as chaperon if you want to go out anywhere while we are away. It is an office in which she delights."

"I won't trouble her. I shall stay at home, and paint all the time. I have a good deal of work to do to my pictures before they will be ready for the winter exhibition, and the time for sending in is drawing dreadfully near. You need have no anxiety as to my gadding about, Martin. You will find me shut up in my painting-room, come home when you will."

Later, when she and her brother were alone in the drawing-room, she went up to him softly and put her arms around his neck.

"Martin, dearest, I know you have some great trouble. Why don't you tell me? Is it anything very bad? Does it mean loss of fortune; poverty to be faced; this pretty home to be given up, perhaps?"

"No, no, no, my dear. The home is safe enough; the house will stand firm as long as you and I live. I am not a shilling poorer than I was yesterday. There is nothing the matter—nothing worth speaking about; blue devils, vapours if you like. That's all."

"You are ill, Martin. You have found out that there is something wrong with you—heart, lungs, something—and you are going to London to consult a physician. Oh, my dear, dear brother," she cried, with a look of agony, her arms still clasped about his neck, "don't keep me in the dark; let me know the worst."

"There is no worst, Allegra. I am out of sorts, that's all. I am going to town to see my lawyer."

CHAPTER XV.

"MY LIFE CONTINUES YOURS, AND YOUR LIFE MINE."

They started by the eleven-o'clock train from Fowey next morning, husband and wife, in a strangely silent companionship—Isola very pale and still as she sat in a corner of the railway carriage, with her back to the rivers and the sea. Naturally, in a place of that kind, they could not get away without being seen by some of their neighbours. Captain Pentreath was going to Bodmin, and insisted upon throwing away a half-finished cigar in order to enjoy the privilege of Colonel and Mrs. Disney's society, being one of those unmeditative animals who hate solitude. He talked all the way to Par, lit a fresh cigar during the wait at the junction, and reappeared just as the colonel and his wife were taking their seats in the up-train.

"Have you room for me in there?" he asked, sacrificing more than half of his second cigar. "I've got the *Mercury*—Jepps is in for Stokumpton—a great triumph for our side."

He spread out the paper, and made believe to begin to read with a great show of application, as if he meant to devour every syllable of Jepps's long exposition of the political situation; but after two minutes he dropped the *Mercury* on his knees and began to talk. There were people in Fowey who doubted whether Captain Pentreath could read. He had been able once, of course, or he could hardly have squeezed himself into the Army; but there was an idea that he had forgotten the accomplishment, except in its most elementary form upon sign-boards, and in the headings of newspaper articles, printed large. It was supposed that the intensity of effort by which he had taken in the cramming that enabled him to pass the ordeal of the Examiners had left his brain a blank.

"You're not going further than Plymouth, I suppose?" he asked.

"We are going to London."

"Are you really, now? A bad time of year for London—fogs and thaws, and all kinds of beastly weather."

And then he asked a string of questions—futile, trivial, vexing as summer flies buzzing round the head of an afternoon sleeper; and then came the welcome cry of Bodmin Road, and he reluctantly left them.

The rest of the journey was passed almost in silence. They had the compartment to themselves for the greater part of the time, and they sat in opposite corners, pretending to read—Isola apparently absorbed in a book that she had taken up at random just before she started, when the carriage was at the door, and while Allegra was calling to her to make haste.

It was Carlyle's "Hero Worship." The big words, the magnificent sentences, passed before her eyes like lines in an unknown language. She had not the faintest idea what she was reading; but she followed the lines and turned the leaf at the bottom of a page mechanically.

Martin Disney applied himself to the newspapers which he had accumulated on the way—some at Par, some at Plymouth, some at Exeter, till the compartment was littered all over with them. He turned and tossed them about one after the other. Never had they seemed so empty—the leaders such mere beating the air; the hard facts so few and insignificant. He glanced at Isola as she sat in her corner, motionless and composed. He watched the slender, white hands turning the leaves of her book at regular intervals.

"Is your book very interesting?" he asked, at last, exasperated by her calmness.

He had been attentive and polite to her, offering her the papers, ordering tea for her at Exeter, doing all that a courteous husband ought to do; but he had made no attempt at conversation—nor had she. This question about the book was wrung from him by the intensity of his irritation.

"It is a book you gave me years ago at Dinan," she answered, looking at him piteously. "'Hero Worship.' Don't you remember? I had never read anything of Carlyle's before then. You taught me to like him."

"Did I? Yes, I remember—a little Tauchnitz volume bound in morocco—contraband in England. A cheat—like many things in this life."

He turned his face resolutely to the window, as if to end the conversation, and he did not speak again till they were moving slowly into the great station, in the azure brightness of the electric light.

"I have telegraphed for rooms at Whitley's," he said, naming a small private hotel near Cavendish Square, where they had stayed for a few days before he started for the East.

"Do you think it would be too late for us to call at Hans Place before we go to our hotel?"

She started at the question. He saw her cheeks crimson in the lamplight.

"I don't think the lateness of hour will matter," she said, "unless Gwendolen is dining out. She dines out very often."

"I hope to-night may be an exception."

"Do you want very much to see her?" asked Isola.

"Very much."

"You are going to question her about me, I suppose?"

"Yes, Isola, that is what I am going to do."

"It is treating me rather like a criminal; or, at any rate, like a person whose word cannot be believed."

"I can't help myself, Isola. The agony of doubt that I have gone through can only be set at rest in one way. It is so strange a thing, so impossible as it seems to me, that you should have visited your sister while I was away, although no letter I received from you contained the slightest allusion to that visit—an important event in such a monotonous life as yours—and although no word you have ever spoken since my return has touched upon it; till all at once, at a moment's notice, when I tell you of your journey from London and the slander to which it gave occasion—all at once you spring this visit upon me, as if I ought to have known all about it."

"You can ask Gwendolen as many questions as you like," answered Isola, with an offended air, "and you will see if she denies that I was with her in the December you were away."

Colonel Disney handed his wife into a station brougham. The two portmanteaux were put upon the roof, and the order was given—99, Hans Place—for albeit Mr. Hazelrigg's splendid mansion was described on his cards and his writing-paper as The Towers, it is always as well to have a number for common people to know us by.

No word was spoken during the long drive from Paddington; no word when the neat little brougham drew up in front of a lofty flight of steps leading up to a Heidelberg doorway, set in the midst of a florid red-brick house, somewhat narrow in proportion to its height, and with over much ornament in the way of terra cotta panelling, bay and oriel, balcony and pediment.

A footman in dark green livery and rice powder opened the door. Mrs. Hazelrigg was at home. He led the way to one of those dismal rooms which are to be found in most fine houses—a room rarely used by the family—a kind of pound for casual visitors. Sometimes the pound is as cold and cheerless as a vestry in a new Anglican church; sometimes it affects a learned air, lines its walls with books that no one ever reads, and calls itself a library. Whatever form or phase it may take, it never fails to chill the visitor.

There was naturally no fire in this apartment. Isola sank shivering into a slippery leather chair, near the Early English fender; her husband walked up and down the narrow floor space. This lasted for nearly ten minutes, when Gwendolen came bursting in, a vision of splendour, in a grey satin tea-gown, frothed with much foam of creamy lace and pale pink ribbon, making a cascade of fluffiness from chin to slippered toes.

"What a most astonishing thing!" she cried, after kissing Isola, and holding out both her plump, white hands to the colonel. "Have you dear, good people dropped from the clouds? I thought you were nearly three hundred miles away when the man came to say you were waiting to see me. It is a miracle we are dining at home to-night. We are so seldom at home. Of course you will stay and dine with us. Come up to my room and take off your hat, Isa. No, you needn't worry about dress," anticipating Disney's refusal; "we are quite alone. I am going to dine in my tea-gown, and Daniel is only just home from the city."

"You are very kind; no, my dear Mrs. Hazelrigg, we won't dine with you to-night," answered Disney. "We have only just come up to town. We drove across the park to see you before going to our hotel. Our portmanteaux are waiting at the door. We are in town for so short a time that I wanted to see you at once—particularly as I have—a rather foolish question to ask you."

His voice grew husky, though he tried his uttermost to maintain a lightness of tone.

"Ask away," said Gwendolen, straightening herself in her glistening grey gown, a splendid example of modern elegance in dress and demeanour, and altogether a more brilliant and imposing beauty than the pale, fragile figure sitting in a drooping attitude beside the fireless hearth. "Ask away," repeated Gwendolen, gaily, glancing at her sister's mournful face as she spoke. "If I can answer you I will—but please to consider that I have a wretched memory."

"You are not likely to forget the fact I want to ascertain. My wife and I have had an argument about dates—we are at variance about the date of her last visit to you—while I was away—and I should like to settle our little dispute, though it did not go so far as a wager. When was she with you? On what date did she leave you?"

All hesitation and huskiness were gone from manner and voice. He stood like a pillar, with his face turned towards his sister-in-law, his eyes resolute and inquiring.

"Oh, don't ask me about dates," cried Gwendolen, "I never know dates. I buy Letts in every form, year after year—but I never can keep up my diary. Nothing but a self-acting diary would be of any use to me. It was in December she came to me—and in December she left—after a short visit. Come, Isa. You must remember the dates of your arrival and departure, better than I. You don't live in the London whirl. You don't have your brains addled by hearing about Buenos Ayres, Reading and Philadelphias, Berthas, Brighton A's, and things."

Martin Disney looked at her searchingly. Her manner was perfectly easy and natural, of a childlike transparency. Her large, bright, blue eyes looked at him—fearless and candid as the eyes of a child.

"You ought to remember that it was on the last day of the year I left this house," said Isola, in her low, depressed voice, as of one weary unto death. "You said enough about it at the time."

"Did I? Oh, I am such a feather-head, *tête de linotte*, as they used to call me at Dinan. So it was—New Year's Eve—and I was vexed with you for not staying to see the New Year in. That was it. I remember everything about it now."

"Thank you, Mrs. Hazelrigg," said Martin Disney, and then going over to his wife, he said gravely, "Forgive me, Isola, I was wrong."

He held out his hands to her with a pleading look, and she rose slowly from her chair, and let her head fall upon his breast as he put his arms round her, soothing and caressing her.

"My poor girl, I was wrong—wrong—wrong—a sinner against your truth and purity," he murmured low in her ear; and then he added laughingly, to Gwendolen, "Were we not fools to dispute about such a trifle?"

"All married people are fools on occasion," answered Mrs. Hazelrigg. "I have often quarrelled desperately with Daniel about a mere nothing—not because he was wrong, but because I wanted to quarrel. That kind of thing clears the air—like a thunderstorm. One feels so dutiful and affectionate afterwards. Dan gave me this sapphire ring after one of our biggest rows," she added, holding up a sparkling finger.

Daniel Hazelrigg came into the room while she was talking of him, a large man, with a bald head and sandy beard, a genial-looking man, pleased with a world in which he had been permitted always to foresee the rise and fall of stocks. The Hazelriggs were the very type of a comfortable couple, so steeped in prosperity and the good things of this world as to be hardly aware of any keener air outside the gardenia-scented atmosphere of their own house; hardly aware of men who dined badly or women who made their own gowns; much less of men who never dined at all, or women who flung themselves despairing from the parapets of the London bridges.

Mr. Hazelrigg came into the room beaming, looked at his wife and smiled, as he held out his hand to Colonel Disney, looked at his sister-in-law and smiled again, and held out his hand to her, the smile broadening a little, as if with really affectionate interest.

"I'm very glad to see you, my dear Mrs. Disney; but I can't compliment you upon looking as well as you did when we last met."

"She is tired after her long journey," said Gwendolen, quickly. "That's all there is amiss."

"The sooner we get to our hotel the better for both of us," said Disney. "We are dusty and weather-beaten, and altogether bad company. Good night, Mrs. Hazelrigg."

"But surely you'll stop and dine; it's close upon eight," remonstrated Hazelrigg, who was the essence of hospitality. "You can send on your luggage, and go to your hotel later."

"You are very good, but we are not fit for dining out. Isola looks half dead with fatigue," answered Disney. "Once more, good night."

He shook hands with husband and wife and hurried Isola to the door.

"Be sure you come to me the first thing to-morrow," said Gwendolen to her sister. "I shall stay in till you come, and I can drive you anywhere you want to go for your shopping—Stores, Lewis and Allanby's—anywhere. I want to show you my drawing-room. I have changed everything in it. You'll hardly know it again."

She and her husband followed the departing guests to the hall, saw them get into the little brougham and drive off into the night; and then Gwendolen put her arm through her husband's with a soft clinging affectionateness, as of a Persian cat, that knew when it was well housed and taken good care of.

"Poor Isa! how awfully ill she looks," sighed Gwendolen.

"Ghastly. Are all women alike, I wonder, Gwen?"

"I think you ought to know what kind of woman I am by this time," retorted his wife, tossing up her head.

---

Martin Disney and his wife were alone in their sitting-room at the hotel, somewhat bare and unhomelike, as hotel rooms must always be, despite the march of civilization which has introduced certain improvements. He had made a pretence of dining in the coffee-room below, and she had taken some tea and toast beside the fire; and now at ten o'clock they were sitting on each side of the hearth, face to face, pale and thoughtful, and strangely silent.

"Isola, have you forgiven me?" he asked at last.

"With all my heart. Oh, Martin, I could never be angry with you — never. You have been so good to me. How could I be angry?"

"But you have the right to be angry. I ought not to have doubted. I ought to have believed your word against all the world; but that man raised a doubting devil in me. I was mad with fears and suspicions, wild and unreasonable — as I suppose jealousy generally is. I had never been jealous before. Great God! what a fearful passion it is when a man gives himself up to it. I frightened you by my vehemence, and then your scared looks frightened me. I mistook fear for guilt. Isola, my beloved, let me hear the truth from your own lips — the assurance — the certainty," he cried with impassioned fervour, getting up and going over to her, looking down into the pale, upturned face with those dark, earnest eyes which always seemed to search the mysteries of her heart. "Let there be no shadow of uncertainty or distrust between us. I have heard from your sister that you were with her when you said you were. That is much. It settles for that vile cad's insinuated slander; but it is not enough. Let the assurance come to me from your lips — from yours alone. Tell me — by the God who will judge us both some day — Are you my own true wife?"

"I am, Martin — I am your own true wife," she answered, with an earnestness that thrilled him. "I have not a thought that is not of you. I love you with all my heart and mind. Is not that enough?"

"And you have never wronged me? You have been true and pure always? I call upon God to hear your words, Isola. Is that true?"

"Yes, yes; it is true."

"God bless you, darling! I will never speak of doubt again. You are my own sweet wife, and shall be honoured and trusted to the end of my days. Thank God, the cloud is past, and we can be happy again!"

She rose from her low seat by the fire, and put her arms round his neck, and hid her face upon his breast, sobbing hysterically.

"My own dear girl, I have been cruel to you—brutal and unkind; but you would forgive me if you knew what I have suffered since noon yesterday; and, indeed, my suffering began before then. That man's harping on Lostwithiel's name in all his talk with you—his air of meaning more than he said—and your embarrassment, awakened suspicions that had to be set at rest somehow. Remember the disadvantages under which I labour—the difference in our ages; my unattractiveness as compared with younger men. These things predisposed me to doubt your love. I have not had a moment's peace since the night of that odious dinner-party. Yes; I have felt a new sensation. I know what jealousy means. But it is past. Praise be to God, it is past. I have come out of the cloud again. Oh, my love, had it been otherwise! Had we been doomed to part!"

"What would you have done, Martin?" she asked, in a low voice, with her face still hidden against his breast, his arms still round her.

"What would I have done, love? Nothing to bring shame on you. Nothing to add to your dishonour or sharpen the agony of remorse. I should have taken my son—my son could not be left under the shadow of a mother's shame. He and I would have vanished out of your life. You would have heard no more of us. The world would have known nothing. You would have been cared for and protected from further evil—protected from your own frailty. So far, I would have done my duty as your husband to the last day of my life; but you and I would never have looked upon each other again."

---

Colonel Disney and his wife stayed in London two days; perhaps to give a colour to their sudden and in somewise unexplained journey;

but Isola refused all her sister's invitations, to lunch, to drive, to dine, to go to an afternoon concert at the Albert Hall, or to see the last Shakespearean revival at the Lyceum. She pleaded various excuses; and Gwendolen had to be satisfied with one visit, at afternoon teatime, when husband and wife appeared together, on the eve of their return to Cornwall.

"It was too bad of you not to come to me yesterday morning, as you promised," Gwendolen said to her sister. "I stayed indoors till after luncheon on your account; and the days are so short at this time of year. I couldn't do any shopping."

Mrs. Hazelrigg was one of those young women for whom life is flavourless when they have nothing to buy. She was so well supplied with everything that women desire or care for that she had to invent wants for herself. She had to watch the advertisements in order to tempt herself with some new wish; were it only for a patent toast-rack, or a new design in ivory paper-knives. The stationers helped to keep life in her by their new departures in writing-paper. Papyrus, Mandarin, Telegraphic, Good Form, Casual, mauve, orange, scarlet, verdigris green. So long as the thing was new it made an excuse for sitting in front of a counter and turning over the contents of a show-case.

"You never came to look at my drawing-room by daylight," she went on complainingly. "You can't possibly judge the tints by lamplight. Every chair is of a different shade. I think you have treated me shamefully. I have sent you more telegrams than I could count. And I had such lots to talk about. Have you heard from Dinan lately?"

"Not since August, when mother wrote in answer to our invitation for her and father to spend a month with us. I felt it was hopeless when I wrote to her."

"Utterly hopeless! Nothing will tempt her to cross the sea. She writes about it as if it were the Atlantic. And Lucy Folkestone tells me she is getting stouter."

"You mean mother?"

"Yes, naturally. There's no fear of Lucy ever being anything but bones. Mother is stouter and more sedentary than ever, Lucy says. It's really dreadful. One doesn't know where it will end," added Gwendolen, looking down at her own somewhat portly figure, as if fearing hereditary evil.

"I shall have to take Isa and the boy to Dinan next summer," said Disney. "It is no use asking the father and mother to cross the channel; though I think they would both like to see their grandson."

"Mother raved about him in her last letter to me," replied Gwendolen. "She was quite overcome by the photograph you sent her, only she has got into such a groove—her knitting, her novel, her little walk on the terrace, her long consultations with Toinette about the smallest domestic details—whether the mattresses shall be unpicked to-day or to-morrow, or whether the *lessive* shall be a week earlier or a week later. It is dreadful to think of such a life," added Gwendolen, as if her own existence were one of loftiest aims.

## CHAPTER XVI.

## "SORROW THAT'S DEEPER THAN WE DREAM, PERCHANCE."

Life flowed on its monotonous course, like the Fowey river gliding down from Lostwithiel to the sea; and there seemed nothing in this world that could again disturb Martin Disney's domestic peace. Vansittart Crowther made no further attempt to avenge himself for the night attack upon his gates; nor did he demand any apology for the vulgar abuse which he had suffered in the sanctuary of his own library. This he endured, and even further outrage, in the shape of the following letter from Colonel Disney:—

"SIR,

"As you have been pleased to take a certain old-womanish interest in my domestic affairs, I think it may be as well to satisfy your curiosity so far as to inform you that when your solicitor travelled in the same train with my wife, she was returning from a visit to her married sister's house, a visit which had my sanction and approval. I can only regret that her husband's modest means constrained her to travel alone, and subjected her to the impertinent attentions of one cad and to the slanderous aspersions of another.

"I have the honour to be,

"Yours, etc.,

"MARTIN DISNEY."

Mr. Crowther treated this letter with the silent contempt which he told himself it merited. What could he say to a man so possessed by uxorious hallucinations, so steeped in the poppy and mandragora of a blind affection, that reason had lost all power over his mind.

"I spoke plain enough—as plain as I dared," said Mr. Crowther. "He may ride the high horse and bluster as much as he likes. I don't think he'll ever feel quite happy again."

Yet in spite of hints and insinuations from the enemy at his gates, Martin Disney was happy—utterly happy in the love of his young wife, and in the growing graces of his infant son. He no longer doubted Isola's affection. Her tender regard for him showed itself in every act of her life; in every look of the watchful face that was always on the alert to divine his pleasure, to forestall his wishes. Mrs. Baynham went about everywhere expatiating on the domestic happiness of the Disney family, to whom she was more than ever devoted, now that she felt herself in a manner related to them, having been elevated to the position of godmother to the firstborn — a very different thing to being godmother to some sixth or seventh link in the family-chain, when all thought of selection has been abandoned, and the only question mooted by the parents has been, "What good-natured friend *can* we ask this time?"

Captain Hulbert took his yacht to other waters in November, only to come sailing back again in December, when he finally laid up the *Vendetta* in winter quarters, and took up his abode at the Mount, where he availed himself of his brother's stud, which had been reduced to two old hunters and a pair of carriage-horses of mediocre quality. And so the shortening days drew on towards Christmas; baby's first Christmas, as that small person's adorers remarked — as if it were a wonderful thing for any young Christian to make a beginning of life — and all was happiness at the Angler's Nest. All was happiness without a cloud, till one morning — Allegra and her brother being alone in the library, where she sometimes painted at her little table-easel, while he read — she put down her palette and went over to him, laying her hand upon his shoulder as he sat in his accustomed place in the old-fashioned bow-window.

"Martin, I want to speak to you about Isola," she said, rather tremulously.

"What about her? Why, she was here this minute," he exclaimed. "Is there anything amiss?"

"I do not think she is so strong as she ought to be. You may not notice, perhaps. A woman is quicker to see these things than a man — and she and I used to walk and row together — I am able to see the difference in her since last year. She seems to me to have been going back in her health for the last month or two, since her wonderful recovery from her illness. Don't be anxious, Martin!" she said, answering his agonized look. "I feel sure there is nothing that a little care cannot cure; but I want to put you on your guard. I asked her to let me send for Mr. Baynham, and she refused."

"Why, he sees her two or three times a week—he is in and out like one of ourselves."

"But he doesn't see her professionally. He comes in hurriedly late in the evening—or between the lights—to fetch his wife. He is tired, and we all talk to him, and Isa is bright and lively. He is not likely to notice the change in her in that casual way."

"Is there a change?"

"Yes, I am sure there is. Although I see her every day, I am conscious of the change."

"Baynham shall talk to her this afternoon."

"That's right, Martin—and if I were you I'd have the doctor from Plymouth again."

Life had been so full of bliss lately, and yet he had not been afraid. Yes, it was the old story. "Metuit secundis." That is what the wise man does. Fools do otherwise—hug themselves in their short-lived gladness, and say in their hearts, "There is no death."

---

Mr. Baynham came in the afternoon, in answer to a little note from Martin Disney, and he and Isola were closeted together in the library for some time, with baby's nurse in attendance to assist her mistress in preparing for the ordeal by stethoscope. Happily that little instrument which thrills us all with the aching pain of fear when we see it in the doctor's hand, told no evil tidings of Isola's lungs or heart. Thero was nothing organically wrong—but the patient was in a very weak state.

"You really are uncommonly low," said Mr. Baynham, looking at her intently as she stood before him in the wintry sunlight. "I don't know what you've been doing to yourself to bring yourself down so much since last summer—after all the trouble I took to build you up, too. I'm afraid you've been worrying yourself about the youngster—a regular young Hercules. I don't know whether he'd be up to strangling a pair of prize pythons; but I'm sure he could strangle you. I shall send you a tonic; and you'll have to take a good deal more care of yourself than you seem to have been taking lately."

And then he laid down severe rules as to diet, until it seemed to Isola that he wished her to be eating and drinking all day—new-laid eggs, cream, old port, beef-tea—all the things which she had loathed in the dreary days of her long illness.

Mr. Baynham had a serious talk with the colonel after he left Isola, and it was agreed between them that she should be taken to Plymouth next day to see the great authority.

"You are giving yourself a great deal too much trouble about me, Martin," she said. "There is nothing wrong. I am only a little weak and tired sometimes."

Her husband looked at her heart-brokenly. Weak and tired. Yes; there were all the signs of failing life in those languid movements of the long, slender limbs, in the transparent pallor of the ethereal countenance. Decay was lovely in this fair young form; but he felt that it was decay. There must be something done to stop Misfortune's hastening feet.

He questioned his wife, he questioned his own memory, as to when the change had begun, and on looking back thus thoughtfully it seemed to him that her spirits and her strength had flagged from the time of Captain Hulbert's arrival at Fowey. She had seemed tolerably cheerful until then, interested in life, ready to participate in any amusement or occupation of Allegra's; but from the beginning of their yachting excursions there had been a change. She had shrunk from any share in their plans or expeditions. She had gone on board the yacht—on the two or three occasions when she had been persuaded to go—with obvious reluctance, and she had been silent and joyless all the time she was there. Within the last fortnight, when Captain Hulbert had pressed her to go to luncheon or afternoon tea at the Mount, she had persistently refused. She had begged her husband to take Allegra, and to excuse her.

"The walk up the hill would tire me," she said.

"My love, why should we walk? I will drive you there, of course."

"I really had rather not go. I can't bear leaving baby so long; and there is no necessity for me to be with you. Allegra is the person who is wanted. You must understand that, Martin. You can see how much Captain Hulbert admires her."

"And I am to go and play propriety while you do baby-worship at home. Rather hard upon me."

This kind of thing had occurred three or four times since the sailor's establishment at the Mount, and Colonel Disney had attached no significance to the matter; but now that he had begun to torture himself by unending speculations upon the cause of her declining health, he could but think that Captain Hulbert's society had been distasteful to her. It might be that Mr. Crowther's insulting allusions to Lord Lostwithiel had made any association with that name painful; and yet this would seem an overstrained sensitiveness, since her own innocence of all evil should have made her indifferent to a vulgarian's covert sneers.

## CHAPTER XVII.

## "THE YEAR OF THE ROSE IS BRIEF."

Mr. Baynham accompanied his patient and her husband to Plymouth, where the family adviser of Trelasco had a long and serious talk with the leading medical light of the great seaport. The result of which consultation—after the tossing to and fro of such words as anæmia, atrophy, family history, hysteria, between the two doctors, as lightly as if diseases were shuttle-cocks—was briefly communicated to Colonel Disney in a sentence that struck terror to his heart, carefully as it was couched. It amounted in plain words to this: We think your wife's condition serious enough to cause alarm, although there are at present no indications of organic disease. Should her state of bodily weakness and mental depression continue, we apprehend atrophy, or perhaps chronic hysteria. Under these circumstances, we strongly recommend you to give her a change of scene, and a milder winter climate even than that of the west of England. Were she living in Scotland or Yorkshire we might send her to Penzance; but as it is we should advise either a sea voyage, or a residence for the rest of the winter at Pau, Biarritz, or on the Riviera.

Modern medicine has a high-handed way of sending patients to the uttermost ends of the earth; and although Martin Disney thought with a regretful pang of the house and stables that he had built and beautified for himself, the garden where every shrub was dear, yet he felt grateful to the specialist for not ordering him to take his wife to the banks of the Amazon or to some sheltered valley in Cashmere. Pau is not far—the Riviera is the beaten track of civilized Europe, the highway road to Naples and the East. He thought of the happy honeymoon, when he and his bright young wife had travelled along that garden of oranges and lemons, between the hills and the sea, and how there had been no shadow on their lives except the shadow of impending separation, about which they had talked hopefully, trying to believe that a year or two would not seem very long, trying to project their thoughts into that happy future when there should be no more parting.

This—this dreary present—was that future which they had pictured as a period of unalloyed bliss. What had the future brought to that hopeful husband, going forth at the call of duty, to return with fondest expectations when his work was done? What but a year and a half of wedded life overshadowed by disappointment, darkened by vague doubts? And now came the fear of a longer parting than had lain at the end of his last Italian journey.

The patient herself was told nothing except that change to a warmer climate would be good for her, and that her husband had promised to take her to the South soon after Christmas.

"You will like to go, won't you, Isola?" he asked her tenderly, as they drove back to the station alone, leaving Mr. Baynham to follow his own devices in the town. "You will enjoy seeing the places we saw together when our marriage was still a new thing?"

"I shall like to go anywhere with you, Martin," she answered. "But is it really necessary to go away? I know you love Trelasco."

"Oh, I have the Cornishman's passion for his native soil; but I am not so rooted to it as to pine in exile. I shall be happy enough in the South, with my dear young wife; especially if I see the roses come back to your cheeks in that land of flowers."

"But it will cost you such a lot of money to take us all away, Martin; and you could not leave Allegra or the baby. Doctors have such expensive ideas."

"Allegra, and the boy! Must we take them, do you think, love?"

"We could not leave him," said Isola, horrified at the bare suggestion; "and it would be very hard to leave Allegra. She bore all the burden of my illness. She has been so good and unselfish. And she will so revel in the South. She has never travelled, she, for whom Nature means so much more than it can for you or me."

"Well, we will take Allegra, and the boy, whose railway ticket will cost nothing, and his nurse. There is a shot in the locker still, Isa, in spite of last year's building operations, which cost a good deal more than I expected. We will all migrate together. Consider that settled. The only question that remains is the direction in which we shall go.

Shall we make for the Pyrenees or the Maritime Alps? Shall we go to Pau, and Biarritz, or to the Riviera, Hyères, Cannes, Nice?"

Isola was in favour of Pau, but after much consultation of books recording other people's experiences, it was finally decided that of all places in the world, San Remo was the best winter home for Martin Disney's wife.

"You can take her up to the Engadine in June," said Mr. Baynham, who had a superficial familiarity with the Continent from hearing his patients talk about their travels, he himself never having left Cornwall, except for a plunge into the metropolitan vortex during the Cattle Show week. "Or you may spend your summer in Auvergne—unless you want to come home as soon as the cold weather is over."

"I shall do whatever may be best for her—home or otherwise," answered Disney. "You may be sure of that."

The doctor went back to his wife, with whom he always discussed everything, except purely professional matters—there were even occasions when he could not refrain from enlarging upon the interesting features of some very pretty case—and was enthusiastic in his praise of Colonel Disney.

"I never saw such devotion," he said. "Any other man would think it hard lines to have to strike his tent at a day's notice, and go off to winter at a strange place, among invalids and old women; but Disney says never a word of his own inclinations or his own inconvenience. He positively adores that young woman. I only hope she's worth it."

"She's very fond of him, Tom," replied Mrs. Baynham, decisively. "There was a time when I was rather doubtful about that. She seemed listless and indifferent. But since the baby came she has been growing fonder and fonder of her husband. I flatter myself I am a pretty good judge of countenances, and I can read hers. I've seen her face light up when the colonel came into the room. I've seen her go over to him shyly, as if it were still their honeymoon. She's a very sweet creature. I took to her from the first; and I shall be dreadfully upset if she goes into a decline."

The doctor shook his head despondently.

"There's nothing to fight with in her case," he said, "and there's very little to fall back upon. I can't make her out. She has gone off just like a girl who was simply fretting herself to death; and yet, if she's fond of her husband, what in Heaven's name is there for her to fret about?"

"Nothing," answered his wife. "It's just a delicate constitution, that's all. She's like one of those grape hyacinths that never will stand upright in a vase. The stem isn't strong enough."

Allegra was all sympathy and affection. She would go with them — yes, to the end of the world. To go to San Remo would be delightful.

"It is a deliciously paintable place, I know," she said, "for I have seen bits of the scenery often enough in the exhibitions. I shall work prodigiously, and earn a small fortune."

She told her brother in the most delicate way that she meant to pay her own expenses in this Italian tour; for of course when Isola should be strong enough they would go about a little, and see the Wonderland of Italy.

Martin protested warmly against any such arrangement.

"Then I shall not go," she exclaimed. "Do you think me one of the incapable young women of the old school—unable to earn a sixpence, and wanting to be paid for and taken care of like a child? I would have you to know, sir, that I am one of the young women of the new school, who travel third-class, ride on the tops of omnibuses, and earn their own living."

"But I shall take a house at San Remo, Allegra. Do you expect me to turn innkeeper—charge you for your bed and board?"

"Oh, you are monstrously proud. You can do as you like in your own house, I suppose. But all travelling and hotel expenses will be my affair, remember that."

"And you don't mind leaving Trelasco?"

"I am like Ruth. You are my home and my country. Where thou goest I will go."

"And Captain Hulbert—how will he like to lose you?"

"What am I to Captain Hulbert?" she asked, trying to laugh off the question, but blushing deeply as she bent over her colour-box, suddenly interested in the littered contents.

"A great deal, I fancy, though he may not have found plain speech for his feelings yet awhile."

"If—if you are not a very foolish person, and there is any foundation for your absurd idea, Captain Hulbert will know where to find us. He can spread his wings and follow."

"The *Vendetta*? Yes, she is pretty familiar with the bays and bights of the Mediterranean. No doubt he will follow us, dear. But I should like him to speak out before we go."

"Then I'm afraid you will be disappointed. He likes coming here—he likes you and Isola, and perhaps he likes me, pretty well, after a fashion; but sailors are generally fickle, are they not? And if he is at all like his brother, Lord Lostwithiel, who seems to have a dreadful reputation, judging by the way people talk of him here——"

"He is not like his brother in character or disposition. If he were, I should be sorry for my sister to marry him."

"Have you such a very bad opinion of his brother?" asked Allegra, shocked and grieved that any one closely allied to John Hulbert should bear an evil repute.

"Perhaps that would be too much to say. I know so little about him. I have scarcely seen him since he was a lad—only I have heard things which have prejudiced me," continued Disney, lapsing into moody thoughtfulness.

Was it not Mr. Crowther's insolence, and that alone, which had prejudiced him against Lostwithiel—had made the very name hateful to him? Yes, that was the cause of his aversion. He had disproved those insolent insinuations; he had exploded the covert slander and rebuked the slanderer; but he had not forgotten. The wound still rankled.

## CHAPTER XVIII.

### "NO SUDDEN FANCY OF AN ARDENT BOY."

It was Christmas Eve. All things were arranged for departure on the 28th, which would give time for their arrival at San Remo on New Year's Day. They were to travel by easy stages, by Amiens, Basle, and Lucerne. A good deal of luggage had been sent off in advance, and trunks and portmanteaux were packed ready for the start; so that the travellers could take their ease during the few days of Christmas church-going and festivity. Isola's spirits had improved wonderfully since the journey had been decided upon.

"It seems like beginning a new life, Martin," she told her husband. "I feel ever so much better already. I'm afraid I'm an impostor, and that you are taking a great deal of unnecessary trouble on my account."

It was such a relief to think that she would see Vansittart Crowther no more, that she could wander where she pleased without the hazard of meeting that satyr-like countenance, those pale protruding eyes, with malevolent stare—such a relief to know that she would be in a new country, where no one would know anything about her, or have any inclination to gossip about her. Something of her old gaiety and interest in life revived at the prospect of those new surroundings.

They were to put up at an hotel for the first few days, so as to take their time in looking for a villa. Two servants were to go with them—the colonel's valet and handy-man, who was an old soldier, and could turn his hand to anything in house, or stable, or garden; and the baby's nurse, a somewhat masterful person of seven and twenty, from the Fatherland, surnamed Grunhaupt, but known in the family by her less formidable domestic diminutive Löttchen. Other hirelings would be obtained at San Remo, but these two were indispensable—Holford, the soldier-servant, to bear all burdens, and Löttchen to take charge of the baby, to whom life was supposed to be impossible in any other care.

It was Christmas Eve—the mildest Christmas that had been known for a long time, even in this sheltered corner of the coast. Allegra had been busy all the morning, helping in the church decorations, and co-operating with Mr. Colfox in various arrangements for the comfort of the old and sick and feeble, among the cottages scattered over the length and breadth of a large parish. She had walked a good many miles, and she had stood for an hour in the church, toiling at the decoration of the font, which had been assigned to her, and which she covered with ferns, arbutus, and berberis foliage, in all their varieties of colour, from darkest bronze to vivid crimson, starred with the whiteness of Christmas roses; while the Miss Crowthers lavished the riches of the Glenaveril hothouses upon the pulpit, keeping themselves studiously aloof from Miss Leland.

Not a jot cared Allegra for their aloofness. She disliked their father, and she knew that her brother detested him, without having any clear idea of the cause. She was so thoroughly loyal to Martin that she would have deemed it treason to like any one whom he disliked; so had the daughters of Glenaveril been the most companionable young women in Cornwall she would have considered it her duty to hold them at arm's length. Glenaveril and all its belongings were taboo.

She was very tired when she went home at four o'clock, just on the edge of dusk here—pitch dark, no doubt, in London and other great cities, where the poor, pinched faces were flitting to and fro in the fitful glare of the butcher's gas, intent on finding a Christmas joint to fit the slenderest resources. Here, in this quiet valley, the reflected sun-glow still brightened sky, sea, land, and river, and the lamps had not yet been lighted in hall or drawing-room at the Angler's Nest.

There was a pleasant alternation of firelight and shadow in the long double room, the flames leaping up every now and then, and lighting wall and bookcase, picture and bust, the blue and red of the Mandarin jars, and the golden storks on the black Japanese screen; but it was such a capricious light that it did not show Allegra some one sitting *perdu* in Martin Disney's deep elbow chair, a person who sat and watched her with an admiring smile, as she flung off her little felt hat and fur cape, and stretched her arms above her head in sheer weariness, a graceful, picturesque figure, in her plain brown serge gown, belted round the supple waist, and clasped at the throat, like Enid's, and with never an ornament except the oxydized silver clasps, and the serviceable chatelaine hanging at her side.

The tea-table was set ready in front of the fire, the large Moorish tray on bamboo legs. But there was no sign of Isola; so Miss Leland poured out a cup of tea and began to drink it, still unconscious of a pair of dark eyes watching her from the shadow of the big armchair.

"And am I to have no tea, Miss Leland?" asked a voice out of the darkness.

Allegra gave a little scream, and almost dropped her cup.

"Good gracious!" she exclaimed. "How can you startle any one like that? How do you know that I have not heart disease?"

"I would as soon suspect the goddess Hygeia of that, or any other ailment," said Captain Hulbert, rising to his full six feet two, out of the low chair in the dark corner by the bookcase. "Forgive me for my bearishness in sitting here while you were in the room. I could not resist the temptation to sit and watch you for a minute or two while you were unconscious of my presence. It was like looking at a picture. While you are talking I am so intent upon what you say, and what you think, that I almost forget to consider what you are like. To-night I could gaze undistracted."

"What absolute nonsense you talk," said Allegra, with the sugar-tongs poised above the basin. "One lump—or two?"

"One, two, three—anything you like—up to a million."

"Do you know that you nearly made me break a tea-cup—one of mother's dear old Worcester tea-cups? I should never have forgiven you."

"But as you didn't drop the tea-cup, I hope you do forgive me for my stolen contemplation, for sitting in my corner there and admiring you in the firelight?"

"Firelight is very becoming. No doubt I looked better than in the daytime."

"And you forgive me?"

"I suppose so. It is hardly worth while to be angry with you. I shall be a thousand miles away next week. I could not carry my resentment so far. It would cool on the journey."

"A thousand miles is not far for the *Vendetta*, Miss Leland. She would make light of crossing the Pacific—for a worthy motive."

"I don't know anything about motives; but I thought you were fairly established at the Mount, and that you had made an end of your wanderings."

"The Mount is only delightful—I might say endurable—when I have neighbours at the Angler's Nest."

"Martin will let this house, perhaps, and you may have pleasant neighbours in the new people."

"I am not like the domestic cat. It is not houses I care for, but individuals. My affections would not transfer themselves to the new tenants."

"How can you tell that? You think of them to-night as strangers—and they seem intolerable. You would like them after a week, and be warmly attached to them at the end of a month. Why, you have known us for less than three months, and we fancy ourselves quite old friends."

"Oh, Miss Leland, is our friendship only fancy? Will a thousand miles make you forget me?"

"No, we could not any of us be so ungrateful as to forget you," answered Allegra, struggling against growing embarrassment, wondering if this tender tone, these vague nothings, were drifting towards a declaration, or were as simply meaningless as much of the talk between men and women. "We can't forget how kind you have been, and what delightful excursions we have had on the *Vendetta*."

"The *Vendetta* will be at San Remo when you want her, Allegra. She will be as much at your command there as she has been here; and her skipper will be as much your slave as he is here—as he has been almost ever since he saw your face."

This was not small talk. This meant something very serious. He had called her Allegra, and she had not reproved him; he had taken her hand and she had not withdrawn it. In the next instant, she knew not how, his arm was round her waist, and her head, weary with the long day's work and anxieties, was resting contentedly on his shoulder, while his lips set their first kiss, tenderly, reverently almost, on her fair broad brow.

"Allegra, this means yes, does it not? Our lives have flowed on together so peacefully, so happily, since last October. They are to mingle and flow on together to the great sea, are they not, love—the sea of death and eternity."

"Do you really care for me?"

"Do I really adore you? Yes, dear love. With all my power of adoration."

"But you must have cared for other girls before now. I can't believe that I am the first."

"Believe, at least, that you will be the last, as you are the only woman I ever asked to be my wife."

"Is that really, really true?"

"It is true as the needle to the north."

"Yet they say that sailors——"

"Are generally tolerable dancers, and popular in a ball-room, especially when they are the givers of the ball—that they can talk to pretty women without feeling abashed—and that they contrive to get through a good deal of flirting without singeing their wings. I have waltzed with a good many nice girls in my time, Allegra, and I have sat out a good many waltzes. Yet I am here at your side, honestly and devotedly your own; and I have never loved any other woman with the love I feel for you. No other woman has ever held my whole heart; no, not for a single hour."

"You make nice distinctions," said Allegra, gently disengaging herself from his arm, and looking at him with a faint, shy smile, very doubtful, yet very anxious to believe. "I am dreadfully afraid that all this fine talk means nothing more than you would say to any of your partners, if you happened to be sitting out a waltz."

"Should I ask any of my partners to be my wife, do you think?"

"Oh, you can withdraw that to-morrow—forget and ignore it. We may both consider it only a kind of under-the-mistletoe declaration, meaning no more than a mistletoe kiss. I believe when English people were domestic and kept Christmas, the head of the family would have kissed his cook if he had met her under the mistletoe."

"Allegra, is it not cruel of you to be jocose when I am so tremendously serious?"

"What if I don't believe in your seriousness?"

"Is this only a polite way of refusing me?" he asked, beginning to be offended, not understanding that this nonsense-talk was a hasty defence against overpowering emotion, that she was not sure of him, and was desperately afraid of betraying herself. "Am I to understand that you don't care a straw for me?"

"No, no, no," she cried eagerly, "as a friend, I like you better than any one else in the world; only I don't want to give you more than friendship till I can trust you well enough to believe in your love."

"Prove it, Allegra," he cried, clasping her waist again before she was aware. "Put me to any test or any trial—impose any duty upon me. Only tell me that if I come through the ordeal you will be my wife."

"You are not in a great hurry to fetter yourself, I hope?" she said.

"I am in a hurry—I long for those sweet fetters by which your love will hold me. I want to be anchored by my happiness."

"Give me a year of freedom, a year for art and earnest work in Italy, a year for Martin and Isola, who both want me; and if this night year you are still of the same mind, I will be your wife. I will not engage you. You may be as free as air to change your mind and love some one else; but I will promise to be true to you and to this talk of ours till the year's end—one year from to-night."

"I accept your sentence, though it is severe; but I don't accept my freedom. I am your slave for a year. I shall be your slave when the year is out. I am yours, and yours alone for life. And now give me that cup of tea, Allegra, which you have not poured out yet, and let us fancy ourselves Darby and Joan."

"Darby and Joan," echoed Allegra, as she filled his cup. "Must we be like that: old and prosy, sitting by the fire, while life goes by us outside? It seems sad that there should be no alternative between slow decay and untimely death."

"It is sad; but the world is made so. And then Providence steeps elderly people in a happy hallucination. They generally forget that they are old; or at least they forget that they ever were young, and they think young people so ineffably silly that youth itself seems despicable to their sober old minds. But you and I have a long life to the good, dear love, before the coming of grey hairs and elderly prejudices."

And then he began to talk of ways and means, as if they were going to be married next week.

"We shall have enough for bread and cheese," he said. "I am better off than a good many younger sons; for a certain old grandfather of mine provided for the younger branches. It is quite possible that Lostwithiel may never marry—indeed, he seems to me very decided against matrimony, and in that case those who come after us must inherit title and estate in days to come."

"Pray don't talk so," cried Allegra, horrified. "It sounds as if you were speculating upon your brother's death."

"On Lostwithiel's death? Not for worlds. God bless him, wherever he may be. You don't know how fond we two fellows are of each other. Only when a man is going to be married it behoves him to think even of the remote future. I shall have to talk to the colonel, remember; and he will expect me to be business-like."

"I hope you don't think Martin mercenary," said Allegra. "There never was a man who set less value on money. It wouldn't make any difference to him if you had not a penny. And as for me, I have a little income from my mother—more than enough to buy frocks and things—and beyond that I can earn my own living. So you really needn't trouble yourself about me."

There was a touching simplicity in her speech, mingled with a slight flavour of audacity, as of an emancipated young woman, which amused her lover, reminding him of a heroine of Murger's, or

Musset's, a brave little grisette, who was willing to work hard for the *ménage à deux*, and who wanted nothing from her lover but love. He looked into the candid face, radiant in the fire-glow, and he told himself that this was just the one woman for whom his heart had kept itself empty, like a temple waiting for its god, in all the years of his manhood. And now the temple doors had opened wide, the gates had been lifted up, and the goddess had marched to her place, triumphant and all-conquering.

The clock on the mantelpiece struck six, and the old eight-day clock in the hall followed like a solemn echo. Captain Hulbert started up. "So late! Why, we have been talking for nearly two hours!" he exclaimed, "and I have a budget of letters to write for the night mail. Good-bye, darling—or I'll say *au revoir*, for I'll walk down again after dinner, and get half an hour's chat with Disney, if you don't think it will be too late for me to see him."

"You know he is always pleased to see you—we are not very early people—and this is Christmas Eve. We were to sit round the fire and tell ghost-stories, don't you remember?"

"Of course we were. I shall be here soon after nine, and I shall think over all the grizzly legends I ever heard, as I come down the hill."

He went reluctantly, leaving her standing by the fire, a contemplative figure with downcast eyes. At a little later stage in their engagement no doubt she would have gone with him to the door, or even out to the garden gate, for a lingering parting under the stars—but there was a shyness about them both in this sweet dim beginning of their union, when it was so strange to each to have any claim upon the other.

"How lightly she took the whole business," Captain Hulbert said to himself as he went up the hill. "Yet her voice trembled now and then—and her hand was deadly cold when first I clasped it. I think she loves me. A year,"—snapping his fingers gaily at the stars—"what is a year? A year of bliss if it be mostly spent with her. Besides, long engagements are apt to dwindle. I have seen such engagements—entered on solemnly like ours to-night—shrink to six months, or less. Why should one linger on the threshold of a new life, if one knows it is going to be completely happy?"

The blissful lover had not been gone five minutes when Isola came creeping into the room, and put her arm round Allegra's neck and kissed her flushed cheek.

"Why, Isa, where have you been hiding all this evening?"

"I had fallen asleep in my room, just half an hour before tea, and when I awoke it was five o'clock, and Löttchen told me you and Captain Hulbert were in the drawing-room. And as I know you two have always so much to talk about, I thought I wouldn't disturb you. So I let Löttchen make tea for me in the nursery, and I stayed there to play with baby. And here you are all in the dark."

"Oh, we had the firelight—Parker forgot to bring the lamp."

"And you forgot to ring for it," said Isola, going over to the bow-window, and drawing back a curtain. "What a lovely sky! Who would think it was Christmas-time?"

The moon was in her second quarter, shining brilliantly, in the deep purple of a sky almost without a cloud.

"Will you put on your hat and jacket and come for a stroll in the garden, Isa?" asked Allegra. "It is a mild, dry night, and I don't think the air can hurt you."

"Hurt me! It will do me all the good in the world. Yes, I shall be ready in a moment."

They went out into the hall, where Allegra packed her sister-in-law carefully in a warm, fur-lined jacket, and flung a tartan shawl round her own shoulders. Then they went out into the garden, and to the lawn by the river. The moon was shining on the running water, brightly, coldly, clear, while the meadows on the opposite bank were wrapped in faint, white mists, which made all the landscape seem unreal.

"Are you not too tired for walking here after your long day, Allegra?" Isola asked, when they had gone up and down the path two or three times.

"Tired, no. I could walk to Tywardreath. I could walk to the Mausoleum. Shall we go there? The sea must be lovely under that moon."

"My dearest, it is nearly seven o'clock, and you have been tramping about all day. If you are not very tired, you must be very much excited, Allegra. I am longing to hear what it all means."

"Are you really, now? Do you care about it, Isola? Can you, who are firmly anchored in the haven of marriage, feel any sentimental interest in other people, tossing about on the sea of courtship? Martin is to be told everything to-night—so you may as well know all about it now. You like Captain Hulbert, don't you, Isola?"

"I do, indeed. I like him, and believe in him."

"Thank Heaven! I should have been miserable if you had doubted or disliked him. He is to be my husband some day, Isa, if Martin approve—but not for a year, at least. Tell me, dear, are you glad?"

"Yes, I am very glad. God bless you, Allegra, and make your life happy—and free—from—care."

She broke down with those last faltered words, and Allegra discovered that she was crying.

"My dearest Isa, don't cry! I shall fancy you are sorry—that you think him unworthy."

"No, no, no. It is not that. He is worthy. He is all that I could desire in the man who is to be your husband. No, I was only thinking how completely happy you and he must be—how cloudless your life promises to be. God keep you, and guard you, dear! And may you never know the pain of parting with the husband you love—with your protector and friend—as I have known it."

"Yes, love; but that is all past and done with. There are to be no more farewells for you and Martin."

"No, it is past, thank God! Yet one cannot forget. I am very glad Captain Hulbert has left the navy—that his profession cannot call him away from you."

"No, he is an idle man. I dare say the time will come when I shall be plagued with him, and be almost obliged to suggest that he should keep race-horses, or go on the Stock Exchange, to occupy his time. I have heard women say that it is terrible to have a stay-at-home husband. Yet Martin is never *de trop*—but then Martin can bury himself in a book. He has no fidgety ways."

"How lightly you talk, Allegra."

"Perhaps that is because my heart is heavy—heavy, not with grief and care, but with the burden of perplexity and surprise, with the fear that comes of a great joy."

"You do love him, then?" said Isola, earnestly. "You are glad."

"I am very glad. I am glad with all my heart."

"God bless you, dearest! I rejoice in your happiness."

They kissed again, this time with tears on both sides; for Allegra was now quite overcome, and sobbed out her emotion upon her sister's neck; they two standing clasped in each other's arms beside the river.

"When I am dead, Allegra, remember always that I loved you, and that I rejoiced in your happiness as if it were my own."

"When you are dead! How dare you talk like that, when we are taking you away to get well and strong, and to live ever so many years beyond your golden wedding? Was there ever such ingratitude?"

The odour of tobacco stole on the evening air, and they heard Martin's firm tread approaching along the gravel path.

Isola put her arm through his, while Allegra ran into the house, and husband and wife walked up and down two or three times in the darkness, she telling him all about the wonderful thing that had happened.

"You are glad, are you not, Martin? You are as glad as I am?"

"Are you so very glad?"

"Yes, for I know that Allegra loves him, has loved him for a long time."

"Meaning six weeks or so—allowing a fortnight for the process of falling in love. Is that what you call a long time, Isola?"

"Weeks are long sometimes," she answered, slowly, as if her thoughts had wandered into another channel.

"Well, if Allegra is pleased, I suppose I ought to be content," said Disney. "Hulbert seems a fine, frank fellow, and I have never heard anything to his discredit. He was popular in the navy, and was considered a man of marked ability. I dare say people will call him a good match for Allegra, so long as Lostwithiel remains a bachelor."

"No one can be too good for Allegra, and only the best of men can be good enough. If I had my own way, I should have liked her to remain always unmarried, and to care for nothing but her nephew and you. I should have liked to think of her as always with you."

The triangular dinner-party was gayer that evening than it had been for a long time. Isola was in high spirits, and her husband was delighted at the change from that growing apathy which had so frightened him. The ladies had scarcely left the table when Captain Hulbert arrived, and was ushered into the dining-room, where Martin Disney was smoking his after-dinner pipe in the chimney corner—the old chimney corner of that original Angler's Nest, which had been a humble homestead two hundred years ago.

The two men shook hands, and then John Hulbert seated himself on the opposite side of the hearth, and they began to talk earnestly of the future, Martin Disney speaking with fond affection of the sister who had been to him almost as a daughter.

"Her mother was the sweetest and truest of women," he said, "and her father had one of the most refined and delicate natures I ever met with in a man. I do not know that he was altogether fitted for the Church. He was wanting in energy and decision, or force of character; but he was a firm believer, pure-minded and disinterested, and he was an artist to the tips of his fingers. It is from him Allegra inherits her love of art; only while he was content to trifle with art she has worked with all the power of her strong, resolute temperament. She inherits that from her mother's line, which was a race of workers, men with whom achievement was a necessity of existence—men who fought, and men who thought—sword and gown."

Disney smiled at the stern condition of a year's probation which Allegra had imposed upon her lover.

"Such sentences are very often remitted," he said.

"I own to having some hope of mercy," replied Captain Hulbert. "People have an idea that May marriages are unlucky; and perhaps we had better defer to a popular superstition. But it seems to me that June is a capital month for a yachtsman's honeymoon; and if I can persuade my dearest to remit half my period of probation, and fix the 1st of June for our wedding, I should be just half a year happier than I am now."

"Have you any notion yet what kind of life you are to lead after your marriage? I hope it will not be a roving life. Isola and I would like to have our sister near us."

"And Allegra and I would like to study your liking," laughed Hulbert. "We may wander a little on summer seas, but we will have our fixed abode, and it shall be near you. So long as Lostwithiel is a bachelor, we can make our home at the Mount; but fond as I am of that dear old place, I should be glad to see my brother married. There is something amiss in his present mode of life; and I have but too strong reason to fear that he is not a happy man."

"Have you any idea of the cause of his unhappiness?"

"Only speculative ideas—mere theories that may be without foundation in fact. I fancy that he has burnt the lamp of life a little too furiously, and that the light has grown dim in the socket. The after-taste of a fiery youth is the taste of dust and ashes. There may be memories, too—memories of some past folly—which are bitter enough to poison his life. I know that he is unhappy. I have tried to find out the cause; and it all ends in this—an obstinate reserve on his part, and mere theorizing on mine."

"I have heard that he lived in a bad set after he left the University?"

"A bad set—yes, that is it. A man who begins life in a certain circle is like a workman who gets his arm or his leg caught unawares in a machine worked by steam power. In an instant he is entangled past rescue. He is gone. A man takes the wrong road. Ten years afterwards, perhaps, when he is bald and wrinkled, he may pull himself up on the downward track and try to get rid of a bad reputation and make a fresh start; but those fresh starts rarely end in a winning race. I am very sorry for my brother. He is a warm-hearted fellow, with a good deal of talent; and he ought not to have made a bad thing of his life."

"Let us hope that he has pulled up in time, and that he may get a young wife before he is many years older. I have no desire that my sister's son should be a peer. I only want to see her happy with a husband who shall be worthy of her."

CHAPTER XIX.

"I HAVE YOU STILL, THE SUN COMES OUT AGAIN."

The new year was just a week old, and Isola and Allegra were standing on a terraced hillside in a country where January has noontides as brilliant and balmy as an English June. They had travelled up that almost perpendicular hill in a roomy landau drawn by a pair of strong horses, and now, near the summit of the hill, on the last of those many terraces that zig-zag up the face of the cliff, they had alighted from the carriage, and were standing side by side upon the broad white road, at an angle where the cliff dipped suddenly, clothed with the wild growth of stunted olive and bushy pine, down and down to the abyss where the blue sea looked like a sapphire at the bottom of a pit. They stood and gazed, and gazed again, almost bewildered by the infinite beauty and variety of that dazzling prospect.

Below them, in the shelter of the land-locked bay, Ospedaletti's pavilioned Casino shone whitely out of a garden of palm and cactus, with terrace and balustrade vanishing down by the sea. To the right, the steep promontory of Bordighera jutted far out into the blue; and over the rugged crest of the hill Mentone's long white front lay in a gentle curve, almost level with the sea—a strip of vivid white between the blue of the water and the gloom of that great barren mountain wall which marks the beginning of modern Italy. And beyond, again, showed the twin towers of Monaco; and further still, in the dim blue distance, rose the battlemented line of the Esterelles, dividing the fairyland of the Riviera from the workaday realities of shipbuilding Toulon and commercial Marseilles.

On this side of those pine-clad mountains there were only pleasure and fancy, wealth, fashion, the languid invalid, and the feverish gambler; on the other side there were toilers and speculators, the bourse and the port, the world of stern fact.

To the left, deep down within the hills, lay the little harbour of San Remo, with its rugged stone pier and its shabby old houses, and the old, old town climbing up the steep ascent to that isolated point where the white dome of the Sanctuary shone out against the milky azure of the noontide sky; and further and further away stretched the long line of the olive-clothed hills, to the purple distance, where the seamen's church of Madonna della Guardia stands boldly out between sky and sea, as if it were a half-way house on the road to heaven.

"How lovely it all is!" cried Allegra. "But don't you feel that one careless step upon that flowery edge yonder would send us whirling down the cliffs to awful, inevitable death? When that man passed us just now with his loaded cart, I felt sick with fear—the wheels seemed to graze the brink of the abyss as the horse crept slowly along—poor stolid brute!—unconscious of his danger. It is a dreadful drive, Isola, this zig-zag road to Colla—slant above slant, backwards and forwards, up the face of this prodigious cliff. I had to shut my eyes at every turn of the road, when the world below seemed to swim in a chaos of light and colour—so beautiful, so terrible! Do you see the height of those cliffs, terrace above terrace, hill above hill? Why, that level road at the very bottom is the top of a taller cliff than those I used to think so appalling at Broadstairs and Ramsgate!"

"I don't think it would make much difference to a man who fell over the edge whether he fell here or in the Isle of Thanet," said Martin Disney, as he stood, with his arm drawn through his wife's, sweeping the prospect with his field glass.

"Oh, but it would! One would be only a sudden shock and a plunge into the sea, or swift annihilation on the rocks below; but from this awful height—think of the horror of it! To go whirling down, plucked at here by an olive branch, or there by a jagged rock, yet always whirling downward, rebounding from edge to edge, faster, and faster, and faster, till one were dashed into a shapeless mass on that white road yonder!"

"And to think of people living up there in the clouds, and going to sleep every night with the knowledge of this mighty wall and that dreadful abyss in their minds!" she concluded, pointing upward to where the little white town of Colla straggled along the edge of the hill.

They were going up to see the pictures and books in the little museum by the church. It was their first excursion, since their arrival in Italy, for Martin Disney had been anxious that his wife should be thoroughly rested after her long journey, before she was called upon to make the slightest exertion. She was looking better and stronger already, they were both agreed; and she was looking happier, a fact which gave her husband infinite satisfaction. They had come by the St. Gothard, had rested a night at Dover and a night at Basle, and had stopped at Lucerne for three days, and again a couple of days at Milan, and again at Genoa, exploring the city, and the Campo Santo in a leisurely way; Allegra exalted out of herself almost by the delight of those wonderful collections in the palaces of the Via Balbi—the Veroneses, the Titians, the Guidos—Isola languidly admiring, languidly wondering at everything, but only deeply moved when they came to the strange city of the dead, the scenic representation of sickness, calamity, grief and dissolution, in every variety of realistic representation or of classic emblem. Sculptured scenes of domestic sorrow, dying fathers, kneeling children, weeping widows—whole families convulsed in the throes of that last inevitable parting; the death of youth and beauty; the fallen rose-wreath; the funeral urn; the lowered torch; hyacinth and butterfly; Psyche and Apollo; the fatal river and the fatal boat; grimness and beauty—the actual and the allegorical curiously mixed in the sculptured images that line the cold white colonnades, where the footsteps of holiday-makers echo with a sepulchral sound under the vaulted roof. Here Isola was intensely interested, and insisted on going up the marble steps, flight after flight, and to the very summit of the hill of graves, with its wide-reaching prospect of mountain, and fort, and city, and sea.

"Think how hard it must be to lie here and know nothing of all that loveliness," she said, her eyes widening with wonder as they gazed across the varied perspective of vale and mountain, out to the faint blue sea. "How hard, how hard! Do they feel it and know it, Allegra? Can this I—which feels so keenly, which only sleeps in order to enter a new world of dreams—busier and more crowded and more eventful than the real world—can this consciousness go out all at once like the flame of a candle—and nothing, nothing, nothing be left?"

"They are not here," said Allegra, with gentle seriousness. "It is only the husk that lies here—the flower-seed has been carried off in God's great wind of death—and the flower is blossoming somewhere else."

"One allegory is as good as another," said Isola. "We can but console ourselves with symbols. I don't like this crowded city of the dead, Allegra. For God's sake, don't let Martin have me buried here, if I should die at San Remo!"

"Dearest, why will you harbour such ghastly thoughts?"

"Oh, it was only a passing fancy. I thought it just possible that if I were to die while we are in Italy, Martin might think to honour me by having me laid in this splendid cemetery. He seemed so struck by the grandeur and beauty of the monuments, just now, when we were in those colonnades down yonder."

Colonel Disney had lingered a little way off to look at Mazzini's monument. He came up to them now, and hurried them back to the gate, where their carriage was waiting. And so ended their last afternoon in Genoa; and the most vivid picture of the city and its surroundings that Isola carried away with her was the picture of those marble tombs upon the hill, and those tall and gloomy cypresses which are the trees of death.

---

Yes, she was better, gayer, and more active—more like the girl-wife whom Martin Disney had carried home to Cornwall, prouder than Tristram when he sailed away with Irish Isolt.

The Italian sunshine had revived his fading flower, Disney told himself, ready to love all things in a land that had brought the smiles back to his wife's pale lips, and a delicate bloom to her wan cheeks. Yes, she was happier than she had been of late in Cornwall. He saw and rejoiced in the change.

They stayed at a hotel for more than a week, while they deliberated upon the choice of a villa. They found one at last, which seemed to realize their ideas of perfection. It was not a grand or stately dwelling. No marble bell-tower or architectural loggia attracted the eye of the passing pedestrian. It was roomy, and bright, and clean, and airy, built rather in the Swiss than the Italian style, and it stood upon the slope of the hill on the west side of the town, with nothing but olive-woods between its terraced garden and the road that skirted the sea. It was a reminiscence of the Alps, built by a retired merchant of Zurich, and its owner had called it Lauter Brunnen. The house was at most two years old; but life's vicissitudes had left it empty for a year and a half, and the rent asked of Colonel Disney was much less than he had been prepared to pay.

The installation was full of delight for Isola and her sister-in-law. The house afforded innumerable surprises, unexpected nooks and corners of all kinds. There were lovely views from every window—east, west, north, or south—and there was a garden full of roses, a garden made upon so steep a slope that it was a succession of terraces, with but little intervening level ground, and below the lowest terrace the valley stretched down to the sea, a tangle of gnarled old olive trees, wan and silvery, with a ruined gateway just seen among the foliage at the bottom of a dim grey glade.

To the right, straggling along the edge of the wooded hill, appeared the white houses and churches, cupola, pinnacle, and dome of Colla, so scattered as to seem two towns rather than one, and with picturesque suggestions of architectural splendour that were hardly borne out by the reality, when one climbed those rugged mule-paths, and crossed the romantic gorge above the waterfall, and then upward and upward to the narrow alleys and crumbling archways, and the spacious old church with its lofty doorway standing high above the stony street.

---

Only a few paces from Colonel Disney's villa there was a stately house that had gone to ruin. The roof was off in some places; there were neither floors nor windows left; and the walls were open to the wind and rain—frescoed walls, upon which might be traced figures of saint and martyr, angel and madonna. There was a spacious garden, with an avenue of cypresses—a garden where the flowers had been growing wild for years, and where Isola and Allegra wandered and explored as they pleased. It was higher on the hillside than their own villa, and from the eastward edge of this garden they looked—across a yawning gulf in which lay all the lower town of

San Remo—to the Sanctuary and the Leper Hospital, conspicuous on the crest of the opposite hill.

The need for Citadel and Sanctuary had passed with the fiercer age in which they were built. Neither Saracen nor pirate menaced San Remo nowadays; but the old white walls made a picturesque note in the landscape, and the very name of Sanctuary had a romantic sound.

The first week in the new house was like a week in fairyland. The weather was peerless—a climate that makes people forget there is such a season as winter in the world—and the two girls wandered about in the olive woods and climbed the mule-paths all through the fresh balmy hours or in the hottest noontides sat in the deserted garden or in a sheltered corner near an old stone well—one of those wells which suggest the meeting of Isaac and Rebecca—and Allegra painted while Isola read to her, in the low sweet voice which lent new and individual music to the sweetest verse of her favourites, Byron, Keats, and Shelley.

In these sequestered spots, where only a peasant woman laden with a basket of olives, or a padre, going from Colla to San Remo, ever passed within sight of them, they read the Eve of St. Agnes and the Pot of Basil—the Prisoner of Chillon, Manfred, and all those familiar lyrics and favourite passages of Shelley which Isola held in her heart of hearts. The wonder-dream of Alastor—the passionate lament of Adonaïs, could not seem purer or more spiritual than the life of these young women in those calm days through which January slipped into February, unawares, like a link in a golden chain—a chain of sunshine and flowers.

In February came the Carnival; and pretty little rustic San Remo decked itself with bunting and greenery, and made believe to hold a Battle of Flowers, which had a certain village simplicity as compared with the serried ranks of carriages, the fashion, and beauty, and wealth of floral displays, along the Promenade des Anglais or the Croisette. With the Carnival came the mistral, which generally seems to be waiting round the corner ready to leap out upon the flower-throwers, to blight their bouquets, and blow dust into the eyes of beauty, and make the feeble health-seekers cower in the corners of their rose-decked carriages. This Lenten season was no exception to other seasons; and the calendar—which had been as it were in abeyance since New Year's Day—came into force again—and stern and sterile Winter said, "Here am I. Did you think I had forgotten you?" The invalids were roughly awakened from their dream of Paradise, to discover that February even in San Remo meant February, and could not always be mistaken for May or June.

Isola felt the change, though she was hardly conscious of it on the day of the floral battle, when she was sitting in a roomy landau, covered with the dark shining foliage and pale yellow fruit from some of those lemon trees in the orchard where she and Allegra had spent their morning hours. Allegra had planned the decorations, and had gone down to the coach-house to assist in the work, delighted to chatter with the coachman in doubtful Italian, groping her way in a language in which her whole stock-in-trade consisted of a few quotations from Dante or Petrarch—and all the wise saws of Dr. Riccabocca.

"I would have none of that horrid pepper tree which pervades the place with its floppy foliage, and dull red fruit," she told Isola, descanting on the result of her exertions. "I was rather taken with the pepper trees at first, but I am satiated with their languid grace. They are like the weeping ash or the weeping willow. There is no real beauty in them. I would rather have one of those cypresses towering up among the grey-green olives in the valley below Colla than all the pepper trees in the public gardens. I have used no flowers but narcissus; no colour but the pale gold of the lemons and the dark green of the leaves; except one bit of audacity which you will see presently."

This was at noon, after two hours' work in the coach-house. An hour later the carriage was at the door.

Allegra's audacity was an Algerian curtain, a rainbow of vivid colour, with which she had draped the back of the landau, hiding all the ugliness of rusty leather. The carriage, or it might have been the two girlish faces in it, one so pale and gentle, the other so brilliant and changeful in its lights and shadows, made the point of attraction in the little procession. Everybody spoke of the two girls in the lemon landau, with the nice-looking, middle-aged man. Were they his daughters, people wondered, or his nieces; and at what hotel were they staying? It was a disappointment to discover that they were living in that villa to the west of the town, out of the way of everything and everybody, and that they were seldom to be seen in public, except at the new church, where they were regular worshippers.

"The man is Colonel Disney, and the tall, striking-looking girl is his wife," said one person better informed than the rest, but making a wrong selection all the same.

CHAPTER XX.

"THOU PARADISE OF EXILES, ITALY."

Isola was not quite so well after that drive in the February wind and dust. She developed a slight cough—very slight and inoffensive; but still it was a cough—and the kind and clever physician of San Remo, who came to see her once a week or so, told her to be careful. Mr. Baynham had written him a long letter about his patient, and the San Remo doctor felt a friendly interest in Isola and her sister-in-law, and the baby son in whom the whole family were so intensely interested. The infant had accepted the change in his surroundings with supreme complaisance, and crowed and chirruped among the lemons and the olives, and basked in the Southern sunshine, as his nurse wheeled his perambulator to and fro upon the terraced road behind the villa—the road which lost itself a little way further on amidst a wilderness of olives, and dwindled into a narrow track for man or mule.

The flower-battle was over, and the mistral had gone back to the great wind-cavern to lie in wait for the next golden opportunity; and the sun was shining once again upon the hills where the oil mills nestled, clinging to some rough ledge beside the ever-dropping waters, upon the labyrinthine lanes and alleys, the queer little flights of stone steps up which a figure like Ali Baba might generally be seen leading his heavily-laden, long-suffering donkey; upon arch and cupola, church and market-place, and on the triple rampart of hills that shuts San Remo from the outer world. The Disneys had been in Italy nearly seven weeks, and it seemed as natural to Isola to open her eyes upon the broad blue waters of the Mediterranean, the gorgeous sunrise, and the lateen sails, as on the Fowey river and the hills towards Polruan. She had taken kindly to this Italian exile. The sun and the blue sky had exercised a healing influence upon that hidden wound which had once made her heart seem one dull, aching pain. She loved this new world of wood and hill, and most of all she loved the perfect liberty of this distant retreat, and the consolations of solitude. As for the cough, or the pain in her side, or any of those other symptoms about which the doctor talked to her so gravely, she made very light of them. She was happy in her husband's love, happy in his society, strolling with him in the olive wood, or the deserted garden, or down to the little toy-shop parade by the sea, where the band played once a week; or to the other garden in the town, where the same band performed on another day, and which was dustier and less airy than the little plantation of palm and cactus upon the edge of the sea. She went for excursions with him to points of especial beauty high up among the hills—to the chocolate mill, to San Romolo, she riding a donkey, he at the animal's side, while the guide trudged cheerily in the dust at the edge of the mountain road. In the evening she played to him, or sat by his side while he smoked the pipe of rest, or worked while he read to her. They had never been more devoted to each other, never more like wedded lovers than they were now. People who only knew them by sight talked of them admiringly, as if their love were an interesting phenomenon.

"He must be twenty years older than his wife," said Society, "and yet they seem so happy together. It is quite refreshing to see such a devoted couple nowadays."

People always seem ready and rather pleased to hold their own age up to contempt and ridicule, as if they themselves did not belong to it; as if they were sitting aloft in a balloon, looking down at the foolish creatures crawling and crowding upon the earth, in a spirit of philosophical contemplation.

Only one anxiety troubled Isola at this time, and that was on Allegra's account rather than her own. They had left England nearly two months, and as yet there had been no sign or token of any kind from Captain Hulbert, not so much as a packet of new books or new music—not so much as a magazine or an illustrated paper.

"He asked if he might write to me, and I told him no," Allegra said, rather dolefully, one morning, as they sat a little way from the well, Allegra engaged in painting a brown-skinned peasant girl of ten years old, whom she had met carrying olives the night before, and had forthwith engaged as a model. "I said it would never do for us to begin the folly of engaged lovers, who write to each other about nothing, sometimes twice a day. He has been wonderfully obedient: yet I think he ought to have written once or twice in two months. He ought to have known that though I told him not to write, I should be very anxious to hear from him."

"You mustn't be surprised at his obeying you to the letter, Allegra. There is a kind of simplicity about him, although he is very clever. He is so thoroughly frank and honest. It is for that I honour him."

"Yes, he is very good," sighed Allegra. "I ought not to have told him I would have no letter-writing. I really meant what I said. I wanted to give myself up to art, and you, for the unbroken year—to have no other thought, no distractions—and I knew that his letters would be a distraction—that the mere expectation of them—the looking for post time—the wondering whether I should have his letter by this or that post—I knew all that kind of thing would unnerve me. My hand would have lost its power. You don't know what it is when all depends upon certainty of touch—the fine obedience of the hand to the eye. No, his letters would have been a daily agitation—and yet, and yet I should like so much to know what he is doing—if he is still at the Mount—if he has any idea of coming to San Remo later—with his yacht—as he talked of doing."

"I have no doubt he will come. It will be the most natural thing for him to do. You will see the white sails some afternoon, glorified in the sunset, like that boat yonder with its amethyst-coloured sail."

Isola was right in her prophecy, except as to the hour of Captain Hulbert's arrival. They were taking a picnic luncheon in a little grove of lemon and orange, wedged into a cleft in the hills, on the edge of a deep and narrow gorge down which a mountain torrent rushed to the sea. Suddenly across the narrow strip of blue at the end of the vista came the vision of white sails, a schooner with all her canvas spread, dazzling in the noonday sun, sailing towards San Remo. Allegra sat gazing at the white sails, but said never a word. Neither Martin Disney nor his wife happened to be looking that way, till the child in his nurse's lap gave a sudden crow of delight.

"Did he see the pretty white ship, then?" said the nurse, holding him up in the sunshine. "The beautiful white ship."

No one took any notice. The colonel was reading his *Times*, the chief link between the exile and civilization. Isola was intent upon knitting a soft white vestment for her firstborn.

Two hours later the garden gate gave a little click, and Captain Hulbert walked in. Allegra heard the click of the latch as she sat in the verandah, and ran out to meet him. She had been watching and expectant all the time, though she had held her peace about the vision of white sails, lest she should be suspected of hoping for her lover's coming, and, above all, lest she should be compassionated with later in the day, if the ship were not the *Vendetta*.

Yes, it was he. She turned pale with delight at the realization of her hope. She had hardly known till this instant how much she loved him. She let him take her in his arms and kiss her, just as if he had been the commonest sailor whose "heart was true to Poll."

"Are you really glad to see me, darling?" he whispered, overcome by the delight of this fond welcome.

"Really glad. I feel as if we had been parted for years. No letter to tell me where you were or what you were doing! I began to doubt if you ever cared for me."

"Heartless infidel, you told me not to write; and so I thought the only alternative was to come. And I have been coming for the last five weeks. We had a stiffish time across the bay—nothing to trust to but canvas; and I had to waste a week at Toulon while my ship was under repairs. However, here I am, and the *Vendetta* is safe and sound; and I am your most obedient slave. How is Mrs. Disney?"

"Not quite so well as she was two or three weeks ago. She improved wonderfully at first, but she caught cold one bleak, blowy day, and she has started a little nervous kind of cough, which makes us anxious about her."

"Better spirits, I hope. Not quite so mopy?"

"Her spirits have revived wonderfully. This lovely land has given her a new life. But there are times when she droops a little. She is curiously sensitive—too impressionable for happiness. We have a very fine preacher here—Father Rodwell; you must have heard him."

"Yes, I heard of him at Oxford. He was before my time by some years; but he was a celebrity, and I heard men talk of him. Well, what of your preacher? Has he fallen in love with my Allegra—is he in the same boat as poor Colfox?"

"Fallen in love! No, he is not that kind of man. He is as earnest and enthusiastic as a mediæval monk. We have all been carried away by his eloquence. He preaches what people call awakening sermons; and I fear they have been too agitating for Isola. She insists on hearing him; she hangs upon his words; but his preaching has too strong an influence upon her mind—or upon her nerves. I have seen the tears streaming down her poor pale cheeks; I have seen her terribly overcome. She is too weak to bear that kind of strain. She is depressed all the rest of the day."

"She ought not to be allowed to hear such sermons. Take her to another church, where some dozy old bird will send her comfortably to sleep."

"I have tried to take her to the other church—you must not talk of a clergyman as a dozy old bird, sir—but she looked so unhappy at the mere idea of missing Father Rodwell's sermons that I dare not press the matter. He comes to see us occasionally, and he is the cheeriest and pleasantest of men, nothing of the zealot or ascetic about him; so that I am in hopes his influence will be for good in the long run. How long shall you be able to stop at San Remo?"

"Till the lady for whose sake I came shall take it into her head to leave the place. I have been thinking, Allegra," putting his arm through hers, and pacing up and down the terrace, with the bright expanse of sea in front of them, and at their back the great curtain of hills encircling and defending them from the wintry world—"I have been thinking that Venice would be a charming place for you and me to spend next summer in—if—if—you meant six months instead of twelve for my probation—as I really think you must have done. We could be married on the first of June—such a pretty date for a wedding! So easy to remember! You would want to be married in Trelasco Church, of course; on our native soil. The church in which my great-grandfather was married, and in which I and all my race were christened! We could have the yacht at Marseilles ready to carry us off on our travels, through the delicious summer days and nights, all along this lovely coast, and away by Naples to the

Adriatic. Allegra, why should we wait for the winter, the dreary winter, to begin our life journey? Let us begin it in the time of roses."

"Look, John!" cried Allegra, laughing, as she pointed to the hedge of red roses in front of them, and the clusters of creamy bloom hanging over the verandah. "The roses have been blooming ever since we came to Italy. It is always rose-time here. You remember our reading in the dedication of 'To Leeward' how Marion Crawford strewed his wife's pathway with roses on Christmas Day at Sorrento. We can find a flowery land for our honeymoon at any season of the year."

"But why wait a year? Can you not prove me trusty and true in less than a year?"

"You are so impatient," she said, plucking a handful of roses, and scattering the petals at her feet. "A year is so short a time."

"Short, love! why, eight weeks have seemed an eternity to me without you; and you honoured me just now by saying that the time had appeared long, even to you—even to my liege lady, sitting serene in her palace of art, painting contadinas and their olive-faced offspring—even to you, whose love is as a thread of silk against a cable, compared to mine. Even to you, my mistress and my tyrant."

"That was because you were so far away. But there will be nothing to hinder our seeing each other, as often as you may find convenient. I have set my heart upon painting steadily for a twelvemonth, without any distractions."

"There is no such place as Venice for a painter. Think of the Miss Montalbas, and the splendid work they have done at Venice. Would you not like to be like them?"

"Would I not like to be like Apelles?"

"Well, Venice will be your treasury; Venice will fill that busy brain with ideas. You shall be fed upon pictures old and new—the new living pictures in the narrow streets and canals; the old masters in the churches and palaces. You shall learn of Tintoret and Veronese. You shall paint as much as you like. You shall have no distractions. We shall be strangers there, can live as we choose. Summer is the time for Venice, Allegra. Benighted English people have an idea that Italy is a place to winter in, and they go and shiver in marble palaces, and watch the torrential rain beating against windows that were never meant to shut out bad weather. The Italians know that their land is a land of summer, and they know how to enjoy sunny days and balmy nights. You don't know how delicious life is on the Lido when the night is only a brief interval of starshine betwixt sunset and dawn. You don't know what a dream of delight it is to float along the lagoons and watch the lamp-lit city melt into the mists of evening, breathing faint echoes of music and song. A great many things of beauty have been turned to ugliness, Allegra, since printing and the steam engine were invented; but, thank God! Venice is not one of them. You will think of my plan, won't you, love? At the least, it is a thing to be considered."

"Anything you say is worthy to be considered, John. And now come in and see Isola and Martin."

He felt that he had gone far enough—he felt that it were unwise to press the question too much at first. He meant to be gently persistent; and he meant to have his own way.

He followed Allegra into the drawing-room—a room full of light and sunshine, which had been beautified and made home-like by the addition of a few Japaneseries and a little old Italian furniture which Martin Disney had picked up at a bric-à-brac shop in the Via Vittorio Emanuelo. There were flowers everywhere, in the bright Italian pottery, so artless, so cheap, so gay, in its varieties of form and colouring. To Hulbert's fancy it was the prettiest room he had seen for an age.

"You seem to have made yourself uncommonly comfortable here," he said, after cordial greetings, settling down into a bamboo chair near Isola's little olive-wood table, littered with Tauchnitz novels and fancy work. "It is a pleasant sensation for a rolling stone who has hardly ever known what home means to drop into such a nest as this. You will have too much of my company, I'm afraid. You'll be shocked to hear that I have taken rooms at the Anglais, down there," pointing down the valley, "within a stone's throw of you."

"We are not shocked. We are very glad you will be near us," said Isola, smiling at him. "It has been a dull life for Allegra, I'm afraid."

"Dull! dull in this land of beauty!" cried Allegra. "I have never known a dull hour since I came here; though, of course," with a shy glance at her lover, "I have naturally thought sometimes of absent friends, and wished they were with me to revel in the loveliness of these woods and hills."

"Well, one of your friends has come to you, one who would as gladly have come had you been in regions where the sun never shines, or where his chariot wheels scorch the torrid sands."

Captain Hulbert stayed with them all the evening, and planned a sail to Mentone for the following day, Isola again begging to be left out of their plans, as she had done at Fowey.

"You need feel no compunction about leaving me," she paid. "I shall be perfectly happy in the woods with nurse, and baby, and my books."

They obeyed her, and the little excursion was arranged. They were to start soon after the early breakfast, carrying what their Italian cook called a pique-nique with them, in the shape of a well-provided luncheon-basket. Isola sat in the olive wood, watching the white sails moving slowly towards Bordighera. It was an exquisite day—a day for dreaming on the water rather than for rapid progress. The yacht scarcely seemed to move as Isola watched her from the cushioned corner which Löttchen had arranged in an angle of the low stone wall—all amongst ferns and mosses, brown orchises and blue violets—an angle sheltered by a century-old olive, whose gnarled trunk sprawled along the ground, rugged and riven, but with another century's life in it yet. Far down in the valley, below the old gateway, a company of cypresses rose dark against the blue of the sea, and Isola knew that just on that slope of the shore where the cypresses grew tallest the graves of English exiles were gathered. Many a fair hope, many a broken dream, many a disappointed ambition lay at rest under those dark spires, within the sound of that summer sea.

This was one of many days which the young mother spent in the woods or in the garden with her baby for her companion, while Allegra and the colonel sailed east or west in the *Vendetta*. Her doctor would have liked her to go with them, but she seemed to have an absolute aversion to the sea, and he did not press the point.

"Nothing that she dislikes will do her any good," he told Colonel Disney. "There is no use in being persistent about anything. Fancies and whims stand for a great deal in such an illness as hers."

A week or two later the same kind doctor discovered that his patient was fast losing ground. Her strength had flagged considerably in a short time. He recommended change of scene.

"This quiet life suited her wonderfully well for the first month or so, but we are no longer making any headway. You had better try a gayer place—a little more life and movement."

Martin Disney was ready to obey. He and Allegra took counsel together, and then—in the lightest strain, one evening after dinner— they discussed the notion of a change.

"Shall we strike our tents, Isola? Are you tired of San Remo?"

"No, Martin. I am tired of myself, sometimes—never of these olive woods and lemon groves. Sometimes the stillness and the silent beauty of the place make me feel unhappy, without knowing why; but that is a kind of unhappiness no one can escape."

"Is there any place in the world within tolerable easy reach of this that you would like to see?" asked her husband.

"Yes, there is one city in the world that I have been longing to see ever since I began to have thoughts and wishes."

"And that is ——"

"Rome! I should like to see Rome before I die, Martin; if it were not too troublesome for you ——"

"Troublesome! My dearest, can anything be troublesome to me if it can but give you pleasure? You shall see Rome—not once—but again and again, in the course of a long and happy life, I hope. I am more than twenty years older than you; but I count upon at least thirty years more upon this planet, before I blow out my candle and say 'Bon soir.'"

"God grant that you may live to a good old age, Martin. The world is better for such a man as you."

"The world would be no place for me without my wife," he said. "And so you would like to see Rome, Isa? What has put that fancy into your head?"

"Oh, it is an old dream, as I said just now. And lately I have been talking to Father Rodwell, who knows Rome as well as if he were a Roman citizen, and he has made me more and more anxious to go there. If it would not be a great plague to you, Martin."

"On the contrary, it would be a great pleasure. We will go to Rome, Isa, if your doctor approve. Allegra will like it, I know."

"Like it?" echoed Allegra, "I shall simply be intoxicated with delight. I know the catalogues of all the picture-galleries by heart. I think I know every one of the seven hills as well as if I had walked upon them from my childhood. I have read so many descriptions of the place and its surroundings—so many raptures penned by people whom I have envied for nothing else than that they have known Rome; they have lived in Rome."

The whole business was easily settled. Captain Hulbert was the only person who regretted the change. He had been a month at San Remo, a month of summer idleness in February and March, a month of summer sails on an azure sea; of mountain walks and rides, high up from stage to stage, until the region of lemon groves and olive woods gave place to the pines on the loftier hills. He had been able to spend all his days in Allegra's society.

There were no pictures, except in that one little gallery at Colla. There was nothing to distract her from her lover. In Rome there would be all the wonders of the most wonderful city in the world. It would be art first and love second.

The doctor approved; Father Rodwell wrote to an agent in Rome, and after some negotiation a suite of apartments was found on the high ground near the Trinità de' Monti, which seemed to meet all the requirements of the case. The priest vouched for the honesty and good faith of the agent, and on his responsibility the rooms were taken for the month of April, with liberty to occupy them later if it were so desired.

## CHAPTER XXI.

### "THE WOODS ARE ROUND US, HEAPED AND DIM."

It was their last day at San Remo. Everything had been packed for the journey, and the drawing-room at Lauter Brunnen had a dreary look now that it was stripped of all those decorations and useful prettinesses with which Allegra had made it so gay and home-like.

The morning was brilliant, and Martin, Allegra, and Captain Hulbert set off at nine o'clock upon a long-deferred expedition to San Romolo. They would be home in good time for the eight-o'clock dinner; and Isola promised to amuse herself all day, and to be in good spirits to welcome them on their return.

"You have a duty to do for your sister," she said, when her husband felt compunction at leaving her. "Think of all she has done for us, her devotion, her unselfishness. The least we can do is to help her to be happy with her lover; and all the burden of that duty has fallen upon you. I think you ought to be called Colonel Gooseberry."

She looked a bright and happy creature as she stood on the mule-path in the olive wood, waving her hand to them as they went away—Allegra riding a donkey, the two men walking, one on each side of her bridle, and the guide striding on ahead, leading a second donkey which was to serve as an occasional help by-and-by, if either of the pedestrians wanted a lift. Her cheeks were flushed with walking, and her eyes were bright with a new gladness.

She was full of a childish pleasure in the idea of their journey, and the realization of a dream which most of us have dreamt a long time before it assumed the shape of earthly things—the dream of Rome.

Isola stood listening to their footsteps, as they passed the little painted shrine on the hill path. She heard them give the time of day to a party of peasant women, with empty baskets on their heads, going up to gather the last of the olives. Then she roamed about the wooded valley and the slope of the hill towards Colla for an hour or two, and then, growing suddenly tired, she crept home, in time to sit beside her baby while he slept his placid noontide sleep. She bent over the little rosebud mouth and kissed it, in a rapture of maternal love.

"So young to see Rome," she murmured. "And to think that those star-like eyes will see and take no heed; to think that such a glorious vision will pass before him, and he will remember nothing."

The day was very long, something like one of those endless days at Trelasco, when her husband was in Burmah and she had only the dog and the cat for her companions. She thought of those fond friends to-day with a regretful sigh—the sleepy Shah, so calm and undemonstrative in his attachment, but with a placid, purring delight in her society which seemed to mean a great deal; the fox-terrier, so active and intense in his affection, demanding so much attention, intruding himself upon her walks and reveries with such eager, not-to-be-denied devotion. She had no four-footed friends here; and the want of them made an empty space in her life.

In the afternoon the weather changed suddenly. The sky became overcast, the sea a leaden colour; and the mistral came whistling up the valley with a great rustling and shivering of the silver-green foliage and creaking of the old bent branches, like the withered arms of witch or sorceress. All the glory of the day was gone, and the white villas on the crest of the eastward hill stood out in livid distinctness against the blackened sky.

Isola wandered up the hill-path, past the little shrine where the way divided, the point at which she had seen her husband and his party vanish in the sunny morning. She felt a sudden sense of loneliness now the sun was gone; a childish longing for the return of her friends, for evening and lamplight, and the things that make for cheerfulness. She was cold and dull, and out of spirits. She had left the house while the sun was shining, and she had come without shawl or wrap of any kind, and the mistral made her shiver. Yet she had no idea of hurrying home. The loneliness of the house had become oppressive before she left it; and she knew there would be some hours to wait for the return of the excursionists. So she mounted the steep mule-path, slowly and painfully, till she had gone two-thirds of the way to Colla; and then she sat down to rest on the low stone wall which enclosed a little garden in a break of the wood, from which point there was a far-stretching view seaward.

She was very cold, but she was so tired as to be glad to rest at any hazard of after-suffering. Drowsy from sheer exhaustion, she leant her head against a great rugged olive, whose roots were mixed up with the wall, and fell fast asleep. She awoke, shivering, from a confused dream of sea and woods, Roman temples and ruined palaces. She had been wandering in one of those dream-cities that have neither limit nor settled locality. It was here in the woods below Colla, and yet was half Rome and half Trelasco. There was a classic temple upon a hill that was like the Mount, and the day was bleak, and dark, and rainy, and she was walking on the footpath through Lord Lostwithiel's park, with the storm-driven rain beating against her face, just as on that autumn evening, when the owner of the soil had taken compassion upon her and had given her shelter. The dream had been curiously vivid—a dream which brought the past back as if it were the present, and blotted out all that had come afterwards. She woke bewildered, forgetting that her husband had come back from India, and that she was in Italy, thinking of herself as she had been that October evening when she and Lostwithiel met for the first time.

The sea was darker than when she fell asleep. There was the dull crimson of a stormy sunset yonder, behind the jutting promontory of Bordighera, while the sky above was barred with long, black clouds, and the wind was howling across the great deep valley like an evil spirit tortured and imprisoned, shrieking to his gods for release. Exactly opposite her, as she stood in the deep cleft of the hills, a solitary vessel was labouring under press of canvas towards the point upon whose dusky summit the chapel of the Madonna della Guardia gleamed whitely in the dying day. The vessel was a schooner yacht, of considerable tonnage, certainly larger than the *Vendetta*.

Isola stood, still as marble, watching that labouring boat, the straining sails, the dark hull beaten by the stormy dash of the waves. She watched with wide, open eyes, and parted lips, quivering as with an over-mastering fear, watched in momentary expectation of seeing those straining sails dip for the last time, that labouring hull founder and vanish betwixt black wave and white surf. She watched in motionless attention till the boat disappeared behind the shoulder of the hill; and then, shivering, nervous, and altogether over-strung, she hurried homewards, feeling that she had stayed out much too long, and that she had caught a chill which might be the cause of new trouble.

If those narrow mule-paths had been less familiar, she might have lost her way in the dusk; but she had trodden them too often to be in any difficulty, and she reached the villa without loss of time, but not before the return of the picnic party.

Allegra and Captain Hulbert were watching at the gate. Colonel Disney had gone into the wood to look for her, and had naturally taken the wrong direction.

"Oh, Isola; how could you stop out so late, and on such a stormy evening?" remonstrated Allegra.

"I fell asleep before the storm came on."

"Fell asleep—out-of-doors—and at sunset! What dreadful imprudence."

"I went out too late, I'm afraid; but I was so tired of waiting for you. A kind of horror of the house and the silence came upon me—and I felt I must go out into the woods. I walked too far—and fell asleep from sheer fatigue; and when I woke I saw a yacht fighting with the wind. I'm afraid she'll go down."

"What, you noticed her too?" exclaimed Hulbert. "I didn't think you cared enough about yachts to take notice of her. I was watching her as we came down the hill; rather too much canvas; but she's right enough. She's past Arma di Taggia by this time, I dare say. I'll go and look for Disney, and tell him you're safe and sound. Perhaps I shall miss him in the wood. It's like a Midsummer Night's Dream, isn't it, Allegra?" he said, laughing, as he went out of the gate.

"If it were only mid-summer, I shouldn't care," answered his sweetheart, with her arm round Isola, who stood beside her, pale and shivering. "Come in, dear, and let me make you warm, if I can."

"If they should all go down in the darkness!" said Isola, in a low, dreamy voice. "The boat looked as if it might be wrecked at any moment."

Allegra employed all her arts as a sick-nurse in the endeavour to ward off any evil consequence from that imprudent slumber in the chill hour of sunset; but her cares were unavailing. Isola was restless and feverish all night, yet she insisted on getting up at her usual hour next morning, and declared herself quite capable of the journey to Genoa. Allegra and her brother, however, insisted on her resting for a day or two. So the departure was postponed, and the doctor sent for. He advised at least three days' rest, with careful nursing; and he reproved his patient severely for her imprudence in exposing herself to the evening air.

Captain Hulbert appeared at teatime, just returned from a railway journey to Allassio.

"I've a surprise for you, Mrs. Disney," he said, seating himself by the sofa where Isola was lying, surrounded by invalid luxuries, books, lemonade, fan, and eau de Cologne flask, her feet covered with a silken rug.

"A surprise!" she echoed faintly, as if life held no surprises for her. "What can that be?"

"You remember the yacht you saw last night?"

"Yes," she cried, roused in an instant, and clasping her hands excitedly. "Did she go down?"

"Not the least little bit. She is safe and sound at Allassio. She is called the *Eurydice*, she hails last from Syracuse, and my brother is on board her. He wired to me this morning to go over and see him. I'm very glad I went, for he is off to Corfu to-morrow. The *Flying Dutchman* isn't in it with him."

There was a curious silence. Martin Disney was sitting on the other side of his wife's sofa, where he had been reading selected bits of the *Times*, such portions of the news of men and nations as he fancied might interest her. Allegra was busy with a piece of delicate needlework, and did not immediately reply; but it was she who was first to speak.

"How frightened you would have been yesterday evening had you known who was on board the boat," she said.

237

"I don't know about being frightened, but he was certainly carrying too much canvas. I told him so this morning."

"What did he say?"

"Laughed at me. 'You sailors never believe that a landsman can sail a ship,' he said. I wanted to talk to his sailing-master, but he told me he was his own sailing-master. If his ship was doomed to go down, he meant to be at the helm himself."

"That sounds as if he were foolhardy," said Allegra.

"I told him I did not like the rig of his boat, nor the name of his boat, and I reminded him how I saw the *Eurydice* off Portland with all her canvas spread the day she went down. I was with the Governor of the Prison, a naval man, who had been commander on my first ship, and we stood side by side on the cliff, and watched her as she went by. 'If this wind gets much stronger, that ship will go down,' said my old captain, 'unless they take in some of their canvas.' And a few hours later these poor fellows had all gone to the bottom. I asked Lostwithiel why he called his boat the *Eurydice*. 'Fancy,' he said; he had a fancy for the name. 'I've never forgotten the old lines we used to hammer out when we were boys,' he said—'Ah, miseram, Eurydicen! anima fugiente vocabat; Eurydicen toto referebant flumine ripæ.'"

"I don't think the name matters, if she is a good boat," said Allegra, with her calm common sense.

"Well, she is, and she isn't. She is a finer boat than the *Vendetta*; but I'd sooner handle the *Vendetta* in a storm. There are points about his new boat that I don't quite like. However, he had her built by one of the finest builders on the Clyde, and it will be hard if she goes wrong. He has given me the *Vendetta* as a wedding-present—in advance of the event—on condition that I sink her when I'm tired of her; and he said he hoped she'd be luckier to me than she had been to him."

Martin Disney sat silent by his wife's sofa. He could never hear Lord Lostwithiel's name without a touch of pain. His only objection to Hulbert as a brother-in-law was the thought that the two men were of the same race—that he must needs hear the hated name from time to time; and yet he believed his wife's avowal that she was pure and true. His hatred of the name came only from the recollection that she had been slandered by a man whom he despised. He looked at the wasted profile on the satin pillow, so wan, so transparent in its waxen pallor, the heavy eyelid drooping languidly, the faintly coloured lips drawn as if with pain—a broken lily. Was this the kind of woman to be suspected of evil—this fair and fragile creature, in whom the spiritual so predominated over the sensual? He hated himself for having been for a moment influenced by that underbred scoundrel at Glenaveril, for having been base enough to doubt his wife's purity.

He had pained and humiliated her, and now the stamp of death was on the face he adored, and before him lay the prospect of a life's remorse.

They left San Remo three days afterwards, Isola being pronounced able to bear the journey, though her cough had been considerably increased by that imprudent slumber in the wood. She was anxious to go; and doctor and husband gave way to her eagerness for new scenes.

"I am so tired of this place," she said piteously. "It is lovely; but it is a loveliness that makes me melancholy. I want to be in a great city where there are lots of people moving about. I have never lived in a city, but always in quiet places—beautiful, very beautiful, but so still—so still—so full of one's self and one's own thoughts."

## CHAPTER XXII.

## ECCO ROMA.

The agent had proved himself worthy of trust, and had chosen the lodging for Colonel Disney's family with taste and discretion. It was a first floor over a jeweller's shop in a short street behind the Piazza di Spagna, and under the Pincian Gardens. There were not too many stairs for Isola to ascend when she came in from her drive or walk. The gardens were close at hand, and all around there were trees and flowers, and an atmosphere of verdure and retirement in the midst of the great cosmopolitan city.

It was dark when the train came into the terminus; and Isola was weary and exhausted after the long hot journey from Pisa, the glare of the sun, and the suffocating clouds of dust, and the beautiful monotony of blue sea and sandy plains, long level wastes, where nothing grew but brushwood and osier, and stretches of marshy ground, with water pools shining here and there, like burnished steel, and distant islets dimly seen athwart a cloud of heat. Then evening closed in, and it was through a grey and formless world that they approached the city whose very name thrilled her.

The railway station was very much like any other great terminus; like Milan, like Genoa. There was the same close rank of omnibuses. There were the same blue blouses and civil, eager porters, far too few for the work to be done, rapacious but amiable, piling up the innumerable packages of the Italian traveller, loading themselves like so many human beasts of burden, and with no apparent limit to their capacity for carrying things. Two flys were packed with the miscellaneous luggage, nurse and baby, and then Isola was handed to her place in another, with Allegra by her side, and through the narrow streets of tall houses, under the dim strip of soft April night, she drove through the city of heroes and martyrs, saints and apostles, wicked emperors and holy women, the city of historical contrasts, of darkness and light, refinement and barbarism, of all things most unlike each other, from Nero to Paul, from Gregory the Great to the Borgias.

The glory and the beauty of Rome only began to dawn upon her next morning, in the vivid sunlight, when she climbed the steps of the Trinità de' Monti, and then with Allegra's arm to lean upon went slowly upward and again upward to the topmost terrace on the Pincian Hill, and stood leaning on the marble balustrade, and gazing across the city that lay steeped in sunshine at her feet—over palace and steeple, pinnacle and tower, to the rugged grandeur of Hadrian's Tomb, and to that great dome whose vastness makes all other temples seem puny and insignificant. This was her first view of the world's greatest church.

The air was clear and cool upon this height, although the city below showed dimly through a hazy veil of almost tropical heat. Everywhere there was the odour of summer flowers, the overpowering sweetness of lilies of the valley, and great branches of lilac, white and purple, brimming over in the baskets of the flower-sellers.

On such a morning as this one could understand how the Romans came to call April the joyous month, and to dedicate this season of sunshine and flowers to the Goddess of Beauty and Love.

Isola's face lighted up with a new gladness, a look of perfect absorption and self-forgetfulness, as she leant upon the balustrade, and gazed across that vast panorama, gazed and wondered, with eyes that seemed to grow larger in their delight.

"And is this really Rome?" she murmured softly.

"Yes, this is Rome," cried Allegra. "Isn't it lovely? Isn't it all you ever dreamt of or hoped for? And yet people have so maligned it—called it feverish, stuffy, disappointing, dirty! Why, the air is ether—inspiring, health-giving! April in Rome is as fresh as April in an English forest; only it is April with the warmth and flowers of June. I feel sure you will grow ever so much stronger after one little week in Rome."

"Yes, I know I shall be better here. I feel better already," said Isola, with a kind of feverish hopefulness. "It was so good of Martin to bring me. San Remo is always lovely—and I shall love it to the end of my life, because it was my first home in Italy—but I was beginning to be tired—not of the olive woods and the sea, but of the people we met, and the sameness of life. One day was so like another."

"It was monotonous, of course," agreed Allegra; "and being a little out of health, you would be bored by monotony sooner than Martin or I. It was such a pity you did not like the yacht. That made such a change for us. The very olive woods and the mountain villages seem new when one sees them from the water. I was never tired of looking at the hills between San Remo and Bordighera, or the promontory of Monaco, with its cathedral towers. It was a pleasure lost to you, dear; but it could not be helped, I suppose. Yet once upon a time you used to be so fond of the sea, when you and I went in our row-boat, tempting danger round by Neptune Point."

"I may have been stronger then," Isola faltered.

"Oh, forgive me, darling! What an inconsiderate wretch I am! But Rome will give you back your lost strength; and we shall round Neptune Point again, and feel the salt spray dashing over our heads as we go out into the great fierce Atlantic. I confess that sometimes, when that divine Mediterranean which we are never tired of worshipping has been lying in the sunshine like one vast floor of *lapis lazuli*, I have longed for something rougher and wilder—for such a sea as you and I have watched from the Rashleigh Mausoleum."

Colonel Disney and his wife and sister went about in a very leisurely way in their explorations. In the first place, he was anxious to avoid anything approaching fatigue for his wife; and in the second place it was only the beginning of April, and they were to be in Rome for at least a month; there was therefore no need for rushing hither and thither at the tourist pace, with guide-books in their hands, and anxious, heated countenances, perspiring through the streets, and suffering deadly chills in the churches. Allegra's first desire was naturally to see the picture-galleries, and to these she went for the most part alone, leaving Isola and her husband free to wander about as they pleased, upon a friendly equality of ignorance, knowing very little more than Childe Harold and Murray could teach them. Isola's Rome was Byron's Rome.

There was one spot she loved better than any other in the city of mighty memories. It was not hallowed by the blood of saint or hero, sage or martyr. It had no classical associations. He whose heart lay buried there under the shadow of the tribune's mighty monument, perished in the pride of manhood, in the freshness and glory of life; and that heart—so warm and generous to his fellow-men—had hardened itself against the God of saint and martyr, the God of Peter and Paul, Lawrence and Gregory, Benedict and Augustine. Yet for Isola there was no grave in Rome so fraught with spiritual thoughts as Shelley's grave, no sweeter memory associated with the eternal city than the memory of his wanderings and meditations amidst the ruined walls of the Baths of Caracalla, where his young genius drank in the poetry of the long past, and fed upon the story of the antique dead.

She came to Shelley's grave as often as she could steal away from the anxious companions of her drives and walks.

"I like to be alone now and then," she told her husband. "It rests me to sit by myself for an hour or two in this lovely place."

There was a coachman in the Piazza who was in the habit of driving Colonel Disney's family—an elderly man, sober, steady and attentive, with intelligence that made him almost as good as a guide. He was on the watch for his English clients every morning. They had but to appear on the Piazza, and he was in attendance, ready to take them to the utmost limit of a day's journey, if they liked. Were they in doubt where to go, he was always prompt with suggestions.

He would drive Isola to the door of the English cemetery, leave her there, and return at her bidding to take her home again. Disney knew she was safe when this veteran had her in charge. The man was well known in the Piazza, and of established character for honesty. She took a book or two in her light basket, buying a handful of flowers here and there from the women and children as she went along, till the books were hidden under roses and lilac. The custodian of the cemetery knew her, and admitted her without a word. He had watched her furtively once or twice, to see that she neither gathered the flowers nor tried to scratch her name upon the tombs. He had seen her sitting quietly by the slab which records Shelley's death—and the death of that faithful friend who was laid beside him, sixty years afterwards. Sixty years of loving, regretful memory, and then union in the dust. Shall there not be a later and a better meeting, when those two shall see each other's faces and hear each other's voices again, in a world where old things shall be made new, where youth and its wild freshness shall come back again, and Trelawney shall be as young in thought and feeling as Shelley?

The English burial-place was a garden of fairest flowers at this season—a paradise of roses and clematis, azaleas and camelias—and much more beautiful for its wilder growth of trailing foliage and untended shrubs, the pale cold blue of the periwinkle that carpeted slope and bank, and for the background of old grey wall, severe in its antique magnificence, a cyclopean rampart, relic of time immemorial, clothed and beautified with weed and floweret that grew in every cleft and cranny.

Here, in a sheltered angle to the left of the poet's grave, Isola could sit unobserved, even when the custodian brought a party of tourists to see the hallowed spot, which occurred now and then while she sat there. The tourists for the most part stared foolishly, made some sentimental remark if they were women, or if they were men, betrayed a hopeless ignorance of the poet's history, and not unfrequently confounded him with Keats. Isola sat half-hidden in her leafy corner, where the ivy and the acanthus hung from the great grey buttress against which she leant, languid, half-dreaming, with two books on her lap.

One was her Shelley—her much-read Shelley—a shabby, cloth-bound volume, bought in her girlhood at the book-seller's in the Place Duguesclin, where English books could be got by special order, and at special prices. The other was an Italian Testament, which her husband had bought her at San Remo, and in which she had read with extreme diligence and with increasing fervour as her mind became more deeply moved by Father Rodwell's sermons. It was not that she had ever been one of those advanced thinkers who will accept no creed which does not square with their own little theories and fit in to their own narrow circle of possibilities. She had never doubted the creed she had been taught in her childhood, but she had thought very little about serious things, since she was a young girl, preparing for her confirmation, touched with girlish enthusiasm, and very much in earnest. In these fair spring days, and in this city of many memories, all young thoughts had reawakened in her mind. She pored over the familiar Gospel-stories, and again, as in the first freshness of her girlhood, she saw the sacred figure of the Redeemer and Teacher in all the vivid light and colour of a reality, close at hand. Faith stretched a hand across the abyss of time, and brought the old world of the Gospel-story close to her; the closer, because she was in Rome, not far from that church which enshrines the print of the Divine footstep, when He who was God and Man, appeared to His disciple, to foreshadow approaching martyrdom, to inspire the fortitude of the martyr. Yes, although the Saviour's earthly feet never entered the city, every hill and every valley within and without those crumbling walls has interwoven itself so closely with the story of His life—through the work of His saints and martyrs—that it is nowise strange if the scenes and images of the sacred story seem nearer and more vivid in Rome than in any other place on earth, not excepting Jerusalem. It was from Rome, not from Jerusalem, that the Cross went out to the uttermost ends of the world. It is the earth of the Colosseum and the Borgo that is steeped in the blood of those who have died for Christ. It was Rome that ruled the world, through the long night of barbarism and feudal power, by the invincible force of His name.

It might seem strange that Isola should turn from the story of the Evangelists to the works of a poet whose human sympathies were so wrung by the evil that has been wrought in the name of the Cross that he was blind to the infinitely greater good which Christianity has accomplished for mankind. Shelley saw the blood of the martyrs, not as a sublime testimony to the Godlike power of faith, not as a sacrifice rich in after-fruits, sad seed of a joyous harvest—but as the brutal outcome of man's cruelty, using any name, Christ, or Buddha, Mahomet, or Brahma—as the badge of tyranny, the sanction to torture and to slay.

Shelley's melancholy fate seemed brought nearer to her now that she sat beside his grave, in the summer stillness, and in the shadow of the old Aurelian Wall. It was only his heart that was lying there, the imperishable heart, snatched by Trelawney's hand from the flame of the Greek pyre, from the smoke of pine-logs and frankincense, wine and oil. Sixty years had passed before that hand lay cold in the grave beside the buried heart of the poet, sixty years of severance, and fond faithful memory, before death brought re-union.

What a beautiful spirit this, which was so early quenched by the cruelest stroke of Fate—a light such as seldom shone out of mortal clay, a spirit of fire and brightness, intangible, untamable, not to be shut within common limits, nor judged by common laws!

CHAPTER XXIII

"SEEK SHELTER IN THE SHADOW OF THE TOMB."

Of the people who came to look upon the grave, some to lay a tributary flower upon the stone, and some to pluck a leaf or two of acanthus or violet, all hitherto had been strangers to Isola, had gone away without seeing her, or had glanced indifferently, as at one more unfortunate with a sketching-block, spoiling paper in the pursuit of the unattainable. There were so many amateur artists sitting about in the outskirts of the city, that such a figure in a romantic spot challenged nobody's attention. So far people had come and gone, and had taken no notice; but one afternoon a figure in a long black cassock came suddenly between her and the golden light, and Isola looked up with a cry of surprise on recognizing Father Rodwell.

"You did not expect to see me here," he said, holding out his hand.

She had risen from her seat on the low grassy bank, and she gave him her hand, half in pleasure, half in a nervous apprehension which his keen eye was quick to perceive. His life had been spent in dealings with the souls of men and women, and he had learnt to read those living pages as easily as he read Plato or Spinosa.

"No," she said. "I had no idea you were in Rome. You told us you were going back to London."

"I meant to go back to London and hard work, but my doctor insisted upon my prolonging my holiday for a few weeks, so I came here instead. Rome always draws me, and is always new. Rome gives me fresh life and fresh power when my heart and brain have been feeling benumbed and dead. I am glad they brought you here, Mrs. Disney. You were looking languid and ill when you left San Remo. I hope Rome has revivified you."

He looked at her earnestly. Her face had been in shadow until now, but as she moved into the sunlight, he saw that the lines had sharpened in the pale, wan face, and that there was the stamp of wasting disease in the hollow cheeks, and about the sunken eyes, and in the almost bloodless lips. As he looked at her in friendliest commiseration those pathetic grey eyes—whose expression had baffled his power of interpretation hitherto—filled suddenly with tears, and in the next moment she clasped her hands before her face in an agony of grief.

The Italian Testament which she had been reading when he approached dropped at her feet, and stooping to pick it up Father Rodwell saw that it was open at the fourth chapter of St. John, the story of the woman of Samaria, the sinner with whom Christ talked at the well. A leaf from Shelley's grave lay upon the book, as if to mark where Isola had been reading, and Father Rodwell's quick glance saw that the page was blotted with tears.

"My dear Mrs. Disney," he said gently, "is there anything wrong at home? Your husband, your boy are well, I hope?"

"Yes, thank God, they are both well. God has been very good to me. He might have taken those I love. He has been merciful."

"He is merciful to all His creatures; though there are times when His dealings with us seem very hard. Oh, Mrs. Disney, you can't think how difficult a priest's office is sometimes when he has to reconcile the afflicted with the Providence that has seen fit to lay some heavy burden on them. They cannot understand; they cannot say it is well. They cannot kiss the rod. But as you say, God has been good to you. Your lines have been set in pleasant places. You are hedged round and sheltered by love. I never saw greater affection in husband for wife than I have seen in your husband. I never saw sister more devoted to sister than your sister-in-law is to you."

She had sunk again into a sitting position on the low bank at the foot of the wall. Her face was still hidden, and her sobs came faster as he spoke to her.

"Why should you grieve at the thought of their love? Is it because it may please God to take you from them in the morning of your life? If it is that dread which agitates you I entreat you to put it aside. There is nothing in your case that forbids hope, and hope will do much to help your recovery. You should tell yourself how valuable your life is to those who love you. The thought of their affection should give you courage to struggle against apathy and languor. Believe me, invalids have their condition a great deal more in their own power than they are inclined to believe. So much can be overcome where the spirit is strong and brave, where faith and hope fight against bodily weakness. You ought not to be sitting alone here in this saddening spot. It is lovely, but with the beauty of death. You ought to be driving out to Frascati or to Tivoli with your husband. You ought to be watching the carriages in the Pincian Gardens, or amusing yourself in one of the picture galleries."

"I had rather be alone," she said, wiping away her tears, and in some degree recovering her self-possession.

"That is a morbid fancy, and one that hinders your recovery."

"I have no wish to recover. I only want to die."

"My dear Mrs. Disney, it is your duty to fight against these melancholy moods. Can you be indifferent to your husband's feelings? Have you not the mother's natural desire to watch over your child's early years, to see him reach manhood?"

"No, no, no!" she cried passionately. "I have had enough of life. They are dear to me, very dear. No wife ever loved and honoured her husband more than I love and honour mine—but it is all over, it is past, and ended. I am more than resigned to death—I am thankful that God has called me away."

He watched her closely as she spoke, watched her with his hand upon hers, which was cold as ice. He had heard such words before from the early doomed, but they had been accompanied by religious exaltation; they had been the outpouring of a faith that saw the gates of heaven opened and the Son of man sitting in glory—of a love that longed to be with God. Here there was no sign of hope or exaltation. There were only the tokens of despair.

He remembered how agitated he had seen her many times in the little church at San Remo, and how, although hanging eagerly upon his preaching, she had persistently avoided anything like serious conversation with him upon the few occasions when he had found himself alone with her.

He had her Testament still in his hand, and looking down at the tear-stained page it seemed to him that there lay the clue to her melancholy.

"You have been reading the story of the woman of Samaria," he said.

"Yes."

"And you have read that other story of her who knelt in the dust at her Saviour's feet, and to whom He said, 'Neither do I condemn thee.'"

"Yes."

"Is there anything in either of those stories to sadden you more than the thought of sin and sorrow saddens all of us?"

She looked at him shrinkingly, pale as death, as if he had a dagger in his hand ready to strike her.

"No, I don't suppose there is anything that goes home to my heart any more than to other hearts," she said, after a pause, trying to speak carelessly. "We are all sinners. The Gospel teaches us that in every line! We are none of us altogether worthy—not even my husband, I suppose, although to me he seems a perfect Christian."

"I can believe that he is a Christian, Mrs. Disney, and a man of strong convictions. If he had wronged anybody, I do not think he would rest till he had atoned for that wrong."

"I am sure he would not. He would do his uttermost to atone. And so would I—although I do not pretend to be half so good a Christian as he is. I would do all in my power to atone for any wrong I had done to one I loved."

"As you love your husband, for instance."

"Yes, as I love him. He is first in the world for me. Dear as my child is, Martin must always be first."

"And you would not for the world do him any wrong?" pursued the priest, more and more earnest as he went on, pale with emotion, his whole power of observation concentrated upon the whitening face and lowered eyelids of the woman sitting at his feet.

"Not for the world, not for my life," she said, with her hands tightly clasped, her eyes still hidden under the heavy lids, tearless now—and with dry and quivering lips, from which the words came with a dull and soulless sound. "I would die to save him an hour's pain. I would fling away this wretched life rather than grieve him for a moment."

"Poor soul!" murmured the priest, pitying that debt of self-abasement which he understood so well, under whatsoever guise she might hide her contrition. "Poor soul, you talk too lightly of that great mystery which we should all face in a spirit of deep humility. Do you feel that you can contemplate that passage through death to a new life without fear of the issue? Have you no reckoning to make with the God who pardons repentant sinners? Do you stand before Him with a clear conscience—having kept nothing back—cherished no hidden sin?"

"No one can be without sin in His sight. Do you suppose that I am sinless, or that I have ever believed myself sinless? I know how weak and poor a thing I am—a worm in the sight of Him who rules the universe. But if—if He cares for such as I, He knows that I am sorry for every sinful thought and every sinful act of my life."

She spoke in short sentences, each phrase broken by a sob. She felt as if he were tearing out her heart, this man who had been heretofore so kindly and indulgent in his speech and manner that he seemed to make religion an easy thing, a garment as loose and expansive as philosophy itself. And, now, all at once he appeared before her as a judge, searching out her heart, cruel, inflexible, weighing her in the balance, and finding her wanting.

"If I am sorry," she murmured, between her sobs, "what more can God or man require of me?"

"Nothing, if your sorrow is that true sorrow which means repentance, and goes hand-in-hand with atonement. Forgive me, my dear friend, for presuming to speak unreservedly to you. If I try to find out the nature of your wound it is only that I may help you to heal it. Ever since I have known you I have seen the tokens of a wounded heart, a bruised and broken spirit. I saw you surrounded with all the blessings that make woman's lot happy. It was hardly possible to conceive fairer surroundings and truer friends. Can you wonder, then, if my compassionate interest was awakened by the indications of a deep-rooted sorrow for which there was no apparent cause? I saw your emotion in church, saw how quickly your heart and mind responded to the appeal of religion—saw in you a soul attuned to heavenly things, and day by day my interest in you and yours grew stronger. The hope of seeing you again, of helping you to bear your burden, of ultimately lightening it, was one of my reasons for coming to Rome. I felt somehow that you and I had not met in vain—that my power to move you was not without a meaning in both our lives; that if, as I thought, you needed spiritual help and comfort, it was my vocation to help and comfort you. And so I came to Rome, and so I found out where you spent your quiet hours, and so I have followed you here this afternoon. Tell me, Mrs. Disney, did I presume too much? Was it the preacher's vanity or the priest's intuition that spoke?"

"It was intuition," she said. "You saw that I had sinned. None but a sinner could shed such tears—could so feel the terror of God's wrath."

"It is of His love I want you to think. Of His immeasurable love and pity. Of His Son's Divine compassion. If you have any special need of His pardon; if there is any sinful secret locked in your heart; do not let the golden hours go by—the time meet for repentance."

"I have repented," she cried piteously. "My life has been one long repentance ever since my sin."

"And your husband—he who so fondly loves you—he knows all, and has forgiven all?"

"Knows!" The word broke from her lips almost in a shriek of horror. "He knows nothing—he must never know. He would despise me, leave me to die alone, while he went far away from me, to the very end of the world. He would take his son with him. I should be left alone—alone to face death—the most desolate creature God ever looked upon. Oh, Father Rodwell, why have you wrung my secret from me?" she cried, grovelling on her knees in the long grass beside him, clinging to his hand as he bent over her, gravely compassionate, deeply moved by her distress. "How cruel to question—to torture me—how cruel to use your power of reading guilty hearts. You will tell my husband, who so loves and trusts me. You will tell him what a guilty wretch I am."

"Tell him, Mrs. Disney! Can you forget that I am a priest—for whom the sinner's confession is sacred? Do you think I have never talked with the tempted and the sorrowing before to-day? Do you think that grief such as yours can be an unknown experience to a man who has worked in a crowded London parish for nearly twenty years? I wanted to know the worst, so that I might be able to advise and to console you. If I have questioned you to-day, it has been as a priest has the right to question; and this place where you and I have met to-day is in my sight as sacred as the confessional. You need have no fear that I shall tell your husband the secret of your sorrow. All I will do is to help you to find strength to tell him yourself."

"Oh no, no, no!" she cried piteously. "Never! never! I can die, I am prepared to die; but I can never tell him—I cannot, I dare not."

"Yet you could dare to die with a lie upon your lips—you who are ready to meet your Judge—you whose whole life is a lie—you who have cheated and betrayed the best of men. Oh, Mrs. Disney, reflect what this thing is which you are doing; reflect what kind of sin it is you are committing. If, as your own sorrowing words acknowledge, you have been a false wife—a false wife to the best and truest of husbands, can you dare to act out that falsehood to the last, to die with that guilty secret locked in your heart, from him who has a right to know,—and who alone upon earth has a right to pardon."

"Oh, how cruel you are!" she said, lifting up her streaming eyes to his earnest, inflexible face. "Is it a Christian's part to be so cruel, to break the bruised reed, to crush anything so weak and wretched as I am? Is not repentance enough? I have spent long nights in penitence and tears, long days in dull aching remorse. I would have given all my future life to atone for one dreadful hour—one unpremeditated yielding to temptation. I *have* given my life—for my secret has killed me. What more can man or God demand of me? What more can I do to win forgiveness?"

"Only this—tell your husband the truth—however painful, however humiliating the confession. That will be your best atonement. That is the sacrifice which will help to reconcile you with your God. You cannot hope for God's love and pardon hereafter, if you live and die as a hypocrite here. God's saints were some of them steeped in the

253

darkness of guilt before they became the children of light—but there was not one of them who shrank from the confession of his sins."

"You are a man," sobbed Isola. "You do not know what it is for a woman to confess that she is unworthy of her husband's love. You do not know. It is not possible for a man to know the meaning of shame."

"You are wrong there," he said, gently lifting her from the ground, and placing her beside him on the bank. "What chastity is to a woman, honour is to a man. Men have had to stand up before their fellow-men and acknowledge their violation of man's code of honour; knowing that such acknowledgment made them dirt, and very dirt, in the sight of honourable men. You, as a woman, know not how deep men's scorn cuts a man who has sinned against the law which governs gentlemen. A woman thinks there is no such sting as the sting of her shame. Men know better. Yes, I know that it will be most bitter, more bitter than death—for you to tell Colonel Disney that you are not what you have seemed to him; but apart from all considerations of duty, do not his love and devotion deserve the sacrifice of self-love on your part? Can you bear yourself to the last, as a virtuous wife—enjoying his respect—knowing that it is undeserved——"

"I will tell him—at the last," she faltered. "In that parting hour I shall not shrink from telling him all—how I sinned against him—almost unawares—drifting half unconsciously into a fatal entanglement—and then—and then—against my will—in my weakness and helplessness—alone in the power of the man I loved—betrayed into sin. Oh God! why do you make me remember?" she cried wildly, turning upon the priest in passionate reproachfulness. "For years I have been trying to forget—trying to blank out the past—praying, praying, praying that my humble, tearful love for my husband and my child might cancel those hours of sin. And you come to me, and question me, and on pretence of saving my soul, you force me to look back upon that bygone horror—to live again through that time of madness—the destruction of my life. Cruel, cruel, cruel!"

"Forgive me!" said Father Rodwell, very gently, seeing that she was struggling with hysteria. "I have been too hard, perhaps, too eager to convince you of the right! There are some men, even of my sacred calling, who would judge your case otherwise—who would say the husband is happy in his ignorance; the wife has repented of her sin. *Non quieta movere.* But it is not in my nature to choose the easy pathways; and it may be that I am too severe a teacher. We will not talk any more about serious things to-day. Only believe that I am your friend—your sincere and devoted friend. If I have spoken hard things, be assured I would have spoken in the same spirit had you been my own sister. Let us say no more yet awhile—and perhaps when you have thought over our interview to-day you will come to see things almost as I see them. I won't press the matter. I will leave your own heart and conscience to plead with you. And now may I walk home with you, before the beauty of the afternoon begins to fade?"

"The vetturino will be waiting for me at the gate," Isola answered, with a dull, dead voice, rising languidly, and adjusting the loosened hair about her forehead with tremulous fingers.

She had thrown off her hat a little while before, and now she took it up, and straightened the loops of ribbon with a nervous touch here and there, and then put the hat on again, and arranged the gossamer veil, which she hoped might hide her swollen eyelids and tear-stained cheeks.

"If Martin should come to meet me, what will he think? she said piteously.

"Let me go with you, and I may be able to distract his attention—if you don't want him to see that you have been crying."

"No, no. He must not see. He would wonder, and question me—and guess, perhaps—as you did just now. How was it you knew—what made you guess?" she asked, with a sense of rebellion against this man who had pierced the veil behind which she had been hiding herself so long.

"I saw your sorrow; and I knew that there could scarcely be so deep a sorrow if there were no memory of sin. Will you take my arm down this steep path?"

"No, thank you. I know every step. I could walk about this place in my sleep. You have been cruel to me, Father Rodwell, very cruel.

Promise me one thing by way of atonement for your cruelty. Promise me that if I die in Rome I shall be buried in this place, and as near Shelley's grave as they can find room to lay me."

"I promise. Yes, it is a sweet spot, is it not? It was down yonder in the old burial-ground that Shelley looked upon the grave of Keats, and said it was a spot to make one in love with death. But I would not have you think yourself doomed to an early death, Mrs. Disney. Have you never read in the 'Lives of the Saints' how some who were on the point of death have revived at the touch of the holy oil, and have lived and have renewed their strength, and re-entered the world to lead a holier and nobler life than they had led before? Who knows if you were to confess your sin, and patiently suffer whatever penance you were called upon to bear, new vistas might not open for you? There is more than one way of being happy in this world. If you could never again know the sweetness of a domestic life—as trusted wife and happy mother—there are other and wider lives in which you would count your children and your sisters by hundreds. There are sisterhoods in which your future might be full of usefulness and full of peace. Or if you had no vocation for that wider life, it might be that touched by your helplessness in the past, and your remorse in the present, your husband might find it in his heart to forgive that bygone sin, and still to cherish, and still to hold you dear."

"No, no," she cried impatiently. "I would not live for an hour after he knew. I know what he would do. He has told me. He would leave me—at once, and for ever. I should never see his face again. I should be dead to him, by a worse death than the grave; for he would only think of me to shudder at my name. Oh, Father Rodwell, Christianity must be a cruel creed if it can demand such a sacrifice from me. What good can come of his knowing the truth? Only agony to him and shame and despair to me. Can that be good?"

"Truth is life, and falsehood is death," answered the priest, firmly. "You must choose your own course, Mrs. Disney; but there is one argument I may urge as a man of the world rather than as a priest. Nothing is ever hidden for very long in this life. There is no secret so closely kept that some one has not an inkling of it. Better your husband should hear the truth from you, in humble self-accusation, than that he should learn it later—perhaps after he has mourned you for years—from a stranger's lips."

"Oh, that would be horrible—too horrible. But I will confess to him; I will tell him everything—on my deathbed. Yes, when life is ebbing, when the end is close, I will tell him. He shall know what a false and perjured creature I am. I swore to him—swore before God that I was true and faithful—that I loved him and no other. And it was true, absolute truth, when I took that oath. My sin was a thing of the past. I had loved another, and I had let my love lead me into sin. And then my husband asked me if I had been true and pure always; always. 'Is that true, Isola? I call upon God to hear your answer,' he said. And I answered yes, it was true. I lied before God rather than lose my husband's love; and God heard me, and the blight of His anger has been upon me ever since, withering and consuming me."

They went down the steep pathway, Father Rodwell first, Isola following, between the crowded graves, the azaleas and camelias, veronica and guelder rose, lilac and magnolia, and on either hand a wilderness of roses, red and white.

The shadows of the cypresses closed over them in that deep alley, and the twilight gloom might seem symbolic of the passage through death to life; for beyond the gates, and through a gap in the cypress screen, the level landscape and the city domes and bell-towers were shining in the yellow light of afternoon.

CHAPTER XXIV.

"OH, OLD THOUGHTS THEY CLING, THEY CLING!"

Colonel Disney and Allegra were both pleased to welcome Father
Rodwell to their home in the great city; pleased to find that his own
rooms were close by in the Via Babuino, and that he was likely to be
their neighbour for some weeks. His familiarity with all that was
worth seeing in the city and its surroundings made him a valuable
companion for people whose only knowledge had been gathered
laboriously from books. Father Rodwell knew every picture and
every statue in the churches and galleries. There was not a building
in Christian or Pagan Rome which had not its history and its
associations for the man who had chosen the city as the holiday
ground of his busy life long before he left the university, and who
had returned again and again, year after year, to tread the familiar
paths and ponder over the old records. He had seen many of those
monuments of Republic and Empire emerge from the heaped-up
earth of ages; had seen hills cut down, and valleys laid bare; some
picturesque spots made less picturesque; other places redeemed
from ruin. He had seen the squalor and the romance of Mediæval
Rome vanish before the march of improvement; and he had seen the
triumph of the commonplace and the utilitarian in many a scene
where the melancholy beauty of neglect and decay had once been
dear to him.

With such a guide it was delightful to loiter amidst the Palace of the
Cæsars, or tread the quiet lanes and by-paths of the Aventine, that
historic hill from whose venerable church the bearers of Christ's
message of peace and love set out for savage Britain. Allegra was
delighted to wander about the city with such a companion, lingering
long before every famous picture, finding out altar-pieces and
frescoes which no guide-book would have helped her to discover;
sometimes disputing Father Rodwell's judgment upon the artistic
value of a picture; sometimes agreeing with him—always bright,
animated, and intelligent.

Isola joined in these explorations as far as her strength would allow.
She was deeply interested in the churches, and in the stories of priest

and pope, saint and martyr, which Father Rodwell had to tell of every shrine and tomb, whose splendour might otherwise have seemed colourless and cold. There was a growing enthusiasm in the attention with which she listened to every record of that wonder-working Church which created Christian Rome in all its pomp and dignity of architecture, and all its glory of art. The splendour of those mighty basilicas filled her with an awful sense of the majesty of that religion which had been founded yonder in darkness and in chains, in Paul's subterranean prison—yonder in tears where Paul and Peter spoke the solemn words of parting—yonder in blood on the dreary road to Ostia, where the headsman's axe quenched the greatest light that had shone upon earth since the sacrifice of Calvary.

Isola went about looking at those things like a creature in a dream. These stupendous tabernacles impressed her with an almost insupportable sense of their magnitude. And with that awestricken sense of power in the Christian Church there was interwoven the humiliating consciousness of her own unworthiness; a consciousness sharpened and intensified by every word that Father Rodwell had spoken in that agonizing hour of her involuntary confession.

He was so kind to her, so gentle, so courteous in every word and act, that she wondered sometimes whether he had forgotten that miserable revelation; whether he had forgotten that she was one of the lost ones of this earth, a woman who had forfeited woman's first claim to man's esteem. Sometimes she found herself lifting her eyes to his face in an unpremeditated prayer for pity, as they stood before some exquisite shrine of the Madonna, and the ineffable purity in the sculptured face looking down at her struck like a sharp sword into her heart. That mute appeal of Isola's seemed to ask, "Has the Mother of Christ any pity for such a sinner as I?"

Colonel Disney was full of thoughtfulness for his wife in all their going to and fro; and before their day's rambles were half done he would drive her to any quiet spot where she might choose to spend a restful hour in the afternoon sunshine—in this or that convent garden, in some shaded corner on the Aventine, or among the wild flowers that flourish and grow rank amidst the ruins of palace and temple on the Palatine. Her favourite resort was still the English cemetery, and she always begged to be set down within reach of that familiar gate, where the custodian knew her as well as if she had been some restless spirit whose body lay under one of those marble urns, and whose ghost passed in and out of the gate every day.

It was in vain that her husband or her sister offered to be her companion in these restful hours. She always made the same reply.

"I am better alone," she would say. "It does me good to be alone. I don't like being alone indoors—I get low-spirited and nervous—but I like to sit among the flowers, and to watch the lizards darting in and out among the graves. I am never dull there. I take a book with me; but I don't read much. I could sit there for hours in a summer dream."

Martin Disney made a point of giving way to her will in all small things. She might be capricious, she might have morbid fancies. That was no business of his. It was his part to indulge her every whim, and to make her in love with life. All that he asked of Heaven was to spin out that attenuated thread. All that he desired was to hold her and keep her for his own against Death himself.

The *Vendetta* was at Civita Vecchia, from which port her skipper frequently bore down upon Rome, distracting Allegra from her critical studies in the picture-galleries, and from her work in her own studio, a light, airy room on the fourth floor, with a window looking over the Pincian Gardens. Captain Hulbert was a little inclined to resent Father Rodwell's frequent presence in the family circle, and his too accomplished guidance in the galleries. It was provoking to hear a man talk, with an almost Ruskinesque enthusiasm and critical appreciation, of pictures which made so faint an appeal to the seaman. Here and there John Hulbert could see the beauty and merit of a painting, and was really touched by the influence of supreme art; but of technical qualities he knew nothing, and could hardly distinguish one master from another, was as likely as not to take Titian for Veronese, or Tintoret for Titian.

He looked with a sceptical eye at the Anglican priest's cassock and girdle. If Father Rodwell had been a Papist it would have been altogether a more satisfactory state of things; but an Anglican—a man who might preach the beauty of holy poverty and a celibate life one year and marry a rich widow the year after—a man bound only by his own wishes.

Had Allegra been a thought less frank—had she been a woman whom it was possible to doubt—the sailor would have given himself over to the demon of jealousy; but there are happily some women in whom truth and purity are so transparently obvious that even an anxious lover cannot doubt them. Allegra was such an one. No suspicion of coquetry ever lessened her simple womanliness. She was a woman of whom a man might make a friend; a woman whose feelings and meanings he could by no possibility mistake.

He had pleaded his hardest and pleaded in vain for a June wedding. Isola's state of health was too critical for the contemplation of any change in the family circle.

"She could not do without me, nor could Martin either," Allegra told her lover. "It is I who keep house and manage their money, and see to everything for them. Martin has been utterly helpless since this saddening anxiety began. He thinks of nothing but Isola, and her chances of recovery. I cannot leave him while she is so ill."

"Have you any hope of her ever being better, my dear girl?"

"I don't know. It has been a long and wearing illness."

"It is not illness, Allegra. It is a gradual decay. My fear is that she will never revive. There is no marked disease—nothing for medicine to fight against. Such cases as hers are the despair of doctors. A spring has been broken somehow in the human machine. Science cannot mend it."

Allegra was very much of her sweetheart's opinion.

The English doctor in Rome was as kind and attentive as the doctor at San Remo; but although he had not yet pronounced the case hopeless, he took a by no means cheerful view of his patient's condition. He recommended Colonel Disney to leave the city before the third week in May, and to take his wife to Switzerland, travelling by easy stages, and doing all he could to amuse and interest her. If on the other hand it were important for Colonel Disney to be in England, he might take his wife back to Cornwall in June. But in this case she must return to the south in October. Lungs and heart were both too weak for the risks of an English winter.

"We will not go back to England," decided Disney. "My wife is not fond of Cornwall. Italy has been a delight to her; and Switzerland will be new ground. God grant the summer may bring about an improvement!"

The doctor said very little, and promised nothing.

Closely as they watched her, with anxious loving looks, it may be that seeing her every day even their eyes did not mark the gradual decline of vitality—the inevitable advance of decay. She never complained; the cough that marked the disease which had fastened on her lungs since February was not a loud or seemingly distressing cough. It was only now and then, when she tried to walk uphill, or over-exerted herself in any way, that her malady became painfully obvious in the labouring chest, flushed cheek, and panting breath; but she made light even of these symptoms, and assured her husband that Rome was curing her.

Her spirits had been less equable since Father Rodwell's appearance. She had alternated between a feverish intensity and a profound dejection. Her changes of mood had been sudden and apparently causeless; and those who watched and cherished her could do nothing to dispel the gloom that often clouded over her. If she were questioned she could only say that she was tired. She would never admit any reason for her melancholy.

CHAPTER XXV.

"WE'LL BIND YOU FAST IN SILKEN CORDS."

Captain Hulbert was not selfish enough to plead for his personal happiness in the midst of a household shadowed by the foreboding of a great sorrow. Martin Disney's face, as he looked at his wife in those moments which too plainly marked the progress of decay, was in itself enough to put a check upon a lover's impatience. How could any man plead for his own pleasure—for the roses and sunshine of life—in the presence of that deep despair?

"He knows that he is doomed to lose her," thought Hulbert; "knows it, and yet tries to hope. I never saw such intense, unquestioning love. One asks one's self involuntarily about any woman—Is she worth it?"

And then he thought of Allegra, truthful and impulsive, strong as steel, transparent as crystal. Yes, such a woman as that was worth the whole of a man's heart—worthy that a man should live or die for her. But it seemed to him that to compare Isola with Allegra was to liken an ash sapling to an oak.

He resigned himself to his disappointment, talked no more of Venice and the starlit lagunes, the summer nights on the Lido, and quoted no more of Buskin's rhapsodies; but he came meekly day after day to join in the family excursion, whatever it might be. He had enough and to spare of ecclesiastical architecture and of the old masters during those summer-like mornings and afternoons. He heard more than enough of the mad Cæsars and the bad Cæsars, of wicked Empresses and of low-born favourites, of despotism throned in the palace and murder waiting at the gate, of tyranny drunken with power long abused, and treason on the watch for the golden opportunity to change one profligate master for another, ready to toss up for the new Cæsar, and to accept the basest slave for master, would be but open the Imperial treasury wide enough to the Prætorian's rapacious hands.

"People gloat over these hoary old walls as if they would like to have lived under Caligula," said the sailor, with a touch of impatience, when Father Rodwell had been expatiating upon a little bit of moulding which decorated an imperial staircase.

"It would have been at least a picturesque time to have lived in," said Allegra. "Existence must have been a series of pictures by Alma Tadema."

Captain Hulbert was startled out of his state of placid submission by the intervention of a most unexpected ally.

It was one of the hottest days there had been since they came to Rome. To cross the Piazza in front of St. Peter's was like plunging into a bath of molten gold; while to enter the great Basilica itself was like going into an ice-house. Father Rodwell was not with them upon this particular morning. They were a party of four, and a roomy landau had been engaged to take them to the Church of St. Paul beyond the walls, and thence to the tomb of Cecilia Metella. Isola and Allegra had made pilgrimages to the spot before to-day. It was a drive they both loved, a glimpse of the pastoral life outside the gates of the city, and a place for ever associated with the poet whose verse was written in their hearts.

They dawdled over a light luncheon of macaroni and Roman wine at a *café* near the great cold white church, and then they drove through the sandy lanes in the heat of the afternoon, languid all of them, and Isola paler and more weary-looking than she had been for some time. Her husband watched her anxiously, and wanted to go back to Rome, lest the drive should be too exhausting for her.

"No, no, I am not tired," she answered impatiently. "I would much rather go on. I want to see that grim old tower again," and then she quoted the familiar lines, dreamily, with a faint pleasure in their music—

> "Perchance she died in youth: it may be bowed
> With woes far heavier than the ponderous tomb
> That weighed upon her gentle dust."

"Besides," she added confusedly, "I want to have a little private talk with Captain Hulbert, while Allegra is busy with her everlasting memoranda in that dirty little sketchbook which is stuffed with the pictures of the future. May I?"

She looked from her husband to Captain Hulbert pleadingly. The latter was first to answer.

"I am at your service, Mrs. Disney; ready to be interrogated, or lectured, or advised, whichever you like."

"I am not going to do either of the three. I am going to ask you a favour."

"Consider that to ask is to be obeyed."

They alighted in the road by the tomb a few minutes afterwards. Allegra's note-book was out immediately, a true artist's book, crammed with every conceivable form of artistic reminiscence.

"Go and talk," she said, waving her hand to Isola and Hulbert; and then she clambered up a bank opposite that tower of other days to get a vantage ground for her sketch.

She had made a score of sketches on the same spot, but there were always new details to jot down, new effects and ideas, on that vast level which frames the grandeur of Rome. Yonder the long line of the aqueduct; here the living beauty of broad-fronted oxen moving with stately paces along the dusty way, the incarnation of strength and majesty, patience and labour.

"Stay here and smoke your cigar, Martin," said Isola, "while Captain Hulbert and I go for a stroll."

Her husband smiled at her tenderly, cheered by her unwonted cheerfulness. His days and hours alternated between hope and despair. This was a moment of hope.

"My dearest, you are full of mystery to-day," he said, "and I am as full of curiosity. But I can wait. Consider me a statue of patience standing by the way-side, and take your time."

She put her hand through Hulbert's arm, and led him away from the other two, sauntering slowly along beside the grassy bank.

"I want to talk about your wedding," she said, as soon as they were out of hearing. "When are you and Allegra going to be married?"

"My dear Mrs. Disney, you know that I pledged myself to wait a year from the time of our engagement—a year from last Christmas—you must remember. That was to be my probation."

"Yes, I remember; but that is all foolishness—idle romance. Allegra knows that you love her. I don't think she could know it any better after another half-year's devotion on your part."

"I don't think she could know it better after another half century. I know I could never love her more than I do now. I know I shall never love her less."

"I believe that you are good and true," said Isola. "As true and—almost—as good as he is"—with a backward glance at her husband. "If I did not believe that I should not have thought of saying what I am going to say."

"I am honoured by your confidence in me."

"I love Allegra too well to hazard her happiness. I know she loves you—has never cared for any one else. She was heart-whole till she saw you. She had no more thought of love, or lovers, than a child. I want you to marry her soon, Captain Hulbert—very soon, before we leave Rome. Would you not like to be married in Rome?"

"I would like to be married in Kamtchatka, or Nova Zembla—or the worst of those places whose very names suggest uncomfortableness. There is no dismallest corner of the earth which Allegra could not glorify and make dear. But, as you suggest, Rome is classic—Rome is mediæval—Rome is Roman Catholic. It would be a new sensation for a plain man like me to be married in Rome. I suppose it could not be managed in St. Peter's?"

"Oh, Captain Hulbert, I want you to be serious."

"I am serious. Why, this is a matter of life or death to me. But I pleaded so hard for a June wedding—and to no purpose. I talked with the artfulness of the first Tempter—I tried to play upon her vanities as an artist. All in vain!"

"Tell her that I have set my heart upon seeing her married," said Isola, in a low voice.

"Why, of course, you will see her married, whether she be married in Rome or at Trelasco. That is no argument."

"But it is; indeed it is. Tell her that, if I am to be at her wedding, it must be soon, very soon. Life is so uncertain at best—and, although I feel well and strong, sometimes—to-day, for instance—there are other times when I think the end is nearer than even my doctor suspects. And I know by his face that he does not give me a long lease of life."

"My dear Mrs. Disney, this is morbid. I am grieved to hear you talk in such a strain."

"Don't notice that. Don't say anything depressing to Allegra. I want her to go off to her Venetian honeymoon very happily—with not one cloud in her sky. She has been so good and dear to me. It would be hard if I could not rejoice in her happiness. I have rejoiced in it always; I shall take pleasure in it to the end of my life. It is the one unclouded spot——." She stopped with a troubled air. "Yes, it is a happy fate—to have cared for one, and one only, and to be loved again. Will you do what I ask you, Captain Hulbert? will you hurry on the wedding—for my sake?"

"I would do anything difficult and unwelcome for your sake—how much more will I hasten my own happiness—if I can. But Allegra is a difficult personage—as firm as rock when she has once made up her mind. And she has made up her mind to stay with you till you are quite well and strong again."

"She need not leave me for ever, because she marries. She can come back to me after a long honeymoon. We can all meet in Switzerland in August—if—if I go there with Martin, as he proposes."

"Well, I will try to bend that stubborn will."

"And you don't mind having a quiet wedding, if she consents to a much earlier date?"

"Mind? The quieter the better for me! I think a smart wedding is a preventive of matrimony. That sounds like a bull. I will say I think there are many wretched bachelors living in dismal chambers, and preyed upon by landladies, who might have been happily married, but for the fear of a smart wedding. We will have as quiet a wedding as you and Disney can desire; but I should like Lostwithiel to be present. He is my only near relation, and I don't want to cut him on the happiest day of my life. Why, Mrs. Disney, you are trembling! You have agitated yourself about this business; you have talked too much for your strength. Let me take you back to the carriage."

"Presently—yes, yes. The heat overcame me for a moment, that's all. Would you mind not waiting for Lord Lostwithiel? I want the marriage to be at once—directly—as soon as Father Rodwell can get it arranged. And you don't know where a telegram would reach your brother?"

"Indeed, I do not; but by speculating a few messages of inquiry I could soon find out the whereabouts of the *Eurydice*."

"Don't wait for that. There would be delay. There must be delay if you have to consult any distant person's convenience. We are all here—you and Allegra, and Martin and I—and Father Rodwell would like to marry you. What do you want with anybody else?"

"Upon my word, I think you are right! Allegra is a creature of impulse—where principle is not at stake. If I asked her to marry me six weeks hence she would parley and make terms. If I ask her to marry me in a few days—before we leave Rome—she may consent. Have you talked to your husband? Is he of your opinion?"

"I have said nothing to him; but I know he would be pleased to see you and Allegra bound together for life."

"I will talk to him this afternoon. One can get everything one wants in Rome, I believe, from a papal dispensation down to an English solicitor. If we can but rattle through some kind of marriage settlement to your husband's satisfaction we can be married on the earliest day to which my darling will consent. God bless you, Mrs. Disney, for your unselfish thought of other people's happiness! You are not like most invalids, who would let a sister languish in lifelong spinsterhood rather than lose her as a nurse. God grant that your unselfishness may be recompensed by speedy recovery!"

"There will be a weight off my mind when you and Allegra are married," said Isola, gravely.

They walked slowly back to the spot where they had left their companions. A pair of oxen, with an empty cart, were standing in the road below the tomb, their driver lounging across the rough vehicle—man and beasts motionless as marble. Allegra sat on a hillock opposite, sketching the group. She had bribed the man to draw up for a brief halt while she made her sketch. The massive heads were drooping under the afternoon sun; the tawny and cream-hued coats were stained with dust and purpled with the sweat of patient labour. The creatures looked as gracious and as wise as if they had been gods in disguise.

"Now, Allegra," said her brother, emptying the ashes out of his pipe, "are you ready to go home?"

"Yes, I have just jotted down what will serve to remind me of those splendid beasts; but I should like to have them standing there all day, so that I could paint them seriously. They are the finest models I have seen in Rome. Have you two quite finished your secrets and mysteries?" she asked, smiling at Isola, who was looking brighter than usual.

"Yes; I have said all I had to say, and have been answered as I wished to be answered. I shall go home very happy."

"That's a good hearing," said Disney, as he helped her into the landau.

Allegra had talked of wanting to revisit Caracalla's Baths, a wish of which Isola reminded her as they drove back to the city, along the Appian Way: whereupon Captain Hulbert suggested that he and his sweetheart should stop to explore the ruins, while Disney and Isola went home.

Allegra blushed and consented, always a little shy at being alone with her lover, especially since he had pleaded so earnestly for a summer honeymoon.

"Mrs. Disney, your right place in Rome would be the Embassy," murmured Hulbert as he shut the carriage door; "you are a born diplomatist."

"What makes my dearest look so pleased and happy this afternoon?" asked Disney, as he changed to the seat beside his wife.

"I am glad because I think Captain Hulbert will persuade Allegra to marry him before we leave Rome. I begged him to hasten their marriage. That was my mystery, Martin. That was what he and I were talking about."

"But why wish to hasten matters, dear? They are very happy as it is—and a year is not a long engagement."

"Too long for me, Martin. I want to see her happy—I want to see them married before——"

"Before what, dear love?" he asked tenderly.

"Before we leave Rome."

"That would be very short work. We leave in a fortnight. The weather will be growing too hot for you if we linger later."

"Yes, but everything can be settled in less time than that. Ask Father Rodwell. He knows Rome so well that he can help you to arrange all details."

"I thought that every young woman required at least six months for the preparation of her trousseau?"

"Not such a girl as Allegra. She is always well dressed, and her wardrobe is the perfection of neatness—but she is not the kind of girl to make a fuss about her clothes. I don't think the trousseau will create any difficulty."

"And when she is gone, what will you do without your devoted companion? Who will nurse you and take care of you?"

"Löttchen, or any other servant," she answered, with a kind of weary indifference. "It would be very hard if my bad health should stand in the way of Allegra's happiness. So long as you will stay with me and be kind to me, Martin, I need no one else."

Tears were streaming down her cheeks as she turned from him, pretending to be interested in the convent walls on the edge of the hill below which they were driving.

"So long as I stay with you! My darling, do you think business or pleasure, or any claim in this world, will ever take me from you any more? All your hours are precious to me, Isola. I hardly live when I am away from you. Wherever your doctor may send you, or your own fancy may lead you, I shall go with you, unhesitatingly— without one regret for anything I leave behind."

"Don't say these things," she cried suddenly, with a choking sob; "you are too good to me. There are times when I can't bear it."

## CHAPTER XXVI.

### "SO, FULL CONTENT SHALL HENCEFORTH BE MY LOT."

Allegra was not inexorable. There, in the ruins of the Imperial baths, where Shelley dreamed the wonder-dream of his Prometheus, Captain Hulbert pleaded his cause. Could love resist the pleading of so fond a lover? Could art withstand the allurements of Venice—Titian and Tintoret, the cathedral of St. Mark and the Palace of the Doges, the birthplace of Desdemona and of Shylock, the home of Byron and of Browning?

She consented to a Roman marriage.

"I can't help wishing I could be a Papist just for that one day," she said lightly. "An Anglican marriage seems so dry and cold compared with the pomps and splendours of Rome."

"Dearest, the plainest Christian rites are enough, if they but make us one."

"I think we are that already, John," she answered shyly; and then, nestling by his side as they sat in the wide solitude of that stupendous pile, she took his hand and held it in both her own, looking down at it wonderingly—a well-formed hand, strong and muscular, broadened a little by seafaring.

"And you are to be my husband," she said. "Mine! I shall speak of you to people as my own peculiar property. 'My husband will do this or that.' 'My husband has gone out, but he will be home soon.' Home. Husband. How strange it sounds!"

"Strange and wonderful now, love. Sweet and familiar before our honeymoon is ended."

They went out of the broad spaces that were once populous with the teeming life of Imperial Rome, splendid with all that art could create of beauty and of grandeur—wrapt in the glamour of their dream. They walked all the way to the Piazza di Spagna in the same happy dream, as unconscious of the ground they trod on as if they had been floating in the air.

They were a very cheerful party at dinner that evening. Father Rodwell dined with them, and was delighted at the idea of having to marry these happy lovers. He took the arrangement of the ceremony into his own hands. The English chaplain was his old friend, and would let him do what he liked in his church.

"It is to be a very quiet wedding," said the colonel, when the three men were smoking together in a loggia, looking on the little garden of orange trees and oleanders, in the grey dim beginning of night, when the thin crescent moon was shining in a sky still faintly flushed with sunset. "Isa could not stand anything like bustle or excitement. Luckily we have no friends in Rome. There is no one belonging to us who could be aggrieved at not being invited."

"And there is no one except Lostwithiel on my side who has the slightest claim to be present," said Hulbert. "I am almost as well off as the Flying Dutchman in that respect. I am not troubled with relations. All the kinsfolk I have are distant, and I allow them to remain so. My dear Disney, so far as I am concerned, our wedding cannot be too quiet a business. It is the bride I want, mark you, not the fuss and flowers, wedding-breakfast, and bridesmaids. Let us be married at half-past ten, and drive from the church to the railway station in time for the noonday train. I have given up my dream of taking Allegra round Southern Italy to the Adriatic. We shall go to Florence first, and spend a few days in the galleries, and thence to Venice, where we will have the *Vendetta* brought to us, and anchored near the arsenal, ready to carry us away directly we are tired of the city of old memories."

Father Rodwell left them and went into the drawing-room, where Isola and her sister-in-law were sitting in the lamplight—Isola's hands occupied with that soft, fluffy knitting which seemed to exercise a soothing influence upon her nerves; Allegra leaning over the table, idly sketching random reminiscences of the Baths, the Tomb, the grave-eyed oxen, with their great curving horns and ponderous foreheads.

The priest was interested in watching Isola this evening. He saw a marked change in the expression of her countenance, a change which was perceptible to him even in her voice and manner—a brightness which might mean a lightened heart, or which might mean religious exaltation.

"Has she told him?" he wondered, studying her from his place in the shadow as the lamplight shone full upon her wasted features and hectic colouring. "Has she taken courage and confessed her sin to that loyal, loving husband, and is the burden lifted from her heart?"

No; he could not believe that she had lifted the veil from the sad secret of her past. Martin Disney's unclouded brow to-night was not that of a man who had lately discovered that the wife he loved had betrayed him. There might be pardon—there might be peace between husband and wife after such a revelation; but there could not be the serenity which marked Martin Disney's manner to his wife to-night. Such a thunder-clap must leave its brand upon the man who suffered it. No; her secret was still locked in her impenitent heart. Sorry—yes. She had drunk the cup of remorse in all its bitterness; but she knew not true penitence, the Christian's penitence, which means self-abasement and confession. And yet she seemed happier. There was a look of almost holy resignation upon the pale and placid brow, and in the too-lustrous eyes. Something had happened—some moral transformation which made her a new being.

Father Rodwell drew his chair nearer to her, and looked at her earnestly with his cordial, almost boyish smile. He was a remarkably young-looking man, a man upon whom long years of toil in the dark places of the earth had exercised no wasting or withering influence. He had loved his work too well ever to feel the pressure of the burdens he carried. His gospel had been always a cheerful gospel, and he had helped to lighten sorrows, never to make them heavier. He was deeply interested in Isola, and had been watchful of all her changes of mood since their conversation in the shadow of the old Roman wall. He had seen her impressed by the history and traditions of the church, moved by the pathos of holy lives, touched almost to tears by sacred pictures, and he saw in her character and disposition a natural bent towards piety, exactly that receptive temperament which moves holy women to lives of self-abnegation and heroic endeavour. He had lent her some of those books which he loved best and read most himself, and he had talked with her of religion, careful not to say too much or with too strong an emphasis, and never by any word alluding to her revelation of past guilt. He wanted to win her to perfect trustfulness in him, to teach her to lean upon him in her helplessness; until the hour should come when she would let him lead her to her husband, in the self-abasement of the penitent sinner.

He knew that in this desire he exceeded the teaching of churchmen; that another priest in his place might have bade her keep her sad secret to the end, lie down with it in her early grave, be remembered as a saint, yet die knowing herself a sinner. If he had thought of the husband's peace first, he would have counselled silence. But he thought most of this stricken soul, with wings that spread themselves towards heaven, held down to earth by the burden of an unpardoned sin.

He looked at her in the lamplight, and her eyes met his with a straighter outlook than he had seen in them for a long time. She looked actually happy, and that look of happiness in a face on which death has set its seal has always something which suggests a life beyond the grave.

"The excitement of this marriage question has brightened you wonderfully, Mrs. Disney," he said. "We shall have you in high health by the wedding-day."

"I am feeling better because I am so glad," Isola answered naively, putting her hand into Allegra's.

"I consider it positively insulting to me as a sister," exclaimed Allegra, bending down to kiss the too-transparent hand—such a hand as she had seen in many a picture of dying saint in the Roman galleries. "You are most unaffectionately rejoiced to get rid of me. I have evidently been a tyrannical nurse, and a dull companion, and you breathe more freely at the prospect of release."

"You have been all that is dear and good," Isola answered softly, "and I shall feel dreadfully lonely without you; but it won't be for long. And I shall be so comforted by the knowledge that nothing can come between you and your life's happiness."

The two men came in from the loggia, bringing with them the cool breath of night. Isola went to the piano and played one of those Adagios of Mozart's which came just within the limit of her modest powers, and which she played to perfection, all her soul in the long lingering phrases, the tender modulations, with their suggestions of shadowy cathedral aisles, and the smoke of incense in the deepening dusk of a vesper service. Those bits of Mozart, the slow movements from the Sonatas, an Agnus Dei, or an Ave Maria from one of the Masses, satisfied Captain Hulbert's highest ideas of music. He desired nothing grander or more scientific. The new learning of the Wagnerian school had no charm for him.

"If you ask me about modern composers, I am for Verdi and Gounod," he said. "For gaiety and charm, give me Auber, Rossini, and Boieldieu—for pathos, Weber—for everything, Mozart. There you have the whole of my musical education."

The question of settlements was opened seriously between Martin Disney and his future brother-in-law, early on the following morning. Hulbert wanted to settle all the money he had in the world upon Allegra.

"She is ever so much wiser than I am," he said. "So she had better be my treasurer. My property is all in stocks and shares. My grandfather was fond of stock-jobbing, and made some very lucky investments which he settled upon my mother, with strict injunctions that they should not be meddled with by her trustees. My share of her fortune comes to a little over nine hundred a year. I came into possession of it when I came of age, and it is mine to dispose of as I like, trusts expired, trustees cleared off—in point of fact, both gone over to the majority, poor old souls, after having had many an anxious hour about those South American railway bonds, and Suez Canal shares, which turned up trumps after all. I've telegraphed to the family lawyer for a schedule of the property, and when that comes, just tie it all up in as tight a knot as the law can tie, and let it belong to Allegra and her children after her. Consider me paid off."

Martin Disney laughed at the lover's impetuosity—and told him that he should be allowed to bring so much and no more into settlement. Allegra's income was less than two hundred a year, a poor little income upon which she had fancied herself rich, so modest is woman's measure of independence as compared with man's. It would be for the lawyer to decide what proportion the husband's settlements should bear to the wife's income. Father Rodwell had given Colonel Disney an introduction to a solicitor of high character, a man who had occupied an excellent position in London until damaged lungs obliged him to seek a home in the south.

With this gentleman's aid, matters were soon put in train, and while the men were in the lawyer's office, the two women were choosing Allegra's wedding-gown.

The young lady had exhibited a rare indifference upon the great trousseau question. She was not one of those girls whose finery is all external, and who hide rags and tatters under æsthetic colouring and Raffaelle draperies. She was too much of an artist to endure anything unseemly in her belongings, and her everyday clothes, just as they were, might have been exhibited, like a Royal trousseau, without causing any other comment than, "How nice!" "What good taste!" "What exquisite needlework!"

The hands which painted such clever pictures were as skilful with the needle as with the brush, and Allegra had never considered that a vocation for art meant uselessness in every feminine industry. She had attended to her own wardrobe from the time she learnt plain sewing at her first school; and now, as she and Isola looked over the ample array of under-linen, the pretty cambric peignoirs, and neatly trimmed petticoats, they were both of one mind, that there was very little need of fuss or expenditure.

"I have plenty of summer frocks," said Allegra. "So really there is only my travelling gown to see about, that is to say, the gown I am to be married in."

"But you must have a real wedding-gown, all the same, a white satin gown, with lace and pearls," pleaded Isola. "When you go to dinner-parties, by-and-by, you will be expected to look like a bride."

"Dinner-parties! Oh, those are a long way off. We are not likely to be asked to any parties while we are wandering about Italy. I can get a gown when I go home."

Allegra's wedding-day had dawned—a glorious day—a day to make one drunken with the beauty of sky and earth; a day when the vetturini in the Piazza di Spagna sat and dreamt on their coach-boxes—narcotized by the sun—when the reds and blues in the garments of the flower-women were almost too dazzling for the eye to look upon, and when every garden in the city sent forth tropical odours of roses steeped in sunlight.

The church in which the lovers were to be made one was a very homely temple as compared with the basilicas yonder on the hills of Rome. But what did that matter to Allegra this morning as she stood before the altar and spoke the words which gave her to the man she loved? A flood of sunshine streamed upon the two figures of bride and bridegroom, and touched the almost spectral face of the bride's sister-in-law, a face which attracted as much attention as the bride's fresh bloom and happy smile. It was a face marked for death, yet beautiful in decay. The large violet eyes were luminous with the light of worlds beyond the world we know. There was something loftier than happiness in that vivid look, something akin to exaltation—the smile of the martyr at the stake—the martyr for whom Heaven's miraculous intervention changes the flames of the death-pile into the soft fanning of seraphic wings; the martyr unconscious of earthly pains and earthly cruelties; who sees the skies opening and the glorious company of saints and angels gathered about the great white throne.

Father Rodwell saw that spiritual expression in the pale, wasted face, and he told himself that a lost soul could not look out of eyes like those. If death were near, as he feared, the true repentance for which he had prayed many an earnest prayer was not far off.

---

Bride and bridegroom were to leave Rome by the mid-day train. Colonel Disney was going to see the last of them at the station, but Isola and her sister-in-law were to say good-bye in the vestry, and to part at the church door. And now Father Rodwell's brief, but fervent, address had been spoken, the Wedding March pealed from the organ, and the small wedding-party went into the vestry to sign the registers.

Isola was called upon for her signature as one of the witnesses. She signed in a bold, clear hand, without one tremulous line, her husband looking over her shoulder as she wrote.

"That doesn't look like an invalid's autograph, does it, Hulbert?" he asked, snatching at every token of hope, unwilling to believe what his doctors and his own convictions told him—expecting a miracle.

They had warned him that he could not keep her long. They had advised him to humour her fancies, to let her be present at the wedding, even at the hazard of her suffering afterwards for that exertion and excitement. She would suffer more perhaps—physically as well as mentally—if she were thwarted in her natural wish to be by Allegra's side on that day.

All was finished. Neither Church nor law could do anything more towards making the lovers man and wife. The law might undo the bond for them in the time to come, but the part of the Church was done for ever. In the eye of the Church their union was indissoluble.

Isola clung with her arms round the bride's neck.

"Think of me sometimes, dearest, in the years to come. Think that I loved you fondly. Be sure that I was grateful for all your goodness to me," she said tearfully.

"My own love, I shall think of you every day till we meet again."

"And if we never meet again on earth—will you remember me kindly?"

"Isa, how can you?" cried Allegra, silencing the pale lips with kisses.

"You may be glad to think how much you did towards making my life happy—happier than it ought to have been." Isola went on in a low voice. "Dearest, I am more glad of your marriage than words can say; and, Allegra, love him with all your heart, and never let your lives be parted—remember, dearest, never, never let anything upon this earth part you from him."

Her voice was choked with sobs, and then came a worse fit of coughing than she had suffered for some time; a fit which left her exhausted and speechless. Her husband looked at her in an agony of apprehension.

"Let me take you home, Isa," he said. "You'll be better at home, lying down by your sunny window. This vestry is horribly cold. Hulbert, if you and Allegra will excuse me, I won't see you off at the station. Father Rodwell will go with you, perhaps. He'll be of more use than I could be; and we shall see each other very soon again in Switzerland, please God."

"Yes, yes, There is no need for you to go," Hulbert answered, grasping his hand, distressed for another man's pain in the midst of his own happiness. There death, and the end of all joy—here the new life with its promises of gladness just opening before him. Such contrasts must needs seem hard.

They all went to the church door, where the carriages were waiting. Only a few idlers loitered about the pavement, faintly interested in so shabby a wedding—a poor array of one landau and one brougham, the brougham to take the travellers to the station, where their luggage had been sent by another conveyance.

The two women kissed each other once more before Allegra stepped into the carriage, Isola too weak for speech, and able only to clasp the hands that had waited on her in so many a weary hour; the clever hands, the gentle hands, to which womanly instinct and womanly love had given all the skilfulness of a trained nurse.

Disney lifted his wife into the landau, Father Rodwell helping him, full of sympathy.

"You'll dine with us to-night, I hope," said the colonel. "We shall be very low if we are left to ourselves."

"I've an engagement for this evening—but—yes, I'll get myself excused, and spend the evening with you, if you really want me."

"Indeed we do," answered Disney, heartily; but Isola was dumb. Her eyes were fixed upon the distant point at which the brougham had disappeared round a corner, on its way to the station.

## CHAPTER XXVII

### "GONE DEEPER THAN ALL PLUMMETS SOUND."

Church bells are always ringing in that city of many churches, and there were bells ringing solemnly and slowly as Isola walked feebly up the two flights of stairs that led to Colonel Disney's lodging. She walked even more slowly than usual, and her husband could hear her labouring breath as she went up, step by step, leaning on the banister rail. He had offered her his arm, but she had repulsed him, almost rudely, at the bottom of the stairs.

They went into the drawing-room, which was bright with flowers in a sunlit dusk, the sun streaming in through the narrow opening between the Venetian shutters, which had been drawn together, but not fastened. All was very still in the quiet house; so still that they could hear the splash of the fountain in the Piazza, and the faint rustling of the limes in the garden.

Husband and wife stood facing each other, he anxious and alarmed, she deadly pale, and with gleaming eyes.

"Well, she is gone—she is Mrs. Hulbert now, and she belongs to him and not to us any more," said Disney, talking at random, watching his wife's face in nervous apprehension of—he knew not what. "We shall miss her sadly. Aren't you sorry she is married, Isola, after all?"

"Sorry! No! I am glad—glad with all my heart. I have waited for that."

And then, before he was aware, she had flung herself at his feet, and was kneeling there, with her head hanging down, her hands clasped—a very Magdalen.

"I waited—till they were married—so that you should not refuse to let her marry—his brother—waited to tell you what I ought to have told you at once, when you came home from India. My only hope of pardon or of peace was to have told you then—to have left you for ever then—never to have dared to clasp your hand—never to have dared to call myself your wife—never to have become the mother of your child. All my life since that day has been one long lie; and nothing that I have suffered—not all my agonies of remorse—can atone for that lie, unless God and you will accept my confession and my atonement to-day."

"Isola, for God's sake, stop!"

Again the racking cough seized her, and she sank speechless at his feet.

He lifted her in his arms and carried her to the sofa, and flung open the shutters and let the light and air stream in upon her, as she lay prostrate and exhausted, wiping her white lips with a blood-stained handkerchief. He looked at her in a kind of horrified compassion. He thought that she was raving, that the excitement of the morning had culminated in fever and delirium. He was going to ring for help, meaning to send instantly for her doctor, when she stopped him, laying her thin cold hand upon his arm, and holding him by her side.

"Sit down by me, Martin—don't stop me—I must tell you—all—the truth."

Her words came slowly, in gasps; then with a great effort she gathered up the poor remnant of her strength, and went on in a low, tremulous voice, yet with the tone of one whose resolve was strong as death itself.

"There was a time when I thought I could never tell you—that I must go down to my grave with my sin unrevealed, and that you would never know how worthless a woman you had loved and cherished. Then, on my knees before my God, I vowed that I would tell you all, at the last, when I was dying—and death is not far off now, Martin. I have delayed too long—too long! There is scarcely any atonement in my confession now. I have cheated you out of your love."

He looked at her horror-stricken, their two faces close to each other as he bent over her pillow.

No; this was no delirium—there was a terrible reality in her words. The eyes looking up at him were not bright with fever, but with the steady resolute soul within—the soul panting for freedom from sin.

"You have cheated me out of my love," he repeated slowly. "Does that mean that you lied to me that night in London—that you perjured yourself, calling God to witness that you were pure and true?"

"I was true to you then, Martin. My sin had been repented of. I was your loving, loyal wife, without one thought but of you."

"Loving, loyal!" he cried, with passionate scorn. "You had deceived and dishonoured me—you had made your name a by-word—a jest for such a man as Vansittart Crowther—and for how many more? You had lied, and lied, and lied to me—by every look, by every word that made you seem a virtuous woman and a faithful wife. My God, what misery!"

"Martin, have pity!"

"Pity! Yes, I pity the women in the streets! Am I to pity you, as I pity them? You, whom I worshipped—whom I thought as pure as the angels—wearing nothing of earth but your frail loveliness, which to me always seemed more of spirit than of clay. And you were false all the time—false as hell—the toy of the first idle profligate whom chance flung into your path? It was Lostwithiel! That man was right. He would hardly have dared to talk to you as he did if he had not been certain of his facts. Lostwithiel was your lover."

"Martin, have pity!" she repeated, with her hands clasped before her face.

"Pity! Don't I tell you that I pity you—pity you whom I used to revere! Great God! can you guess what pain it is to change respect for the creature one loves into pity? I told you that I would never hurt you—that I would never bring shame upon you, Isola. You have no unkindness to fear from me. But you have broken my heart, you have slain my faith in man and woman. I could have staked my life on your purity—I could have killed the man who slandered you—and you swore a false oath—you called upon Heaven to witness a lie!"

"I was a miserable creature, Martin. I could not bear to lose your love. If death had been my only penalty I could have borne it, but not the loss of your love."

"And your sister and her husband? They were as ready with their lies as you were," he exclaimed bitterly.

"Don't blame Gwendolen. I telegraphed to her, imploring her to stand by me—to say that I was in London with her."

"And you were not in London?"

"No, except to pass through, when—when I had escaped from him, and was on my way home."

"Escaped! My God! What villainy must have been used against you—so young, so helpless! Tell me all—without reserve—as freely as you want to be forgiven."

"I was not utterly wicked, Martin. I did not sin deliberately—I did not know what I was doing when I wrecked my life and destroyed my peace of mind for ever. I never meant to forget you—or to be false to you—but I was so lonely—so lonely. The days were so dreary and so long—even the short autumn days seemed long—and the evenings were so melancholy without you. And he came into my life suddenly—like a prince in a fairy tale—and at first I thought very little about him. He was nothing more to me than any one else in Trelasco—and then somehow we were always meeting by accident—in the lanes—or by the sea—and he seemed to care for all the things I cared for. The books I loved were his favourites. For a long time we talked of nothing but his travels, and of my favourite books. There was not a word spoken between us that you or any one else could blame."

"A common opening," said Martin Disney, with scathing contempt. "One of the seducer's favourite leads."

"And then, one evening in the twilight, he told me that he loved me. I was very angry—and I let him see that I was angry, and I did all I could to avoid him after that evening. I refused to go to the ball at Lostwithiel, knowing that I must meet him there. But they all persuaded me—Mrs. Crowther, Mrs. Baynham, Tabitha—they were all bent upon making me go—and I went. Oh, God, if I had but stood firm against their foolish persuasion, if I had but been true to myself! But my own heart fought against me. I wanted to see him again—if only for the last time. He had talked about starting for a long cruise to the Mediterranean. His yacht was ready to sail at an hours notice."

"You went, and you were lost."

"Yes, lost, irretrievably lost! It is all one long, wild dream when I look back upon it. He implored me to go away with him—but I told him no, no, no, not for worlds, nothing should ever make me false to my husband—nothing. I swore it—swore an oath which I had not the strength to keep. Oh, it was cruel, heartless, treacherous—the thing he did after that. When I was going away from the dance, he was there at my side—and he put me into the wrong carriage—his own carriage—and when I had been driven a little way from the hotel, the carriage stopped and he got in. I thought that he was driving me home. I asked him how he could be cruel as to be with me, in his own carriage, at the risk of my reputation—but he stopped me—shut my lips with his fatal kiss. Oh, Martin, how can I tell these things? The horse went almost at a gallop. I thought we should be killed. I was half fainting when the carriage stopped at last, after rattling up and down hill—and he lifted me out, and I felt the cold night-air on my face, the salt spray from the sea. I tried to ask him where I was,—whether this was home—but the words died on my lips—and I knew no more—knew no more till I woke from that dead, dull swoon in the cabin of the *Vendetta*, and heard the sailors calling out to each other, and saw Lostwithiel sitting by my side—and then—and then—it was all one long dream—a dream of days and nights, and rain, and tempest. I thought the boat was going down in that dreadful night in the Bay of Biscay. Would to God that she had gone down, and hidden me and my sin for ever! But she lived through the storm, and in the morning she was anchored near Arcachon, and Lostwithiel went on shore, and sent a woman in a boat, to bring me clothes, and to attend upon me; and I contrived to go on shore with the woman when she went back in the boat that had brought her, and I borrowed some money on my ring at a jeweller's in Arcachon, and I left by the first train for Paris, and went on from Paris to London, and never stopped to rest anywhere till I got home."

"May God bring me face to face with that ruffian who imposed upon your helplessness!" cried Martin Disney.

"No, no, Martin; he was not a ruffian. He betrayed me—but I loved him. He knew that I loved him. I was a great a sinner as be. I was his before he stole me from my home—his in mind and in spirit. It was our unhappy fate to love each other. And I forgave him, Martin. I forgave him on that night of tempest, when I thought we were going to die together."

"You don't expect me to forgive him, do you? You don't expect me to forgive the seducer who has ruined your life and mine?"

"His brother is your sister's husband, Martin?"

"I am sorry for it."

"Oh, John Hulbert is good; he is frank and true. He is not like the other. But oh, Martin, pity Lostwithiel and his sin, as you pity me and my sin! It is past and done. I was mad when I cared for him—a creature under a spell. You won my heart back to you by your goodness—you made me more than ever your own. All that he had ever been to me—all that I had ever thought or felt about him—was blotted out as if I had never seen his face. Nothing remained but my love for you—and my guilty conscience, the aching misery of knowing that I was unworthy of you."

He took her hand and pressed it gently in silence. Then, after a long pause, when she had dried the tears from her streaming eyes, and was lying faint, and white, and still, caring very little what became of her poor remnant of life, he said softly—

"I forgive you, Isola, as I pray God to forgive you. I have spent some happy years with you—not knowing. If it was a delusion, it was very sweet—while it lasted."

"It was not a delusion," she cried, putting her arms round his neck, in a sudden rapture at being pardoned. "My love was real."

The door opened softly, and the kindly face of the Anglican priest looked in.

"I have seen the lovers on their way to Florence," he said, "and have come to ask how Mrs. Disney is after her fatiguing morning."

"I am happier than I have been for a long time," answered Isola, holding out her hand to him. "I am prepared for the end, let it come when it may."

He knew what she meant, and that the sinner had confessed her sin.

"Come out for a stroll with me, Disney," he said, "and leave your wife to rest for a little while. I'm afraid she'll miss her kind nurse."

Disney started up confusedly, like a sleeper awakened, and looked at his watch.

"I believe I have a substitute ready to replace Allegra by this time," he said, ringing the bell.

"Has the person from England arrived?" he asked the servant.

"Yes, sir. She came a quarter of an hour ago."

"Ask her to come here at once."

"Oh, Martin, you have not sent for a hospital nurse, I hope," cried Isola, excitedly. "Indeed I am not so bad as that. I want very little help. I could not bear to have a stranger about me."

"This is not a stranger, Isola."

There came a modest knock at the door as he spoke.

"Come in," he said; and a familiar figure in a grey merino gown and smart white cap with pink ribbons entered quietly and came to the sofa where Isola was lying.

"Tabitha!" she cried.

"Don't say you're sorry to see an old face again, Mrs. Disney. I told Mr. Martin that if you should ever be ill and want nursing I'd come to nurse you—if you were at the other end of the world—and Mr. Martin wrote and told me you wanted an old servant's care and experience to get you over your illness—and here I am. I've come every inch of the way without stopping, except at the buffets, and all I can say is Rome is a long way from everywhere, and the country I've come through isn't to be compared with Cornwall."

She ran on breathlessly as she seated herself by that reclining figure with the waxen face. It may be that she talked to hide the shock she had experienced on seeing the altered looks of the young mistress whose roof she had left in the hour of shame. She had left her, refusing to hold commune with one who had sinned so deeply. The faithful servant had taken leave of her mistress in words that had eaten into Isola's heart, as if they had been written there with a corrosive acid.

"I am very sorry for you, Mrs. Disney," she said. "You are young and pretty, and you are very much to be pitied—and God knows I have loved you as if you were my own flesh and blood. But I won't stay under the roof of a wife who has brought shame upon herself and has dishonoured the best of husbands."

Isola had denied nothing, had acknowledged nothing, and had let Tabitha go. And now they met again for the first time after that miserable parting, and the servant's eyes were full of pitying tears, and the servant's lips spoke only gentlest words. What a virtue there must be in death, when so much is forgiven to the dying!

Martin Disney went out with the priest, but at the corner of the Piazza he stopped abruptly.

"Isola's coughing fit has upset me more than it has her," he said; "I'm not fit company for any one, so I think I'll go for a tramp somewhere, and meet you later at dinner, when I've recovered my spirits a little."

"*A riverderci*," said the priest, grasping his hand. "I felicitate you upon this day's union; a happy one, or I am no judge of men and women."

"I don't know," Disney answered gloomily. "The woman is true as steel—the man comes of a bad stock. You know what the Scripture says about the tree and the fruit."

"There never was a race yet that was altogether bad," said the priest. "Virtues may descend from remote ancestors as well as vices,—I think you told me moreover that Captain Hulbert's mother was a good woman."

"She was. She was one of my mother's earliest and dearest friends."

"Then you should have a better opinion of her son. If ever I met a thoroughly good fellow in my life, I believe I met one the day I made Captain Hulbert's acquaintance."

"Pray God you may be right," said Disney, with a sigh. "I am no judge of character."

He turned abruptly, and skirted the hill on his way to the gardens of the Villa Borghese, where he found shade and seclusion in the early afternoon. The carriages of fashionable Rome had not yet begun to drive in at the gate. The cypress avenues, the groves of immemorial ilex, the verdant lawns where the fountains leapt sunward, were peopled only by creatures of fable, fixed in marble, faun and dryad, hero and god. Martin Disney plunged into the shadow of one of those funereal avenues, and—while the sun blazed in almost tropical splendour upon the open lawn in the far distance—he walked as it were in the deep of night, a night whose gloom harmonized with that darker night in his despairing heart.

Great God, how he had loved her! How he had looked up to her, revering even her weakness as the expression of a childlike purity. And while he had been praying for her, and dreaming of her, and longing for her, and thinking of her as the very type of womanly chastity, unapproachable by temptation, unassailable, secure in her innocence and simplicity as Athene or Artemis with all their armour of defence; while he had so loved and trusted her, she had flung herself into the arms of a profligate—as easily won as the lightest wanton. She had done this thing, and then she had welcomed him, with wan, sweet smiles, to his dishonoured home. She had made him drink the cup of shame—a by-word it might be for the whole parish, as well as for that one man who had dared to hint at evil. And yet he had forgiven her—forgiven one to whom pardon meant only a peaceful ending; forgiven as a man holds himself forgiven by an all-merciful God, as he hears words of pity and promise murmured into his ear by the priest upon the scaffold, when the rope is round his neck and the drop is ready to fall. How could he withhold such pardon when he had been taught that God forgives the repentant murderer?

## CHAPTER XXVIII.

## "THOUGH LOVE AND LIFE AND DEATH SHOULD COME AND GO."

Isola was alone in the spacious Roman drawing-room, its wide windows open to the soft, warm air. The sun was off that side of the house now, and the Venetian shutters had been pushed back; and between the heavy stone pillars of the loggia she saw the orange and magnolia trees in the garden, and the pale gold of the mimosas beyond. The sun was shining full upon the Hill of Gardens, that hill at whose foot Nero was buried in secret at dead of night by his faithful freedman and the devoted woman who loved him to the shameful end of the shameful life; that hill whose antique groves the wicked Cæsar's ghost had once made a place of terror. The wicked ghost was laid now. Modern civilization had sent Nero the way of all phantoms; and fashionable Rome made holiday on the Hill of Gardens. A military band was playing there this afternoon in the golden light, and the familiar melodies in Don Giovanni were wafted ever and anon in little gusts of sweetness to the loggia where the vivid crimson of waxen camelias and the softer rose of oleander blossoms gave brightness and colour to the dark foliage and the cold white stone.

Isola heard those far-off melodies faint in the distance—heard without heeding. The notes were beyond measure familiar, interwoven with the very fabric of her life, for those were the airs Martin Disney loved, and she had played them to him nearly every evening in their quiet, monotonous life. She heard, unheeding, for her thoughts had wandered back to the night of the ball at Lostwithiel and all that went after it—the fatal night that struck the death-knell of peace and innocence.

How vividly she remembered every detail—her fluttering apprehensions during the long drive on the dark road, up hill and down hill; her eagerness for the delight of the dance, as an unaccustomed pleasure—a scene to which young beauty flies as the moth to the flame; her remorseful consciousness that she had done wrong in yielding to the temptation which drew her there; the longing to see Lostwithiel once more—Lostwithiel, whom she had vowed to herself never to meet again of her own free will. She had gone home that afternoon resolved to forego the ball, to make any social sacrifice rather than look upon that man whose burning words of love, breathed in her ear before she had enough of nerve or calmness to silence him, had left her scathed and geared as if the lightning had blasted her. She had heard his avowal. There was no room now to doubt the meaning of all that had gone before, no ground now for believing in a tender, platonic admiration, lapping her round with its soft radiance—a light, but not a fire. That which had burnt into her soul to-day was the fierce flame of a dishonouring love, the bold avowal of a lover who wanted to steal her from her husband, and make her a sinner before her God.

She knew this much—had brooded upon it all the evening—and yet she was going to a place where she must inevitably meet the Tempter.

She was going because it was expedient to go; because her persistent refusal to be there might give rise to guesses and suspicions that would lead to a discovery of the real reason of her absence. She had often seen the subtle process, the society search-light by which Trelasco and Fowey could arrive at the innermost working of a neighbour's heart, the deepest mysteries of motive.

She was going to the ball after all, fevered, anxious, full of dim forebodings; and yet with an eager expectancy; and yet with a strange over-mastering joy. How should she meet him? How could she avoid him, without ostentatious avoidance, knowing how many eyes would be quick to mark any deviation from conventional behaviour? Somehow or other she was resolved to avoid all association with him; to get her programme filled before he could ask her to dance; or to refuse in any case if he asked her. He would scarcely venture to approach her after what had been said in the lane, when her indignation had been plainly expressed with angry tears. No, he would hardly dare. And so—in a vague bewilderment at finding she was at her journey's end—she saw the lights of the little town close upon her, and in the next few minutes her carriage was moving slowly in the rank of carriages setting down their freight at the door of the inn.

Vaguely, as in a dream, she saw the lights and the flowers, the satin gowns and the diamonds, the scarlet and white upon the walls, brush and vizard, vizard and brush. He was not there. She looked along the crowd, and that tall figure and that dark head were absent. She ought to have been glad at this respite, and yet her heart grew heavy as lead.

Later he was there, and she was waltzing with him. At the last moment when he was standing before her, cool, self-possessed, as it were unconscious of that burning past, she had no more power to refuse to be his partner than the bird has to escape from the snake. She had given him her hand, and they were moving slowly, softly to the music of the soft, slow waltz. Myosotis, myosotis—mystic flower which means everlasting remembrance! Would she ever forget this night? Their last meeting—safest possible meeting-place here in the shine of the lamps—in the sight of the multitude. Here she could so easily hold him at a distance. Here she might speak to him lightly, as if she too were unconscious of the past. Here she was safe against his madness and her own weak unstable heart, which fluttered at his smallest word.

And so the night wore on, and she danced with him more times than she could count, forgetting, or pretending to forget, other engagements; going through an occasional waltz with another partner just for propriety's sake, and hardly knowing who that partner was; knowing so well that there was some one else standing against the wall, watching her every movement, with the love-light in his eyes.

Then came the period after supper when they sat in the ante-room and let the dances go by, hearing the music of waltzes which they were to have danced together, hearing and heeding not. And then came a sudden scare at the thought of the hour. Was it late?

Late, very late!

The discovery fluttered and unnerved her, and she was scarcely able to collect her thoughts as he handed her into the carriage and shut the door.

"Surely it was a grey horse that brought me!" she exclaimed, and in the next minute she recognized Lostwithiel's brougham, the same carriage in which she had been driven home through the rain upon that unforgotten night when his house sheltered her, when she saw his face for the first time.

Yes, it was his carriage. She knew the colour of the lining, the little brass clock, the reading-lamp, the black panther rug. She pulled at the check-string, but without effect. The carriage drove on, slowly, but steadily, to the end of the town. She let down the window and called to the coachman. There was only one man on the box, and he took no notice of her call.

Yes, he had heard, perhaps, for he drew up his horse suddenly by the road-side, a little way beyond the town. A man opened the door and sprang in, breathless after running. It was Lostwithiel.

"You put me into your carriage!" she cried distractedly. "How could you make such a mistake? Pray tell him to go back to the inn directly."

They were driving along the country road at a rapid pace, and he had seated himself by her side, clasping her hand. He pulled up the window nearest her, and prevented her calling to the coachman.

"Why should you go back? You will be home sooner with my horse than with the screw that brought you."

"But the fly will be waiting for me—the man will wonder."

"Let him wonder. He won't wait very long, you may be assured. He will guess what has happened. In the confusion of carriages you took the wrong one. Isola, I am going to leave Cornwall to-night—to leave England—perhaps never to return. Give me the last few moments of my life here. Be merciful to me. I am going away—perhaps for ever."

"Take me home," she said. "Are you really taking me home? Is this the right way?"

"Of course it is the right way. Do you suppose I am going to drive you to London?"

He let down the glass suddenly, and pointed into the night.

"Isola, do you see where we are? There's the sign-post at the cross roads. There's the tower of Tywardreath Church, though you can hardly see it in this dim light. Are you satisfied now?"

He had drawn up the glass again. The windows were clouded by the mist of their mingled breath; the atmosphere was faint with the odour of the faded chrysanthemums on her gown and the carnation in the lapel of his coat. All that she could see of the outer world was the blurred light of the carriage lamps. The high-spirited horse was going up and down the hills at a perilous pace. At this rate the journey could not take long.

And then—and then—he came back to the prayer he had breathed in her ear more than twelve hours ago in the wintry lane. He loved her, he loved her, he loved her! Could she refuse to go away with him— having woven herself into his life, having made him madly, helplessly in love with her? Could she refuse? Had any woman the right to refuse? He appealed to her sense of honour. She had gone too far—she had granted too much already, granting him her love. She was in his arms in the dim light, in the faint, dream-like atmosphere. He was taking possession of her weak heart by all that science of love in which he was past master. Honour, conscience, fidelity to the absent, piety, innocence were being swept away in that lava flood of passion. Helpless, irresolute, she faltered again and again. "Take me home, Lostwithiel! Have mercy! Take me home."

He stopped those tremulous lips with a kiss—the kiss that betrays. The carriage dashed down a steep bill, rattled along a street so narrow that the wheels seemed to grind against the house-fronts on each side, down hill again, and then the horse was pulled up suddenly in a stony square, and the door opened, and the soft, fresh sea-breeze blew among her loosened hair, and upon her uncovered neck, and she heard the gentle plish-plash of a boat moored against the quay at her feet.

"This is not home!" she cried piteously.

"Yes, it is home, love, our home for a little while—the home that can carry us to the other end of the world, if you will."

The quay, and the water, and the few faint lights here and there grew dark, and she knew no more, till she heard the sailors crying,

"Yeo, heave, yeo," and the heavy sails flapping, and the creak of the boom as it swayed in the wind, and felt the dancing motion of the boat as she cut her way through the waves, felt the strong arm that clasped her, and heard the low, fond voice that murmured in her ear, "Isola, Isola, forgive me! I could not live without you."

---

That which came afterwards had seemed one long and lurid dream—a dream of fair weather and foul; of peril and despair; of passionate, all-conquering love.

To-day, as she lay supine in the afternoon silence—lying as Tabitha had left her, in a fevered sleep—the vision of that past came back upon her in all its vivid colouring, almost as distinctly as it had re-acted itself in her hours of delirium, when she had lived that tragic chapter of her life over again, and had felt the fury of the waves and breathed the chill, salt air of the tempest-driven sea, and had seen the moon riding high amidst the cloud-chaos—now appearing, now vanishing, as if she too were a storm-driven bark in a raging sea.

Oh God! how vividly those hours came back! The awful progress from Ushant to Arcachon; the darkness of the brief day; the horror of the long night; the shuddering yacht, with straining spars, and broadside beaten by a heaving mass of water, that struck her with the force of a thousand battering-rams, blow after blow, each blow seeming as if the next must always be the last—the final crash and end of all things. The pretty, dainty vessel, long and narrow, rode like an eggshell on those furious waters—here a long wall of inky blackness, rising like a mountain-ridge, and bearing down on the doomed ship, and beyond, as far as the eye could reach, a waste of surf, livid in the moonlight. What helpless insignificance, as of a leaf tossed on a whirlpool, when that mountainous mass took the yacht and lifted her on cyclopean shoulders, and shook her off again into the black trough of the sea, as into the depths of hell! And this not once only, nor a hundred times only, but on through that endless-seeming night, on in the sickly winter dawn and in the faint yellow gleam of a rainy noontide—on through day that seemed mixed and entangled with night, as if the beginning of creation had come round again, and the light were not yet divided from the darkness.

Oh, those passionate, never-to-be-forgotten moments, when she had stood with him at the top of the companion, looking out upon those livid waters; fondly believing that each moment was to be their last; that the gates of death were opening yonder—a watery way, a gulf to which they must go down, in a moment, in a little moment, in a flash, in a breath, at the next, or the next, or the next mad plunge of that hurrying bark. Yes, death was there, in front of them— inevitable, imminent, immediate—and life and sin, shame, remorse, were done with, along with the years that lay behind them, a page blotted and blurred with one passionate madness, which had changed the colour of a woman's life. She knew not how she bore up against the force of that tempest; clinging to him with her bare, wet arms; held up by him; crouching against the woodwork, which shook and rattled with every blow of the battering-rams. She only knew that his arms were round her, that she was safe with him, even when the leaping surf rose high above her head, wrapping her round like a mantle, blinding, drowning her in a momentary extinction. She only knew that his lips were close to her ear, and that in a momentary lull of those awful voices he murmured, "We are going to die, Isola! The boat cannot live through such a storm! We shall go down to death together!" And her lips turned to him with a joyful cry, "Thank God!" Then again, in a minute's interval, he pleaded, "Forgive me, love; my stolen love, forgive me before we die!" And again, "Was it a crime, Isola?" "If it was, I forgive you!" she whispered, clinging to him as the blast struck them.

---

Cruel revulsion of feeling, bitter irony of Fate, when the great grim waves—which had seemed like living monsters hurrying down upon them with malignant fury to tear and to devour—when the awful sea began to roar with a lesser voice, and the thunder of the battering-rams had a duller sound, and the bows of the yacht no longer plunged straight down into the leaden-coloured pit; no longer climbed those inky ridges with such blind impetus, as of a cockle-shell in a whirlpool. Bitter sense of loss and dismay when the grey, cold dawn lighted a quieter sea, and she heard the captain telling Lostwithiel that they had seen the worst of the storm, and that there was no fear now. He was going to put on more canvas: and hadn't the lady better go below, where it was warm. She needn't feel anyway nervous now. They would soon be in the roadstead of Arcachon.

She had not felt the chill change from night to morning. She had not felt the surf that drenched her loose, entangled hair. She hardly know when or how Lostwithiel had wrapped her in his fur-lined coat; but she found that she was so enveloped presently when she stumbled and staggered down to the cabin, and flung herself face downward upon the sofa, in a paroxysm of impotent despair.

Death would have delivered her. The tempest was her friend; and the tempest had passed her by, and left her lying there like a weed, more worthless than any weed that over the sea cast up to rot upon the barren rocks. Yes, she was left there; left in a life that sin had blighted; loathsome to herself, hateful to her God.

She locked herself in the cabin, while the hurrying footsteps overhead told her that Lostwithiel was working with the sailors.

An hour later, and he was at the cabin door, pleading for one kind word, entreating her to let him see her, were it only for a few moments, to know that she was not utterly broken down by the peril she had passed through. He pleaded in vain. She would give no answer—she would speak no word. Indeed, in that dull agony of shame and despair it seemed to her as if a dumb devil had entered into her. Her parched lips seemed to have lost the power of speech. She lay there, staring straight before her at all the swinging things on the cedar panel—the books and photographs—and lamps and frivolities, vibrating with every movement of the sea. Her hands were clenched until the nails cut into the flesh. Her heart was throbbing with a dull, slow beat that made itself torturingly audible. Did God create His creatures for such agony? Had she been foredoomed everlastingly—in that awful incomprehensible ante-natal Eternity—foredoomed to this fallen state, to this unutterable shame?

Hours went by, she knew not how. Again and again Lostwithiel came to her door, and talked and entreated—Heaven knows how tenderly—with what deep contrition, with what fond pleading for pardon. But the dumb devil held her still. She wrapped herself in a sullen despair—not anger, for anger is active. Hers was only a supine resistance.

At last she heard him come with one of the sailors, and she could make out from their whispering talk that they were going to force open the door. Then she started up in a fury, and went and flung herself against the cedar panels.

"If you don't leave me alone in my misery I will kill myself!" she cried.

The long night was over; and the sun was high. It seemed as if they were sailing over a summer sea, and through the scuttle port she saw a little foreign town nestling under the shelter of pine-clad hills.

She woke from brief and troubled slumbers to see this smiling shore, and at first she fancied they must have sailed back to Cornwall, and that this was some unknown bay upon that rock-bound coast; but the sapphire sea and the summer-like sunshine suggested a fairer clime than rugged Britain.

While she was looking out at the crescent-shaped bay, and the long line of white villas, the anchor was being lowered. The sea was almost as smooth as a lake, and those tranquil waters had the colour and the sheen of sapphire and emerald. She thought of the jasper sea—the sea of the Apocalypse, the tideless sea beside that land of the New Jerusalem where there are no more tears, where there can be no more sin, a city of ransomed souls, redeemed from all earth's iniquity.

A boat was being lowered. She heard the scroop of the ropes in the davits; she heard footsteps on the accommodation-ladder, and then the dip of oars, and presently the boat passed between her and the sunlit waters, and she saw Lostwithiel sitting in the stern, with the rudder-lines in his hands, while two sailors were bending to their oars, with wind-blown hair and cheery, smiling faces, broad and red in the gay morning sunshine.

He was gone, and she breathed more freely. There was a sense of release in his absence; and for the first time she looked round the cabin, where beautiful and luxurious things lay, thrown here and there in huddled masses of brilliant colour. A Japanese screen, a masterpiece of rainbow-hued embroidery on a sea-green ground, flung against the panelling at one end—Persian curtains wrenched from their fastenings and hanging awry—satin pillows that had drifted into a heap in one corner—signs of havoc everywhere. She stood in the midst of all this ruin, and looked at her own reflection in a Venetian glass riveted to the panelling, about the only object that had held its place through the storm.

Her own reflection. Was that really herself, that ghastly image which the glass gave back to her? The reflection of a woman with livid cheeks and blanched lips, with swollen eyelids, and dark rings of purple round the haggard eyes, and hair rough and tangled as Medusa's locks, and bare shoulders from which the stained satin bodice had slipped away. Her wedding-gown! Could that defiled garment—the long folds of the once shining satin, draggled and dripping with sea-water—could these tawdry rags be the wedding-gown she had put on in her proud and happy innocence in the old bedroom at Dinan, with mother, and servants, and a useful friend or two helping and hindering?

Oh, if they could see her now, those old friends of her unclouded childhood, the mother and father who had loved and trusted her, who had never spoken of evil things in her hearing, had never thought that sin could come near her! And she had fallen like the lowest of womankind. She had forfeited her place among the virtuous and happy for ever. She, Martin Disney's wife! That good man, that brave soldier who had fought for Queen and country—it was his wife who stood there in her shame, haggard and dishevelled!

She flung her arms above her head and wrung her hands in a paroxysm of despair. Then, with a little cry, she plucked at the loose wild tresses as if she would have torn them from her head; and then she threw herself upon the cabin floor in her agony, and grovelled there, a creature for whom death would have been a merciful release.

"If I could die—if I could but die, and no one know!" she moaned.

She lifted herself up again upon her knees, and, with one hand upon the floor, looked round the walls of the cabin—looked at a trophy of Moorish and Italian arms which decorated the panelling, searching for some sharp dagger with which she might take her hated life. And then came the thought of what must follow death, not for her in the dim incomprehensible eternity, but for those who loved her on earth, for those who would have to be told how she had been found, in her draggled wedding-gown, stabbed by her own hand on board Lord Lostwithiel's yacht. What a story of shame and crime for newspapers to embellish, and for scandal-lovers to gloat over! No! She dared not destroy herself thus. She must collect her senses, escape from her seducer, and keep the secret of her dishonour.

She took off her gown, and rolled train and bodice into a bundle as small as she could make them. Then she looked about the cabin for some object with which to weight her bundle. Yes, that would do. A little brass dolphin that was used to steady the open door. That was heavy enough, perhaps. She put it into the middle of her bundle, tied a ribbon tightly round the whole, and then she opened the scuttle port and dropped her wedding-garment into the sea. The keen fresh wind, the wind from pine-clad hills and distant snow mountains, blew in upon her bare neck and chilled her; but it helped to cool the fever of her mind, and she sat down and leant her head upon her clasped hands, and tried to think what she must do to free herself from the toils in which guilty love had caught her.

She must escape from the yacht. She must go back to England—somehow.

She thought that if she were to appeal to Lostwithiel's honour some spark of better feeling would prevail over that madness which had wrecked her, and he would let her go, he would take her back to England, and facilitate her secret return to the home she had dishonoured. But could she trust herself to make that appeal? Could she stand fast against his pleading, if he implored her to stay with him, to live the life that he had planned for her, the life that he had painted so eloquently, the dreamy, beautiful life amidst earth's most romantic scenes, the life of love in idleness? Could she resist him if he should plead—it might be with tears—he, whom she adored, her destroyer and her divinity? No, she must leave the yacht before he came back to her. But how?

There were only men on board. There was no woman to whose compassion she could appeal, no woman to lend her clothes to cover her. She saw herself once again in the Venetian glass, in her long trained petticoat of muslin and lace, so daintily fresh when she dressed for the ball—muslin and lace soddened by the sea, torn to shreds where her feet had caught in the flounces as she stumbled down the companion during last night's storm. A fitting costume in which to travel from Arcachon to London, verily! She opened a door leading to an inner cabin, which contained bed and bath, and all toilet appliances. Hanging against the wall there were three dressing-gowns, the lightest and least masculine of the three being a robe of Indian camel's hair, embroidered with gray silk—a shapeless garment with loose sleeves and a girdle.

Here, within locked doors, she made her hurried toilet, with much cold water. She brushed her long, ragged hair with one of the humblest of the brushes. She would not take so much as a few drops from the great crystal bottle of eau de Cologne which was held in a silver frame suspended from the ceiling. Nothing of his would she touch, nothing belonging to the man who wanted to pour his fortune into her lap, to make his life her life, his estate her estate, his name her name, could she but survive the ordeal of the divorce court, and shake off old ties.

She rolled her hair in a large coil at the back of her head. She put on the camel's hair dressing-gown, and tied the girdle round her long, slim waist, and having done this she looked altogether a different creature from that vision of haggard shame which she had seen just now with loathing. She had a curious Puritan air in her sad coloured raiment, and braided hair.

Scarcely had she finished when she heard the dip of oars, and looking out in an agony of horror at the apprehension of Lostwithiel's return, she saw a boat laden with two big milliner's baskets, and with a woman sitting in the stem. The men who were rowing this boat were not of the crew of the *Vendetta*.

She had not long to wonder. She unlocked her door, and went into the adjoining cabin, while the boat came alongside, and woman and baskets were hauled upon the deck.

Three minutes afterwards the cabin-boy knocked at her door, and told her that there was a person from Arcachon to see her, a dressmaker with things that had been ordered for her.

She unlocked the door, for the first time since she locked it at dawn, and found herself face to face with a smiling young person, whose black eyes and olive complexion were warm with the glow of the south, golden in the eyes, carnation on the plump, oval cheeks.

This young person had the honour to bring the trousseau which Monsieur had sent for Madame's inspection. Monsieur had told her how sadly inconvenienced Madame had been by the accident by which all her luggage had been left upon the quay at the moment of sailing. In truth it must have been distressing for Madame, as it had evidently been distressing for Monsieur in his profound sympathy with Madame, his wife. In the meantime she, the young person, had complied with Monsieur's orders, and had brought all that there was of the best and most delicate and refined for Madame's gracious inspection.

The cabin-boy brought in the two baskets, which the milliner opened with an air, taking out the delicate lingerie, the soft silk and softer cashmere—peignoirs, frilled petticoats, a fluff and flutter of creamy lace and pale satin ribbons, transforming simplest garments into things of beauty. She spread out her wares, chattering all the while, and then looked at Madame for approval.

Isola scarcely glanced at all the finery. She pointed to the only plain walking-gown among all the delicate prettinesses, the silks and cashmeres and laces—a grey tweed tailor-gown, with no adornment except a little narrow black braid.

"I will keep that," she said, "and one set of under-linen, the plainest. You can take all the rest of the things back to your shop. Please help me to dress as quickly as you can—I want to go on shore in the boat that takes you back."

"But, Madame, Monsieur insisted that I should bring a complete trousseau. He wished Madame to supply herself with all things needful for a long cruise in the south."

"He was mistaken. My luggage is safe enough. I shall have it again in a few days. I only want clothes to wear for a day or two. Kindly do what I ask."

Her tone was so authoritative that the milliner complied, reluctantly, and murmuring persuasive little speeches while she assisted Madame to dress. All that she had brought was of the most new—expressly arrived from Paris, from one of the most distinguished establishments in the Rue de la Paix. Fashions change so quickly—and the present fashions were so enchanting, so original. She must be pardoned if she suggested that nothing in Madame's wardrobe could be so new or so elegant as these latest triumphs of an artistic *faiseur*. Madame took no heed of her eloquence, but hurried through the simple toilet, insisted upon all the finery being replaced in the two baskets, and then went upon deck with the milliner.

"I am going on shore to his lordship," she said, with quiet authority, to the captain.

It was a deliberate lie—the first she had told, but not the last she would have to tell.

She landed on the beach at Arcachon—penniless, but with a diamond ring on her wedding finger—her engagement ring—which she knew, by a careless admission of Martin Disney's, to have cost fifty pounds. She left the milliner, and went into the little town, dreading to meet Lostwithiel at every step. She found a complacent jeweller who was willing to advance twenty-five Napoleons upon the ring, and promised to return it to her on the receipt of that sum, with only a bagatelle of twenty francs for interest, since Madame would redeem her pledge almost immediately.

Furnished with this money she drove straight to the station, and waited there in the most obscure corner she could find till the first train left for Bordeaux. At Bordeaux she had a long time to wait, still in hiding, before the express left for Paris—and then came the long, lonely journey—from Bordeaux to Paris—from Paris to London—from London to Trelasco. It seemed an endless pilgrimage, a nightmare dream of dark night and wintry day, made hideous by the ceaseless throb of the engine, the perpetual odour of sulphur and smoke. She reached Trelasco somehow, and sank exhausted in Tabitha's arms.

"What day is it?" she asked faintly, looking round the familiar room, as if she had never seen it before.

"Thursday, ma'am. You have been away ten days," the old servant answered coldly.

It was only the next day that Tabitha told her mistress she must leave her.

"There is no need to talk about what has happened," she said. "I have kept your secret. I have let no one know that you were away. I packed Susan off for a holiday the morning after the ball. I don't believe any one knows anything about you—unless you were seen yesterday on your way home."

Then came stern words of renunciation, a conscientious but rather narrow-minded woman's protest against sin.

## CHAPTER XXIX.

### "I, YOU, AND GOD CAN COMPREHEND EACH OTHER."

It was two months after Allegra's wedding-day, and Martin Disney had been warned that the closing hour of the young life he had watched so tenderly was not far off. It might come to-morrow; or it might not come for a week; or the lingering flame might go flickering on, fainting and reviving in the socket, for another month. He must hold himself prepared for the worst. Death might come suddenly at the last, like a thief in the night; or by stealthy, gradual steps, and slowest progress from life to clay.

He sat beside Isola's sofa in the Roman lodging as he had sat beside her bed in that long illness at Trelasco, when her wandering mind appalled him more than her bodily weakness. He watched as faithfully as he had watched then, but this time without hope.

Father Rodwell had been with her at seven o'clock upon the last three mornings, and had administered the sacrament to her and to her husband, and to the faithful Tabitha, one with them in piety and love. The priest thought that each celebration would be the last; but she rallied a little as the day wore on, and lived till sunset; lived through the long painful night; and another day dawned, and he found her waiting for him in the morning, ready to greet him with her pale smile when he appeared upon the threshold of her room, after going up the staircase in saddest apprehension, dreading to hear that all was over, except the funeral service and the funeral bell.

She insisted upon getting up and going into the drawing-room, feeble as she was. Tabitha was so handy and so helpful that the fatigue of an invalid's toilet was lightened to the uttermost. Tabitha and the colonel carried her from the bedroom to the drawing-room upon her couch, and carried the couch back to the bedside in the evening. Before noon she was lying in the sunlit salon, surrounded with flowers and photographs and books and newspapers, and all things that lighten the monotonous hours of sickness.

Nor was companionship ever wanting. Martin Disney devoted himself to her with an unfailing patience. Upon no pretence would he leave her for more than half an hour at a time—-just the space of a walk to the Hill of Gardens, or the length of the Via de' Condotti and the Corso; just the space of a cigar in the loggia.

He read to her, he talked to her, he waited upon her. Tabitha and he were her only nurses; for Löttchen was a young woman of profound concentration of motive, and had early taken unto herself the motto, One baby, one nurse. She conscientiously performed her duty to her infant charge; but she rarely lifted a finger to help any one else.

It was drawing towards the end of July; the weather had been lovely hitherto—hot, and very hot, but not insupportable for those who could afford to dawdle and sleep away their mid-day and afternoon existence—who had horses to carry them about in the early mornings, and a carriage to drive them in moonlit gardens and picturesque places. In the suburbs of the great city, across the arid Campagna yonder, at Tivoli, and Frascati, and Albano, and Castel Gandolfo, people had been revelling in the summer, living under Jove's broad roof, with dancing and sports, and music and feasting, and rustic, innocent kisses, snatched amidst the darkness of groves whose only lamps are fireflies—deep woods of ilex, where the nightingale sings long and late, and the grasshopper trills his good night through the perfumed herbage.

Here, in Rome, the heat was more oppressive, and the splashing of the city's many fountains was the only relief from the glare and dazzle of the piazzas, the whiteness of the great blocks of houses in the new streets and boulevards. Blinds were lowered, and shops were shut, in the blinding noontide heat, and through the early afternoon the eternal city was almost as silent and reposeful as the sleeping beauty—to awaken at sundown to movement, and life, and music, and singing, in lighted streets and crowded cafes.

Suddenly, in the dim grey of the morning, the slumberous calm of summer changed to howling wind and tropical rain—torrential rain, that filled every gutter, and splashed from every housetop, and ran in wild cascades from every alley on the steep hillsides. The Campagna was one vast lake, illumined with flashes of lightning, and the thunder pealed and reverberated along the lofty parapets of the ruined aqueducts. The tall cypresses in the Pincian Gardens bent like saplings before that mighty wind, which seemed to howl and shriek its loudest as it came tearing down from the hill to whistle and rave among the housetops in the Piazza di Spagna.

"One would think the ghost of Nero were shrieking in the midst of the tempest," said Isola, as she listened to the fitful sobbing of the wind late in the dull grey afternoon, while her husband and Father Rodwell sat near her couch, keeping up that sad pretence of cheerfulness which love struggles to maintain upon the very edge of the grave—the brokenhearted make-believe of those who know that death waits at the door. "There comes a shrill cry every now and then like the scream of a wicked spirit in pain."

"Rome is full of ghosts," answered the priest, "but there are the shadows of the good and the great as well as of the wicked. Walking alone in twilight on the Aventine, I should hardly be surprised to meet the spirit of Gregory the Great wandering amidst the scenes of his saintly life; nor do I ever go into the Pantheon at dusk without half expecting to see the shade of Raffaelle. And there are others—some I knew in the flesh—Wiseman and Antonelli, Gibson, the sculptor, consummate artist and gentlest of men—yes, Rome is full of the shadows of the good and the wise. One can afford to put up with Nero."

"You don't mean me to think that you believe in ghosts?" asked Isola, deeply interested.

It was only five o'clock, yet the sky was grey with the greyness of late evening. Here in this land of sunshine there had been all day long the brooding gloom of storm-clouds, and a sky that was dark as winter.

"I won't analyze my own feelings on the subject; I will quote the words of a man at whose feet it was my happiness to sit sometimes when I was a lad at Oxford. Canon Mozley has not shrunk from facing the great problem of spiritual life in this world—of an invisible after-existence upon the earth when the body is dust. 'Is the mother of our Lord now existing?' he asks, and answers, 'Yes. I believe that all fathers, mothers, sons, and daughters are now existing. Nature has disposed of their bodies as far as we can trace her work; but their souls remain. So I read in Homer, in Virgil, and in the New Testament. This existence I am permitted to believe is a conscious and active existence.' Canon Mozley, the man who wrote those words, and much more in the same strain, was not an idle visionary. If he could afford to believe in the presence of the dead among us, why, so can I. And I believe that Gregory the Great has whispered at the ear of many a Holy Father in the long line of his successors, and has influenced many a Cardinal's vote, and has been an invisible power in many a council."

"I like to believe in ghosts," said Isola, gently. "But I thank God those that I love are still in this life."

She held out her hand with a curiously timid gesture to her husband, who clasped it tenderly, bending his lips to kiss the pale thin fingers. Oh, Death, pity and pardon are so interwoven with thine image that neither pride nor anger has any force against thy softening influence. She had been false. She had wronged him and dishonoured herself, cruelly, cruelly, most cruelly; but she had suffered and repented, and she was passing away from him. Let the broken spirit pass in peace!

---

That day wore itself out in storm and tempest, and the night came on like a fierce death-struggle; and the wind raved and shrieked at intervals all through the night; and again next day there were gloom and darkness, and a sky heaped up with masses of lead-coloured cloud; and again the torrential rain streamed from the housetops and splashed in the streets below; a dreary day to be endured even by the healthy and the happy—a day of painful oppression for an invalid. Isola's spirits sank to the lowest depth, and for the first time since Allegra's marriage she talked hopelessly of their separation.

"If I could only see her once more before I die," she sighed.

"My dear love, you shall see her as soon as the railway can bring her here. Remember, it is you who have forbidden me to send for her. You know how dearly she loves you—how willingly she would come to you. I'll telegraph to her within half an hour."

"No, no, no," Isola protested hurriedly. "No, we can never meet again in this world. I took my farewell of her in the church. I meant it to be farewell. I was very happy for her sake when I saw her married to the man she loved. It was a selfish repining that made me ask for her just now. I would not have her summoned here for worlds. She is so happy at Venice—happy in her honeymoon dream. Tell her nothing, Martin—nothing till you can tell her that my days have ended peacefully. She has borne her burden for me in the past. I want her to be free from all care about me—but not to forget me."

"She will not forget, Isola. She loves you fondly and truly."

"Yes, I am sure of that. She was dearer to me than my own sister— cared for me much more than Gwendolen ever cared, though Gwen and I were always good friends. Poor feather-headed Gwen! She writes me affectionate letters, hoping she may get to Italy in the autumn, though it is impossible for her to come just now. And mother and father write to me just in the same way—mother regretting that her health won't allow her to leave Dinan; father hoping to see me in the autumn. Their letters are full of hopefulness," she concluded, with a faint touch of irony.

Her husband read to her for the greater part of the long gloomy day. He read St. Thomas à Kempis for some part of the time. The book had been on the little table by her side throughout her illness. He read two or three of Frederick Robertson's sermons, and for occasional respite from too serious thought he read her favourite poems—Adonaïs, Alastor, and some of Shelley's lovely lyrics, and those passages in Childe Harold which had acquired a new charm for her since she had grown familiar with Rome.

"Read to me about Venice," she said, "and let me think of Allegra and Captain Hulbert. I love to fancy them gliding along those narrow, picturesque streets, in the great, graceful, ponderous gondola I remember so well. It is so nice to know of their happiness—and to know that they need never be parted."

So the long summer day—without the glow and glory of summer— wore on, and except for her excessive languor and feebleness there were no indications that the patient's state was any worse than it had been for some weeks. The doctor came late in the afternoon, and felt her pulse, and talked to her a little; but it was easy to see that his visit was only a formula.

"You have such an excellent nurse, Mrs. Disney, that I consider my position almost a sinecure," he said, smiling at the faithful Tabitha, who stood waiting for his instructions, and who never forgot the minutest detail.

Tabitha came in from the adjoining bedroom every now and then, and adjusted the pillows on the sofa, and sprinkled eau de Cologne, or fanned the invalid with a large Japanese fan, or arranged the silken coverlet over her feet, or brought her some small refreshment in the way of a cup of soup or jelly, and tenderly coaxed and assisted her to take it, talking just as much or as little as seemed prudent, always careful neither to fatigue nor excite her charge.

---

It was between eight and nine in the evening, and there was a gloomy twilight in the loggia, and in the garden beyond. The wind which had dropped in the afternoon had begun to rage again, as if not only Nero but all the wicked emperors were abroad in the air.

Isola had begged that one of the windows might be opened, in spite of the tempestuous weather; and the cold damp breath of the storm crept into the room and chilled Martin Disney as he sat by his wife's sofa, reading a London paper that had come by the evening post.

The only artificial light in the room was a reading-lamp at the colonel's elbow, shaded from the draught by the four-leaved screen which protected the invalid. The gloomy grey daylight had not quite faded, and through the half-open door opposite him Martin Disney saw the white marble wall of the staircase, and some oleanders in stone vases that stood on the spacious landing.

He had been reading to Isola nearly all day. He was reading to himself now, trying to forget his own grief in the consideration of a leading article which prophecied a European war, and the ultimate extinction of English influence in continental politics.

There was perfect stillness in the room. Isola had been lying with closed eyes a little time before, and he fancied that she was sleeping.

The silence had lasted for nearly an hour, broken only by the shriek of the wind, and by the chiming of the quarters from the Church of La Trinità de' Monti, when Colonel Disney was startled by his wife's hand clutching his arm, and his wife's agitated whisper sounding close to his ear.

"Martin! Did you see him?"

She had lifted herself into a sitting position, she who had not been able to sit up for many days past.

The hectic bloom had faded from her cheeks and left them ashy pale. Her eyes seemed almost starting from her head, straining their gaze as if to penetrate the deepening shadows on the landing beyond the half-open door.

"My love, you have been dreaming," said Disney, soothing her with womanly gentleness. "Lie down again, my poor dear. See, let me arrange the pillows and make you quite comfortable."

"No, no! I was not dreaming. I have not been asleep. He was there. I saw him as plainly as I see you. He pushed the door a little further open and looked in at me. I saw his face in the lamplight, very pale."

Disney glanced at the door involuntarily. Yes, the aperture was certainly wider than when he looked at it last; just as if some one's hand had pushed the door a little further back. The hand of the wind, no doubt.

"My dear girl, believe me, you were dreaming. No one could have approached that doorway without my hearing them."

"I have been lying awake thinking all the time you have been reading your paper, Martin. I never had less inclination to sleep. I know that he was there looking in at me, with a smile upon his pale face. But he has gone. Thank God, he has gone! Only I can't help wondering how he came there, without our hearing his step upon the stone stair."

"Who was it, Isola?"

He knew what the answer would be. He thought her mind was wandering, and he knew there was only one image which could so agitate her.

"Lostwithiel."

"A delusion, Isa. Lord Lostwithiel is far away from Rome. Come, dear love, let me read to you again, and let us have our good Tabitha in to cheer you with a cup of tea, and to brighten up the room a little.

We have been growing low-spirited under the influence of the gloomy weather."

He went out of the room on pretence of summoning Tabitha, and having sent her to watch beside his wife, he ran quickly downstairs to find out if the street door were open or closed. The door was shut and bolted. The servants on the ground floor had not opened the door to any one after five o'clock. There was no possibility of any stranger having entered the house since that hour.

---

The end came that night, with an appalling suddenness. Isola had refused to be carried back to her bedroom at the usual time. She seemed to have a horror of going back to that room, as if the shadows lurking there were full of fear. Even Father Rodwell's presence, which generally had a soothing effect upon her nerves and spirits, failed to comfort her to-night. She refused to lie in her usual position, and insisted upon sitting up, supported by pillows, facing the doorway at which her fancy had evoked Lostwithiel's image. She would not allow the door to be shut, and there was the same strained look in her too brilliant eyes all the evening.

Father Rodwell read aloud to her, continuing a history of St. Cecilia, in which she had been warmly interested; but to-night he could see that her thoughts were not with the book. He read on all the same, hoping that the sound of his voice might lull her to sleep. The wind had gone down as the night advanced, and the stars were shining in the strip of sky above the Pincian Gardens. Colonel Disney was pacing up and down the loggia, smoking his pipe in the cool darkness—full of saddest apprehensions.

Her mind had been wandering, surely, when she had that fancy about Lostwithiel, he told himself. It was something more than a dream. And then he remembered those long nights of delirium after her boy was born—and above all, that one night, when she had fancied herself at sea in a storm, when she had tried to fling herself overboard. He knew now what scene she had re-acted in that delirium, what the vision was which a mind distraught had conjured out of empty darkness.

The priest left them before eleven o'clock, and Martin Disney sat with his wife till long after midnight—Tabitha waiting quietly in the next room—before he could persuade her to go to bed. Isola was more wakeful than usual—though her slumbers had been much broken of late—and there was a restlessness about her which impressed her husband as a sign of evil.

"Is the storm over?" she asked, by-and-by, with her face turned towards the loggia and the starlight above the garden.

"Yes, dearest, all is calm now."

"And the boy?" she said, suddenly looking up at the ceiling above which the child slept with his nurse. "He is asleep, of course."

"I hope so. I went upstairs at nine o'clock, while Father Rodwell was reading to you, and gave him my goodnight kiss. He was fast asleep."

"I wonder whether he will ever think of me when he is a man?" she said musingly.

"Can you doubt that? You will be his most sacred memory."

"Ah," she replied, "he will never know——"

The sentence remained unfinished.

"Will you carry me to my bed, Martin? The room begins to grow dark," she whispered faintly. "I can hardly see your face."

He lifted the wasted form in his arms, and carried her with tenderest care into the next room, and to the pure white bed which had been made ready for her, the long net curtains parted, the coverlet turned down. He laid her there, as he had done many a night during that slow and monotonous journey towards the grave; but her gentle acknowledgment of his carefulness was wanting to-night. Her head sank upon the pillow, her pale lips parted with a fluttering sigh, and all was still.

This was how the end came—suddenly, painlessly. She died like an infant falling asleep.

Colonel Disney laid his wife in the place she had loved, the cemetery under the shadow of the old Roman wall, in a verdant corner near Shelley's grave.

Burial follows death with dreadful swiftness in that southern land, and the earth closed over Isola before noon of the day after her death.

Martin Disney waited to see the new-made grave covered with summer's loveliest blossoms before he left the cemetery and went back to the house to which he had taken his fading wife in the radiant Italian springtime. He paced the desolate rooms, and wandered in and out between the drawing-room and the sunny bedroom, with its snowy curtained bed, and looked at this object and that with tear-dimmed eyes and an aching heart.

---

She was gone. That page of his life was closed for ever. And now he had but one purpose and one desire—to settle his account with the scoundrel who had destroyed her. He had waited till she was at rest: and now the long agony of waiting was over. Nothing could touch *her* more; and he was free to bring her seducer to book.

He had telegraphed in the morning to Captain Hulbert at Venice, but there had been no reply so far; and he could only suppose that Allegra and her husband had left the city upon one of those excursions which his sister had described to him as diversifying their quiet life in their palace on the grand canal. He had not been at home long, and his tired eyes were still dazed and blinded by the flood of sunlight which the servants had let in upon the rooms after the funeral, when a telegram was brought to him.

It was from Brindisi.

"The *Eurydice* went down with all hands last night, off Smyrna. My brother was on board. I am on my way to Greece. If you can be spared go to Allegra.—Hulbert."

Martin Disney knew later that it was between eight and nine o'clock that the *Eurydice* struck upon a rock, and every soul on board her perished.

---

The boy and his nurse went back to Trelasco under Tabitha's escort, and they were followed to Cornwall soon afterwards by the new Lord Lostwithiel and his wife, who established themselves at the Mount, to the great satisfaction of the neighbourhood, where it was felt that the local nobleman had again become a permanent institution. Allegra and her husband took Martin Disney's son under their protection in the absence of his father, who carried a heavy heart back to the jungle and the tent, trying to find distraction and forgetfulness in the pursuit of big game, and who did not revisit the Angler's Nest till two years after his wife's death, when he returned to live a tranquil life among the books in the library which he had built for himself, and to watch the growth of his son, whose every look and tone recalled the image of his dead wife. Sometimes, on drowsy summer afternoons, smoking his pipe under the tulip tree, while the Fowey river rippled by in the sunshine, it seemed to him as if Isola's pensive loveliness, and the years that he had lived with her, and the tears that he had shed for her, and the infinite pity which had blotted out all sense of his deep wrong, were only the transient phases of a long sad dream—the dream of a love that never was returned.

"And yet, and yet," he said to himself, after lengthened meditation, with unseeing eyes fixed upon the movement of the tide, "I think she loved me. I think her heart was mine from the hour her tears welcomed me back to this house, until her last sigh. God help all young wives whom their husbands leave alone in their youth and beauty to stand or fall in the hour of temptation!"

---

Idly exploring the contents of the secretaire in the drawing-room one day, Martin Disney found the telegraphic message which his wife had written—and left unsent—before the Hunt Ball.

THE END.

LONDON: PRINTED BY WILLIAM CLOWES AND SONS, LIMITED,
STAMFORD STREET AND CHARING CROSS.

*At all Booksellers and Bookstalls, price* 2s. 6d. *each, Cloth Gilt.*

THE
AUTHOR'S AUTOGRAPH
EDITION OF MISS
BRADDON'S NOVELS.

Also ready, price 2s. each, Picture Boards.

1. LADY AUDLEY'S SECRET.
2. HENRY DUNBAR.
3. ELEANOR'S VICTORY.
4. AURORA FLOYD.
5. JOHN MARCHMONT'S [LEGACY.]
6. THE DOCTOR'S WIFE.
7. ONLY A CLOD.
8. SIR JASPER'S TENANT.
9. TRAIL OF THE SERPENT.
10. LADY'S MILE.
11. LADY LISLE.
12. CAPTAIN OF THE VULTURE.
13. BIRDS OF PREY.
14. CHARLOTTE'S INHERITANCE.
15. RUPERT GODWIN.
16. RUN TO EARTH.
17. DEAD SEA FRUIT.
18. RALPH THE BAILIFF.
19. FENTON'S QUEST.
20. LOVELS OF ARDEN.
21. ROBERT AINSLEIGH.
22. TO THE BITTER END.
23. MILLY DARRELL.
24. STRANGERS AND PILGRIMS.
25. LUCIUS DAVOREN.
26. TAKEN AT THE FLOOD.
27. LOST FOR LOVE.
28. A STRANGE WORLD.
29. HOSTAGES TO FORTUNE.
30. DEAD MEN'S SHOES.

31. JOSHUA HAGGARD.

32. WEAVERS AND WEFT.

33. AN OPEN VERDICT.

34. VIXEN.

35. THE CLOVEN FOOT.

36. THE STORY OF BARBARA.

37. JUST AS I AM.

38. ASPHODEL.

39. MOUNT ROYAL.

40. THE GOLDEN CALF.

41. PHANTOM FORTUNE.

42. FLOWER AND WEED.

43. ISHMAEL.

44. WYLLARD'S WEIRD.

45. UNDER THE RED FLAG.

46. ONE THING NEEDFUL.

47. MOHAWKS.

48. LIKE AND UNLIKE.

49. THE FATAL THREE.

50. THE DAY WILL COME.

51. ONE LIFE ONE LOVE.

52. GERARD; or, The World, The Flesh, and The Devil.

53. THE VENETIANS.

54. ALL ALONG THE RIVER.

55. THOU ART THE MAN.

56. SONS OF FIRE.

"No one can be dull who has a novel by Miss Braddon in hand. The most tiresome journey is beguiled, and the most wearisome illness is brightened by any one of her books."

LONDON: SIMPKIN & CO., LIMITED.

Milton Keynes UK
Ingram Content Group UK Ltd.
UKHW020920181223
434584UK00001BA/277